Illuminating Darwin

Illuminating Darwin

ARABELLA'S LIGHT

Jill George

AUTHOR OF THE LIGHT AMONG US:
THE ELIZABETH CARNE STORY, CORNWALL

Cover design by Ronaldo Alves

For my incredibly strong and beautiful mother, Janet,
who held up the sky for us and so many others across the country.

Illustration by Arabella Buckley

"Complicated theories don't influence culture.
Simple and crude stories have power on human thinking."

Fabio Prolimatika, Professor of Educational Theory
University of Jyvaskyla, Finland

"...We may perhaps learn the 'struggle for existence' which has taught the ant the lesson of self-sacrifice to the community, is also able to teach that higher devotion of mother to child, and friend to friend, which ends in a tender love for every living being, since it recognizes that mutual help and sympathy are among the most powerful weapons, as they are also certainly the most noble incentives, which can be employed in fighting the battle of life."

ARABELLA BUCKLEY, *LIFE AND HER CHILDREN*

Table of Contents

Preface

In the annals of history, stories of remarkable women have often been overshadowed, their triumphs consigned to the dusty corners of forgotten narratives, if told at all. Often, within these neglected pages we find the tales of unsung heroines, whose contributions to science, literature, and society have remained obscured by the passage of time. It is with great pleasure, and a sense of duty, that I present this historical fiction novel—a testament to the women of Victorian times who defied society norms and the men who support them on their path to greatness.

Throughout the course of my research, I went on journeys that lead me into the hallowed halls of London's prestigious institutions and gardens as well as the idyllic landscapes of Devon, retracing the exact footsteps of those in this story who once graced these historic locations with their historic thoughts and deeds. With each visit, I felt a deep connection to them, a profound sense of walking in the very footsteps of the real people who populate these pages and I hope I pass that feeling on to you.

But it was not merely the physical presence at these places that brought his story to life. It was through the discovery of previously unknown and long forgotten letters, painstakingly gathered and read, from archives far and wide, that I delved into the minds and hearts of those who lived these pivotal lives. Among these correspondences across more than sixty years, I uncovered the voices of the remarkable individuals who dared to challenge the status quo, carving their own path through a world steeped in tradition.

Once such voice, that of Arabella, resounded with particular clarity. Her journey, as depicted in these pages, reflects the resilience and determination of countless women who forged their own destinies in the face of societal constraints. Her spirit is brought to life through her own words, preserved within the letters that have spanned more than six decades, providing an intimate understanding of her dreams, fears, and ambitions.

Within these chapters, readers will witness two key transitions: Arabella's remarkable rise as a scientific writer and Charles Darwin's transformation based in part on Arabella's influence. Both were buoyed by the support and encouragement of each other. Through her collaborations with the likes of Sir Charles Lyell and Charles Darwin, Arabella paved the way for widespread acceptance of revolutionary scientific ideas that continue to shape scientific discussion to this day.

This novel, therefore, seeks to rebalance the scales of history, to shed light on the countless women whose achievements have long been overlooked. I aim to celebrate the enduring partnerships and alliances between strong, visionary women and the enlightened men who championed their cause. Let us celebrate these remarkable women and the men who recognized their value, as we endeavor to reclaim their rightful place in the tapestry of history.

May their stories inspire us to champion equality and recognize the indomitable light that resides within each and every one of us.

Chapter One

A Woman at the Podium

The College, Glasgow,
Edinburgh Philosophical Institute

September, Late 1880s

From my vantage point on stage and at the podium, ready to give one of the most prestigious science lectures of my life, I swallowed hard as I saw before me a sea of scholarly beards. Hundreds of them in various shapes, sizes, and colors each surrounding what looked like dour mouths, which conveyed to me their resistance to my being there. My audience's eyes also spoke volumes about how they felt about me and my place as the guest speaker. Sharp eyes either looked at me with defiance or were downcast, avoiding having to look at me directly. My talks in a forum like this typically began with these perceptions of traditional opposition: male versus female, formal education versus informal, gentry versus non gentry. But they never ended that way.

In the last few seconds as the audience took their seats, and as I awaited my introduction, I overheard two older gentlemen exchanging their views on me as they sat down in the front row. I watched as they settled into their seats, thinking that while they were enjoying their own anonymity, I on the other hand, waited on the stage for all to critique. They gazed around the room with amazement at the clattering crowd in the large auditorium at The College, Glasgow. The September meeting of the Edinburgh Philosophical Institute was very well attended indeed. Apparently, they needed to speak loudly because one or both of them were hard of hearing.

The first man, his beard streaked with grey, croaked to his companion in disbelief, his arms folded over his chest. "A woman speaker? This is unheard of! Who is she?"

The second man shook his head. "Not sure, but she can certainly not be any Sir William Hamilton who spoke here in January and February on *Man and His Philosophy*!" He huffed, clearly skeptical about me and my worth. The host briefly introduced me. I pushed away anxious thoughts, stiffened my jaw, and ignited my mind.

Setting aside my notes, I launched into my talk with an energetic flourish. I hurled the logic and artistry I had prepared on my topic, "Progress of Life On Earth," towards my skeptical audience. Effortlessly, I told a story that wove together the findings and theories of the giants of science I had worked with over the last thirty years—Lyell, Darwin, Wallace, Huxley, Hooker, Spencer, and others. I laid the groundwork for my major premise, that mutualism, or collaboration within and between species, and driven by a higher deity, was critical for survival. Then I built example upon example, layer upon layer on that argument, until formerly resistant eyes turned bright with excitement and curiosity. Dour mouths turned into questions for the man seated to his left or right. Previously silent pens scratched on note pads. Hands stroked beards in concentration.

I felt myself in a kind of a mental flow, as if all my years of study and writing had culminated in this lecture, streaming out of my mind like a current or beam of light, calmly and naturally. I so enjoyed myself that I wanted to continue after I gave my conclusion. I could have stood there talking for days about mutualism. The applause at the end was more than cordial and could even be considered thunderous, I thought.

I had no sooner stepped off the podium when I was met with several requests for questions and follow up, to my delight. But from the corner of my eye, I saw a dark-haired man lurking by the side of the stage near the crimson curtains. Savoring my initial success would not last for long. The man was none other than Samuel Butler, my long-time nemesis and would-be novel writer; a rival to, and irreverent critic of, Charles Darwin, my acclaimed mentor and friend. I felt my skin crawl as he slowly sidled up to me, with the same black, pointed beard he had worn for years, still every bit the spider he had always been.

Our history together was littered with unpleasant confrontations. Was this to be yet another one, here, on the stage? Panic began to build inside me as I prepared for him to challenge the points I had just made, to shout out what he thought were my mistakes or worse, to criticize Mr. Darwin as a fraud yet again in front of any remaining in the audience. My insides clenched as he approached me, and his expressionless face hid whatever his intentions were.

He looked down on me from his tall stature. An attempt to intimidate, I was sure.

"How did you do it, Miss Buckley?" he hissed in an ugly tone. "How did you, a woman, manage to get into their inner circle, when most men, certainly your betters, could not? How?" He wore his envy so clearly on his dark suit sleeve it was unnerving to see it out in the open in this very public place.

I pitied the man's jealousy of Mr. Darwin and his inner circle of the giants of science—and his jealousy of me, after all these years. My upbringing called on me to forgive his obvious weaknesses, and the years had softened my loathing of him and his cloying attempts at success. Or perhaps it was the happiness I felt after my presentation, having realized that all my hard work and diligence of years of writing books with painstaking, meticulous research had paid off, and I was in fact achieving my life's mission of bringing Charles Darwin's scientific theories to light.

I looked up at him with all sincerity and said, "How did I do it? How did I achieve what few men and almost no women have achieved? Simple. I did not choose a life of science. It chose me."

Chapter Two

More Than a Pawn

1 St. Mary's Terrace,
Paddington, London

April 1864

I did not fully understand, to be honest, the leap I had taken. I stood before my somber, traditionally minded parents who were about to severely chastise me for taking it. I had jettisoned myself from the family chess board, controlled by my foreboding mother and the times. My fragile dreams, the source of the leap, fought for existence as I struggled to think of how to protect them against what would happen next at this, my moment of reckoning.

As I stood in the parlour, with hands trembling, facing Mother, the queen of the family chess pieces, and Father, the king, they scrutinized me and weighed the options for my next role, my fate. I was but a lowly, plain, and pale pawn, subjected to their power and influence as my siblings had been before me. My goal? To treat the difficult subject of my future in a short and simple way with as much truth as my secrets would allow.

Their straight backs and dark, immaculate, profusely buttoned, high-collared dinner clothes added to their part as the family chess piece royals as they sat on the maroon brocade sofa in our parlour, ready to rule over the seemingly limited and menial paths my life could take as a young and yet unmarried twenty-four-year-old woman. But I had different ideas. The trouble was, how would I possibly be able to put my unusual and socially undesirable plans into action? Women, especially young women, were invisible, with no opinion, voice, rights, and certainly no ability to make decisions on their own, which is exactly what I had done and was about to pay for.

On the outside, I was the perfect picture of modesty for my role as pawn: long, thin, and shiny dark hair, braided and coiled around the top of my head, like my mother's, and perfectly parted down the center; a perfectly trim physique by my family's standards—an energetic and helpful physique, they would say. Not too plain but not overly pretty, either—ideal for a vicar's daughter. What I understood about myself was that my insides posed the real problem: my brain and my disposition collided to form a headstrong, curious, voracious reader who longed for more than what was typical or expected. What was more, I had a courage about me that people noted. All of this led me to what I had done and to why I was now here eyeing my balefully staring parents. I dreaded the thought of the six a.m. to eleven p.m. drudgery of a governess. And nothing and no one could change the boiling pot that was my insides. Not even me.

Mother, never someone to trifle with, was about to deliver a possibly fatal blow to the next step in my life. I stood tensely before her and Father, afraid she would see right through me, her shrewd eyes piercing directly into the key reason why I was about to argue with her in complete defiance, if it came to that. Out of mutual respect, neither of us wanted to argue with the other, but it was in our nature, or so my grammar school instructors would have me believe, given that I seemed to adamantly espouse any topic except for the one being taught at the moment, and therefore often causing them great annoyance and frustration. I could see the words forming in her mind by the tenacity in her eyes and the way she drew her breath in, confident of her next sentence and her ability to win not only the argument—her word, not mine—but the next move.

"I will not have you be seen as a burden to the parishioners, Arabella. At twenty-four and unmarried, you will now need to take a governess position, which I am arranging for you," she said stiffly, her lips turning white as she pursed them. A clear sign that I had no room for negotiation. "Your father and I have already discussed an opportunity for such a position with long-time family friends in Brighton."

"I believe, as head of this household," my father said, a bit annoyed at mother's jump to her own conclusions, "that I am free to deploy my stipend as Vicar of St. Mary's as I deem fit, regardless of what the squabbling women on the church beautification committee that you lead, say," my father said, with his vibrant voice.

Undaunted, my mother eyed me as the pawn I was, obviously considering how to move me as she thought proper, as she had done with all eight of her children. My older sisters, Elsie, Julia, and Janie were suitably positioned about the chess board and my five younger siblings—a sister and four brothers—were waiting to be moved from their starting positions. My youngest brother, Henry, lived with us at our lovely white three-story brick house with a covered porch at One St Mary's Terrace in Paddington and was completing University here in London and then would be sent to study law upon graduation.

"I will not have tongues wagging that one of my daughters lounges here reading on the vicarage dole while others must raise funds to maintain the grounds and interior," Mother retorted to Father without turning to face him. "Furthermore," she snapped, "we have been seeking a position or a suitor for you for six years now, and since you have found no suitor that is to your liking, we have run out of options of eligible matches from our long-time family friends." She clamped her teeth firmly in her jaw, which made the contours of her cheeks look like soft, buttery, creased, leather cushions that you might see in carriage seating. Her dark thin hair was coiled on the top of her head in a braid, tightly wound and in control. Nothing out of place, much like her.

I winced at her barb, digging my nails into my palm, hoping she would not notice, as she had hit precisely on the secret I was desperately trying to hide from her and Father. I prayed she would not notice my reaction to her mention of old family friends. *If I could just focus on the position, move on and make it past the marriage suitor question, my secret will remain thus and my parents will not be broken, shattered, as a result.*

"You do recall, Mother, when my older sisters left home, much of the education of the the younger ones fell to me," I said as softly as I could in my own defense, trying to control my rising defiance.

"Yes, which called upon your remarkable industry and faculties of organization," Father chimed in. Father was in his late fifties, and I could smell a hint of his fetid breath from where I stood. His lanky body seemed to overflow from the sofa as his bony knees jutted out towards me. Father often came to my defense as he considered me one of his brightest offspring. Mother sat unmoved, focused on the points she was making.

"And therefore, I have paid my so-called 'dues' in that arena, having been a governess to my own siblings." I nodded at Father.

I quickly remembered the recent advice Henry, my closest ally and best friend, had given me. He had warned me against sparring with Mother. Since being at university had promoted him from bald-headed pawn to stately knight in the chess game, I took his advice seriously.

"Mother is the queen in our family chess game. It is as if she polishes the black- and tan-coloured squares and pieces by hand each night," he had quipped. "Her strategy, it appears to me, is to think several moves ahead of any of us children when planning and managing our destinies. I suggest you do the same." Henry said these words weeks ago on a Sunday after supper, stroking his newly formed, patchy brown beard.

My brother's advice was key to my thinking and planning in advance of being called in front of Mother and Father. A few days after Henry gave me the advice, I relayed my predicament to my dear friend, Frederica Rowan, herself secretary to Sir Francis Goldsmid. She mentioned that Sir Charles Lyell, the world-famous geologist and author of the hallmark tome *Principles of Geology*, was in need of a literary assistant. I had written to Sir Charles immediately and I had apparently received his letter of interest in my application in return, which my mother now produced from the tabletop beside her. The letter had come into her hands before I could intercept it. Would Henry's advice and my strategy work?

Mother held out the letter by the corner as if it was laced with some type of poison. "We have received this in the post, Arabella. From a certain Sir Charles Lyell. Explain this letter and your impertinence, please," she said, curtly as she snapped the folded sheet of the letter open.

"Yes, I admit I submitted a letter of inquiry to Sir Charles Lyell regarding his position for a literary assistant. That letter is from him, I daresay," I replied, the air thick with tension. "You see, Mother, I know you have thought about a governess position for me. But I have another calling in this life. I have more to offer than being a governess, that is," I said, firmly. I felt a drop of sweat trickle slowly down through my corset and down my back. I was very tense, and the room still contained the humidity of the spring day. "That is why I applied for the position Sir Charles has open," I said, not without some anxiety.

"A literary assistant?" Mother scoffed in shocked disbelief. "You applied for this position without consulting us? Is this position suitable for a woman of your upbringing? Why did you think it proper to apply without consulting us?" Her voice rang with alarm. "John, were you aware of this, this *position* and this *inquiry* to Sir Charles?" She flicked her hand out in Father's direction and then to me. He motioned back to her, palm down, as if to say, "Calm down and let her speak."

"You feel strongly about a governess position, Mother," I continued in a placating tone. "But I feel I have more to offer the world, and I thought this position might be a road to that something more. I am of age and thought I should be more in charge of my own affairs. Sir Charles is a gentleman, a scholar, and a very reputable man. His position may lead to greater knowledge and greater good." I paused. "What does he say in his response?" I asked, my eyes pleading with her.

"What more is it that you think you can offer the world, Arabella?" Mother fairly spat at me. "Your correspondence is a form of defiance I will not tolerate."

"Oh no, Mother!" I replied in alarm. "Not defiance, only investigation. I do not know exactly how I might contribute more to the world, Mother," I said slowly and earnestly. "I simply know in the depths of my being that I can do more with myself than merely teach children, although I do admire and even love that work."

With a heavy sigh, she said, "Ah. Well, it says here, from what I can make out from this atrocious penmanship, that Sir Charles is interested in your application and that he admires your handwriting, which is the best of all the applicants he has seen." Her nose was buried in the words of the letter. "Furthermore, he would like to extend you an offer of employment immediately," she said with surprise, folding the letter. She laid it lightly back on the table and then folded her hands in her lap. "But that does not mean that this position, this secretarial role, is suitable for a young woman such as yourself," she stated again with irritation.

"I see. That being the case, Mother, I can see that you will have to decline his interest in me as a literary assistant, even though it is a higher-paid position than that of governess." I declared, looking her directly in the eyes. As I had tried to use Henry's advice, I now felt compelled to play Mother at her own game. I was so tense that I imagined that the letter in her hand, while merely made of thick cream-coloured paper with its unfamiliar, black scrolling ink, seemed to quiver with its own heartbeat as if it had its own life and breathed my dream of a larger future yet unknown.

"What in heaven's name do you mean, child, *decline*? What is your point, exactly?" she asked, squinting at me as she grabbed the letter off the table and thrust it towards Father, making a cracking sound with the paper.

I could smell the burning candles as I tried to hold fast to my thoughts. A drop of wax helplessly dripped down a long cream-coloured candle, unable to stop itself. "By that I mean, that you seem to be fixed on my being a governess, which could mean much travel outside of London, as you suggested, Brighton possibly, and perhaps even permanent relocation." I tried to quell the edge in my tone. *Quite a risky game I am playing here,* I thought to myself, trying to steady my nerves with Henry's advice.

She said nothing, clearly pausing as she considered her next move. "I sense there is something at play here that I yet do not fully comprehend. Is that the case, child?"

"Why, no, Mother. Not at all..." I stammered, trying to think of what to say next and floundering. I glanced at Father, silently beseeching him to intervene.

Father took his cue to interject. "Initiative. Well done, Arabella. An attempt to better oneself. Right. But would you be able to help others in such a position? Is that not the most important quality of our work here in this life?"

"Exactly so, Father," I echoed, recovering. "I believe helping a man of science is helping other people in the most righteous of ways—education on a world scale as he is a world scholar."

Mother gave me a scowling look and was about to give her opinion of whether helping a man of science was helping in the Christian way Father intended, but Father intervened once more.

"And such a position appeals to you, does it not? It would allow for your own continued education, is that correct?" Father asked, clearly lacking his own knowledge about such a position.

"In fact, it does appeal to me, Father, for several reasons. I would remain living here in London with you both and have access to the museums that I love. I would only be working four hours a day in Marylebone, which, being only two miles away, is easily walkable. I would be able to continue my studies. Lastly, not only does it pay more than a full-time governess position, but I would be able to learn from one of the greatest minds in London, nay the world!" I exclaimed.

"This Lyell must be an honourable man, Elizabeth, given his stature as a gentleman." Father turned to Mother, tapping the letter on her forearm. "I think this position might be an excellent short-term solution to our lack of supply of eligible suitors," he exclaimed, twisting his gold-handled walking stick back and forth lightly on the floor.

Not wanting to seem to overrule Father, Mother gave me a slight nod of her head, conceding my victory. "Indeed, I am inclined to agree with you, John. When would you begin, Arabella?" she asked. "I am quite relieved a solution has presented itself," she said, graciously agreeing with Father.

"This exact month, Mother," I said happily, as I gave a small curtsey to be excused. "Thank you both for your consent."

"Just one moment," Mother frowned, just as I had turned to return to my bedchamber.

As innocently as I could muster, I said, "Yes, Mother?"

"If at the end of one year, this position with Sir Charles is terminated or for any reason is not meeting our expectations, you will either marry a man of our choosing or take a governess position that we arrange. Those are my terms. Is that clear?" She warned, giving me her most stern gaze, jaw set, like the shrewd Queen in the chess set that she was.

"Very clear. Yes, Mother." I gave a small curtsey and quickly departed before any additional terms came to Mother's mind.

Bring the king's pawn forward two paces! I sighed with self-congratulation as I went along the passage to my bedchamber. I could not wait to tell Henry! He would be quite pleased for both of us, at least in the short term of the next calendar year. I could hear my mother and father still conversing in the parlour. On to their next chess piece, I presumed. My shoes clacked loudly on the hall hardwood floor. I tried to slow my gait so that it did not appear as if I was hurrying to my bedroom with something to hide. Because that was precisely what I was doing.

With heavy guilt, I stood at my bedroom door, my forehead resting on the door and my hand squeezing the bronze doorknob. I did, in fact, have the most egregious secret. I hated having to hide it from my parents and bringing dishonesty and a lack of integrity into my family. But exposing myself would ruin my reputation and that of my family and instantly bring dishonour to us all. I shuddered at the prospect.

The doorknob felt cold and heavy in my hand as I opened

the door to my clean white bed chamber. I threw myself down on the edge of my bed, covered in a white quilt, recently laundered and freshly scented. I had more than my response to Sir Charles to worry about. What burned through my mind and heart, and what my mother had yet to discover, was that I did know of the old family friend to whom she had just generally referred. And she was right in suspecting that there was more to the situation. So keen was Mother's sharp mind! A man ineligible for marriage and twenty years my senior...but with whom I had been kindling a deep love, kept secret for the better part of this year. I had always been a dutiful, devoted daughter. Devoted to family and our Lord. Never had I lied about anything substantial. Until this. What had happened to me?

I walked over to my desk, ignoring the lovely sunset melting into the ground just outside my window, and pulled out my small desk chair. I sat at my walnut desk and opened my writing box, thinking about next steps. Yes, I would accept the position Sir Charles had offered me. Come what may, a literary assistant would be an interesting and different, as well as a more lucrative position than a governess. I would be able to stay in London, not only to be with my parents but, if I were honest, to be near the man who intrigued me to no end. I withdrew a plain sheet of stationery and wrote the date and 1 St Mary's Terrace, Paddington, at the top right corner. The page looked clean and full of promise, and with a few effortless strokes of my pen, I leapt onto the page and into the unknown.

Chapter Three

Into the Gullet of Science

53 Harley Street,
London

April 1864

As I made the right turn onto Harley Street, briskly walking just under two miles from Paddington to Marylebone, I wondered who would be more anxious for my first day on my new job, me or Sir Charles. He was one of the most famous scientists in the world, and I had barely any experience but had gotten this job because I had the neatest handwritten letter of all the applicants. Apparently, Sir Charles, age sixty-four, suffered from poor eyesight. *My penmanship is not a very lofty skill from which to start a challenging position that is a chance of a lifetime,* I thought, sighing.

I looked down at the tarred wood block paving of Harley Street, which formed a surface much quieter than granite setts under the clatter of hooves and wheels, and I saw a long, neat row of elegant pale townhouses trimmed with lovely cream-coloured scrolls. It seemed as if each house was a well-shaped, beautiful white tooth, all in alignment on either side of a wide mouth, the street being the tongue. I had the feeling, as I did about much of London, despite the fact that I had lived here my whole life, that Harley Street could drag me down its throat, overwhelming me with a sense that I was drowning.

My steps quickened to overcome my feelings of anxiety and nervousness. Harley Street appeared to be much cleaner than other streets in London, for which I was grateful. I did not want to arrive at Sir Charles' office with dirty shoes. The crossing sweepers, usually boys or old men with brooms, shovels, and buckets for carrying away horse droppings, were apparently well-paid on this street. Marylebone was known for its many doctors and medical offices, so cleanliness was essential here, as was the quietness of the paving. The pleasantness of the surroundings still did not detract from the nervousness leaping up into my throat.

I am a clever enough woman, I said to myself with conviction and straightened my posture. *When I speak, people typically listen. I can be persuasive, and I am punctual. I am energetic, strong, and fit. I am no statuesque beauty, but neither am I plain. I have a small but pleasant figure. My hair is neatly combed. And most of all, I am determined to help others.* I would simply carry on with my best aspects here with Sir Charles as I had done in other circumstances, shallow as those might be.

And after all, what other options did I have? To be a governess or a wife, perhaps? Was I ready to be a wife? Mother kept insisting I was. Despite our agreement, if an opportunity for marriage arose, I knew she would bring it up for discussion. Several family friends whom we had known since early childhood had become available over the last seven years, and some were handsome and intelligent. Another of our family friends, Dr. Thomas Fisher, a married man with a child, had captured my full attention and was the cause of my secrecy with my family. *It is a sin to be desirous of another woman's husband,* I chastised myself.

Yet even now I couldn't stop thinking about him. We had

met at the Collections of Natural History at the British Museum two years ago when he was on a trip back to London from Timaru, New Zealand. Henry and I were visiting the collections so that I could study different species of birds, a fond hobby at the time. I quite literally bumped into Thomas as he was examining the birds of the upper reaches of the tropical Asia collection and I the lower.

He was very tall with an athletic, rugged air about him. He wore a long tan woollen jacket that hung loosely at his sides. I could tell from his posture and gait that he was an agile sort, strong and lithe, but polished like a gentleman. His tanned face and lightened blond hair gave away that he had spent time outside London, somewhere in the sun.

We exchanged opinions and pleasantries about the various species on display and how birds are similar to humans. I recall the museum smelling that special mixture of ancient things and pine floor cleaner. He had often used medical terms to describe the features of the birds we saw, and his observations fascinated me. In due course, he introduced himself to me and Henry, who had reappeared, and I did likewise. He said he knew of me as an old family friend and he had visited our home many years ago, but I had not remembered his visits. I remember that afternoon and our initial conversations with much tenderness, often helplessly repeating them over and over in my mind.

The museum was very crowded that day, and we struggled to make our way from exhibit to exhibit. Families with small children jumped with delight and pressed their hands against the glass, peering into the exhibits. Groups of what appeared to be students huddled and took notes in leather-bound books. We walked past the exhibit of local British garden birds and then went on to another featuring birds of Southeast Asia. Henry meandered off, lost again in the crowd. The high ceilings were cool and dark, creating an atmosphere that added to this new man's allure and intrigue.

"I note that the Tailor bird prefers a very clean but complex nest. Do you see it there? The specimen has a white abdomen and olive-coloured posterior." He extended his long arm and forefinger over my head and out towards the exhibit's glass to a tiny spot of a nest, barely discernable. "The placard says that the Tailor bird sews. Can you imagine? The bird sews large leaves on the branch together and then builds its nest within that sewn-together pouch of leaves. Ingenious." He spoke almost in a whisper, completely lost in his thoughts about the marvels of the Tailor bird and barely audible above the din of the crowds. "For me, neither is important. Give me a rucksack and a tent out in the open wilderness and I am at my happiest." Wistfulness was in his voice. "I am quite similar to the common Goldcrest we passed in the British bird exhibit, a bird who is quite happy with a mess of a nest."

"Yes, a Goldcrest can live in a large forest or a small garden and mates for life," I said. "Oh, I do see that Tailor bird specimen. Is it that the Goldcrest just tires easily and therefore is happy with that nest? His mate keeps him quite busy, helping with the feeding, you see." I spoke playfully as I sidestepped a group of children, heads connected, looking down with fingers pointed to words in a book.

Thomas looked into my eyes and said, "Yes, my wife would do the same." His green eyes reminded me of the green found in nature—slopes of summer grass, grasshoppers, and pond water rimmed with algae—and they were fringed with long lashes. His face was replete with finely chiseled cheeks, chin, nose, and forehead. I wondered if his female patients swooned over him making excuses and appointments just to see him.

"Ah. Many other birds mate for life, such as the Skylark, which is not as gorgeous to look at as a Goldcrest," I said, lightly.

Thomas grimaced at my "mating for life" comment. "I

know through your family that you are as yet unwed. Stay out of that business as long as you can. Be like animals that experience multiple mates before you make a fateful and everlasting decision, one that you may regret." His candidness startled me, but I pretended to have a level of sophistication that I did not.

"That sounds a bit scandalous. And you? Do you regret being married?" I asked innocently, but something in me was starting to rise up to meet him.

"Marriage is a tough business. Especially now that I know someone as intriguing as you, with interests similar to mine, exists. An unconforming woman with a curiosity in all natural phenomena," he said, with a slight, wistful smile.

"That much is true. I truly enjoy natural history and all its glory." I said, ignoring his flirtations. "You and I have much in common with these exhibits, I think."

"Oh, and how is that?" He looked at me with curiosity, shifting his weight from one leg to another.

"One is local, common, and known. The other is from a faraway land, unexplored and mysterious." I replied. "Do you see my meaning?"

"What I see locally is even more captivating than those in a faraway land," he replied, grasping my analogy more quickly than I expected. He added, "And in no way do I consider what is local to be common. More like extraordinary. In fact, my favorite bird is the native British bird, the Skylark, which you mentioned moments ago."

"Oh, the Skylark is my favorite as well. How in particular does the Skylark capture your admiration?" I asked enthusiastically.

"The Skylark has incredible skills that make all who know it happy, such as flying high in the sky and singing for hours. Unique, like you, whom I also admire," he said, tucking his large hands into his pockets, his eyes fixed on me.

I looked over his shoulder at the top of my brother Henry's head, which was all that was visible of him in the crowd as he stood, not far away, in the next section of the exhibition. "Tell me about your home in New Zealand. What is it like?" I asked, trying to choose a very neutral topic.

"I own sheep farming land inland from Timaru called the Grampians. My cottage in Lyttleton is where I see patients from around Christchurch and host medical meetings. I have quite a few Merino sheep—aiming towards owning 25,000 of them. I have a red barn next to my cottage with an ambulance carriage that I use to transport patients. I lead a busy but quiet life, as I prefer," he said, in a sort of brooding tone, walking leisurely on to the next exhibit.

"It sounds lovely, out in the country." I smiled.

"Oh, I arrange social outings to visit my neighbors, such as a friend, Samuel Butler, who was living on a sheep farm some twenty miles away. Have you heard of him? He's an author. We play Whist, talk about science and the like. However, he was considering leaving New Zealand when I last saw him and may have already done so. And I am involved with the local politics there, where we are attempting to change the hostile stance that many of the settlers maintain against the Māori."

"That all sounds fascinating. Your life is quite full. How dreadful for the Māori, given the pride they must have in their homeland." I admired the adventures and the vehement conversations in favor of the Māori I imagined him having. "I admire your jacket. Did the wool come from your sheep?" I asked, sizing up the thick softness of the material.

"Yes, it did. Are you feeling a chill? Would you like to wear it?" He asked, earnestly.

He started to take off his jacket. As he did so, I smelled a clean, soapy fragrance as his scent whiffed toward me. His chest was broad and angled and his waist was very narrow, I noticed.

"Oh, no thank you," I said, rather too quickly, embarrassed. "I think I must rejoin my brother before he becomes..." My sentence broke off and I found it difficult to choose the right words. I looked at the floor.

"Alarmed that you are in close contact with a man, an obviously older man, whose eyes can barely leave you?" He reached out his hand quickly and gave my chin the briefest and lightest touch. "I have known your family for donkey's years, Miss Buckley. I am an old family friend, one who would like to tour another exhibition with you again soon." He hoped, it seemed, to show no malintent, but I was guarded.

"Oh, but I am afraid that is not possible. It would not be seemly." I resisted but at the same time could not help but feel incredibly drawn toward him.

Without hesitation and his mood shifting excitedly, he said, "I have an idea. You and Henry meet me to take in the fossil exhibition here next week, about this time. Meet me at the entrance on Great Russell Street. Then we can go round the exhibition, discuss it, and perhaps take some coffee or tea somewhere afterwards—somewhere where they serve a lovely and proper tea. Perhaps at the Montague? Or, if you like and weather permitting, we could take some fresh air and a stroll around Regent's Park. The flower gardens are truly lovely. Have you seen them?"

While I was sure this was not his intent, my mind flicked to situations of him and me alone in a flower garden. I could feel my pulse in my throat. I managed to say, "I am flattered. Truly. But I do not think my family would approve."

"Oh, I think they will. They know my impeccable reputation as a physician. Meet me here. Please say you will. I will be here, waiting for you." He looked down at me. We were so close, given the crowds pressing in, that I could feel the strength of his arm against mine. His confidence was compelling, like a beautiful, warm sunny spot shining on a thick cushioned chair in a cold room, beckoning me to join it. I was smitten and intrigued.

Thomas was correct. My parents did approve of Henry and me visiting museums and parks with him, and we did so often. I was astounded that Mother agreed to these outings with the three of us. Being engrossed in the law, Henry was not much interested in science but was happy to get out of the office and out of the house. I believe my parents saw the much older Thomas as an uncle or perhaps a family tutor and never suspected any other form of a relationship as an option.

As odd as it was, our considerable age difference—he was forty-seven and I was twenty-two—never became an issue with Thomas and me. Through our outings, the adoration between us grew, to the point where I never seriously considered another man. Yet I wasn't sure about marriage, even if by some miracle he were to become available. I had too much I wanted to do and become and see. Marriage sounded nice in the abstract, but it really wasn't my driving ambition—and I was getting the impression that marriage troubled Thomas as well. It was as if he wanted more than a safe marriage. And I yearned to make something more of myself. Therefore, I did not truly consider marriage as an option.

Not only was Thomas married to his wife, Eliza, but he was also very obviously married to his way of life in the frontier of New Zealand. "In New Zealand, a man can be free of the petty societal demands for propriety in London," he often said. He had the blood of a rugged outdoor life in his veins, and the confinements of family life seemed for him to be like having to wear a suit of clothes that are two or three sizes too small.

Best to forget him, I told myself repeatedly as I walked down Harley Street toward my new place of employment. If this new position was worth its weight, it would help me forget him all the more quickly. I was determined to make a success of my own abilities.

"You are every bit as bright as your brothers," Father had told me over the years. His advice had always been: "Help others do their best and by doing so, you will be doing your best as well." And "Make an asset out of your abilities and do good for the world. You are an incredibly intelligent woman. Go where other women cannot go by helping others do their best." Being the vicar of St. Mary's of Paddington, he tended to feel his advice had some elements of divine intervention, and I tended to agree. I wanted to listen and follow his advice over my mother's very traditional outlook on life. Marriage was not the right choice for me, given my yearning to be something more. What that something was I had no idea, but I would have to create it with my own wit and my bare hands, that was certain.

When I arrived at number fifty-three Harley Street, I paused at the front door to catch my breath and get a feeling for the place. People passed by me, but I was oblivious to their rushing and the hindrance I was causing on the pavement. I stared up at the white ornate archway over the door, the beautiful set stone at the entrance, the slender cream columns. *Through the teeth and jaws and down deep into the belly of science I go!* I thought. With all the grit I could muster, I rang the bell.

Lady Lyell answered the door and introduced herself, quite pleasantly.

"Hello and welcome. I am Mary Lyell," she said. "We have been expecting you. Please, do come in." She had a full round face and mouth and deep-set, intelligent eyes. She held the door wide open, and it was as if I had entered another world. I warmed to her immediately.

The first thing I noticed about the office was the smell of ink in wells, ink on paper, books open on tables, and books on shelves. I breathed it all in as I entered the hallway and then walked back into the first large room, equipped as an office with a lovely white fireplace. The soaring ceiling had a lovely crown molding in the center and an elegant dado rail around the room as well. I was immediately inspired by these architectural features, and then I was energized by the work in progress on display on every desk and table. Leather-bound books with gold engravings. Sparkling purple and gray minerals on shelves. Ammonites of varying sizes were displayed in lovely white porcelain trays. Lovely groupings of pale white and pink shells as well as sketches of shells adorned the walls. Paintings of people and places I did not recognize. The office and its adjacent rooms each contained a couple of desks and tables and had an atmosphere that appeared to me to be somewhere in between a museum and library.

The man I would be working for stood next to a desk, holding a pair of eyeglasses in his hand. He was introduced to me as Sir Charles, and he held out his hand for me to shake it. I did not recollect a thing he said. His Scottish accent was so entertaining and kindly that I stared into his eyes. He was tall and thin and had one of the most beautiful faces for a man that I had ever seen. I was not at all expecting such a handsome and charming man as a geologist. I hoped that thought was not going to burst forth out of my mouth.

Sir Charles ushered me into an adjacent office, just as lovely as the others, and asked, "Could you start by proofreading this set of letters please? I need them to be posted today if at all possible. They are already late."

I was surprised that Sir Charles expected me to dive right in, but I didn't hesitate. "Of course, I would be happy to," I said, nodding as I accepted the letters. I sat holding the fine paper of the first one in my fingers. The paper felt thick and slightly textured. The handwriting was a bit slanted and almost like copperplate in style. I had a difficult time reading the jumble at first. But my eyes adjusted to the writing, and soon it was as if I could see it quite clearly and make out every letter. It was as if his writing resembled an accent to which my ears had to become accustomed—except that, with the handwriting, it was my eyes that had to become adjusted. Apparently, this letter had been waiting to be edited and had been written two months previously. I was immediately impressed with the language and became lost in the content, fascinated by every sentence I was reading.

To W. Pengelly, Esq.

February 19, 1864

My dear Sir, Mr. Alfred Wallace, whom you know by name, told me the other day that there are limestone caves in Borneo, within reach of Rajah Brooke's jurisdiction, which deserve more than any in the whole world to be explored, as he feels sure they must contain the bones of extinct species of anthropomorphous apes most nearly allied to man, just as the Australian caves afford us fossil species of extinct kangaroos and other marsupials. He proposed to me to get the Royal Society to make a grant for the exploration of some one of these caves and asked if I knew anyone prepared to undertake it and could be sure that Sir James Brooke would encourage the exploration, if I would only do my best. Do you not sometimes meet Sir James at Miss Coutts's, or is he not somewhere at

Torquay? No one could better explain than you the peculiar interest of such an inquiry, and if I could get Wallace into correspondence with him, we might perhaps find some adventurer with competent knowledge to undertake the enterprise and get the scheme into such shape as to enable us to appeal to the Royal and Geographical Societies, and perhaps get up a private subscription in aid of the object. It is precisely the kind of investigation which no surveyor sent out to find gold or tine or coal, or other products of economic value, would be justified in following up, or even giving to it a small portion of his time, and you well know how much time and patience it would require. Believe me, my dear sir.

Ever most truly yours,
Charles Lyell

When I had finished, I duly advised my employer. "Sir, I found only two small things with the letter which I have amended, and I have put it in the post. What else can I assist with, sir?" I asked him.

He smiled. "Efficiency. I like that. In future, you will write the letters for me, as my eyesight is so bad it makes it difficult for me to see what I have written!" He laughed heartily. "And it is Sir Charles, and nothing as formal as merely 'sir.' Understood?"

"Very well. Yes, Sir Charles. I would be happy to start on your next assignment."

"Good. Then I would like you to read my *Principles of Geology*, second edition, and begin to insert the many changes and upgrades I have done here. It is my most important work and has been neglected and delayed while we have been trying to find you." He pointed to a stack of papers about an inch deep. "Each has a notation as to where it should be placed in the original edition. You will understand it once you get started."

"Yes, sir." I trailed off. He looked at me, his bushy eyebrows arched in question. "I meant, yes Sir Charles. I will get started."

"Oh, and I also need your assistance in gathering together several pieces I have written in preparation for a meeting with a friend coming in from Kent next week. His name is Charles Darwin. Have you heard of him?" He asked in his kindly manner, rifling through a stack of folders on the nearest table.

"You mean the author of *Origin of Species*? *The* Charles Darwin is coming *here*?" My eyes had flown open. Charles Darwin was the most eminent, important man of science in the world, in my opinion. I wondered where my copy of *Origin* was, as I would have to study it immediately.

"So, you have heard of him. Yes, he is a dear friend who has weathered quite a few storms," he said, pulling a thick tan file out of the stack. "He is coming to breakfast on Wednesday. I would like you to join us to capture notes from our discussions and take down conclusions, agreements, and that sort of thing. Would that be suitable for you?" He intoned as if he was asking me to join a routine meeting with routine guests.

"Of course. It would be my pleasure," I said, delightedly.

"Here is the list of materials I would like to have at hand for the meeting with Darwin," was all he said as he placed the list of eleven items in my hand and left the room.

What comes first, the Principles of Geology book or the Darwin list? I wondered. *Where will I find the items on the list? And how do I find them quickly? You said you were clever.* I told myself. *It is time to find out how clever.* I tried to tamp down the panic that had started bubbling up inside my mind.

Fortunately, I had read the second edition of the *Principles* in preparation for the position. I immediately skimmed through the current book and the inserts and changes to gain a sense of how much work the revisions might be. *Significant,* I thought. *If I work towards getting two chapters done a day, I believe that would represent sufficient progress on the revisions while I sort out the Darwin list.* I felt better now that I had a plan to attack the book revisions.

I paused for a moment and looked around my new, quiet, and beautiful world. I felt a sense of belonging and inspiration welling up inside me. Here I was, sitting inside the hallowed office of Charles Lyell, reading what no one on earth had read before from one of the top thinkers and men of science of our day.

"How many students at university and their professors would love to be in my chair right now?" I wondered out loud.

Then I heard another voice coming from another part of myself. *If you would like to stay here, perhaps you should get to work instead of basking in the glory of the office.* Duly chastised, I dipped my nib pen back in its inkwell and tapped the excess ink off in the well so as not to create a blot on the paper. Sir Charles Lyell, no less! Neither the job nor the man would be easy.

Chapter Four

The Man and the Mission

1 St. Mary's Terrace and
53 Harley Street, London

1864 – 1865

In the following days, I familiarized myself with all the offices by making a map of the desks and cabinets. I opened every drawer and looked in every box, folder, and pile, noting down what was where, making a list. I then rearranged items by subject, year, and alphabetical order. Piles and piles of papers and folders were now in an organized system, just the way I liked them.

Sir Charles was pleased, for he had begun having difficulty seeing where his papers were and finding them was becoming a frustrating challenge. I quickly found the items on the list for the meeting with Mr. Darwin and organized them by topic in folders. I read through *Principles* and gained an understanding of the corrections and additions and where they should be placed in the text to create the next edition, which took almost two weeks, and then I began that work in earnest. When I had any spare time during my four-hour sessions, I read and reread the second edition of the *Principles* and the corrections for the third, so that I would fully understand the topics being discussed.

Lady Lyell often floated by my desk, offering me the history of the place as well as words of encouragement. She had a lovely rose scent about her, and her skin was transparent and frail looking, quite the opposite of her strong demeanor.

"I admire the varieties of fossils you have on display," I commented during one of her visits.

"Quite so," she agreed. "Sir Charles and I catalogued thirty-six boxes of fossils and shells from our trip in 1842 and brought them here from America. Since my father was a professor of geology, I also made a study of that field of inquiry, in addition to pursuing my love of mollusks.

"We gathered a great many from the riverbeds in faraway places like Mississippi, Ohio, and Georgia."

I soaked up her words like a sponge. "That sounds like quite heavy work, Lady Lyell," I said, hesitantly.

She chuckled. "You do not picture me as a field study worker? Well, I have been Sir Charles' scientific partner in every way. I have helped with his collections, documentation, interpretation, his papers, and his lectures. He is quite shy, you see. His lectures, and even his papers, needed a bit of assistance with regard to finding their ready acceptance and pleasing his audiences. That is where I have been of most help." She whispered here, to be sure that no one heard her. "I have even insisted that women be allowed to attend his lectures," she said breathlessly. "And I intend to be your advocate too, Miss Buckley, if you will allow it."

Stunned, I replied, "That would be my greatest delight, Lady Lyell."

I felt like the luckiest woman in the world.

At night in my bedchamber by candlelight, I studied Darwin's *Origin of Species,* which had been published six years before and had caused a giant storm of controversy ever since. Sitting at my desk at home, hours flew by as I carefully handled the emerald-green leather binding and reconsidered the logic Darwin had used to form his theory of evolution and natural selection.

Having no real guidance on how to do the job, I decided to take notes in a separate notebook. By doing so, I was sure that I would have the basic tenets fully memorized and therefore could edit any inconsistencies that I might find in Sir Charles' papers. I had no idea how other literary assistants went about the job but in my heart I knew this was how I was meant to go about it. And by so doing, I learned everything in great detail.

Mr. Darwin's work in *Origin* was some of the best scientific writing of our time. I marveled to myself as I looked through the book. *Just imagine. He compiled observations and conclusions for this work for twenty years before he was ready to submit it for publication. Twenty years! What if something had happened to him and his work was never published?* That thought was horrifying to me. I summarized key tenets from some of his chapter headings:

1. *Origin* convinces the reader by using specific evidence that existing animals and plants cannot have been each individually and separately created in their present forms but must have evolved from earlier forms through slow transformation. *How? Why?*

2. The creation process takes place by <u>natural selection</u>, which is the mechanism that automatically produces the transformations. Artificial selection, therefore, is merely the form of the selection process that is carried out by horticulturalists when

they choose particular plants to graft and cross-pollinate, or when poultry breeders select breeding traits to create a desired type of hen, for example.

3. It follows, then, that all living organisms must be related through their common descent from simpler forms, or an original stock. Because in the act of living, there is always competition for life between variants, natural selection and evolution are universal. That is, they apply to all organisms.
4. Natural selection brings about improvement in the conditions of life; the transformations reduce the struggle and allow some organism(s) to "win."
5. Any organism that is able to successfully transform itself diverges into more types, each of which adapts to a particular environment that fits its niche way of life. A key example is the Galapagos turtle, whose shell behind the neck is curved to accommodate additional leveraging of the neck to reach leaves that are higher above the ground than other giant turtles can reach.

My back began to ache as I was leaning in my chair over my book. Maybe my neck needed to be more like the turtle's! Just then, there was a knock on my door.

"Can this lowly barrister enter?" It was Henry, looking for some company.

"I will allow it," I replied in a humorous, lofty, and regal voice.

"My! We are coming up in the world, are we not?" he quipped. "Meeting with Charles Darwin no less!" he said, proudly.

"Bella dear, may I also come in?" Mother was also at the door, peering around the corner.

"Of course, Mother, come in please," I said, wondering why she was appearing at my door this late in the evening.

Mother bustled in wearing her nightgown and cap with a large basket of flowers in her arms. "Someone was just at the door and delivered these flowers," she said. "At this hour! They are for you." She presented me with the basket with a lovely sky-blue ribbon tied around the base. I laid the basket on the desk and looked at the card on the front.

"Oh, who would send me flowers?" I wondered aloud.

"Quite a pretty bouquet," Henry commented, one eyebrow shooting up curiously.

I took the tiny cream-coloured card from its envelope. I forced my voice not to tremble. "Ah," I said with certainty, putting the card and envelope down on the desk. "They are from Dr. Fisher in thanks for our many informative trips to the museum." I slid the basket of flowers across the desk and sought to change the topic of conversation.

But Mother went on and on, pointing at the bouquet, to my frustraton. "I see Clover, blue Clematis, tiny white Edelweiss, and if I am not mistaken, Forget-Me-Not."

"Yes, undoubtedly in support of my meetings with Sir Charles," I said, looking up from my seat with a steady gaze at nothing in particular.

"Hmmm. Indeed." Mother sniffed. "I also see one lone Tulip. A bit odd looking, do you not think so? All these groups of flowers and then one Tulip?" She nodded lightly at the pink petals.

"Since Tulips or any of the flowers are not in season, perhaps the greenhouse he uses had a limited supply." I responded calmly.

"Well, enjoy them. They are lovely. I will leave you two now; I am on my way to bed. Goodnight, dears." With that, she turned and walked into the dark hall, holding her ceramic candle stick.

After mother had gone, Henry turned to me with a wary eye. "A lone Tulip? A good thing for you Mother is tired. In the morning she will remember the flower code, and then where will you be?"

"I doubt Mother has time for floriographical dictionaries, Henry. Besides, it means nothing."

"Nothing. Nothing? A man sends you flowers with hidden meanings, and you say it means nothing? Do you know what Tulips mean in the flower code of the gentry? A profession of love!" Henry was nearly wailing at me, clearly frustrated with the direction Thomas seemed to be taking the relationship.

"Hush! Keep your voice down," I whispered. "Dr. Fisher has no regard for flower codes. He is a man of science. I am sure there is no hidden meaning." Inwardly I was ignoring my own advice, busily trying to determine what the flowers might mean if they were actually meant as a code.

"I will get the floriography dictionary that we have on a shelf somewhere and..."

I interrupted his plan to decode the flowers. "Thank you, kindly. Now if you will excuse me, I am preparing for quite a substantial scientific meeting with Mr. Darwin and Sir Charles Lyell in the morning." I said, standing and gently shooing him towards the door.

Making a face like he had just tasted a bitter tea, he said, "Oh, bother science. Never did understand that whole business in the least at school. And I must say, our trips through the British Museum with Dr. Fisher, while entertaining, have not made a man of science of me yet. Speaking of 'old man Fisher,' do you know when he will be back in town? I could do with a bit of an outing. I find our little jaunts to be like a palette cleanser for me. After I toil through endless displays of dead scientific artifacts, the legal field seems quite invigorating in comparison. When will he be in London next?"

"Yes, he is well and will come up from Buckfastleigh next

week. He would like to go round the gardens in Regent's Park again, perhaps in the Inner Circle, with us and perhaps visit a tea house nearby. Does that sound suitable to you? I think it is a lovely idea," I said, stacking several papers to neaten my desk.

"Sounds like a grand plan, indeed," he said, his arms folded across his chest, leaning nonchalantly against the door frame. "You know, I think he does rather adore you," Henry said as if he was hoping to get information from me about the nature of my relationship with Thomas. "The Tulip?" He asked, nodding his head toward the flower in question.

"He adores us both, it seems to me," I said, neutrally, looking at him with a solid gaze, hoping he would not see right through me.

"Really? Because it seems to me that he takes on a brighter shine when speaking to you. I think he is smitten with you, Bella." Henry spoke with a quiet and serious tone, his eyebrows knitting together in concern.

I paused and turned back to the papers and books on my desk. I gathered up several books as if to reshelve them. I could not look him in the face for fear of giving myself away. I knew it would do no good to act shocked, either. As my brother, he would guess my true feelings immediately.

"He will be leaving within a few months to return to Christchurch and then Timaru," I said, "back to his sheep farm, his property, his political ambitions to help rewrite their constitution to be at peace with the native people, his horse racing, his life. So, we have no need to worry about him. He is returning to the life to which he is committed and loves." I tried to sound matter of fact.

"And his wife? And child? Is he committed to them?" He walked over to me and placed his hands on my shoulders as I sat down at my desk, gripping my hands in my lap in the awkwardness of the conversation.

"He is and always will be committed to them," I fairly snapped back.

"Be careful with yourself, Bella. That is all I ask. I do not want you toyed or tampered with in the process," Henry implored, with tender brotherly concern.

"No, nothing of the sort. Now, can we please return to my life of science? I am trying to sort out Darwin's *Origin of Species*." I paused. An idea struck me like a sharp jolt. "Hold on! An idea has occurred to me. Lend me that overly large brain of yours so that I might..." I stopped. At that instant, he started to walk back towards the door and quickly, apparently to avoid any further discussion.

I jumped up before he could escape. "Hold on." I grabbed his sleeve and tugged him back over to my desk.

"What are you on about now?" He looked confused.

"I am conducting an experiment of sorts. Yes, on you." I said, as he pointed to himself, eyes wide. Then I read aloud to him the key tenets of Darwin's *Origin of Species* as Darwin had originally written them, using the original headings. When I completed the reading, I said, primly, "Now. Describe for me the five tenets I have just read, please."

"Ah. Yes. The first one was something about slow transformation? The second..I cannot remember the second. Well, you see, I find them a bit arcane, and after a long day at work reading the law, I find that I cannot. Fancy a game of whist before bed? I find I sleep better having beaten you at something."

"We would really need more players for Whist unless you want to play German style. Sadly, as I have said, I have work to do before morning. I shall have to play you and win another time," I said with a sisterly smile.

"As you wish. I am now leaving," he said, with a light kiss on the top of my head. It had been a long day and he smelled as if he was in need of a washing.

As the door closed, I had an inspiration of sorts. I sat in my chair and pondered my "experiment," which had turned out exactly as I had expected. Henry had confirmed how murky and conceptual it all sounded. Sir Charles had mentioned in the office that Mr. Darwin had taken great care to write *Origin* with the general public in mind so that it could be understood by all. It seemed to me that in addition to the general public, he was also trying to write to please the scientific community. And, in addition to that, perhaps interested amateurs, such as me. *Yes,* I thought, *it is as if he wrote* *<u>Origin</u>* *to please three audiences at once. A grand purpose which I applaud—but three audiences at once are two too many!*

The fact seemed patently obvious to me: *Origin* was too difficult to digest. As this little experiment with Henry demonstrated, there remained a barrier to understanding for anyone who might not be an educated man of science. My own brother, a highly educated man, could not remember them immediately after I read them aloud to him. My own notes seemed much clearer and to the point. I made a quiet resolution. *Tomorrow, I will continue my experiment with Henry. I will read him my own summary of the tenets and see if he can remember them better than the originals written by Mr. Darwin.* His expressions were lovely and well-written, but not at all digestible by most people. And what good was a published book if only a small handful of people could understand it? Books were expensive and a luxury.

I looked at the volume in my hands. Why, even this book had cost Father fifteen shillings, which he grumbled mightily about when I insisted he buy it as we walked past the bookshop. And, as I recalled, that was how much Charles Dickens said Bob Cratchit made for a week's wage. Of course, that was about twenty years ago, but even now, fifteen shillings was still a week's wages for many people. An indigestible and expensive book was a waste of time and money. I pondered further. Word will get around the public at large that the book is difficult to understand. It may even become a form of intellectual snobbery for some to claim they understand it. The priceless scientific findings of our age will be ignored! Sir Charles was certainly no scientific snob. Did he and Mr. Darwin even see how difficult the book was to grasp and the implications of that opacity? But this was not something to bring to the surface at tomorrow's meeting—I was sure of that.

I began to draw little pictures next to and on top of the numerals I had written in my notebook so that I could better remember each one. I had always been a tolerably proficient artist. If it helps me to have a sketch of something that makes the principle easier to remember, in addition to having more lucid forms of expression, then perhaps this would be useful to Sir Charles at some point, I thought. Perhaps I could help with his illustrations. A capital idea! I would find the appropriate time to make such an offer.

Time was precious and I had little left that evening. I hurriedly returned to my review of *Origin of Species*. Midway through, I rediscovered the section entitled "Special Instincts." Always a source of fascination for me, I thought. Since I am something of a layperson in science, I find it a leap to move from Darwin's discussion of "habit" in animals to "instinct." Is a repeated habit an instinct? I wondered. No, because it can become manifest from birth, even if a parent is not present to guide the behaviour or demonstrate it. Consider an abandoned kitten. Even a kitten knows very early on to jump and hiss when it hears a loud noise and is frightened. It may never have heard another cat hiss, but it knows to make that alarming noise. How? Does the kitten hiss naturally and then repeat it every time it is frightened? I pushed my chair back from my desk and flipped through more pages of *Origin*. I read the following passage:

> *"We shall, perhaps, best understand how instincts in a state of nature have become modified by selection by considering a few cases. I will select only three, namely the instinct which leads the Cuckoo to lay her eggs in other birds' nests, the slave-making instinct of certain ants; and the cell making power of the hive-bee. These two latter instincts have generally and justly been ranked by naturalists as the most wonderful of all known instincts."*

How? I repeated, still trying to use the pages to answer my question. But no answer came to me. If a mother did not teach the kitten to hiss, and no other cat or animal demonstrated a similar alarm as a defense mechanism, then that is instinctual. Is that passed down through the brain to the kitten? Darwin stated that the offspring of the common European Cuckoo, having been raised in another nest, lay their own eggs similarly in another nest and receive the same benefit of having another bird rear their young as a matter of inherited behaviour. Darwin also cited American and Australian species of Cuckoo also laying their eggs in other birds' nests. The eggs seem to vary in size, so the mother bird lays the larger egg in another nest and therefore enables the smaller eggs to benefit from her assistance when she lays them after dispersing the larger eggs to other birds' nests. But how does she know this ingenious technique?

I did not see where Mr. Darwin provided an explanation for this curious egg and nest swapping behaviour. I would have to ask this question in the morning during our breakfast meeting. Doing so, I hoped, would demonstrate that I understood the basic principles, at least.

I turned my attention back to the flowers on my desk, having found a sturdy vase in my father's study next door to my bedroom. I also found our book on floriology in Father's study, with its lovely, flowery cover in shades of pink, violet, and blue.

I arranged the flowers with the tall Tulip in the back of the arrangement, attempting to hide it behind the Clematis. I opened the floriology book which said that Clematis meant ingenuity and cleverness, and that the flower was named after its cunning ability to climb up walls and trellises. That vine never fails to find its way up difficult terrain, I thought. Well, that was encouraging, given my endeavors to understand Mr. Darwin. I would find my way up, no matter what the difficulties. Clover for good luck—that one is easy. I did remember that one.

I turned to the page in the book for Edelweiss. *Let me see,* I said to myself. It meant courage and daring. The star-shaped, white flower bloomed high in the Alps, on dangerous mountainsides. Therefore, procuring Edelweiss was thought to be a feat of great courage and devotion. Yes, I could see his logic here where he and I were concerned. Now for the Tulip. I flipped through the pages again: *When love is forbidden, Tulips spring up as symbols of devotion as did the blood of a man from a Turkish legend who killed himself in order to be with his beloved for eternity...*

Rapidly I closed the floriography dictionary, the only one we had in the house that I knew of. I blew the candle on my desk out sharply, splashing a little wax onto the book. So, he did use the flower code after all. While I was thrilled that his feelings rose to meet mine, I was terribly frightened at the same time. His Tulip was more than a flower. Those dainty pink petals were a powerful explosion waiting to go off in my very restrictive vicarage home.

THE LYELL'S HOUSE, 53 HARLEY STREET, LONDON

The next morning, I arrived a few minutes early to offer my assistance to the Lyells in setting up breakfast, if needed. The young maid, Tess, greeted me at the door.

"Come with me, please," she said as she beckoned me inside. The interior of the Lyells' home on the ground floor consisted of a spacious hallway, a large dining room off to the right, the library to the left, and toward the back, Sir Charles's large office. Then there was a small study that I used for my office, and large room that served as specimen storage.

"Is there anything I can do to assist in the preparation of the meeting?" I asked her as we wove through the first floor to the paneled dining room.

I could hear the kitchen downstairs bustle with life which was just past a large and well-organized pantry with wide plank flooring. Colourfully woven rugs were placed throughout to protect the floor from spills. The three top stoves and black bellows were on the rear wall by the back door of the house, and the stocky cook, Mary, was most likely busy preparing a pan full of sizzling sausages with what smelled like fresh rosemary. My nostrils perked up as I inhaled the delicious aroma that had wafted up to the dining room. My mouth watered. My eyes roamed around to the left side of the dining room, and there, seated alone at the large round table, was Charles Darwin, sipping a cup of tea from a white porcelain teacup.

"None that I am aware of, Miss. Her ladyship asked that you take your seat here." Tess spoke in a lovely Cornish accent as she pointed to a specific chair. On the left side of the dining room table, which was covered with a thick, white tablecloth.

"Good morning," he said, carefully setting down his cup and preparing to stand to meet me. "I am Charles Darwin."

One of the most famous men of my time, and certainly the

most famous man of science, had just introduced himself to me. "It is an honor to meet you, sir," I said, not taking my eyes off his in what was certainly the most profound moment of my life. I gave a slight curtsey and remained standing.

"And your name is...?" he asked, blue eyes twinkling, a smile visible through his bushy white mustache.

"Oh. Yes, forgive me. I am Arabella Buckley. Sir Charles's literary secretary," I said with a quick smile, recovering from my initial stunned reaction. I sat down to his right so that the Lyells could sit directly across the table from him.

Charles Darwin looked like any other middle-aged man I might see on the streets of London. He was tall, about six feet, I guessed. Slightly stooped over. A bit of a belly rounded his black waistcoat and suit jacket, which had a velvet trim collar.

He said, "Lyell tells me you are quite the wonder with editing," and took another sip of the steaming tea.

"It is fascinating work that I enjoy," I responded, a bit nervously. Luckily, Sir Charles and Lady Lyell entered the dining room and Sir Charles pulled out a chair for Lady Lyell and motioned for tea. Tess quickly approached and poured tea for us all.

"Charles! Delighted to see you, my friend!" Sir Charles beamed and shook Mr. Darwin's hand fervently.

"Charles, Mary, always a joy to be here in the calm and out of the storm that is London!" Mr. Darwin replied with equal exuberance.

"Charles, we do hope you will stay with us for a while. You have met our Arabella, I presume? And how is that lovely wife of yours, Emma? Is she well?" Having sat down at the table across from Mr. Darwin, Lady Lyell stirred cream into her tea.

"Oh, yes, I have. Delighted," he said again to me. "Emma and the children are all fine and flourishing. All is well at Down House; I am grateful to report." Mr. Darwin said, smiling.

Mary the cook appeared in her immaculate white apron

spread broadly across her middle, her salt and pepper curls just peeking out of her kerchief, and served our breakfast of poached eggs, sausages, potatoes, and baked apples while the Lyells chatted with Mr. Darwin about family, friends, and local politics. I noticed several green ivy branches swaying in the breeze from the side windows and asked Lady Lyell about them.

"Yes, I like to keep window boxes along with the kitchen garden as well as open patches that we use for experimentation from time to time." She responded pleasantly, as if the gardens held a special place in her heart. Mary Lyell and I had built a particularly cordial relationship in a fairly short amount of time, and I treasured it. She was also a woman of science, being a conchologist or student of shells, and she seemed to understand the demands of a literary assistant quite well. She made me feel so welcome as to feel that I was filling a role as her own adult child. I knew her likes and dislikes as well as those of Sir Charles, I thought.

"In April we had Elizabeth, Francis, and Leonard home from school, which was quite a treat for Emma and me," Darwin said. "We have missed them so! Their minds are quite open and filled with vast amounts of knowledge. It is quite gratifying to see and makes for lively conversations out on the veranda."

"What a wonder they are!" Mary agreed. The Lyells had no children of their own and seemed to welcome news of the eight children in Darwin's brood.

"I am confounded as to how you actually get any work completed in such a boisterous house!" Sir Charles commented. We all laughed. "I was pleased to read your paper on climbing plants in the *Journal of the Proceedings of Linnean Society of London.* Well done, Charles."

"Thank you. I may continue that paper in book form. Would that be useful, do you think?" Mr. Darwin asked, slicing another brown sausage.

"Quite useful, yes. I think you should proceed with that idea. Perhaps, if you need a hand with the editing, inserting additional sections and what have you, Arabella could assist you. If she is willing, of course," Sir Charles added.

"Of course. I would be delighted," I responded, making a note in my book.

"Yes, perhaps. Let me think about what would be needed. I am staying here in London with my brother Erasmus for about ten days and may be able to sort that out over the course of my stay." Mr. Darwin nodded.

"Ten days!" Lady Lyell exclaimed. "Why, we must have a reception for you, here at our house. I will have my own secretary contact you and we will make all the arrangements. I will not take no for an answer. I simply must play you in a game of backgammon at the party." She was quite pleased.

All Mr. Darwin could manage to say was "Wonderful," "Yes," and "Delighted," in response to her vivacious planning. "But not in my honor, please, Mary. I do not want any fuss or acclaim."

"No fuss, just scientific discussion in a sociable atmosphere surrounded by friends, I assure you. And of course, you will attend as well, Miss Buckley, as I will be inviting other women of science," she added.

"I would be thrilled!" I replied with genuine excitement.

Mr. Darwin now sat more upright in his chair. "I have received several delightful letters from Hooker. We have been exchanging opinions on climbing plants and Lubbock's accusations of you. He can not seem to let that argument go."

"Is that so? Not that old truk again. What does Hooker say?" Sir Charles asked.

"Oh, that Lubbock's chapters are short and neglectful, in an almost juicy way. He supports you entirely, of course. We all know that you never would lift full sentences from anyone without giving reference," Mr. Darwin said emphatically.

"Absolutely not!" Sir Charles retorted. "The nerve of the man. I am glad he has turned over to politics from science. It suits him! Ha!" Both men laughed.

"On a different topic, you have heard of course about Admiral Fitzroy. Mary and I were saddened by the news. A nasty business." Sir Lyell said, buttering a slice of toast.

Lady Lyell nodded, swallowed, and said, "Yes, we are sorry for that loss."

"It came as a shock to me. I knew him so well during our voyage together on the *Beagle*, and did not think him capable of it. The suicide, I mean,' he sighed and stroked his long, white beard. "He did suffer from anxiety during our voyage and for a long time afterwards. Left his wife and daughter penniless, you know. Many of us contributed to a fund for his family. Well, at least he is at peace now, God rest him." Mr. Darwin took a sip of his tea. "Free from the anxieties. The murder on board and all that business afterwards with *Origin*. He was never quite happy that his voyage was the start of what he perceived were false accusations on the Bible." Mr. Darwin looked sadly down at his plate. "A hard business."

"And how is your work *Domestic Animals* coming along?" Sir Charles said quickly, changing the subject.

"Ah yes. I had been quite ill with my stomach distress in April, but I am managing work on chapters nine and ten now. I expect to be working on my edits soon."

"Very interesting, indeed. And what about your fourth edition of *Origin*? Has that been finished?" Sir Charles was trying to keep the discussion to more productive topics. "I understand *Origin* continues to be very popular with the public, as it should be."

"Not finished in the least. I must find the time to carry on with the revision. It is long overdue." Ruefully, he added, "I am hoping to expand on my connections to geology, and I am referring to your work now, and some of the discrepancies I see."

Sir Charles gave a quick snort. "If you mean discrepancies in the connections between geological changes through time and natural selection changes also occurring over great lengths of time, I am not there yet, Charles." He folded his arms and regarded Mr. Darwin with his bushy brows furrowed.

"I do, indeed. I must say that I am a bit confounded by your lack of acceptance of natural selection. But we can save that continued discussion for another time, later this week. But I will not quit the line of thinking, Charles." Mr. Darwin said, holding his index finger pointed in the air.

"Like a dog with a bone!" Sir Charles responded and both men laughed. We all smiled. I knew that Mr. Darwin was frustrated that Sir Charles had not officially accepted evolution as part of his explanation for variations found in animal skeletons. Sir Charles preferred to use geological reasoning to account for these changes. The topic had become quite awkward, and I was glad to see the two of them finding humor in the discord. The conversation paused as everyone relaxed with happy stomachs from the delicious breakfast.

"May I ask a question about *Origin*, sirs?" I asked during the pause, looking at Sir Charles for permission to speak. All three of my breakfast companions looked in my direction, surprised.

"Certainly. Please do," Sir Charles encouraged.

I pulled out my copy of *Origin* with the notes I had placed as markers sticking out of the top and placed throughout the book. On my notes, my words and images appeared like some kind of salad sprouting from within.

"My aim in asking is only to improve myself so that I may better assist you," I said.

"Yes, of course, go on," Sir Charles prodded, eyeing my book and notes with a curious interest.

"My question is this," I said. "How do we use the properties of natural selection to explain that which could be termed collaborative or sacrificial behaviour of one creature towards another? By way of example, I mean ants uniting in their work or cats feeling sympathy for other animals outside their species. Or even mothering behaviour, previously unseen by the creature?" I looked around the table at wide eyes staring back at me.

"Have I said something impertinent? If I have, I..." I stammered.

"Not at all," said Darwin, clearly amused.

"Are you thinking what I am thinking, Darwin?" Sir Charles asked.

"If you are thinking that these breakfast meetings have just become rather more interesting, then yes." Mr. Darwin replied with the light of learning burning in his blue eyes.

What was becoming clear was that our conversations had just begun.

Chapter Five

A Curious Specimen

Erasmus Darwin's House, London

1864 – 1865

"Charles do sit down and join me for a proper lunch. You look tired, dear fellow," said Erasmus Darwin, Charles's older brother by five years. Seated at the dining room table, the elder Darwin cleaned his round spectacles with his napkin. He was dressed in a white shirt with a black bow tie and black waistcoat with a charcoal grey jacket. His long, bushy whiskers filled out the sides of his face but were trimmed short at the beard, giving him a squarish-looking chin.

"London always tires me out so," Charles sighed as he flopped down in his appointed chair. He picked up his napkin and arranged it in his lap. "And it muddles my brain!"

"How was your time with Sir Charles yesterday? Productive, I hope?" Erasmus inquired, thanking his servant for his steaming bowl of chicken soup, which he eyed heartily.

"Yes and no," Charles replied. "We discussed work and family, but mostly work. Sir Charles approves of my turning my climbing plants paper into a book. That is the productive part." He paused as his bowl of soup was placed before him. "The less productive part was that he still refuses to expand geology to include the theory of evolution. We did not debate the issue, in the company that was present, but it frustrates me to no end, truly."

"Give him time. He will come around, surely. What do you mean, 'the company'?" Erasmus asked.

"Oh, Lady Lyell was present, as she usually is for our breakfast meetings. And another woman joined us, as well." Charles glanced up from his spoon.

"Is that so?" Erasmus, fully engrossed in his soup, did not look up at his brother.

"Yes. A new literary assistant. Sir Charles's eyesight is poor, you know. A Miss Arabella Buckley. About twenty-five years of age, I would guess. A most curious specimen," Charles added, stressing the word *specimen*.

Erasmus finally put his spoon down. "You speak of her as if she is some wild creature or something you are holding captive in a petri dish. Do tell!"

"I have never encountered another woman like her, I can truly say. Young, but the mind of a scholar. Her insight into evolution is formidable, even after discussing it in only one meeting. I cannot stop thinking about how unusual I find her." Charles explained as if he had found an outlier of a species out in the wilds of the Galapagos Islands. He dipped his spoon back into his bowl.

"Perhaps you can find some use for the girl," Erasmus said, pushing his empty bowl to the side and wiping his lips and beard with his napkin.

"As my older and mostly wiser brother, I defer to you, Ras. What do you have in mind? Some editing?"

"Perhaps. But if she is that unique and talented, should you not think larger, connect her to something more? Think beyond what is typical, like our grandfather did, Charles," Erasmus said, as he sat back in his chair, waiting for his next course to come.

Chapter Six

Darwin's Reception

The Lyell's House,
53 Harley Street, London

1864 – 1865

"There he is! The most dangerous man in all Britain!" a guest at the reception shouted as Mr. Darwin stepped through the wide front door and into the Lyells' hallway.

"Hardly," he said under his breath as he took off his tall black hat and quickly looked about the room. His cheeks were rosy, and his blue eyes shone brilliantly against his black suit and white cravat. As he took stock of the guests milling about, Tess, the maid, took his coat, hat, and walking stick as he thanked her. Seeing Mr. Hooker and Mr. Huxley standing in the dining room, Mr. Darwin went straight in and joined them, shaking hands with his long-time colleagues. I enjoyed watching how these friends and colleagues interacted with each other because it gave me deeper insight into them as men and not just as authors.

I was standing in the dining room with Sir Charles and Lady Lyell, and we went over and greeted Mr. Darwin with sincere affection. Soon we had formed one large circle with the Lyells naturally playing their parts as the hosts. Looking around at the guests, I felt that I knew a little more about each of them. I transcribed many letters a week from Sir Charles to the group—Huxley, Hooker, Wallage, and others—so in a way I was privy to their inner world as no one else was. I knew of the concerns, the arguments, the key points and counterpoints in the written correspondence among these incredibly intelligent men. Sir Charles had all of these insights, too, of course—after all, they were *his* letters. But none of the other members of the group besides the two of us were fully aware of all the goings on within the group through their correspondence. Sir Charles and I were at the center of a great whirling wheel of science, with spokes reaching out to the other men. In my new situation, I had gained access to an intangible library of these men's thoughts, opinions, hypotheses, and ideas. The realization of this insight intoxicated me as if I was the one drinking drams of whiskey.

Around us, glasses clinked, and silver trays whisked by in the hands of waiters dressed in black trousers and jackets and maids in white ruffled aprons, their heads covered in kerchiefs.

Smells of different men's perfumes wafted by—some were soapy smelling and some were spicy. Mingled together, they gave me a heady feeling as they mixed with the typical canopy of pipe and cigar smoke overhead. In the library, a quartet of two violins, a viola, and a cello—together with someone on the Lyells' piano—played selections from Johannes Brahms, Franz Liszt, and Anton Rubinstein. Delightful tunes were the final sparkling accessories to the evening's magical ensemble. The melodies reached through my body and touched my heart, leaving an impression I would never forget.

I was glad of my choice of attire that evening. I wore a green, three-tiered, ruffled frock with edges trimmed in white lace with a green brocade-fitted bodice. Lady Lyell was dressed similarly in a blue-tiered gown and white gloves. A blue gemstone graced her throat with a matching smaller stone on her wrist, both of which glimmered as she turned to talk to her guests.

I also took note of the men's cravats. Not having to tie one myself, I had always found them a bit of a mystery, and I marveled at the intricacy of a properly tied knot. My hypothesis had been that men of science, being particular about every single written word, would also be particular about the tying of their cravats, expecting perfection. This was not the case, however, as I studied the men about me. Mr. Darwin's cravat was expertly tied and flawless, while Mr. Huxley's, I noted, was a bit sloppy and crooked. Perhaps he was too busy to be bothered with trifling with a knot, I thought. After all, a knot is not a scientific paper.

Noticing the men's cravats and the couples happily mingling together brought Thomas to mind, as he was never far from my thoughts. How I would have loved to have been on his arm at this party! I thought of him daily and missed him painfully. Would he be on a horse, riding through his land about now? Or would he be playing cards or seeing patients? He was in his own world, and I was in a quite fine world of my own. A lovely, glittering party was a perfect distraction from wondering about Thomas. For now, at least. I took comfort in Lady Lyell, my friend and mentor.

I leaned towards her, as she was still next to me, and asked, "Someone said Mr. Darwin was "the most dangerous man" when he came in. What was that about?"

She nodded. "After *Origin* was published, I am sure you recall the negative reaction many Christians initially had about Natural Selection, especially in view of your family's connection at St. Mary's."

"Yes, I do recall that it struck deep at the heart of Christians who take a literal view of the Bible."

"Yes, well, during that time, Mr. Darwin was called out as the most dangerous man in all of Britain by those who feared he was taking aim at the Bible and Christian beliefs about Adam and Eve and how the Bible describes Creation. The rumors are that there is a secret society, even today, here in London that aspires to do him in," she whispered.

"But that is absurd! The idea of a great Creator and Natural Selection can occupy one space together…"

"Not everyone would agree with you, my dear. Not even everyone in this room." She angled her head in the direction of a woman across the room. "Mrs. Gatty there is an example. I had difficulty getting her to accept my invitation, so strong are her views against evolution. But feel free to discuss and debate the idea, Arabella. That is why we are all here. To advance scientific thinking. And I believe your mind is naturally keen."

The Lyells both looked radiantly happy to be among friends and men of science, and their party was very well attended. With a few exceptions, the guests were mostly men of middle age. I had been introduced to many men in Sir Charles's circle of friends, including Mr. Babbage, a portly man with a fascinating calculating machine, and Mr. Wallace, whom Lady Lyell and I had met during lunch several weeks ago with Sir Charles.

Throughout the party, Sir Charles's main group of friends—Mr. Darwin, Mr. Huxley, Mr. Hooker, Mr. Wallace, Lady Lyell, with me, always at her side—had mingled freely amongst the guests, but near the end of the evening we came together again, as if afraid to miss out on precious time together.

"Do tell the story of your adventure with the Bishop of Oxford, Mr. Huxley. You tell it with such delightful animation," Lady Lyell requested, her face taking on a youthful glow.

Mr. Huxley cleared his throat, his chin down to his chest,

and looked around at the circle of people whose eyes were now on him. Clearly, he enjoyed the role of storyteller and being the center of attention.

"Very well. It was in 1860, about a year after *Origin* shook the world. You will recall the story of "Soapy Sam," as we referred to him, or Samuel Wilberforce, *contra* Mr. Darwin. Soapy Sam was a slippery fellow; he knew nothing about the natural sciences but pretended he did, with the help of Richard Owen. Very well; I'll continue." The crowd looked pleased in anticipation of a good story, one that they all knew, but enjoyed the retelling of greatly. Charles Darwin gave a faint chuckle and looked down at his shoes.

"Charles here was seen as a terrible radical as he had undermined everything the world believed in up to that point." Mr. Huxley prominently said. The crowd nodded solemnly. "We were in a meeting of the British Association in 1860 on the thirtieth of June, I believe it was. Richard Owen and I had already clashed on man's position in nature two days earlier at the Oxford University Museum of Natural History. You see, Wilberforce, a bulldog of a man but a great speaker, had criticized Darwin's implication that humans and various species of apes share common ancestors. Two days later, here we were with about seven hundred people, in a heated debate about church and science. There were students, men of science, your old friend here, Darwin—and Robert Fitzroy who was present to lecture on storms and weather. And, of course, the Bishop of Oxford, who at one point said loudly during the debate, 'Have turnips turned into men?'" Mr. Huxley did a grand imitation of the old bishop's voice; the crowd pealed with laughter. "I believe it was at that point that Fitzroy, a grey-haired, Roman-nosed old man, held up the Bible and said something like, 'The truth is here! Believe in God, not man!'"

Huxley paused to make sure his audience was with him. "The room was so tense," he continued. "I could feel it as if electric. I responded to the old bulldog, 'Well, it is clear you have not even read the book!' I had dared to challenge them both. The bishop—Soapy Sam—was not pleased at all to be chastised in front of such a large, raucous crowd. He sputtered at that and then burst out, clearly speaking to me, 'Was your grandmother or your grandfather an ape?'" Again, the circle of guests laughed in an uproar. "I simply replied that I would not be ashamed to have a monkey for my ancestor, but I would be ashamed to be connected with a man who used his great gifts to obscure the truth. The bishop was immediately crest-fallen! Having gotten the better of old Soapy, we all went off cheerfully to dine together afterwards." The crowd laughed and said, "Quite right!" and "Cheers to that!"

"The bishop claimed that Darwin here was the greatest heretic on earth," Huxley concluded. "The Devil's Chaplain. But we know him as our Charles, the greatest man of science in the world." He held up a short glass.

"Hear! Hear!" the crowd exclaimed, holding up their glasses in a toast to Mr. Darwin.

"My next work will be about earthworms, I believe," Mr. Darwin offered quietly to the crowd. Everyone laughed heartily at his good humor and good nature. Lady Lyell laughed so heartily that she spilled some of her champagne, but no one seemed to notice.

As our little crowd of Darwin supporters broke into smaller conversations, I glanced around the room filled with people chatting, the occasional empty glass and plate left unattended on a side table. Seated in the corner of the large office were two women dressed in modest attire. Other than the servants, Lady Lyell, myself, and one other with Mr. Wallace, these were the only women at the reception, I noticed.

"Lady Lyell, who are those women seated in the corner?" I asked.

She smiled. "Yes, let us go and meet them straight away

before they become occupied in conversation, dear. I invited Mary Somerville, too, but since she lives in Italy now and is getting a bit older, she has difficulties traveling great distances, so she declined. But I hope to introduce you to her at some point. She is a marvel!"

As we walked across the room, I observed and admired the two women. Both had thick, dark brown hair and were dressed conservatively. But what stood out to me about them was how intelligent they appeared to be. Their heads were bent down in conversation, and I could tell just by looking at their faces and attentive expressions that they were intelligent, and that intrigued me.

Lady Lyell took the initiative to introduce us, of which I was glad. "Ladies, may I introduce to you a young woman of science here in London and one of our own colleagues, Miss Arabella Buckley." I gave a modest curtsey, my gown billowing out at my sides.

"And Arabella, this is Miss Elizabeth Carne, a geologist from Cornwall with banking concerns here in London, and with her is Mrs. Margaret Gatty, who has published her studies of seaweeds."

"Very pleased to meet you," we all said. I forced myself to stifle a snigger. The study of seaweed was all of a sudden quite laughable to me, as it seemed to me to be quite a boring thing to study. I would soon be proven wrong.

"Geology is one of my current interests," I said, trying to regain my composure. "I am working with Sir Charles on the third edition of *Principles of Geology*."

"I admire his work very much," said Mrs. Gatty. "And it is very gratifying to see another young face amongst the sea of men of science." With a smile, she added, "And while I have never supported Darwin's theories, being a Christian woman, I look forward to seeing Sir Charles's new edition."

"I quite agree. How wonderful to have another woman of

science amongst the group. And yes, I do admire *Principles of Geology* as well," echoed Miss Carne. "We have many examples in Penzance of changes to rock formations over time, which I know is one of his areas of conviction. My father and I have keenly studied various formations in Cornwall and have evidence of rapid transformation. Perhaps we could discuss that in the future. I would be interested in hearing your thoughts on that firsthand—and Sir Charles's, as well."

"You do us a great honor of complimenting his work. Thank you. I, for one, would love to discuss rapid transformation. Though I am not sure Sir Charles would be as easily convinced..." I trailed off.

"That is understandable," Miss Carne replied with some mirth in her tone. "But my father was equally steadfast in his beliefs of rapid transformation based on fissures in Bodmin Moor, for example, that appear as evidence of huge rocks rapidly thrust up through the earth."

"I believe you both have papers written to this effect, do you not?" Mrs. Gatty offered, politely.

"Yes, we do. In the *Transactions of the Royal Geological Society of Cornwall*. And what of your latest works, Mrs. Gatty? Do fill us in," Miss Carne suggested with interest.

"I usually work from my home near York, but lately I have been by the sea at Hastings in Sussex," she began. "I write up my findings when I return."

"Is that difficult? I prodded. "To work at home?"

"Only when one of my ten children is there to cause interruptions," she explained, laughing. "I am finishing an introductory book on my seaweed collections to follow my book of short stories aimed at young readers, *Parables from Nature*." She explained. "I am quite busy and fond of my topics, as mundane as seaweed sounds." Again, we laughed. Her genuine nature was endearing. Maybe seaweed wasn't quite as dull as I'd assumed.

"My friend's too modest," Miss Carne said. "Your books are quite popular, Mrs. Gatty. You are practically a household name throughout Britain."

Mrs. Gatty gave a short sigh. "Thank you. I have been blessed. To think that it all came from my boredom during an illness after my seventh child!" She paused and looked at me. "Tell me, Miss Buckley, will Sir Charles write about Mr. Darwin's theory of evolution in his new edition?"

Not wanting to turn the happy gathering sour with the obvious dichotomy of opinion regarding evolution, I responded, lightheartedly, "I believe the debate continues, Mrs. Gatty." The two women laughed heartily. Miss Carne's large brown eyes told me that she understood my meaning completely.

When several men I did not know approached us, clearly wanting to talk with Mrs. Gatty, I excused myself, even though I had become instantly fond of these two women. I made a mental note to correspond with each of them later. I felt I had a great deal I could learn from their thinking. Books for younger readers. A capital idea! I thought.

I looked around at the crowd, which by this time had divided again into several groups, each embroiled in fervent discussion. Mr. Babbage was discussing his latest progress on his counting machine with several men. Mr. Hooker and Mr. Huxley were deep in conversation, their heads tilted towards one another so that they could be heard over the din of the clanking dishes and mixed laughter. They were soon joined by Mr. Darwin, with whom I was hoping to have another discussion following our breakfast meeting.

Mr. Darwin was a very popular guest. There always seemed to be someone by his side demanding his attention. I had marshalled my thoughts on collaboration, sacrifice, and mothering as parts of evolution, but it seemed that I would have no access to share my thoughts with him at this gathering. Moreover, I did not want to seem brash by pushing my way towards him. He must have seen me skulking, though, because suddenly he called me over, inviting me to join their discussion.

"Miss Buckley, shall we continue our conversation of the other morning about the evolution of collaboration in ants? Please, come and join us."

"I would love nothing more," I said and walked over. "Good evening," I said to the men standing next to Mr. Darwin. The other men seemed to draw closer in, curious as to what Mr. Darwin would say next.

"When we last spoke, I mentioned that in *Origin*, you discuss repeated behaviours becoming habits that are then passed on as instincts. For example, bees make honey with the least waste of material and time, and then the swarm that has succeeded the best transmits those economical instincts to new swarms. Is that correct?" I asked, concentrating hard on my subject.

"Yes, I think you have it verbatim, Miss Buckley." Mr. Darwin said.

"The part that I think could be explained a bit more is the transmission process. How does that work? How do you account for the similarity in heredity for those nonphysical elements?"

The men around Mr. Darwin looked on, quickly becoming fascinated by this exchange.

"Ah. You have correctly identified a difficulty that requires explanation in another book. *Origin* does focus on the physical attributes, as you identify," he answered. "Sir Charles, what say you to Miss Buckley's question?" Mr. Darwin turned to him.

"Certainly, to your point, there are other mammals and even insects that cooperate, Miss Buckley." My employer gave me a friendly smile of encouragement. "What say we put the question to those here to come up with an answer. Hooker, what do you think?"

"I think Miss Buckley is a natural lady of science," Hooker said.

With that, the men gave friendly chuckles. I knew being called a lady of science would strike a nerve with some, considering the raucous arguments in the scientific world about what true science is and who is allowed to study or be affiliated with it.

I quickly continued, while I had their attention. "Mr. Darwin, I agree that more explanation would augment your next book. Quite so. It seems to me that you hint that natural selection also includes nonphysical attributes like motivation and collaboration, which would mean that those nonphysical but observable features are transferred. For example, the kitten who has never mothered and has no mother indeed knows how to mother instinctively, and possibly transfers mothering via the spirit or soul of the creature. I have been thinking about this and wonder what you think about the transference of the soul?"

He nodded. "As you may know, I began questioning Christian teachings when I lost my daughter, Annie, at the age of only ten," he said, forlornly.

"Perhaps a greater being, then. A deity," suggested Mr. Wallace to the group.

"Yes, who gives the power to start the process of evolution and includes the evolution of a creature's spirit as well? I have always thought that Christianity and evolution can go hand in hand," I offered.

One of the men whispered to another behind his hand, just barely audible, "Is she not Sir Charles's secretary?" The other man shrugged.

Just then, a small tray of glasses slipped from a servant's hand as she tried to navigate around the corner and among the people in the room. Several glasses fell with a great *crash* on the floor.

She quickly bent down to scoop up the glass in her hand.

"No, not with your..." I blurted out, too late. A crimson ribbon of thick blood streamed out of the right side of her right hand.

The men stood frozen, not knowing what to do in this particular situation.

"Allow me," I said, bending over with a clean cloth napkin that I grabbed from the nearest table. I quickly checked the wound for any remaining glass.

"Oh!" groaned Mr. Darwin as he turned and looked away. He then moved away from the group.

A curious reaction, I noted to myself.

"Let me wrap this for now. Go back to the kitchen and wash this with clean water and then have the cook bandage it for you. Ask one of the other servants to attend to the mess," I suggested.

"Yes, miss," she said, meekly, as she turned towards the kitchen stairs.

The men had reconvened some feet away from where we now stood and away from the glass.

"Now, where were we?" I asked Mr. Darwin, not missing a beat.

Having recovered from the bloody accident, Mr. Darwin said, "You were very kind to step in to help that maid," he said. "I dislike the sight of blood myself. You proved your mettle, Miss Buckley," he looked at me as if he sincerely admired my effort with the servant.

"Not a serious injury, so all is well. I had younger siblings growing up," I replied.

He nodded and said to me. "Now, regarding our discussion. The topic raises a kettle of fish that perhaps we should discuss more. When the Lyells next come to Down House, I invite you to come as well. We can better continue this discussion in the solitude of my gardens," Mr. Darwin concluded. "London makes my brain go higgledy-piggledy; you understand." He said with a smile. With that, he excused himself for more food and drink and Lady Lyell flew up to my side. I could barely contain my excitement given this invitation to not only be at Down House, but to actually discuss my own area of interest which seemed to also interest Mr. Darwin was beyond my wildest dreams. I was ecstatic.

"That poor clod of a man Wallace is standing alone like a solitary crustacean trying to blend in with its environment," Lady Lyell observed. "Be a dear and go speak with him, Miss Buckley, and bring him out of his shell."

"Certainly. I will do my best," I replied, with a kind smile. "He is a quiet man, but is clearly capable of genius, in view of his first paper on natural selection at the Linnean."

"How generous of you, my dear." With that, she left me with a smile and a swish of her skirts to entertain more of her guests.

I walked over to him slowly, trying not to look like a hungry crustacean-eating octopus about to snatch its prey.

"Hello, Mr. Wallace. We met at luncheon with the Lyells. I am Arabella Buckley, if you recall?"

"Oh yes, Miss Buckley," he said, relieved as the last woman at the reception who I had not yet met appeared by his side. "This is my fiancée, Miss Leslie."

"Very nice to meet you," I said with a smile. "And how are you enjoying the reception?"

"Older men, talking about science, can be a bit..." Miss Leslie fumbled, searching for the right word.

"Dull?" I asked. She and I both burst into laughter. Miss Leslie and I appeared to be about the same age, and I could tell she was a great deal livelier than Mr. Wallace.

"The real advancement and discussion should be on Spiritualism. Now *that* is a fascinating area of work," Mr. Wallace broke in.

"Oh, and by work do you mean that you are conducting scientific experiments in this area, and do you mean contacting the deceased?" I asked.

"Yes. We contact the dead via people who serve as mediums. I would call it more like observations and documentation at this point." Mr. Wallace leaned in, clearly eager to discuss the subject.

"I see. Can you tell me about some of your observations?" I wondered if this work could truly be called science, for many in scientific circles were disbelievers.

"Yes, we are in the process of identifying mediums, and I have found several known to be reliable and steeped in the ways of spiritualism. We are using them to collect information and contact loved ones, such as my brother, Herbert."

"That all sounds incredible. I wonder what is required to be a medium. Could I, for example, be a medium?" I asked.

"Not everyone is equipped to be a medium, Miss Buckley," Mr. Wallace replied with a bit of a scoff.

"I truly am interested to learn more about Spiritualism, Mr. Wallace. How would I go about acquiring more knowledge?" I was thinking of my dear sister, Jane, who had passed and how I would dearly love to contact her.

"Perhaps you would like to come over for dinner," he said. " I could show you more of what I am working on." He seemed willing to include those interested in learning about this innovation. "In addition, you may be interested in my phrenology work," he added. "Have you heard of it?"

"Why, let me think. The study of bumps on the head, is it not?" I pondered, wondering how I would react if Mr. Wallace wanted to feel my own head.

Miss Leslie interjected. "Oh yes, please do come to dinner.

It is not often that Alfred invites a woman to join us, and I would love to have you come..."

I decided to snap up the opportunity before Mr. Wallace could change his mind. "Then it is settled!" I replied. "I will come to dinner at your convenience. Now, I must carry on assisting Lady Lyell in entertaining her guests. I will await your invitation."

I returned to Lady Lyell's side in one of the smaller rooms where desks were removed and additional seating was placed about the room. Lady Lyell leaned over to me from her seat and asked, "How did you fare with Mr. Wallace and Miss Leslie?"

"Quite well, actually. I am invited for dinner to discuss Spiritualism in greater detail, as I am quite interested in the topic."

"Stuff and nonsense, that Spiritualism. Talking to the dead, indeed. Be careful, Miss Buckley," Lady Lyell warned. "Spiritualism is not a recognized science, shall we say. Sir Charles and Mr. Darwin do not share Mr. Wallace's opinion of Spiritualism being a worthy endeavor, if you take my meaning."

"I see. Thank you for the advice. But it seems to me it could be quite a breakthrough in our thinking."

"There is a difference between 'hope' and 'science.' Best to keep your new interest to yourself, dear," she said quickly and quietly.

Mr. Huxley was standing by the large marble fireplace in Sir Charles's office where several guests congregated in the room's pleasant seating, his forearm on the mantle and his other hand holding a dram of whiskey. From the look of him, he had already had several that evening. His necktie was loose and his hair slightly disheveled.

"Ah. Miss Buckley," he said as I entered the room. "What do you think about the free love debate? Do you think we should reform our marital practices and allow multiple willing partners, doing away with the institution of marriage?" He asked this question with a wide sweep of his arm, throwing him off balance just a bit. His face was red, and he seemed to be sweating from the heat of the fire.

Possibly the rudest thing ever said to me and certainly unexpected, but I did not cower. I had never done anything to him or anyone here that would elicit this topic. I assumed they had been discussing the topic as I entered. The crowded room became quiet, and all eyes were on me. I knew Mr. Huxley's harsh and argumentative reputation from his letters to Sir Charles, which I had reviewed. He was reputed to be an atheist and he looked like the devil himself, disheveled and wild-eyed from drink. I also knew that he was trying to shock and embarrass me, the youngest female at the party. His glass was almost empty; I needed to have a care in my response. I wondered if he had seen or had knowledge of my outings with Thomas. I responded quickly.

"I believe that love takes many forms, Mr. Huxley," I said, pleasantly and with a smile.

Several people in the room clapped for my reply. Someone said, "She is a quick wit, that one."

"Well said, Miss Buckley," cheered Alfred Wallace as he and Miss Leslie took seats close to the fire. A maid offered them cheese from a tray. Mr. Wallace took several pieces and devoured them before the servant had stepped away.

Huxley had me in his sights. "In that case, Miss Buckley, do tell us about your own situation. Do you see and entertain gentlemen guests? Are you in love? Are you committed to one man or perhaps one woman, or perhaps several of each? Do tell us," he said aggressively. The conversation had at once gone very wrong. Clearly, he was trying to provoke me in front of the crowd. I would not give him the satisfaction.

"Stand down, Huxley. You are way out of line," a man in

the back of the room called out.

"Let her answer. It is a party, after all, and is supposed to be entertaining," Mr. Huxley slurred back.

I tried to quell my inner panic. Should I stay quiet and hope he will lose interest in me or risk trying to back him down as the bully he was? I looked around the room for help and found none. The quiet in the room became uncomfortable. I had to say something. I did not want to seem the simpering type.

"Very well then. If you must know," I said, hesitantly, as if I was about to reveal a secret. "Yes, I do enjoy and in fact love many prominent and up-and-coming suitors. And I am committed to all of them, I would say," I said, a little defiantly so that I would be perceived as conversing in earnest as I began to toy with Mr. Huxley.

"Oh ho!" The crowd gasped and eyed me with great interest now. Mr. Huxley was enjoying the banter and I could see his face light up, an indication that he thought he was about to get the better of me. He took another swig of his whiskey, finished it, and set the glass down on a tray. The servant whisked it away. He paused for effect.

"Then pray, do tell us who these lucky admirers are, where you meet them, and how you manage so many!" he called out.

"Yes, how am I to explain...hmm," I parried. "My suitors are very challenging. I find it difficult on occasion to find time for them all, separately and as a group. I do try to integrate them. I often sit with them in quiet, dark corners, and I almost always take them to my bedchamber each night."

"Yes, go on." Mr. Huxley was practically drooling now, pathetically enjoying my self-disclosure.

"I sometimes meet them in the library and sometimes in this very room," I whispered. My suitors that I greatly admire and cavort with daily are..." I paused and quickly looked around the room with flirtatious eyes. Lady Lyell looked at me fearfully, mouthing the word, 'no.' "My suitors are the subjects of science. Geology. Biology. Botany. And I am committed to fulfilling them with all my energy. I am making the sciences my life's mission, Mr. Huxley."

His mouth fell open for a second. He then shook his head in disbelief over what I had just said. The crowd roared and cheered me on. "You have met your match, Huxley!" and "Well said, Miss Buckley!"

Two valuable invitations and one arrogant man of science put in his place. *A productive evening,* I said to myself, happily, as I said my goodnights and walked through the hallway to the front door. The clock on the mantle on the wall was approaching midnight, and I thought to access a Hansom cab before they stopped running for the evening. Tess helped me with my coat and into the cab.

The horse's hooves *clip-clopped* gently along Harley Street and then turned left to head towards Paddington. I couldn't stop thinking about my interaction at the party.

Thomas had his life and his adventures in New Zealand. Now I had mine. I said at the party that my life's mission was the sciences. I had not realized that before tonight. But it was true. I dedicated myself to the advancement of science not knowing where it would take me.

Chapter Seven

Arabella, a Force of Nature

St. Mary's Churchyard,
Downe Village, Kent

1864 – 1865

Charles Darwin sat down on a stone bench under a yew tree in the churchyard of St. Mary's in Downe village, next to several ancient headstones. His children walked directly to the church door, while his wife, Emma, lingered behind to have a word with him.

"Perhaps you will use the time while we are at the service to ponder your blessings under that tree," Emma said with a smile, hoping to cheer him up as their family marched into the church.

Such an incredibly patient wife, Darwin thought, fully intending to obey her request, as he sat on that cool stone bench under the enormous, knotted yew tree. He gave Emma an appreciative smile as she turned and followed the children into the church and became immersed in his contemplations.

For years now I have sat under this Yew tree in the churchyard each Sunday among the tombstones, not attending services since the death of our dear Annie at ten years old in '51. I doubt there can be a God, given what happened to that poor child with such promise, such potential! Instead, I wait for Emma and our remaining children to finish their church duties and return to this tree. The dense foliage provides a dark, opaque shade, for which I am thankful.

My blessings. Emma is truly a blessing. Her abilities and demeanor set her apart among women. I believe her to be a most admirable, model woman. Until I met Emma, I had scant knowledge of women, really. I barely knew anything about them other than their physical properties. Most men of our class are in similar circumstances. We are whisked away from women in childhood to attend boarding schools with other males. To think that when I wrote down the pros and cons of marriage all those years ago, I said that living with a woman would be better than a dog!

All I cared about then was having enough funds to buy books. Ha! I remember back in the early days of my marriage. Lyell and I had a running joke that we would leave our wives and spend our time in the science clubs. I had little appreciation of Emma and women then! I barely appreciated that Emma could play the piano with the skill of Chopin. Or that she could read Jane Austen in a way that keeps me entertained for three or four hours at a time. Much less her skill with keeping our children and household humming along happily, day after day. Especially with my stomach illnesses.

Emma has certainly broadened my outlook on women. For, what exposure did I have prior to marriage? What exposure does any man have of women, for it is seldom and far between. Growing up, my mother dead, I was left to be raised inadequately by overbearing sisters which drove me outdoors to my passion and my truest companions: beetles, worms, and butterflies. Though I do fondly remember the girls of my childhood. Neighbors that played games and I enjoyed their pretty conversations. I was so anxious and nervous as I mixed with them! The little exposure this provided me with gave me no impression of women's abilities. Perhaps companionship, yes. But not equal to that of the companionship of my brothers. They, like my grandfather and father, debated and tested the world, it seemed. No, there is much more to Emma than there was to the girls of my youth, and I do thank whatever deity might exist for her poise, grace, and strength.

What else. I am grateful and thankful for my work. Yes, my work is my lifeblood. With all my multifarious projects, I am perhaps most grateful for the help I receive with my work. My articles and books require much proofing and editing, where assistance is very valuable. I find actually that women are quite capable in this regard, come to think of it. My Hetty is an excellent judge of the merits and accuracy of my work and provides a ready-made and frugal source of assistance. I have paid her a token sum of money to show some monetary appreciation for her fine efforts, haven't I? She has a keen intelligence. Is she an anomaly among women? Certainly, men who could review and edit are plentiful, but they are not cheap, close by, or as willing a worker, are they?

Is that a Hummingbird Hawk Moth? It is! And a lovely specimen. I see it feeding among the church flowers with its long proboscis. It must have come down from the tall woods around Downe. I admire its blueish-grey forewings and its orange hindwings. I can hear it humming! What a joy to behold.

Where was I? Ah yes, my blessings. Women who return my queries about botany and animal behaviour are quite astute as well. I have found they provide very useful experimental data about carnivorous plants, such as Mrs. Mary Treat. And Lady Lyell has provided mollusk specimens for my work..it seems they go out of their way to help me as no man would.

Then again, there is Miss Buckley. What a curious force of nature she is. I cannot recall ever seeing anyone, even a male, learn so quickly. And she is not just learning to recite or inform, but her discourse is uncanny and fascinating to listen to her notations are insightful. Clearly, she has few equals among females, an outlier of her gender, to be sure. Few women could have her intellect. And she has no formal university training that she can fall back on. Her intellect continues to adapt and rise to any challenge given to her, and she is becoming fully engaged and more and more accepted in the scientific environment. I do enjoy our discussions on my theories and experiments, as well as Lyell's, Wallace's, Huxley's, and Hooker's. And was she not so capable when that maid cut her hand? She adroitly dealt with the injury with remarkable speed and kindness. How I hate the sight of blood. I am useless in that kind of situation. Yes, I am grateful for knowing Miss Buckley and will continue to seek her out for my editing needs whenever possible.

My, the bees here are plentiful. There must be a colony up in the eaves of the church. Yes, I see the worker bees buzzing about the garden and then each going back to the same place. I paused in my recollections to stroll over and as I inspect their activity, I see them almost churning in the busy work.

Is Miss Buckley an example of the evolution of women as they slowly change towards overcoming life-threatening barriers to survive, as evolution and natural selection would predict? Which woman is more evolved for the benefit of the survival of the species—Miss Buckley, who seems as capable in thinking as a man, or Emma, who carries skills that augment those of a man? If it is Miss Buckley, would imply that the demands of the whole world really require twice as many skills as men possess? Or will it be women of high intellect that become extinct as women of more nurturing skills provide the continuation of the species? In truth, when I have observed and delved into the evolution of "man," woman was not part of my considerations. Perhaps a few pages in a later book...

Why, George Eliot is one of my favorite authors, and we all originally thought she was a man.

Her books are acclaimed for their skillful plot development, just like a man's. Marian Evans is her real name and she does an excellent job of pulling out the moral and philosophical issues associated with the growing despair and spiritual decline of our society. Among her works, I consider *The Mill on the Floss* unsurpassed in intellectual depth. Is she another outlier, like Miss Buckley? Are their brains equal in size and makeup to a man's?

I remember speaking with John Mill about freedom of speech and freedom of the press when he mentioned that stifled opponents may have valuable information and insight to share. This insight he applied to women, saying that women have ideas but instead are almost enslaved to men. Is it possible that Emma is enslaved to me? If women had more authority, would they have better-articulated opinions?

Still, the large and prevailing thought on women is clearly that their place in public should be a silent one and that their place is in the home, with the brood, so to speak. And I cannot say I disagree with that. In fact, I applaud it. Emma has no time for studying and writing articles and books! Ha! The thought of it. The tenor of this opinion is so strong in male society today and for the last hundred years, that I make no mention of any alternative viewpoints in public. The last thing I need is to be the most hated man in Britain, along with being the most dangerous man. And if I were to echo John Mill here, I would surely be the most hated man among men.

But I do have to ask why. Are women that intimidating to men? No, I believe it is more like annoying and cloying, given that they lack the credentials to make justifiable conclusions about science, for example, which we men have been reading for years, decades, centuries. Admittedly, there have been times when my daughter and sisters provided me with edits on a manuscript, I did become annoyed at their annotations and tried to justify my original words. Do I have that same reaction with Miss Buckley? While I might initially have the hair on my neck rise slightly when my sister or daughter edits and corrects my work, I do attempt to put the corrections in perspective, do I not? Why that is the reason I have them read the work in the first place!

The work must go on despite my vexing and time-consuming stomach problems that cause me to have to spend all too much time on the privy, and Miss Buckley, Hetty, and my women correspondents are a means to that continuation. Ah, everyone is coming out of the church, and here's Emma and the family!

"There now. We are ready to depart. Did you have a proper discussion with yourself about your blessings?" Emma asked, straightening her hat and taking my extended arm.

"I did. And you were at the top of my list!" I truthfully responded. But I kept my other musings to myself. No sense stirring up the pot, I told myself.

Chapter Eight

The Long Goodbye

Regent Park,
London

1864 – 1865

"It is nearly time for me to say goodbye. I board my ship in two days' time for Christchurch," Thomas said, looking down at the gravel path as we walked around the still and green waters of the boating lake in Regent's Park, just a mile from my home in Paddington. Henry was with us, admiring the enormous evergreen trees and waterfowl, lost in his own thoughts.

"I must return to my sheep, my patients, and my partnership with Mr. Williams," Thomas explained.

I barely heard what he was saying. "Yes, I recall you saying so when we saw you last. And how long will the journey be?" I asked, trying to be stoic.

"About seventy to eighty days across the Pacific from Panama, depending on the wind and the currents. A long journey to be sure. First, though we head southwest through the West Indies and Cuba," he replied softly.

"Well, I wish you fair winds and seas." My voice was shaky and cracked a bit as I spoke. Thomas made no reply. "One can imagine that the Boating Lake is a miniature version of the seas you will travel," I said, my hand sweeping outward towards the water. "I have not traveled across the sea, so I try to imagine it thus." I smiled.

He looked out at the water and folded his arms at his chest. "Try imagining that all you can see in any direction is that colour of the water. Only the greenish blue all around you in any direction. At times, especially at night, the sea looks black and shining, like glass. And it can be as high as the green grass there," he said, pointing to the grassy hills surrounding the lake. "In fact, if you imagine the entire topography of the park, with its hills and valleys, as water, you about have the sea captured."

I imagined myself on a ship, the wind in my face and the sound of the waves crashing on the hull. How lovely the sunset must be setting over the sea, reflecting off the water, casting a glow that would infuse the water for miles. But I also tried to imagine the sea's wrath. How it would toss a ship like a toy in a storm, the crew clinging to the rigging, and the waves crashing over the deck. A sea voyage, I imagined, could be both exhilarating and tempt death at the same time. And yet, despite the fear and the uncertainty, I did envy Thomas for his courage and ability to experience its majesty and power. For now, though, I had to content myself with the tales I had heard and the books I could read and wait for the day when I could set sail and experience the wonder of it for myself.

We walked down the long path as a few carriages and a couple, the woman with a lovely purple hat and matching parasol strolled past. We came upon the edge of the large, green waters of the Boating Lake and looked out as some graceful Swans floating effortlessly on top of the water. *That is what I am also doing.* I said to myself. *Trying to make an effortless appearance while churning and flapping wildly inside.*

The clouds overhead spread across the sky like a thick, grey quilt, typical of London. Very few people were about, as the weather was not particularly conducive to strolling in the park. A mother and little boy, perhaps three years old, tossed a ball. An elderly man sat on a wrought iron bench, feeding bread to the ducks. Several older children played at the edge of the lake, floating sticks and lightly splashing each other. Henry tried to entertain us by imitating a swan we saw on the banks of the pond, waddling and swaying to and fro with an occasional flurry of a large wing flap. We laughed at his silly antics.

"Henry is a dear for trying to cheer you up, do you not think so?" I asked Thomas, trying to make conversation.

"Is it only done to cheer me up, and not you as well?" he asked, turning to look at me as we walked along the grassy banks, which reached up to lovely flower beds with tall shrubs behind them, encircling the lake.

Just at that moment a lump of emotion welled up in my throat, and I found I could not speak.

"You are quite young and have many opportunities ahead of you." He smiled faintly as I looked up at him. "I, on the other hand, am older and at a completely different stage of life. Many of my opportunities are now full responsibilities. My land, my practice. But you have your whole life ahead of you."

"If you are trying to say that you are done having adventures, I do not believe you," I said, with a small laugh.

He smiled. "What I am trying to say, and a bit badly, is that many men will want your attention. Men that might be your age, geographically desirable, and eligible, unlike me."

"The only attention I want is from my men of science, who are becoming both my friends and colleagues, and who also happen to be older than you, I might add," I retorted.

"Charles Darwin, is it? He is the one I should be jealous of, if you'll be spending any time you can with him?" I could not tell if Thomas was joking.

"I will be traveling to Downe with Sir Charles and Lady

Lyell very soon to visit Down House," I primly clarified. "I cannot wait to see Mr. Darwin's experimentation firsthand and to further discuss my thoughts on species collaboration with him. Did you know that he has asked to use my data on half-bred pigeons' roosting behaviour in trees? I am still in disbelief that Charles Darwin has any interest in my work. *And* he intends to refer to my data in his paper to be published on this subject. Imagine, my data being used by *the* Charles Darwin, the foremost thinker in natural sciences of our time," I gushed and went on before Thomas could get a word in edgewise.

"Mr. Darwin has been quite upset at Sir Charles for his tepid inclusion of evolutionary theory in Sir Charles's recent book *Geological Evidences of the Antiquity of Man*. Perhaps I can develop a way for them to close their gaps in understanding during the visit to Down House."

Thomas shook his head admiringly. "You are in your element, I daresay. Women of science typically stick to botany. But you! You are going where few women of science have gone, and it is impressive. You have a keen intellect. Perhaps you will go into politics one day," he mused.

"Not I, but perhaps you," I replied. "You would make a fair and accomplished politician, I daresay."

A man walking towards us raised his hand in greeting and seemed determined to interrupt our conversation. Immediately I recognized Mr. Prescott, my neighbor from St Mary's Mansions across the street on St Mary's Terrace. I stifled a groan.

"Unpopular neighbor, dead ahead," I whispered.

Thomas whispered back, "Permission to use ramming speed, Captain." I covered a laugh with my gloved hand.

Mr. Prescott was soon upon us. "Miss Buckley? I am surprised to see you here."

"And I you, Mr. Prescott," I replied.

"May I introduce our neighbor, Mr. Prescott, of the Bank

of London? Mr. Prescott, this is an old family friend, Dr. Thomas Fisher."

"A pleasure," Thomas nodded at the introduction.

"Yes, likewise," Mr. Prescott said, looking Thomas up and down doubtfully.

"Henry is just there at the edge of the lake." I pointed to Henry as my de facto chaperone for the walk.

"I see. Perhaps I will go and have a word with him," Mr. Prescott said as if he suddenly had some key point to make with Henry.

"Yes, please do that, Mr. Prescott. Good day." I said breezily.

"Yes, good day to you both," Mr. Prescott wheezed.

He steered himself down to the edge of the lake to give Henry a piece of his mind about seeming to leave me unchaperoned, most likely.

"An odd fellow, is he not? Now, where were we?" Thomas murmured. "Ah yes, I was about to laud you for what you are doing with Lyell and Darwin and the others. I remember we have spoken about Darwin several times before. You have mentioned that he is soft-spoken and kind. That he loves to have his wife play the piano for him and read Jane Austen to him, for hours at a time. But as one practitioner of science to another, how does he think? How does he accomplish his work?"

I responded easily. "In our breakfast meetings, he listens more than he speaks. I have noticed that he extrapolates from several proven observations to the universal. He only uses carefully recorded data, but he does accept observations from letters written by sources he learns to trust." I went on to explain what I knew from letters, Sir Lyell's conversations, and the time I had personally spent with Mr. Darwin: that Mr. Darwin's schedule was the same every day; he rose fairly early and ate breakfast alone, worked for three or four hours, then had lunch with any visitors and took a turn or two around his Sandwalk. Around three o'clock, he rested briefly, then went back to answering letters and then took another walk before dinner with his family. "He listens to his wife's excellent piano playing or reading of Jane Austen or the latest George Eliot novel in the evening," I concluded. "He adheres to that routine every day. I am looking forward to seeing all of it in person, I can tell you."

The Weeping Willow trees on the other side of the lake gracefully moved back and forth in with undulating beauty. The fronds were soft variations of greens and blues mixed together in a lovely swaying dance where the branches lightly touched the grass and then swept back up lightly in the air.

"The Weeping Willows are just wonderful in the wind; do you not agree?" I asked, entranced by their captivating beauty.

"Yes, they quite capture the imagination. Does Darwin applaud women like you?" he asked suddenly.

Another easy question for me to answer, as I had thought about it before, many times. "In private and in personal conversations, I find him quite engaging and appreciative of my ideas and ambitions," I said. "Publicly, however, I would say he goes along with the usual male perceptions of women in science. In fact, he is not timid in saying publicly that he thinks, given that women are typically smaller than men, that a woman's mental capacity is likely to be smaller as well, and therefore makes a woman less intelligent than a man, who typically has a larger brain." I looked up at Thomas, pretending to measure the circumference of his head; he laughed. "In addition, he has said that since women do not have to compete with men to make a living or support a family, this has placed women in an inferior position to men until they have to do so and are pressed to grow in new directions. But if a woman writes to him with keen ideas about some subject in ornithology or botany, he is most gracious in his response."

"Interesting. Why does he have two sides to his opinion of women, do you think?" Thomas asked, his head turned to me with complete and sincere attention. I appreciated that he was interested in Mr. Darwin and my work, as I was obviously fascinated by Mr. Darwin. Many men would not be very interested in a woman's occupation, I noted, quite pleased.

"My hunch is that he is not quite brave enough to challenge any more of the status quo than he already has. He has weathered quite a few storms already," I replied, recalling how Sir Charles had first mentioned Mr. Darwin to me. "My hope is to illuminate Darwin, so that he becomes more open, even publicly, to women of science."

"And how do you expect to accomplish this?" Thomas asked, squeezing my arm playfully.

"*My* true aim is to help him accomplish his future endeavors, whatever they may be," I said. "I would never dare to say I am in any way close to his abilities. Yet, I can support him and help him along his journey to greatness. In doing so, I will respect and defend his interests to the best of my abilities. That is my purpose. He has grown to trust me in commenting on his work and how I edit Sir Charles's chapters. That is the first step, I believe." I replied with conviction.

We came along the back side of a small, grey boat house perched on the side of the lake. Two very small rowing boats, one painted yellow and the other red, were pulled up alongside the boat house. Mallard ducks swam to and fro, their shiny green heads darting after water bugs and other insects in the water.

"I see a beautiful Bullfinch just there, in the bushes. Do you see it on the branch pointing upward? It has the most beautiful pink breast and blue-grey wings." I said excitedly.

"Yes, I do see it. A male, given the colouring. A quite spectacular little bird. Quite like you. Spectacular and charming." he said kindly.

"I will take that as a compliment, to be compared to something with such great natural beauty." Our eyes met and locked. Suddenly I found myself without words again, for an altogether different reason.

"Would you like to?" Thomas asked, at last, pointing down at two row boats.

"Not today," I said, forcing the words out of my mouth. "When do you think you will return to London?" I said as lightly as I could, as if I did not care what his response was.

"I do not know. It may be quite a while." He said, his hands in the pockets of his jacket, his face again looking down at the path. His eyes held concern.

"Does your wife often accompany you to London?" I ventured.

He spoke very briefly. "No. She prefers hearth and rug to adventures of any kind." We walked further around the lake. The breeze kicked up loose leaves around us, floating carelessly and freely in the air.

"I would like to walk with you in the Avenue Gardens," he said, after a silence. "It is just up the hill and quite close. Shall we?" Thomas touched my elbow gently, guiding me in the direction up the path to the gardens.

"I would love to see their glorious colours today," I said, hoping my voice sounded strong rather than the quivering feeling in my throat.

Thomas led us through a hedge and up a grassy slope. Spread before us were magnificent formal gardens with purple Primrose and pink, red, and white Begonia beds, multi-tiered fountains, and garden statues as ornaments. We walked silently, taking in the garden and pondering our last moments together in equal measure. I loved the soft crunching noises our boots made on the small gravel stones of the middle path.

Thomas stopped walking and pulled his right hand out of his pocket. He had something in his hand, wrapped in a light piece of brown wax paper.

"I want you to think of me in my absence. So, in the meantime, I have something for you," he said, holding it out. I hesitated. He picked up my hand and pressed the parcel into it. "To remember our fond times together."

I looked up at him and then down at the parcel. Silently I opened the paper. A large, circular silver locket lay looking up me, flat on the front and back.

"Oh!" I exclaimed. "It is stunning. But I cannot possibly..." I trailed off. "What would your wife say? I feel it is inappropriate."

"Nonsense. It is a gift to a longtime family friend. Please open it to look inside," he said, gently.

When I pressed the locking button, the locket popped open easily. Inside was a lovely miniature painting of a Skylark. The painting of the plump speckled bird was uncannily lifelike. The short, blunt crest on its head was raised, and its white underbelly was just visible. "How truly lovely," I said. "You remembered our discussion of our favorite bird. Thank you. I will wear it and remember you. I am grateful for our time together but sad at the same time, knowing that I will be waiting quite a long time until you return," I said evenly.

"I do not expect you to wait for me, you understand. You are young and have your whole life ahead of you." He took my gloved hand in his and held it tightly. "You remind me of a wild bird. Innately intelligent, a natural beauty, and strong-willed. It may be quite some time before I return. Years, in fact," he said forlornly, his eyes searching my face for my reaction.

Not knowing what to say, I said, "Oh, I see," I said, dejectedly. I studied the locket in my hand, then looked back up at him. "I almost forgot that I have a gift for you, as well." I pulled a small package from my tan leather reticule and held it out for him.

He removed the light brown wrapping and string on what was obviously a small, pocket-sized book. "How symbolic," he said, with a slight laugh. "*British Birds in Their Haunts* by Rev. C. A Johns. I will treasure this, given our first meeting. "Thank you," he said, and our eyes locked.

"I hope it reminds you of home, here, and that it will inspire you to return soon," I said, taking a few more steps from the boathouse to resume the path around the lake. "Please, do let us know when you are in London next. We have all enjoyed your visits to the house this year." I slipped the locket into my reticule. "Especially your services as a physician each time you visited. I fear that my family abused our friendship by asking for your medical advice and treatment when all you wanted was a relaxing meal!" We laughed, remembering the resistance of the patients during the visits.

"Do you recall the occasion when your father had that nasty inflamed boil on his neck, just by his collar?" he asked. "I knew I had to lance that before it became further inflamed. You were a fabulous assistant. You were not at all fazed by the lancing or the blood. But your father! I thought he might faint from the sight of the scalpel. I had to put alcohol under his nose to prevent him from fainting or vomiting or in some other way making a nuisance of himself. He is an amusing old chap. I shall miss him." He trailed off.

"Yes, you were very skilled with that. And with the mole on Henry's neck, despite his protestations. Quite disgusting all around." I made a face at the memory.

"I only regret that I could not perform some service for you while I was there. You would have made a far more lovely and docile patient than either of those two!" We laughed again at the recollections of the men in my family.

"I shall miss how much we laughed together. In truth, I fear it is likely that I may never see you again," I said, glancing up at him quickly.

"You will see me again," he said. "But regrettably you may well be an old married lady by then. With a baby under each arm." He said, folding his arms across his chest. He stopped walking and stood next to a small wooden shack just off the path.

"Perhaps. I have enjoyed our little excursions, so thank you for those fond times." I hurried to get the words out, trying not to become emotional.

"Is that what I am to you, a fond outing?" He asked a bit tensely, his green eyes flashing at me.

"That is all you can possibly be, do you not see that?" I said firmly. "I am the daughter of a vicar. It is a sin to pine over another woman's husband, as you may recall. I may be young and naïve, but I am not without integrity and some common sense," I huffed, standing next to him.

The shadow of the garden shed added a layer of coldness under the sunless sky. I shivered. He turned to face me, at a loss for words. He took a step closer and put his hands on the outsides of my arms, turning me to face him.

"I would gladly get a divorce if it would not ruin my professional reputation and yours. Please know that," he said, almost whispering.

"I know a divorce would be impossible. Out of the question. I am committing myself to a life of science. I will be busy without you." I looked up at him and felt my eyes beginning to water. "I am making a life for myself knowing you are leaving. Please know that."

He pulled me towards him and in a split second, before I could realise what was happening, his mouth was on mine, fervently, for what seemed an instant but must have been at least ten seconds. His lips were hard and seeking. At that instant, neither of us was concerned about who might have seen us. He squeezed my arms lightly as he released me, his face hovering close for just a moment, and then he quickly stepped back from me, his hands dropping to his sides as he fought to recover his bearing.

"I have no right. My apologies," he said miserably. "I will think of you always and I will write. Please say you will write back in return. Write to me often. Know that I am in agony, for I am besotted with you." His eyes were full of hurt and brooding, and thick, like the clouds that hung over us.

I was unsure of what to say or do. The pain of his leaving was a harsh reality juxtaposed with what were supposed to be happily received words of love for me. The first of their kind that I had ever received from a man.

"Then your departure is well timed, I suppose, for the benefit of us all," I quickly replied as evenly and clearly as I could. "Thank you for the beautiful locket. I will cherish it. But it seems unjust to me for a man to touch a woman's heart knowing all the while that he will sail away." My eyes were filling with tears despite my efforts to hold them back. "You will understand if I find it quite impossible to take tea with you today. Goodbye, Thomas. I will never forget you and I wish you well. Please, be well. And please find your happiness," My voice trembled.

I felt very confused. I turned abruptly and strode off, stomach knotted, hands in fists, back down the slope of the hill. I passed around the lake and the Weeping Willows, back to the sidewalk and the street pavement and the safety of home. I heard Henry shouting my name somewhere behind me, but I did not look back. Large white town houses stood tall and stoically as I passed, showing no emotion, which I tried to emulate.

A few days later, I received a letter from Thomas. He had obviously posted the letter before his ship had sailed. Henry brought the letter to me in my bedchamber, where I was seated at my desk, completing additional work for Sir Charles. My work was the salve that numbed my pain and redirected my mind to something productive instead of the anguish of missing Thomas.

"A letter for you. I believe it is from *him*," Henry said, entering the room, tapping the letter against his hand before he handed it to me. "Can I be of any assistance?" he asked with a tone of brotherly kindness. "I know you are fond of him. You know Mother and Father would not approve." He paused, frowning. "I hesitate to mention this to you, but Mr. Prescott came to me the other day at Regent's Park and asked why I was not paying more attention to you as your official escort. It was obvious to him that you were walking with a man inappropriately. I told him Thomas was just an old friend. To which he replied, 'if that is so, then I am the King of England.'"

"That dreadful man!" I complained, my hand gripping the sides of my forehead in an attempt to stave off a headache.

"I told Prescott that it was my fault you were unattended and that I had meandered to the boating lake shore after thinking I had seen a fish in the water." He shrugged his shoulders at the lame excuse he had given.

"Kind of you to cover for my faults," I said quietly.

"I shan't tell Mother and Father at the moment because Thomas is leaving, and I think it is best to let things fade with the natural course of events. But best to let him go, I am afraid, Bella."

"Of course, you are correct," I said. I didn't believe a word I was now saying. "I am completely focused on my work, as you can see. I shall be fine, and I will move on, as you suggest." Lies, all of it. "And there is no need to mention this to Mother and Father, please."

"Then I will leave you to it." He replied with a sympathetic smile, turning and walking out the door.

I opened the letter. The tan-coloured paper was thick and stiff in my hands and made a crackling noise as I opened it.

My dear Arabella,

My ship will be leaving the dock very soon, so I write this letter in haste. I feel our time will come at some point in the future. Please do not think of me with aspersions as time moves on, but with care, fondness, and even a bit of adoration if possible. I admit, I am a difficult man with many faults. Be that as it may, I am besotted with you, as I said. But what I neglected to say that day in the Park that I wished I had said, is that you are right in purpose to follow your dreams. You have a great intellect that Darwin, Lyell and the rest are lucky to have available. Keep going! And know that you are locked in my heart and will remain there. Have a care with your health and that of your family. Until I see you again, please know that I am thinking of you.

Yours sincerely.

Thomas

Chapter Nine

Spiritualism as a Science

London and Down House, Downe Village, Kent, England

1865 – 1866

The room was completely dark and smelled of a strange incense. We were ready for the séance to begin. Mary Marshall, the most well-known medium and Alfred Wallace's favorite for the job, had advised us all to wear black so that the spirit would not be distracted by colourful attire. We sat in chairs with no armrests, our feet on the floor and our hands laid flat on the table, which was covered with a white lace tablecloth that seemed to glow eerily in the darkness. We—Alfred Wallace, Mary Marshall, Fanny (Alfred's sister), and her tenant, Agnes Nichol (both of whom Alfred knew to be spiritual mediums), a tall man with dark hair and a dark pointed beard (who turned out to be none other than Samuel Butler, Thomas's neighbour in New Zealand), and I—sat as Mary guided us through the procedure of the séance. I, for one, wanted to make scientific observations of both the process and the outcomes.

Mr. Wallace introduced everyone who was around the table, and Mr. Butler sat on my right. We chatted while waiting for Miss Marshall to be seated. Mr. Butler turned his head and regarded me. "Are you a medium as well, Miss Buckley?"

"No, I am the literary assistant to Sir Charles Lyell," I responded politely.

"Ah, then you are here in a secretarial capacity," he nodded, his eyes now avoiding mine—no need to make eye contact with Lyell's secretary!

"No, I am here to learn the science of Spiritualism, the same as you are, I suspect, Mr. Butler," I snapped back at his rudeness.

"Is that so?" was his short reply. He sat in his chair with an air of superiority. Something about him seemed odd. Perhaps it was just a bit of arrogance.

Taking her place at the table, Miss Marshall began by resting a blank piece of paper under the table, showing us both sides first. Then she initiated her process to conjure Herbert, Alfred's deceased brother.

"You must keep your eyes closed at all times, so that the spirit feels free to enter. Is that clear? Your eyes must be closed," she instructed. We all agreed, and I closed mine tightly, resisting the temptation to open them. I didn't want to be accused in front of everyone for ruining the séance.

"I begin by telling the story of his death in Para, where he had been on an adventure in South America," Miss Marshall said. She began the story in a wailing voice. After she finished each part of the tale, she asked each of us around the table to repeat the sentence she last said, keeping our hands still and flat on the table. She said, "He is in grave peril!" Then we each said, one at a time around the table, "He is in grave peril." When she reached the end of the story, she said, "He is dead!" We each repeated, "He is dead!" Suddenly, the table lifted directly up off the floor. There it remained, suspended in midair.

Fanny shrieked. Alfred gasped and whispered fervently,

"It is Herbert. He means to send a message to us!" At this point, all of our eyes had flown open, aghast.

"Silence!" Mary Marshall hissed. "Do not break the signal."

I was stunned. In the complete blackness I tried to look above the table to see if any hidden mechanism was responsible for lifting it. I moved my foot around under the table to determine what could possibly be lifting it off the floor. I felt nothing. The table slowly settled down. Next, across the room, a guitar slid from a bureau top to a lower table.

"Incredible!" Alfred exclaimed, pointing to the guitar. "He is here! His love of the guitar..." Alfred motioned again over to the guitar, now lifeless on the smaller table.

Mr. Butler said, "Perhaps there is more..."

Our leader emitted a loud sigh. "I am afraid you have broken the aura and the transmittance of the message has stopped," Mary Marshall announced.

"What about the paper under the table?" I asked, curiously.

"Yes, yes. The paper!" Alfred echoed, excitedly.

"Everyone remain still," Mary Marshall quietly said as she retrieved the paper. On it was written the word, "Herbert."

Fanny let out a wail. Alfred grabbed the paper. "Proof, if proof were needed! Herbert was here and left his name."

"Let *me* see that," Mr. Butler pompously exclaimed, snatching the paper out of Mr. Wallace's hand. I was intrigued and wanted to believe but was not completely convinced. Had someone slipped the paper under the table? I neither heard nor saw anyone near the table but those of us around it, but in the darkness, it was certainly possible that someone had crept under the table. Both Alfred and Mr. Butler were both singing Mary Marshall's praises, saying that she indeed was a first-rate medium. I, however, felt that we needed more data and scientific proof.

Alfred and Anne Wallace had become my saviors in the wake of Thomas's departure. After being jilted by Miss Leslie, whom I had met at the reception for Charles Darwin at the Lyell's house, Mr. Wallace had met and married the very kind Anne Mitten after only one year of courtship. I had come to know her, too, and we became fast friends. We occasionally encountered each other at spiritualist meetings.

Alfred and I both wanted to attain that next level of scientific discovery—from natural selection and evolution towards a growing spiritualism. After the séance with Mary Marshall, Alfred began to argue that psychic phenomena followed new scientific laws. He began inviting men of science to dinner parties to witness his sister Fanny and her spiritualist tenant Agnes demonstrate their mediumistic powers. At one such dinner—where Miss Marshall would again be joining us—I arrived at the Wallaces' home a little early to see if Anne needed any assistance. I was looking forward to seeing her again. She and I had become great confidantes, in part, I believed, because I knew Alfred very well, as he and I had become good friends. I found her in the parlour setting wine glasses on a tray. We embraced in greeting, and I joined her in bringing the glasses down from the dresser in the dining room.

"It is so kind of you to assist me, Miss Buckley," Anne said. "Alfred is setting up the table and chairs in his study for the séance after dinner."

"I see. And are you now accustomed to married life, Mrs. Wallace?" I asked, wondering what she thought of having friends in her house contacting the dead.

"Yes, I am. Alfred has been very busy with his writing and I with setting up our home. He has been writing papers to defend evolution lately and to be honest with you, has been very frustrated. I know that you and Alfred have become friends through your work on evolution and spiritualism, so I know that I can be frank with you." She spoke looking over my shoulder to make sure Alfred was not within hearing distance.

"I am sorry to hear about his frustrations," I said. "Alfred is quite the genius, in my opinion, so I would like you to know that I have the utmost respect for him." I then made an offer. "Please, I may be of help. I do not want to appear impertinent, but what is the source of these frustrations, if I may ask?"

"Yes, you may," Anne sighed. "He has sold many of his specimens from his voyages in the Malay Archipelago and that source of income has now dwindled. He is very concerned about our finances and is trying to write to support us. I too am quite worried."

"I am most distressed to hear this. Perhaps I could be of some help?" I repeated my offer.

"Please think of avenues we might not have explored, Miss Buckley. Thank you for thinking of me." She quickly picked up the tray as several guests and Alfred strode into the parlour.

"Miss Buckley, how wonderful to see you. We have set up the perfect conditions to contact your deceased sister, Jane, and Miss Marshall will arrive after dinner," Alfred explained.

"Yes, I am quite excited to do so. Excuse me, Mr. Wallace, I see Mr. Butler is here again," I said.

"Why yes. Yes, he is," Mr. Wallace confirmed, looking off in the direction of the parlour, distracted by the preparations.

"What is his interest here, may I ask?" I prodded. "Is he a man of science or simply interested in séances?" I was hoping to hear that this source of arrogance would not become a permanent fixture in our group.

"Oh, he is a writer and something of a critic of science, you might say. I believe he is working on a new book about a utopian society or some such thing. Will you kindly excuse me, Miss Buckley? There is much to do!" With that, Mr. Wallace bolted off to ensure that the preparations were being made properly.

I greeted the other guests, who included Fanny and Agnes, whom I had seen before, and also Richard Spruce, an old friend of Alfred's from Brazil who knew Anne's father, William Mitten, quite well. Mr. Butler and I exchanged polite but strained greetings. Everyone at the party seemed quite excited to begin the séance, which was all we discussed during dinner.

As I ate, I kept thinking about what Lady Lyell had said during the reception in her home. She had warned me that both Mr. Darwin and Sir Charles believed spiritualism to be an untrue science, a falsity. If this were so, and I could not doubt Lady Lyell, then Alfred would be heading down a terrible path for his scientific career. After dinner, I motioned Alfred aside, concerned for his well-being after what Anne had confided to me before dinner.

"Mr. Wallace, have you discussed the findings from your séances with Mr. Darwin or Sir Charles yet?" I asked neutrally, trying not to dampen his excitement.

"No, I have not. I want to present them with true pieces of evidence once I have compiled several to prove my points. And I have a paper in mind that will outline connections to evolution," he responded. "Why do you ask? Would you like to edit the paper, perhaps?"

"Perhaps. But I do wonder about the volume of evidence needed here. At each séance, we derive one or two pieces of evidence, and those are difficult to accurately prove. Mr. Darwin expects large amounts of data from his experiments..." I trailed off.

"Yes. Well, we have spoken many times, you and I, about the volume of data I have from my voyages in Southeast Asia," he said. "I collected more than one hundred twenty-five thousand species of insects, birds, and more with my colleague Ari. And as you know, I found several new species." He paused, one hand on his hip, the other gesturing in mid-air. "And I am working on my book about the Malay Archipelago. But since I decided that the ownership of evolution and natural selection should go to Darwin, who had more data, I have been playing second fiddle to him. These new advances in Spiritualism can help sustain my career."

"True, it could help," I said, "and you have your new wife to consider. But best to finish your book as the top priority and then see how much data you are able to procure for Spiritualism."

He raised an eyebrow at my forthrightness. "All in good time, Miss Buckley. All in good time. Now, shall we enter my study and contact Jane? Miss Marshall is ready to begin."

We entered the darkened parlour and sat around a large rectangular table, brought in to accommodate all the séance guests, and took our seats. I purposefully sat next to Anne at the end of the table to avoid having to make conversation with Mr. Butler, who eyed me with some strange determination from across the table. *That man is up to something*, I said to myself, *but what?*

Miss Marshall began. "This very evening, I will put myself into a trance and summon the spirit of Jane Buckley, older sister of Arabella Buckley. And to further prove the existence of the spiritual world and my abilities as a medium, you all will wear no blindfolds, nor will you close your eyes. We must keep the room dark to coax the spirit to us, since spirits come from a dark place."

The reaction at the table was one of mixed awe and trepidation. I was quite glad that no blindfolds would be used. I would steel my eyes to uncover any activities that would render the séance fraudulent. "Furthermore," Miss Marshall continued as the darkness closed in all around me, "to prove this séance is of good merit and not unholy, you will sing Christian hymns to assist me in gaining my meditative state. I ask that your hands stay on the table and that, if you should see something, you not reach out to it. You must understand that interfering with the spirit could actually kill me, the medium, for I contain spirits within myself." She turned to me. "Miss Buckley, since the spirit is your sister, you should select the hymns that most appealed to her."

"Very well. In that case, I would select 'All Things Bright and Beautiful' and then 'How Great Thou Art,'" I suggested quickly; I was eager to move on to the actual séance.

"Excellent," said Miss Marshall. "Now, I will review the story of her death and you will repeat my last sentence as we did before, and then we will sing. But first, I would like each of you to confirm to me and to the spirits that you believe in their existence this night. Please say in turn, 'I believe.'"

Each of us said, "I believe," some more exuberantly than others.

I had relayed the story of my sister's illness and subsequent death to Miss Marshall in advance so that she would have the appropriate facts, even though there was much we did not know or understand about my sister's death. Miss Marshall began the story of my sister's terrible illness and how she had died suddenly one night.

"She is very ill," Miss Marshall said as she began to relate the story. She lifted a white-gloved hand, signaling us to repeat her phrase. "She is in grave danger," she said.

"She is in grave danger," each one of us said in turn around the table.

The atmosphere was very somber, even eerie, and it was dreadful for me to have to relive the story and hear everyone repeat the phrases about my poor sister's untimely death.

"Yes, I feel the spirit coming!" Miss Marshall slowly whispered. "Time for singing! Commence with singing, Miss Buckley. Lead us off, if you please," she hissed.

I cleared my throat, not expecting to have to sing or lead

any singing. I softly began "All Things Bright and Beautiful," which I felt was in keeping with my love of natural science, and so felt like home to me, a relief in this haunted atmosphere. Fortunately, my voice came out clearly and strongly.

"All things bright and beautiful
All creatures great and small
All things wise and wonderful
The Lord God made them all."

"Louder!" Miss Marshall cried in a hysterical tenor.

"Each little flower that opens
Each little bird that sings
God made their glowing colours
And made their tiny wings."

"Louder still!" Miss Marshall cried again, as I went on to the third verse. Since most of those at the table were not the children of vicars, no one else seemed to know the verses well, or at all even. My voice alone in the dark kept the hymn going.

All at once a chill of cold air rushed past my left ear, like a fluttering breath. This sudden sensation was difficult to take in, as I struggled to sing. My blood ran cold, and I felt frozen in place, my hands still on the table. I temporarily lost my sensibilities and my powers of observation. My shoulders hunched involuntarily. I stopped singing. And then to our shock and considerable horror, a pair of pale green gloved hands appeared in the dark next to me on my left, by the end of the table. I jumped to my right out of fear and gasped. The crowd at the table let out similar responses; some shrieked and some yelped like frightened animals.

Just as quickly as the hands appeared, they were gone in a flash. We sat silently at the table, trying to understand what we had just seen.

"My friends, you have just seen the hands of Jane Buckley, Arabella's sister! Miss Marshall proclaimed.

"Can you believe that? We have actually witnessed the spirit's hands approaching you, Miss Buckley!" Mr. Wallace said, shrilly, like a young girl.

"Yes, I saw the gloved hands, too!" A clearly frightened Anne looked around for confirmation.

They were all gaping at me with questioning faces. "I felt a draught of cold air, and something fluttered by my ear, although I cannot say what," I stammered. "I also smelled a scent. Like a perfume."

"It was likely the spirit arriving and taking a form you would understand, of course." Miss Marshall's elaboration sounded plausible enough. And we all did see the gloved hands.

"Yes, yes. Astounding. But were they your sister's hands?" Here came the obvious question from skeptical Mr. Butler.

"How would one know whose hands those were, Mr. Butler?" I asked rubbing my temple where I had felt the flutter. I was at a loss. I was determined to figure out what just happened but not for Mr. Butler's benefit. How could I defend what I wasn't even sure I had just seen?

Chapter Ten

A Threat to Darwin

53 Harley Street, London, and Downe, Kent

1866 – 1867

I had instructed Emily, our housemaid, to bring any correspondence for me directly to my desk. In the event that I would receive a letter from Thomas, I did not want my parents to start asking questions. He wrote sporadically and infrequently, so I was not particularly worried. But I was glad of those instructions the November day when a letter appeared on my desk. I ran my hand across the front of the letter; excitedly I ripped open the envelope.

November 1866

The Grampians,

Timaru

My dear Arabella,

I am delighted to write to let you know I will be returning to London at the beginning of February for my daughter Rose's wedding, which is to be later that month. She will be married to a fine man, Mackay Andrew Herbert James Heriot in Staverton, Totnes, Devon. I will be spending time with them there but will return to London when I am able. I have been busy here in Timaru preparing and providing vaccinations for many locals at the hospital. I will enjoy time away from patients and sheep during my voyage, and I will think of you en route. My feelings for you have not changed. I hope yours remain the same as well. Until I see you, I wish you and your family well. My fondest regards and sincerity,

Thomas

Heavenly days! He is returning to London, God willing! The post had taken two months to deliver this letter, but what happy news on this cold January morning. I stuffed the letter into my coat pocket and went on my way to Sir Charles' office. *Perhaps I should burn the letter here at the Lyells' to remove any evidence of our relationship*, I thought as I pulled open the door to their home.

Should I agree to see him again? Would it be better for both of us to avoid such a meeting? I wondered. I must stay focused, or I will drive myself insane with worry. I pulled a stack of letters over to read, prioritize, and relay to Sir Charles if needed. Stack in hand, I went into his study.

"Good morning," I said to him. "Is now a good time to review your correspondence?"

"Only if there is something intriguing in that pile of yours," came his gruff response. With his back facing me, he was deeply focused on a large astronomy book. "I have been up late several nights this week studying astronomy to include as a chapter in my new book, and I am quite fatigued today as a result."

"There is something of interest," I said. "A manuscript from a certain 'Mr. Charles Darwin,'" I quipped.

"Ho ho! Let us get on with it then!" he exclaimed, turning to face me, beaming. I handed him the manuscript and the letter that came with it. I sat in the chair adjacent to his and waited for his response.

He read the letter silently. "Yes, Miss Buckley. Prepare to write a reply, please." He leaned back in his chair, arms folded behind his neck. I took out my pen and paper and placed them on the small, round table next to his large desk that overflowed with stacks of letters and books.

He began dictating his letter, and I wrote down everything he said, making little improvements along the way as needed. He crafted his response slowly and methodically.

> *My dear Darwin, Your precious MS has arrived safely. I will return it registered in a few days. I am much obliged to you for the privilege of reading it; and in regard to the notes prepared for the new edition, I am amused to find the Agassiz Mountains, which I believe are only about 7 degrees farther from the equator than the Organ Mountains. It is very interesting to read Hooker's letter dated 1856 and to see the impression that the MS made on him, causing him to feel, as he says, 'shaky as to species' so long before the Origin was published. We certainly ran no small risk of that work never seeing the*

light of day, until Wallace and others would have anticipated it in some measure. But it was only by the whole body of doctrine being brought together, systematized, and launched at once upon the public, that so great an effect could have been wrought in the public mind.

I have been doing my best to do justice to the astronomical causes of former changes of climate, as I think you will see in my new edition, but I am more than ever convinced that the geographical changes are, as I always maintained, the principal and not the subsidiary ones. If you snub them, it will be peculiarly ungrateful in you, if you want to have so much general refrigeration at a former period. In my winter of the great year, I gave you in 1830 cold enough to annihilate every living being. The ice now prevailing at both poles is owing to an abnormal excess of land, as I shall show by calculation. Variations in eccentricity have no doubt intensified the cold when certain geographical combinations favoured them, but only in exceptional cases, such as ought to have occurred very rarely, as palaeontology proves to have been the case.

Ever most truly yours,
Charles Lyell

"Have you taken all that down, Miss Buckley?" Sir Charles asked, heaving a sigh of accomplishment.

“I believe I have, yes. Do you want to include the calculations you mentioned with the letter, Sir Charles?” I asked.

“No, but perhaps I will with the manuscript itself when I return it,” he responded, looking quite fatigued.

“Very well. I can polish this up and send it out directly if you like,” I offered.

“Yes, Miss Buckley. Is that all the pressing correspondence for the moment?”

“I believe it is,” I replied. I wanted to ask him about something that had been on my mind, but he seemed so fatigued that I hesitated. “Would you mind if I asked you a question, as I am still learning how geology and evolution are intertwined?”

“Of course. Please do.” He sat up in his chair and leaned forward on his desk, his jacket crumpling up in front.

“To confirm your intent of this letter, are you saying to Mr. Darwin that you believe that geology and climate have more to do with species variation than evolution?”

“Yes, that is my intent. I still do not believe that Darwin can parcel out the effects of geology and climate change in species variation as opposed to simply using natural selection as the primary cause. Do you understand that Miss Buckley?” he asked, patiently.

“Yes, I do. Is it possible, then, for evolution to be sped up by sudden and catastrophic changes in climate, such as the frigid temperatures you refer to? Is it possible that the two go hand in hand, as opposed to one being subjugated to the other?” I asked, curiously.

“We may never know to what degree. Although advocates of natural selection often ascribe too much to it as a theory alone, it has enabled them, at any rate, to assign a reason for many phenomena which would never have been brought to light by those who are satisfied with saying that all things were pre-ordained to be as they are,” he explained.

"So, the instincts, habits, and colour come to be gradually acquired by each species living in new conditions. Is that your point of view?" I asked.

"Yes, that sums it up nicely. Why, I wonder, do you ask, Miss Buckley?"

I thought about how best to respond. "I continue to be intrigued by instincts, specifically collaboration, within and across species," I replied. "I am intrigued by insects and mammals that collaborate for the betterment of their welfare and even survival. Ants, bees, cats...all have collaborative behaviours. I wonder if these can be acquired spontaneously as well as gradually, as you suggest."

"Excellent question. One we should consider and then ask Darwin on our next visit to Down next month," Sir Charles suggested. But his voice was thin—clearly he was more worn out than usual.

"Very well. It would be my pleasure."

"Thank you, Miss Buckley. That will be all for now," Sir Charles stifled a yawn.

FEBRUARY 1867

We arrived at the railway station at Beckenham, the nearest to Down House which was a lean building being little more than a set of planks with a few stairs. Mr. Darwin's black carriage and team of horses were waiting for us.

Luggage aboard, the three of us, Sir Charles and Lady Lyell and I, traveled the six or so miles from the station to Downe village and then on to the lovely estate of Down House, Mr. Darwin's residence. The drive was a precarious one, through thick and dense woods and down a narrow, twisted, and winding country lane that was more like a foot path. We passed only a few very old-looking cottages and farmhouses before reaching the village and swinging right into the Luxted road that led to Down House. The first sight on approaching the house itself was a welcome one: an orchard of apple trees that were of course bare of leaves but still had a pleasant, welcoming order to them.

While this was my second visit to Down House, I still had a tremendous fascination with the place where *Origin* was written, and I was in awe of the scientific works now in progress there; especially those involving collaboration and mutualism, which I enjoyed discussing with Mr. Darwin. I touched the black wrought-iron bell pull in the shape of a cross with a white center. Down House was relatively isolated, out in the countryside, so the Darwins seemed very happy to see us and have us stay with them, especially since their children were long grown up and out of the house.

"Do come in and welcome. Please, this way to the drawing room. How was your journey?

Mrs. Emma Darwin asked invitingly, looping her arm through mine.

"All according to plan," Sir Charles responded, taking off his hat and coat.

Mr. Darwin greeted us and launched into discussing various recent letters with Sir Charles, the two men putting their two heads together immediately.

"A true demonstration of friendship and collegiality," I smiled at Mrs. Darwin and Lady Lyell.

"Yes, they have been friends and colleagues for thirty years, since before we were married," Mrs. Darwin said proudly.

"May the discussions of geology and animal behaviour begin!" Lady Lyell solemnly pronounced. Mrs. Darwin and I laughed.

"Luncheon will be served shortly. I am sure you are famished." Mrs. Darwin told us to make ourselves comfortable in the drawing room where she kept her piano and oboe. Near the instruments was a charming, three legged, claw footed and double sided music stand which I admired with several open sheets of music waiting to be played. The room was sumptuously decorated with calming floral wallpaper and several light blue chairs. We sat in these comfortable chairs, and I for one was glad to be out of the carriage and off the winding and bumpy roads. My entire body was still swaying and jolting even as I sat still.

"After lunch, I would be pleased to play the piano for you. I have several lovely Chopin pieces prepared," Mrs. Darwin said, her hands folded neatly in her lap, her face lit with eagerness.

"We would be delighted to hear you play, of course, Emma," Lady Lyell, cooed, and I echoed, "How lovely!"

"Mrs. Darwin was classically trained by the master, Chopin, himself," Mr. Darwin declared, proudly, with a loving tone and a puffed-out chest.

"In the evenings, Mr. Darwin delights in my readings aloud of Jane Austen. And if you are also interested, we can read several pieces of your choice," Mrs. Darwin said, smiling.

"I am sure we will be most well entertained!" Lady Lyell proclaimed.

After a few more pleasantries in Mrs. Darwin's drawing room, Mr. Darwin and Sir Charles excused themselves to Mr. Darwin's study. I followed, as was customary since I would be taking notes for Sir Charles as his literary assistant. The study was quite tight for space, crowded with Mr. Darwin's large desk, completely covered with letters, books, bottles containing specimens, and rolled-up maps. A large sea urchin sat on the table next to pairs of shears and additional instruments used in the investigations of insects and other specimens. On a drum table nearby were pillboxes holding more insects and seed specimens. Closer to the door were his large, high-backed leather chair and a lap table for writing.

The shutters and thick red curtains held back the glare of the late morning sun. The paintings on the walls showed various men and women I did not recognize. On the left was a partitioned privy with a washstand—an aid for coping with Mr. Darwin's incessant stomach illnesses, I presumed. *Truly hallowed ground,* I thought. *Only the most highly regarded men of science have set foot in this room.*

"I was very pleased to read your last capital letter including evolution as one of the elements to cause variation, Lyell," Mr. Darwin said.

"Yes, I have accepted that evolution plays a key role over time. But temperature cannot be overlooked," Sir Charles responded kindly.

"Yes. And the key to including evolution is establishing the length of time the world has been in existence," Mr. Darwin mused.

I was thrilled to see that this argument could now be put to rest and the tension between these two famous men alleviated. I could see in Mr. Darwin's face he felt the same way, as he put his feet up on his maple-wood horsehair stool.

"About *Domestic Animals,* I do have several notations. Miss Buckley, can you please retrieve Mr. Darwin's manuscript and read my notes aloud? My eyes, you know."

"Yes, Sir Charles." I opened his portfolio and removed the manuscript with the paper markers we had inserted. Mr. Darwin rolled up to the table—his chair was on casters—and picked up his pocketbook and nib pen to make his own notations. Their discussion went on uninterrupted until we were called to luncheon, much to our dismay.

After we had eaten, the men went on the Sandwalk to discuss recent events in London, and I continued to work in the study. I rewrote the changes to the *Domestic Animals* manuscript that the men had agreed to make, assiduously copying the original text, the changed text inserts, and my notes on the day's discussion as needed. By weaving in the new text and comments to which they had agreed and by deleting the old, I was able to create two chapters in the newest version of the manuscript during the three hours they were gone. Relieved and satisfied with my work, I felt I had proved my worth for the trip.

"The pair of them will be quite pleased with these new chapters. I daresay they are greatly improved, making the trip worthwhile," I muttered to myself. I stood up to stretch my tired neck and back. My right hand cramped and ached from all the writing I had done. I walked over to the table and placed the new manuscript down in front of Mr. Darwin's chair where he would see it when he returned. Then I happened to notice a letter written in feminine handwriting. The envelope was postmarked from London. As it was my normal duty to read and respond to letters and without concern for propriety, I unfolded the letter and began to read it.

London, 1866

Mr. C. Darwin

Your insidious work has seeped through our nation like a hot acid, corroding the very foundations of our religious beliefs. We call upon you to recant your theories of evolution or suffer dire consequences. Consider your family, Mr. Darwin. Take heed as we, the true believers, will not be dismissed by you or your henchmen. You may remit your recantation in writing at the address below and expect to see it in the London newspapers. Do not delay, Mr. Darwin, as we are watching and waiting and will make you pay for your evil lies.

Evangelical Christians Alliance

What was this? What was the Evangelical Christian's Alliance? For pity's sake, what a horrid and threatening letter! Furiously, I wondered if I should tell Sir Charles that I had seen it. *Poor Mrs. Darwin,* I thought. *Does she know about this letter? Do I bring up this threat in the due course of conversation, or do I pretend I saw nothing? Oh, heaven above! What do I do now?*

I attended church services conducted by my father that following Sunday, as I did every Sunday. But on that day, I attended for three specific reasons. One was to pray for the safety of Mr. Darwin and his family. The second was to pray for myself and the sins I was thinking about committing with Thomas. The third was to ask God for clarity so that I might find a solution to the eerie and discomforting green, gloved hands.

I sat with my family and our house staff in our designated pew box at the front of the dimly lit church, which held a congregation of about a hundred, and waited for Father to begin. I tried to look about lovely St. Mary's as if nothing troubled me. Hopefully my family would not notice the worry that surely plagued my expression.

I had always loved this old church. The original structure dated back to the thirteenth century, and had seen many changes and reconstructions over the years. The exterior was particularly picturesque when viewed from the Oxford, Edgeware, and Harrow roads and at one time had boasted the largest churchyard in London. The inside of the church was an octagonal gallery supported by Doric columns. Ancient tablets adorned the walls of families with great achievements and dedication to the church. Next to our pew box, an ornate circle on the floor guarded the crypt below it.

I stared ahead to the carved octagonal lectern where my father stood. I usually enjoyed his sermons. Many of them had been praised as quite memorable. But today, my sins seemed to overwhelm me, so egregious were they that I had difficulty discussing them with God. *I have let myself fall in love with the wrong man. God, please help me find my way to piety. Please bestow your good graces on the Darwin family and keep them from harm,* I prayed silently and fervently, hoping God would hear me.

LONDON, FEBRUARY 1867

As I turned the corner at the end of Harley Street into Marylebone Road, I decided to catch an omnibus rather than walk in the cold back home to Paddington. Even though I was wearing my warmest woollen coat, gloves, and hat, the air was icy and burned my throat. As the omnibus found its way around pedestrians and carriages, I gripped the seat, still bothered by the fact that Sir Charles had recommended we take no action about the letter threatening Mr. Darwin and his family. We had had an intense discussion about it, the three of us, just a few days before, and after a prolonged exchange, Mr. Darwin had burned the letter in the fireplace. He said that no Evangelical Christian Alliance existed: he suspected the diatribe to be the anonymous work of a woman of means named Lady Hope, herself an evangelical, as she had been a loud voice in previous criticisms of his scientific theories.

Where is everyone going? I wondered as I looked up and down the street from the omnibus. Such busy lives everyone led. Just before Baker Street, I noticed something odd, a small group of women gathered by the street corner, an unusual sight this time of year in the fierce cold. They were standing with a tall man. His mannerisms seemed familiar. I was shocked to realise that it was Thomas. The omnibus was about to move on, but I quickly and rather impetuously jumped off.

He stood there laughing with a group of seven women, each dressed very fashionably. I wondered what to do next. Should I stay where I was and observe them unseen? Or, should I walk up to him and ask why I was not notified of his arrival in London? Perhaps he was there to visit these women and not me! My face was hot in my embarrassment. Best to hurry along the pavement undetected.

I turned tail and fled when I heard my name. "Miss Buckley, I presume! Miss Buckley! Miss Buckley, wait!" I could not decide whether to turn around or not. I could have easily continued walking, feigning oblivion to his calls amid all the street noise and traffic. But I turned anyway.

"Arabella, it is a joy to see you!" he exclaimed, out of breath from running after me.

"Thomas! You have returned," I said politely.

"Yes, just. I can still feel the rocking motion of the ship in my legs if I stand still! I sent a message to your house, but you had apparently departed for the Lyells."

"Yes, apparently. I have seen no such message. How was your voyage?" I asked curtly.

"I will tell you all about it later this evening. Your parents have invited me over for dinner. Is something bothering you? You do not seem as happy to see me as I had hoped!" He turned me to face him and looked into my face searchingly.

"I think you have been well met already by the company you are keeping." I looked up into his eyes, my lips trembling.

"They were some of the wedding guests, my darling, shopping here in London prior to my daughter's wedding down in Devon. When we landed at the docks, I made arrangements for my belongings to be sent to the Roseate in Paddington, where I will be lodging, and then went directly to meet with the groom's parents, who came up from Plymouth. You understand, I had to meet them and the other members of the bridal party since I am here in London. I departed saying I had to meet a patient." He soothed.

"I see. I thought..." my voice trailed off and I looked away. "The Roseate? Why stay there?" I asked, curiously.

"It is close to Marylebone, but not as expensive, and closer to Paddington Green and St Mary's Terrace, where someone I have been waiting to see for months lives, and they have let me have an office and two rooms for my patients that I regularly see when I am in London," he replied, his mouth to my ear so that he could be clearly heard over the din. I could feel his warm breath brushing my cheek.

"Now, you are finished with work for the day, and it is time for luncheon, is it not?" he continued. "What say you that we find something to eat that we can carry and walk back to the British Museum? Just you and me. I have waited so very long to see you!" He touched my gloved hand while taking my portfolio to carry.

"I believe we would need a chaperone for that plan," I protested, weakly.

"A chaperone, indeed. What a load of ridiculous rules for two adults to bear," he said, still smiling, however. "It is no wonder that I retreat to New Zealand, away from the proprieties of London society. Can we not be on a research expedition of some sort that will involve a librarian as chaperone, at least temporarily?" He grinned down at me.

The idea wasn't as far-fetched as he thought. "I have, in fact, written several letters to the head of the Reading Room and my friend, Richard Garnett, on behalf of Sir Charles," I said. "I could go in person and collect the articles and take notes on the exhibits in question. But how do we explain your presence?"

His eyes danced. "Leave that to me, my dear." With that, he took my arm and whisked me away in the direction of the British Museum, with no further questions asked, oblivious to the frosty temperature.

Late that evening, after dinner with my parents, Thomas and I lingered in our parlour overlooking the veranda and our small garden. The ferns and other plants were all curled up asleep underground, content as they were awaiting the warmth of spring.

"I enjoyed our time today very much," Thomas said, stretching his feet out and resting them on a maroon velvet ottoman with tiny pale blue tassels. "But I say, you put a man through quite a bit of walking with all that research of yours. I think we walked five miles inside the museum, in addition to walking there and back."

"I believe it was you who requested that we look at several of the bird exhibits," I replied, with a tone of comeuppance.

"Oh, yes. I did. Right. How my feet ache! Be a dear and give them a rub, will you?" He asked, leaning back in the maroon-striped wing-backed chair.

"I will not!" I exclaimed with a laugh. "What do you take me for? A lady of unscrupulous morals? But seriously, Thomas. Earlier at the museum today, our stolen touches and kisses in the dark corners. To go on like this is immoral. I find I am not enjoying church services any longer because of the guilt I feel over our relationship. My father! Your wife! How can we go on like this? It is wrong of us," I said looking at him with despondent eyes.

"I thought our small intimacies were mutually favored, Bella," he whispered back.

"Of course, they are. But we still mustn't. You will be here another six months or so and then you sail yet again. And I am left holding these secrets. I feel the lines of sacred trust are being obscured. I am terribly confused and ashamed. We can no longer continue this, this..." I said, searching for the right words when my voice trailed off as Henry entered the room.

"My apologies. I came in for my book. Am I intruding?" Henry asked, too nonchalantly.

"My word, no, my man. Come in and have a brandy with us and tell us about your day. We can fill you in on our research as well." Thomas said, straightening up in the chair. His shirt and tie pin were crooked.

"Is that what they are calling it these days?" Henry asked in an unsmiling, terse tone of voice, glaring directly at Thomas. He slammed shut the book he had picked up off the drum table and walked out of the parlour, looking back at Thomas with a stern gaze of warning as he left.

Chapter Eleven

Fortune Favors the Bold

Down House,
Downe, Kent

June 1873

"Fortune favors the bold. At least that is what the Romans thought," I said to myself with conviction. "But would he, Charles Darwin, favor my boldness?" We would soon find out.

After an interesting discussion on the topic of collaboration within species, referred to as mutualism, the four of us, Sir Charles and Lady Lyell, Mr. Darwin, and I walked out of the back door of Down House and into the garden, headed for the Sandwalk, where Mr. Darwin had thought through a great many scientific ideas. We passed first through his kitchen garden, vital to the botanical studies that played such a large part of his scientific endeavors. The path was covered in small round buff gravel, and the brick wall on the garden's south perimeter was blanketed by pear and apple trees, mounted and trained on the southern exposure. In the garden beds were hundreds of varieties of plants and herbs, neatly organized and identified, all in their seasonal glory, either having just blossomed or coming into bud on this warm June afternoon.

Next we walked past a large arched greenhouse on the right of the path, where he conducted experiments crossing plant variations, mollusks, and worms.

"I have some interesting findings to show you in the greenhouse, but perhaps after our Sandwalk," he said, gently urging us forward as if we were his flock of geese. The graveled walk began at the edge of the garden, before the start of a large meadow, and further on turned back on itself to form a circuit in a pleasant, wooded area filled with alders, birches, and hornbeams. Mr. Darwin used this circuit daily, even several times a day on occasion, to do his best thinking without distractions. He liked to move about after his morning spent sitting in his horsehair chair in the study with his lap table, nib in hand, corresponding with other men of science, family, and friends.

I turned to look at my employer and mentor, Sir Charles, now in his early seventies, still the most eminent geologist of the day. His *Principles of Geology* had been read by thousands of people the world over during the last forty years. He seemed almost like a god in the scientific world—an accolade with which I heartily concurred. Truly, he was the ideal mentor for every man carrying a geology book, a notebook, a microscope, a magnifying glass, or any other means of gaining expertise in science. And he himself had led me to this critical juncture. He gave me a knowing nod with the tilt of his head as if saying, "Go on. Get on with it." I acknowledged him with a corresponding nod and took a determined breath.

We turned left out of the garden and began to stroll down the Sandwalk. It was here that we would now discuss his book, *The Descent of Man*, second edition, yet another of Mr. Darwin's flashes of scientific lightning, striking at those antagonistic evangelical Christians.

Grateful for the support of Sir Charles, as well as that of

our friend and colleague, Mr. Wallace, I felt as prepared as anyone possibly could be while facing a giant in this field. A field in which I had no legitimate right to be, my thoughts raced, even as I tried to steel myself for an intelligent and thoughtful conversation. For I had no formal education, only what I had absorbed through my work and my own study. Yet here I was. Mr. Darwin and I had become friends, and I believe that I was his only female friend with whom he had seriously discussed ideas and books. For the last seven years, I had also been the only woman dedicated to the review, reconstruction, and bringing up to date of Sir Charles's books and papers. More recently I had often read Mr. Darwin's drafts to give an opinion and advise him if I thought something was missing or given inadequate treatment. It was lost on no one that I had become very knowledgeable as a result.

Of course, Mr. Darwin had had plenty of childhood friends who were now grown women, and it pleased Emma when he made pleasant conversation with them. Through his correspondence, he also conferred with women on more scientific matters, asking them for information pertaining to his scientific endeavors, such as whether their dogs curled up their lips when they appeared happy or at what age their children first cried with wet tears. Yet although I believed myself to be one of the most knowledgeable people, man or woman, concerning the particulars of every article and book written by Lyell, Wallace, Huxley, Hooker, and many other scientific figures of the time, and although I was obviously no threat to him as a woman (after all, I could not hold any job more notable than an administrator or an assistant!), we nonetheless enjoyed bantering his theories about. I was becoming—perhaps—his intellectual interlocutor.

In addition to my knowledge, I was an inexpensive resource, and Mr. Darwin was an extremely frugal man. He kept a ledger of every single expense incurred at Down House. He was meticulous with his money. He was not afraid to spend it, but he abhorred wasting it. Therefore, when it came to assistance with his work, it seemed prudent to him to have women, such as his own daughters and even me, to provide the requisite editorial services as we were cheaper to employ than men—but equally as stringent as any man who might undertake the work.

In the last few months, he and I had discussed mutualism and broached the topic of traducianism—I had a special interest in reconciling my knowledge and conviction in Christianity with evolution. These conversations were the foundation of what I wanted to ask today, about how I could help Mr. Darwin with revisions of *Man*, I thought, trying to calm myself.

He and I entered the woodland section of the Sandwalk, where for about the length of several tennis courts, the natural woodlands had been extended, but otherwise left untouched. Sir Charles and Lady Lyell were some way behind us, not yet in the wood. I found it difficult at first to see where the actual path actually went because the trees and plants were so thick, but of course Mr. Darwin knew the way. I decided that this was the moment to advance my plan, while we were alone and hidden from view.

"Mr. Darwin, as you work on the second edition of *The Descent of Man*, do you envision modifications with regard to mutualism, one of the topics we have previously discussed?" I asked as we stepped over sticks and roots that crossed the rougher part of the path that ran through the wood. The shade was soothing, and we walked slowly.

"Yes, I will refine points leading up to the fifth chapter, which is devoted to the topic. I believe it to be an important piece in *Man*, do you not agree?"

I nodded. "Quite certainly. More specifically, I believe the work would benefit from including the evolution of morals, as we have discussed, through traducianism, which could unify evolution and Christianity, despite objections from Mr. Wallace and others."

"Yes, and your specific conception of how religion ties into evolution via traducianism is what again, exactly?" Darwin asked as our shoes crunched over sticks, stones, and bark.

"Based on my knowledge of Christianity, which I know you have also studied objectively and in some depth," I said, trying not to sound anxious, "I suggest that traducianism, which emphasizes the development of the soul across generations, is actually an evolution of the soul itself. Animals have an internal drive for maternal tradition and social responsibility, such as collaboration, which we see time and again in mammalian species down through the chain to insects, such as bees and ants. Certainly, these same animals face competition and changes in their natural conditions. When such struggles are a critical part of evolution, I contend that one of the laws of life which is as strong, if not stronger than, the law of force and selfishness is that of mutual help and dependence."

He smiled. "I see. But some Christians would say that morality as a law is applicable only to human beings."

"Yes, you are correct. But I disagree with that. I assert that collaboration and mutualism are a gradual development through the animal world as a whole, evolving as attributes which are both natural and divine."

"Divine as in God-given, you say," Mr. Darwin mused.

"Yes, exactly," I said, silently sighing with relief that I had concisely and clearly articulated my position. I had laid the groundwork for the next step, which was my main point. But I would have to let him speak first, of course.

"Your postulations add complexity to evolution," Darwin remarked. "It alludes to a man acting impulsively, as the bee or the ant probably does when it blindly follows its instincts, but for the greater happiness, rather than for personal gain or pleasure. These are social instincts that have developed for the greater good, but which have resulted in a standard of morality for the community rather than merely general happiness, as sought by the utilitarianism of J.S. Mill or Jeremy Bentham."

I clapped my hands in approval. "You give the idea excellent clarification. I believe this extension of evolution to be a key to the understanding of mankind. I believe it will especially satisfy those Christians who seek to destroy your work. Have you had any more angry letters purporting to be from Christian associations?" I asked, fighting through my hesitation to do so.

"No, no more letters of that kind." He replied in his kindly manner. No doubt he thought I was more worried about such letters than he was.

"Even so, I think it would be prudent to ask the stationmaster at Beckenham, if he were willing and able, to check the name and credentials of any strangers asserting that they have business with you at Down House or are attempting to find you here, and to notify the police if he had any suspicions. We would all rest more easily if we knew that you at least had this minimum amount of protection," I suggested, with pleading in my voice.

"I doubt if any protections are needed. We have had no such need before," Mr. Darwin replied calmly.

I thought to summarize my premise and move on. "Very well. In summary of my earlier points, I would argue that mankind would not only survive but thrive with more collaboration and more so for future generations. We should seek to influence Christian theology in ways that would encourage the most ardently religious believers to embrace evolution."

"Well said, Miss Buckley. You have captured the premise exactly," Mr. Darwin said, stopping to examine a leaf fading from green to light yellow.

"Sir, that leads me to a question I would like to pose. I

would like to propose that I follow the publication of the second edition of *Man* with an article of support that I would like to write myself and submit for publication. I would like to use what talent I have to defend and support your work. With your permission, of course," I added hastily.

"I see. That is quite a grand gesture," Mr. Darwin said, his one hand rubbing his white beard, the other tapping his walking stick against the ground. "You have a keen perspective and appreciation of the work. I approve, of course. Your writing is superior to much that is published today. Where are you thinking of seeking publication?" he asked with interest.

"MacMillan's comes to mind. As a woman, I would sign with my initials only. I would be happy to submit the article to you prior to sending it to the editor, of course," I offered.

"No need. I trust your judgement," Mr. Darwin said with a gentle wave of one hand while the other rested firmly on his walking stick, his eyes cast downward in contemplation.

Victory! We rounded the path to find the Lyells had gone no further than where the path rejoined itself, and were seated on the bench that was there. Sir Charles held a striated rock up to the sun, squinting at its layers. Lady Lyell sat holding her parasol. I gave Sir Charles a very slight smile, which I could not contain, as we passed them. He smiled back at me, nodding hopefully.

We had now gone once around the loop of the Sandwalk. Mr. Darwin reached down and picked up a white stone from the path and laid it down on the edge of the walkway. "A way of marking how many times round we have gone," he said, extending his arm to the start of the path again. Shall we go around again, Miss Buckley?"

Chapter Twelve

Science and Faith

Darwin's Study,
Down House, Kent

1874

Alfred Wallace, one of Charles Darwin's particularly favorite colleagues and friends, and Charles Darwin sit in Darwin's study and reflect on Arabella Buckley's first publication in *MacMillan's* monthly periodical.

"Sir Charles Lyell and Miss Buckley were here recently. Sir Charles remarked that no one writes such good scientific reviews as you," Darwin noted to Wallace.

"That was quite kind of him to say, given his expertise," Wallace responded, holding one of Mr. Darwin's papers in one hand and a pen in the other. His long legs were crossed; he was deep in concentration.

"And Miss Buckley added that you delight in picking out all that is good and are very blind to all that is bad. I must admit, Alfred, that your reviews console me, notwithstanding that we differ on several things. I will nevertheless keep your objections to my views in mind," Darwin added.

Wallace looked up from the paper. "Our views are not so far off, are they?"

"I will admit to thinking for long weeks about the inheritance and selection difficulties you raised, and I covered quires of paper with notes, in trying to get out of it, but could not, though clearly seeing that it would be a great relief if I could," Darwin chuckled.

"Speaking of views, what are your views of Miss Buckley's first paper in *Macmillian's*?" Wallace asked, one eyebrow arched, both feet now on the floor as he paid direct attention to his longtime friend and colleague.

"She and I did discuss her writing the paper, as you might have guessed. She writes precisely and correctly about evolution," Darwin explained.

"I agree. I thought her paper was brilliant support for evolution and the idea of a higher deity driving evolution, even thought that is not my own personal view. I do encourage her to express her viewpoints and to write. She has a gift, I would say." Wallace looked about the room as if he was having difficulty finding the right words.

"I must say that I'm somewhat in conflict with myself as I think about your reviews and Miss Buckley's article, and I have realized something troubling," Darwin said, frowning down at his desk.

"What exactly can you mean?"

"I find myself lauding you for your review of *Man* while I have made no acknowledgement at all in writing to Miss Buckley for her recent review in *Macmillian*'s. I rarely mention women in my books or papers, for obvious reasons. Women are like flashes of lightning in society and in public life. It is right and prudent of me to avoid writing about her, is it not?" Darwin asked, clearly perplexed.

Wallace remained silent, not knowing what to say.

After a pause, Darwin went on. "Yet I find that some of the women in my personal world are more than the sum of their talents. Not only are they worthy readers and editors, but they can also make more out of whatever they touch. Give a woman wheat, and she will make bread. Give a woman meat or fish, and she will make a meal. Give a woman your seed, and she will make a child. From that child, she will make a family," Darwin said as Wallace cocked his head to one side, considering his words carefully.

"In Miss Buckley's case," Darwin went on, "if you give her facts and theorems, she expands them verbally and in written form in a way that few men can articulate. She then expands her extension of viewpoints into a published paper, no less! The courage and fortitude of Miss Buckley must be key to her ability to multiply two times two and have six be the outcome. Yet I do not acknowledge Miss Buckley's advocacy of me the way I do for you. Why, I wonder?"

Wallace thought for a moment. "Could it be because it feels as if lauding Miss Buckley is like praising yourself? Or, perhaps, praising a student who is not yet ready for praise?"

"Perhaps. I certainly find you worthy of praise, Wallace, as you are an originator of true science. Is Miss Buckley less deserving of praise?"

Wallace shrugged his shoulders. "A very good question."

"It has been a difficult year for me, with the time spent planning my daughter's marriage and the continued arguments against *Origin* and now *Man*. I have been using the burden of my workload as an excuse not to write a letter extolling Miss Buckley's writing virtues. Why shouldn't we consider Miss Buckley a student, even though she is female? She is a studious, focused, dedicated, logical, and brilliant as any man, if I can be bold enough to admit this. I too am proud of her. Yet, to say so publicly or even in in a simple letter would be to bring upon myself an angry wasps' nest!" Darwin exclaimed.

The two men sat and stared out into the room, thinking. Finally, Darwin said, "Her defense of me, while courageous and loyal, does not quite ring with the same loud tone as that of a seasoned man of science like yourself, Wallace, and in the end, *that* is the difference in my mind. What is more, you are a professional with a family to keep. Miss Buckley is not. I will set the matter aside. Now, where are we on that review in your hand?"

Chapter Thirteen

The Throes

53 Harley Street,
London

1873 – 1875

I opened the front door from Harley Street and entered the hallway, pulling the door shut against a gust of wind and rain, just as I had done so many times before. I walked into the quiet hall, shaking off the rain and happy to be back after a few days' absence. Immediately, however, I noticed something odd about the office. No lamps were lit, for one thing, and no one was there, for another. The house smelled musty, as if it had been closed for some time. Tess emerged from the kitchen entrance wringing her hands in her white apron, expression contorted.

"Good morning, Tess. What is happening here today? Why are no lamps lit?" I asked, searching her ashen face.

"We sent ye a note, Miss. Did you not receive it?" She shivered, her white ruffled maid's cap and apron both trembling.

"No, apparently, I have missed the note somehow. Please tell me what is happening. You look unwell," I added, concerned.

"Yes, Miss. But it is not me, it is Lady Lyell. She came down with the typhoid something terrible only two days ago. She has gone to the Lord, Miss. He took her right quick." Tess explained. "So, she had naught but a bit of sufferin'." She wiped her eyes and sniffed.

"Oh, my heavens, no!" I gasped into my gloved hand. "Gone?" Tears filled my eyes at the thought of her struggle. Typhoid was a cruel illness that in its final throes tortured the body with spasms, ejecting any liquid from its victims. How I would miss her, my true ally, mentor, and friend!

I reached around for a chair, my hand still over my mouth, covering my sobs. Tess gently guided me into the closest one, so I would not collapse on the floor.

"Why, Sir Charles must be inconsolable. I must go to him!" I tried to stand up, but Tess's strong arm pushed me back safely in my seat.

"Quarantine, Miss. No one is allowed upstairs except medical staff for two weeks." Her eyes became stern as was her tone, both emphatic and convincing, telling me that she had seen the illness and its result firsthand. "No one, Miss. Not even you." I sat there in shock, limp with grief. Tess returned to her duties elsewhere in the house.

FEBRUARY 1875

Sir Charles and I toiled away at the twelfth edition of his *Principles,* as best we could through our continuing grief and mourning for Lady Lyell. Sir Charles had been very deeply affected by her death, and remained so even now, over a year since her passing.

"Nothing can ever be the same without her, I am afraid," he said one dark morning. "I lack the drive for the work that I had for so many years, trying to impress my brilliant wife." He darted a glance at me before looking away again. His clothes were askew and wrinkled. His breath was fetid from improper hygiene, and his beard had become matted and soiled. He pushed away any attempts from the servants to help. He had lost interest in more than just his work.

Of course, life in the offices on Harley Street would never be the same. The glimmer and the lively museum-like atmosphere seemed to dim; the specimens collected dust. Sir Charles had become more and more depressed, weary, and even sullen. Gone was the heart of a lion pursuing science. I had never seen a man so weakened by such desolation.

"Come," I said, on a day when we were finishing a list of review items. "Let us venture into the sitting room where you might be more comfortable. I can read your correspondence there and we can work on your responses in a larger, airier place," I said, lightly, trying to encourage him to at least leave his study for a few moments.

"No. I cannot bear to sit in one of her favorite spots while she lies buried." He got up slowly and left the room, writing paper in hand. "Perhaps we could make a bit of progress upstairs."

This directive was now my cue to help Sir Charles up to his bed. There, propped up on pillows, he would dictate letters to me while I sat on a small green felt ladies' chair by his bedside. His bedroom was a lovely, large room with a four-poster bed with a white canopy trimmed in lace, obviously one of Lady Lyell's choices. Now the thick, rose-colored curtains remained closed all the time, even during the day, blocking out the uncaring world that carried on just beyond them. We often worked here in the mornings, lit only by candles, until Sir Charles fell back asleep, his only peace from his heavy grief. I would then carry on with the work downstairs at my desk. I would leave him instructions on his desk for what the manuscript needed next, so that he would know where my work left off and where he would need continue once he returned downstairs. It occurred to me that, as often happens with old age, our positions had become reversed. I had become the instructor and he the student.

I found him there at his desk one rainy morning just days later. He was lying slumped over his desk, pages of the manuscript scattered about his arms and face. Reference books were piled on the carpeted floor at his slippered feet. No servants were about, but that was not unusual—they all had their chores to perform. I walked into his study thinking he had simply fallen asleep while reading.

"Resting on the job again, are we?" I asked him teasingly. I was about to wake him, but when I touched his shoulders, they were stiff and cold. Then I noticed his lips were a faint blue, and a piece of paper touched his open eye. *Oh God,* I thought. Sir Charles Lyell, scientific legend, had died where he lived, working on the twelfth edition of his beloved *Principles of Geology*. I sank to the nearest chair, mouth open, in surreal agony of despair.

As the Lyells had no children, I aided their solicitor in dealing with the notifications, the servants, their belongings, and their remaining scientific work. I dreaded the important notifications I must write to Sir Charles's scientific colleagues, but I dreaded writing to Mr. Darwin the most. I knew exactly where he would be sitting as he read my terrible news and how he would react at losing one of his closest friends and allies. I knew the pain my letter would cause him.

February 22, 1875
Lyell House
53 Harley Street
Marylebone, London

My dearest Mr. Darwin,

It is with shock and deep grief that I must write to you with the gravest news. Sir Charles has gone to our Lord this day. He died as he lived, working on the twelfth edition of his Principles of Geology, which I will ensure reaches the publisher. I offer you my greatest condolences, which are wholly inadequate for our irreplaceable friend and ally, one of the greatest minds of science of our time.

Yours most sincerely,
Arabella Buckley

The very next day, I received the following reply from an anguished Charles Darwin as I sat alone in the Lyell's house, except for the busy servants packing possessions that would not see the light of day again, especially in such grandeur, for who knows how long.

Down Beckenham
Feb. 23. 1875

My dear Miss Buckley,

I am grieved to hear of the death of my old and kind

friend, though I knew that it could not be long delayed, and that it was a happy thing that his life should not have been prolonged, as I suppose that his mind would inevitably have suffered. I am glad that Lady Lyell has been saved this terrible blow. His death makes me think of the time when I first saw him, and how full of sympathy and interest he was about what I could tell him of Coral reefs and South America. I think that this sympathy with the work of every other naturalist was one of the finest features of his character. How completely he revolutionised Geology; for I can remember something of pre-Lyellian days.

I never forget that almost everything which I have done in science I owe to the study of his great works. Well, he has had a grand and happy career, and no one ever worked with truer zeal in a noble cause. It seems strange to me, that I shall never again sit with him and Lady Lyell at their breakfast.—I am very much obliged to you for having so kindly written to me.

Pray give our kindest remembrances to Miss Lyell, and I hope that she has not suffered much in health from fatigue and anxiety.

Believe me, my dear Miss Buckley,
Yours very sincerely
Charles Darwin

I sat there in my office, which I now only occupied temporarily, and let the letter fall to the floor. Along with the emptiness I felt at the loss of the Lyells, a larger question loomed for me. What now? How would I continue my mission to help those who thirsted for science? What would become of me? After all my work, was my worth to science done for? Would I ever see Charles Darwin again?

In the lonely and dark days that followed the death of Sir Charles, I was, of course, at home at my parents' house on Paddington Green much more often than I had been when I was working. Mother and Father had been saddened for the loss of the Lyells, of course. I tried to keep to my room, but conversations with my mother about my future were inevitable. When she and I were alone, her tone and choice of words were much sharper than when Father was also part of the conversation.

"Now that your work with Sir Charles has come to an end, my dear, what will you do next?" she asked as she sat in the parlour with her embroidery hoop, satin stitching the petals of a silken rose with light green leaves. Her hair was coiled around the top of her head in her usual fashion, and I wondered if the tightness of the coils caused—or reflected—the tightness of her attitudes and values.

"I have been thinking that I would like to work beyond another literary assistant position, Mother," I said. "Luckily, I have received requests for editorial projects from people of science of world renown. And Mr. Darwin and I continue to work together on his book *Insectivorous Plants*, which he hopes to publish within the year. I hope that I can use this to launch into my next line of work."

"I see," came her response through pursed lips. "And what

then, Arabella? You are thirty-six years old. Mr. Darwin too is getting on in years. You need to face the reality that you need security, a home of your own. You know that we do not own this house that we all live in. The Church of England does." Her hardened eyes matched the cold tone in her voice.

"Mr. Darwin has a passion for the movement of plants and cross pollination, and I...well, it brings me happiness to continue to follow his investigations," I stammered.

"Happiness is a luxury that you cannot afford, Arabella. You need security, and now it is too late for a husband at your age. Who will want to marry a woman over thirty except an old widower? A fine predicament you have made for yourself," she scoffed.

"A husband can die off quite unexpectedly. Even a husband is not a lifelong, guaranteed solution, Mother," I chided. "I am sorry, but I do not see any husband in my foreseeable future." I thought about Thomas and his wife, Eliza, with a lump in my throat. *Not likely that he will be available as a husband,* I thought ruefully.

While I had always admired her strong and pious values, my mother's opinions of a woman's contribution to society formed a constant source of friction between us. I tried to sound affirming and confident as I conveyed my latest news. I had contacted Sir Charles's publisher, Mr. Murray, who had become a friend of mine through the course of my work. I suggested to him that I was now available for work, and he mentioned the need for a publication on the history of science. "A brilliant and practical idea to help those who thirst for knowledge. I would be honoured to accept," I had told him.

"I am happy to let you know, Mother, that I have also had an offer to write a book from Mr. Murray, Sir Charles's publisher, and I have accepted the offer. With the advance, I now have some security. And once the book is published, I shall have more, I daresay. And the sale of a book can continue indefinitely, unlike the life or funds of a husband." She had gone back to her needle work, and I tried to engage her eyes, but she refused to look up.

She was silent for a moment. Finally, in a swift motion, she tossed her embroidery hoop on the sofa, clearly frustrated. "A book? Writing cannot be the business of a woman's life and ought not to be," she said.

"Nevertheless, Mother," I firmly said. "A book about the history of natural science is underway and will detail the progress of discovery from the time of the Greeks to the present day. Your daughter is writing it. And my aim will be to educate young people. I have firsthand knowledge from a large number of men of science for the book. Now I ask you, what can possibly be improper about that?"

Chapter Fourteen

A Short History Arrives

1 St. Mary's Terrace,
Paddington, London

April 1876

"It is not fitting for women to write books, in my opinion. It is not *ladylike*," said Mr. Prescott, my neighbor from across the street and my nemesis from that walk with Thomas at Regent's Park. His thick brown mustache twitched at his own abrupt and rude greeting. He turned and tapped his finely polished walking cane as he passed me on the pavement leading to my house on St Mary's Terrace on Paddington Green. His arrogant attitude did not surprise me, as he frequently made it a point to suggest that my way of life was aberrant in more ways than one. If he knew the hours, the days I spent toiling through countless books and papers, striving to justify every word on the page, would his lowly opinion of me improve?

"Good day to you, too, Mr. Prescott. Do you happen to know if the early afternoon post has arrived?"

Still a lofty local bank manager, although his former employer, The Bank of London, had failed back in 1866 he made no eye contact with me as he paused at the entrance to his grand town house. "As you seem aware, I am expecting the arrival of my first published book today!" I announced, my taffeta skirts rustling as I slowed to speak with him.

"Oh. Yes, good day, Miss Buckley," Mr. Prescott said in his typically unenthusiastic, persnickety, manner. He was perfectly clad in a tan tweed suit woven with a faint green plaid. He the cherry tobacco smoke from his pipe, his usual, wafted in my direction. I tried not to wrinkle my nose at the repugnant smell.

"Today, is it?" he asked, with one eyebrow arched as he stood at the great, wide stairs under a carved lion's head on the frieze of his building. "Oh, yes. Your brother Henry told me you were writing a book. He looked frostily off into the distance. "Women are suited to more conventional roles in the home, are they not, Miss Buckley?"

"Why on earth is that?" I asked after him, a smile painted on my weary face, though I would honestly rather have snarled like one of those carved lion heads adorning the outside of his townhouse. I had worked late into the night and very early into the morning on a lecture, "Through Magical Glasses." Now I had to summon what little energy I had left to be polite to Mr. Prescott.

Mr. Prescott was an example of a man, like many others, that never ceased to amaze me with their inflexible, stale thoughts about what women ought to do. He gave my parents and me a stale fruitcake from his bank every year at Christmas time. While well intended, we surmised it must have been one that he received as a gift from the bank, which he then gave to us. The tired cake, it seemed to me, was passed around much like the tired traditions passed down for women. As stale as unwanted fruit cakes.

"Why? It gives people wrong ideas." After a long pause, he replied quickly as he walked up the stairs toward his black wrought iron door, his round hat bobbing up and down with each step.

"What type of wrong ideas?" I asked, genuinely interested. He hesitated for a moment and then looked back over his shoulder at me.

"Women are inferior intellectually to men. Charles Darwin said so himself in that book he wrote about the apes," Mr. Prescott said, self-importantly.

"Yes, well I believe, knowing Mr. Darwin quite well, that what he meant is that women who do not have the pressure of earning a living the way men do therefore may not be as intelligent because they have not been forced into learning in the same way and from the same need. But that is all situational. Seeing that I am writing books to help people and so that I can make a living, are we not equal, at least to a certain extent, Mr. Prescott?" I asked in my most light and melodious voice, trying not to raise any ire, as I had long learned to avoid doing. "That is, you help people with their money while you earn your living."

"Miss Buckley, women are too emotional to be trusted to write books." He was starting to get a bit emotional himself, something I would have liked to point out to him.

"I think what gender or what color someone happens to be is far from the point," I said. "If the book advances its cause, then it has value. Oh, surely you know as well as I do those women have been writing books of science for at least the last thirty or forty years. Since the Middle Ages, really. Why, there is Mary Somerville, Maria Mitchell, Janet Taylor, Margaret Gatty, Elizabeth Carne of Cornwall."

He cut me off mid-sentence. "Well, I...What I mean to say is ..." he stammered. "Women ought to be married and tend to the house!"

"I see," I said, most agreeably. "Is there an offer of marriage that you know about that I should like to know as well, Mr. Prescott?"

"Uh, well no, I mean..." He was clearly taken aback.

"Well, when I have an offer, then I shall indeed take it into consideration. But until then, being an unmarried lady of thirty-six, I must do what I can to help people as I make a living to support myself. Is that not what you do, Mr. Prescott?

"Arabella Buckley, you are too direct for a lady. Impertinent if you ask me," he muttered under his breath as he pulled open the door and stepped inside, dismissing me as he often thought he did.

"Have a lovely day, Mr. Prescott," I called loudly after him. To myself, I firmly said, *Never mind him.*

I continued along the pavement and up to the front porch of my house as I was returning home from my lecture at the cheerful yellow church hall in St. John's Wood. I was wearing a blue striped dress that fitted snugly on my frame. The short, tight sleeves worked well during my lecture—not once did they disrupt my notes on the podium, as longer sleeves sometimes did. The white ribbons of my wide brimmed hat flapped in the warm early afternoon breeze. I wore my hair neatly parted down the middle, braided and wrapped around my head. Smoothed back and out of sight—just the way I preferred it. Only a small curl on each side of my face peered out of the large brim of my hat.

I gave lectures to continue to provide knowledge to those who wanted it. Doing so allowed me to escape home for several hours to do something worthwhile. And the lectures provided a small way to repay Sir Charles for all he had taught me. Despite my fatigue from hours of preparation, the lecture earlier that morning had gone very well. Several women came up to me afterwards to ask if I had a paper about the lecture they might read. I was so pleased to be able to report to the crowd that my new book, *A Short History of The Natural Sciences*, would be published and available that very day! Propagating my in-depth knowledge gained from Sir Charles seemed not only the right thing to do to repay him but also a bridge to the unknown for me.

I fumbled with my key to open our door, when suddenly it sprang open as if by itself.

"The crate is here!" My father's eyes gleamed, as he rushed me through the open doorway. I flung off my hat and gloves as I entered the house. "I loosened the top so that you could open it quickly," he said, fairly giddily. "But I was careful not to look inside." We both stared at a wooden crate stuffed with straw. Mother put down her sewing and drew up closer as well. Silent but smiling, she looked at me.

"Hello, Mother," I said, glancing up at her quickly as I drew nearer to the crate. I stood and looked into her eyes briefly. Still cornflower blue but with more creases around the corners and in between them. At seventy-two, the lines in her face resembled a very over ripe apple that had shrunken and shriveled around the edges but still possessed its natural colour and softness. She was beautifully dressed in a blue day frock with a white gauze collar and a modest gold locket hanging from a small strand of pearls. Her salty grey hair was pulled back in one braid that she wound around in a circle on her crown, and pinned, like mine. Her hair always reminded me of a cinnamon bun doused with white powdered sugar. She smelled of the gentlest lavender scent that softly permeated any room that she occupied. I knew that although she remained reluctant to support my book writing, she was as curious to see this book as Father and me. Somehow, however, I no longer needed her support. I was free—and a little wistful in that very freedom.

"Now look at you," Father said, with his deep ringing voice. "A female author of a genuine natural science book at only thirty-six." I looked at him with admiration. He was tall and thin with a handsome face and full head of grey hair and squared beard. I doubted a wiser, more intelligent man existed. His eyes were the color of a greenish brown lake that ran deep with human kindness and insight. His hands, which he held out, palms up with esteem for me, were thick and strong, emanating a peaceful power.

"Well, go on. Open it!" Mother urged, wringing her hands anxiously.

"Should we not wait for Henry to return for the opening?" I asked, politely, not wanting to leave my brother out.

"He will be just as surprised to see your book in person when he comes home from the law firm. Open it before I tear into the box myself!" Father urged.

I reached down and touched the box with my right hand. The crate was just deep enough to hold a stack of books. I lifted the top off and set it gently down on the parlour table. Instantly a strong scent of pine rose from the box and filled my nostrils. I slowly brushed away the crisp, dry straw packing. I saw my hands opening the top of the crate, but I did not believe they were mine when they pulled out a green leather-bound book with my name on it. I was in a dream-like state by this point. My fingers ran across the cover. The book looked thicker than I had imagined it would be, which pleased me, and it was heavier than I had anticipated, too, giving me the impression of rich, weighty content. My very own book on science!

I turned it over in my hand and gazed down at the cover. When I saw my name at the bottom, Arabella B. Buckley, I remembered a discussion I had had with Mr. Murray during the production of the book. He had warned me against using my real name. He had said that women writers should use pseudonyms because they could run into disagreement from the public. He must know Mr. Prescott and his kind, I now thought. That manly attitude is an impenetrable brick wall when it comes to women and their abilities. Since it is men who do most of the writing, they promote their own perceptions and no one else's. The outcome, be it history, interpretations of art, comments on the sexes, or anything else, is always influenced by the author. My aim is to change that. *I want to write science from a woman's point of view, for the masses!*

I recalled standing with my publisher at his print shop, discussing these issues. "I am afraid I do not take your meaning, about the pseudonym, sir." I said, as earnestly as I could, trying to keep the edge out of my voice.

"Words can be misconstrued," he obliquely said. "Things can be misinterpreted. And can get dangerous. Better to use a pseudonym, if you take my meaning."

"There is nothing salacious in this book, Mr. Murray." I responded quickly. "And I wrote about kings and queens in my earlier work to educate people, young people, with illustrations," I added.

"Like I said, Miss. Better to protect yourself with a pseudonym. I know Sir Charles must have provided much in the way of education for this book. How did you manage to put his work into it?" He shuffled the papers of our publishing agreement, searching for details. I refused to be offended by anything he said or inferred.

"Same way as most men, I suspect, sir," I recalled saying. "I read and I listen to lectures, same as any man. Now, can I pay you for the production of my book as we agreed? Surely my money is the same as any man's."

I grinned now as I remembered those parting words with him that day. Father jolted me back to the present. "Oh, it is just beautiful, Bella, my dear. The green leather backing is so striking!" he exclaimed, running his index finger down the side of the book. In the crate were nine more of the book's siblings, exact copies, waiting in line to be held and read.

"For you and Mother" I said, proudly, presenting the book to him with both hands and a curtsey, making the gift official, my skirts swishing as they brushed the floor.

"To think of all those days and nights you were constantly writing!" Mother said, trying to be helpful.

"Yes, and to think of all the scratched out and balled up pages of corrections!" Father added. I laughed.

"And I suppose now you will continue with your lectures in St. John's Wood?" Mother asked.

"Yes, but I would like to do more than a few lectures and a history book, Mother," I said as we stood around the crate. I couldn't stop picking up and holding my books. "Writing this book has given me confidence in my abilities and helped me solidify my hopes. I want to use what I have learned with Sir Charles and Mr. Darwin. Their work is some of the most important scientific thought of this century, yet many have not read it or do not understand it. I want to help shine a light on their work for young people who might not initially understand the complexity of geology, biology, evolution and the sciences represented in their works. I want to carry on their work in a way that sends their knowledge out to the world. And a big step forward is with young people while they are still eager to learn. We have no idea just how important these scientific findings may be to the world in the future." I paused, suddenly embarrassed by my loquaciousness. "Am I too much, do you think?"

"It is an unusual thing for a woman to do," my mother said, biting her bottom lip. "I am not sure of your meaning."

"I, for one, would look forward to a better understanding of those big words like 'evolution,'" Father grumbled, thumbing through the book.

"Well done for remembering the term, Father," I said in praise.

"Perhaps an example, Bella, would aid our understanding." he prompted.

"Yes, certainly. First, though, I would like to read you the acknowledgement I wrote for the Lyells. I owe them a debt of gratitude."

I opened the book, leafed to the acknowledgement page and began to read aloud.

"To the memory of
My beloved and revered friends
SIR CHARLES AND LADY LYELL
To whom I owe more than I can ever express
I dedicate this my first book.
Trusting that it may help
To develop in those who read it that
Earnest and truth-seeking spirit in the study of God's
Works and laws which was the guiding Principle
of their lives."

I looked up at them. "Well said, Bella," Father proclaimed.

"Yes, very appropriate," said Mother. "And what do you suppose Sir Charles, if he were alive now, and Mr. Wallace and Mr. Darwin would all say about your book?" she asked, a bit skeptically.

"A very good question, Mother. Are you suggesting they might take offense at the fact that an uneducated woman is articulating the ideas of the most prestigious scientists the world has yet known?" Turning over the book in my hand, I asked myself the same question, a bit nervously. What would they say? Would they support my book as I have supported their works for years? Or would they dismiss my writing approach as childish, intended to capture hearts and imaginations first and then implant science in their brains?

"No, not implying that exactly, dear. But men are men, and they do see things differently." She was obviously concerned.

"Mr. Darwin will be pleased that I have espoused his theories. I have no doubt," I said optimistically.

"Very well, then. In honour of the moment, dear, please

read us a passage from the book. And tell us a bit about whatever you select," Mother requested, seating herself on the sofa and arranging her dress around her like a party guest awaiting a piano recital. "Do sit down, dear," she motioned to my father, patting the spot on the sofa next to her.

"In honour of this moment...let me see," I responded, flipping through the pages. "Let me find something that would interest you. Perhaps this..." I opened my book about halfway and started to read on page 110.

> *"Harvey's discovery of the circulation of the blood in 1619. In the year 1600, when Galileo and Kepler were still at the beginning of their discoveries, a young Englishman of two and twenty, named Harvey, who was born at Folkestone in 1578, went to Padua to study anatomy under the famous professor Fabricius Aqapendente. Although anatomists had by this time learnt a great deal about the bones and parts of a dead body, yet they were still crying about the working of a living one. They knew that arteries throb, like the pulse in the wrist, which is an artery; and that veins (that is, the blue branching tubes which you can see under the skin in your hand and arm) contain blood and do not throb like arteries, but they had no clear idea of the use of either arteries or veins...that is how the blood was pumped backward or forward."*

"Mother, are you quite well?" I asked, stopping my reading. Mother looked pale and unwell.

"Perhaps a different section would be better," Father suggested, fanning mother with a letter he found on the table.

"Right," I quickly said. Too much blood in that one. "Astronomy, perhaps? Halley's comet? Or the velocity of light?" I suggested, quickly searching. "I know! Benjamin Franklin's experiments with electricity." I turned to page 257, scanning with my finger, and began to read aloud.

> *"Franklin's idea was that if he could send an iron rod up into the clouds to meet the lightning, it would become charged with the electricity, which he believed was there, and would send it down a thread attached to it, so that he might be able to feel it. He too, therefore, two light strips of cedar fastened crossways, upon which he stretched a silk handkerchief tied by the corners to the end of the cross, and to the top of his kite he fixed a sharp-pointed iron wire more than a foot long. He then put a tail and a string to this kite, and at the end of the string near his hand he tied some silk (which is a bad conductor), to prevent the electricity from escaping into his body. Between the string and the silk, he tied a key, in which the electricity might be collected.*
>
> *When his kite was ready he waited eagerly for a heavy thunderstorm, and, as soon as it came, he went out with his son to the commons near Philadelphia and let his kite fly. It mounted up among the dark clouds, but at first no electricity came down, for the string was too dry to conduct it. But by-and-by the heavy rain fell, the kite and string both became thoroughly wet, and the fibers of the string stood out as threads do when electricity passes along them. Directly Franklin saw this and he knew that his experiment had succeeded; he put his finger to the key and drew out a strong bright spark; and therefore, before long he had a rapid current of electricity passing from the key to his finger."*

I snapped the book shut for dramatic effect. Given Mother's frailness, I would omit what came next—even though it was one of my favorite passages: the part about electrical current running through the dissecting knife of a dead frog, producing convulsions in the frog's leg.

"Bravo!" my father said, nodding vigorously.

"Thank you. I do hope you enjoy the book," I said with a happy sigh. I handed the book to Father, and he began to examine the illustrations. "I have given the book to Mr. Garnett," I added, "the head of the Reading Room at the British Museum, and he has promised to give my book to several authors in his circle who will provide friendly criticisms between authors."

"I see," Mother said, waving my comment off as if unimportant. Having recovered from the previous reading, she stood up from the couch and steered me aside with my elbow. "Before I forget to mention this, I received a letter today from our friends the Fishers, who have written to say that their daughter in law, Eliza, has not yet defeated her troubling respiratory illness and has taken a turn for the worse. She is trying to recover in Devon. Does that sound a bit ominous to you, dear? And, her strapping husband, Dr. Thomas Fisher, as you well know, is in New Zealand and not able to care for her." Mother said these words in an odd tone as she eyed me strangely.

"Yes, that does sound troubling indeed," I replied, looking down at the floor so that she would not notice the shock on my face. "If you will excuse me, I have much to do to prepare for a meeting with Mr. Darwin and will work at my desk." Perhaps too casually, I slid through the parlour and down the hall to my bedroom.

Mother nodded as if she knew I had much to think about. Maybe she understood more than I had always thought!

Her news and comments about the Fishers caused an explosion of emotions inside me. Did Mother suspect something about my relationship with Thomas? Had she chosen this exact moment to tell me about his wife to change my mind about book writing? My guess was that Mother was alerting me to her ultimate dream—a possible husband for me at last. Did she know or suspect he had been unhappy in his marriage with Eliza and the confinements of the way of life here in England? Had she finally put the clues together as to why he decided to escape years ago and move to the frontier of New Zealand, where he could more easily roam the great outdoors and practise innovations in medicine that had been seen as unconventional in his practice in Devon? He was fleeing more than close-minded practitioners and patients.

Certainly, Thomas must know about Eliza's condition. They were so estranged at this point that he was not returning to England to be at her side. I hugged a cushion on my bed. What will he do if she dies? Does he even know how serious her condition is? Does he still feel strongly about me after all these years? Will he ask me to marry him? I cannot even think such a thing with Eliza on her own and possibly dying. I have never wished her ill. Poor Eliza! Alone and battling for her life! With her daughter, Rose, at present far away in Scotland while her husband is absent on active service? Will Rose return? My mind was ablaze with questions.

I thought about how far I had come with the great men of science I had been working with, and how I first came to work with them, became friends with them, and was now accepted as a part of their group. Would I have to give up all that I had accomplished if I wed Thomas? I would never want to give up my work, but what would Thomas say? What would he do?

I stared down at the cover of *The History of Natural Science* in my hands. Famous men of science choosing to be friends with a female literary assistant? Hard to believe. A humble woman with no formal education writing a book on the history of science? Even more difficult to believe. I was growing more and more exhausted. Well, I would find out soon enough if my grand scientific friends supported me or not. I had arranged to meet with Mr. Darwin when he came to London next. Questions of love and marriage would have to wait their turn.

Chapter Fifteen

Arabella's Declaration

Erasmus Darwin's House, London

1876

"Through our continued work together, I feel we extend the Lyells' legacy, do you agree, Mr. Darwin?" I pushed a set of papers across the table to him. We were meeting at his brother Erasmus's house, where Mr. Darwin often stayed when he visited London. He picked the papers up and began to leaf through them.

"Yes, it is so. I am happy to have the benefit of your review of my work," he replied, smiling, happy to see all the marking on the pages denoting our progress. "I do miss them both very much." He continued to check the papers, happily noting the changes with his forefinger as he went down the page.

"Yes, they were such pillars of science. I do try to live up to their standards, and yours, in my work," I responded, with my own smile, albeit a more sorrowful one. I waited for him to form questions for me from the papers. I sat with my notepad and pen, ready to take down further instructions from him. Since Sir Charles' death, we were working together more closely.

He set the papers and his pen down, "Thank you for sending me *A Short History of Natural Science*," he said. "I am reading it with delight. And what of your other work these days, Miss Buckley? What do you intend to do? Will I be able to continue to ask for your editorial skills?" His eyes were warm. "I do have several works in progress, even at my advanced age, you know."

"Of course!" I exclaimed, with a nod of my head. "And since you have raised the subject of my future, I would like to discuss with you what I think my course of action will be," I said, with resolution.

I drew in a full breath. "Mr. Darwin, I have begun work on a new book, a scientific work. But that is not all. I intend to write it—and any future books— in a way that people of all educational backgrounds and abilities can understand. That is to say, I would like to use my writing ability as well as my artistic talents to write and illustrate science books that appeal to both children and adults." I paused to observe his reaction.

He considered my words. "Very well. I applaud your writing, as you know," he replied.

"Yes, well, thank you!" I said. "The thing is, I would like to write books in a way that, shall we say, mirror or expand upon, *your* theories of evolution, as well as Sir Charles's and Mr. Wallace's works, for those who thirst for knowledge." I girded up my courage. "Therefore, Mr. Darwin, I ask for your permission to carefully and meticulously write books that espouse your theories specifically to help younger generations know and appreciate your work as I do. I feel compelled to write in this manner as if it is a calling or a vocation—my mission in life, if you will, but I want to know if I have your permission to do so. In effect, I would be using your work like a megaphone or a microscope, bringing it more in view for people from backgrounds that might not see it otherwise. Is that worthy, do you think?"

"Worthy? I think only the readers in the course of time can be the judge of that. But yes, you certainly have my permission; but there really is no need. Why, you explain evolution better than anyone I know," came his gentle reply.

"Wonderful! It is decided then!" I fought to restrain my excitement. "I will be your faithful follower and an authoress of science. Thank you, Mr. Darwin!" I reached out to shake his hand.

ARABELLA BUCKLEY, AGE 43

THE BUCKLEY FAMILY HOME –
1 ST MARY'S TERRACE, PADDINGTON, LONDON, U.K.

The Darwin Family Home – Down House, Downe, Kent, U.K.

IMAGE OF ARABELLA BUCKLEY IN REGENT GARDENS, LONDON – CREATED BY RONALDO ALVES

WALREDDON MANOR HOUSE – BACK VIEW

Letter From Arabella Buckley to Richard Garnett, 1893

~~UPCOTT AVENEL,~~
~~HIGHAMPTON,~~
~~N. DEVON~~

Walreddon Manor
Tavistock
March 19/93.

My dear friend

My young carpenter whom I brought from North Devon finished his work last night & goes home on Monday, so my work to adapting refitting, painting etc is really finished. It has been hard work, for I have adapted everything & only bought <u>one</u> single piece of furniture, a small wash-stand

LETTER FROM ARABELLA BUCKLEY TO RICHARD GARNETT, 1893

The date upon the porch we
believe is 1591 at which time
the house was evidently restored
Parts they say belong to Edward
III —

Now to business. If you have not
settled with anyone else we will
go on as we are with the Times
We are too far from Tavistock to
fetch it at midday, & if any
pressing occurred we can see
it at the Library. So we must
be content with it the second
day. I am going next week
to try & write the article on Sir
Charles Lyell which must be
sent to America in a fortnight

LETTER FROM ARABELLA BUCKLEY TO RICHARD GARNETT, 1893

~~UPCOTT AVENEL,~~
~~HIGHAMPTON,~~
~~N. DEVON.~~

we are also going to
Plymouth one day
next week & to Staverton
to where the Heriots are
now staying — I cannot
write more now as I must
go with the Heriots but
I wanted to answer your
two letters

Yours with sincerest
friendship
Arabella B. Fisher

ARABELLA BUCKLEY AND LILY FISHER –
SIDMOUTH, DEVON, U.K. IN THE EARLY 1900S

ARABELLA BUCKLEY IN THE EARLY 1900S

Arabella and Thomas' Travels from London to the West Country

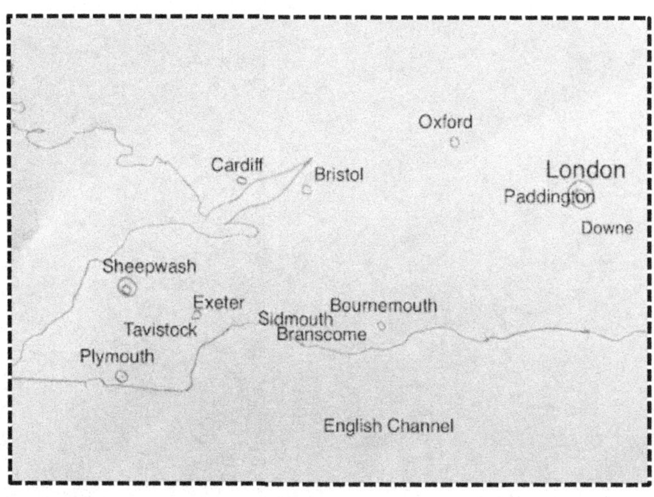

London - Sheepwash via Bristol	233 miles
Sheepwash – Branscombe	64 miles
Sheepwash – Sidmouth	51 miles
Branscombe- Beer	2 miles
Sheepwash – Buckfastleigh	57 miles
Sheepwash – Plymouth	42 miles
Tavistock – Plymouth	15 miles
Sheepwash – Tavistock	26 miles
Paddington – Downe	20 miles

Chapter Sixteen

The Fairyland of Science

Dorking, Surrey, and Paddington and Marylebone, West London

1876 - 1878

"How clever of you, Alfred, to build your own home! I am astonished at the quality of your work, although I really should not be," I said. "It is much like your papers. Very logical and complete with no mistakes!" I gazed around the room, admiring the banister work of his new staircase. I had visited the Wallaces' new home south of London in Dorking, Surrey, several times; and each time I admired their progress.

"Yes, thank you. I have been putting all my time into this house, and we are happy with the results," Alfred sighed. "I will pick some mint for our refreshments from the garden. I shall return in a moment." He smiled.

Annie Wallace set out several glasses and a small cake for our teatime offering. She noticed that I looked surprised at the glasses, rather than the cups for tea that she knew I was expecting.

"I am afraid that we are entirely out of tea just now," she explained. "What with the expenses of the house, we find ourselves..." Hesitating, she gave me a pleading look.

"You find yourselves a bit short of money, with the building expenses coming in all at once," I remarked. "Of course, this is usually the case with a new home." I smiled and offered to fill our glasses with water from the pitcher.

Her response was quiet. "Yes, that is it exactly."

Their unfortunate situation came over me with a shock. I knew Alfred had no fixed situation from which he could garner a salary. But I had assumed that his writings supported and covered his family's needs. From her tone, I could see that the Wallaces were clearly penniless. I shut my eyes and drew a deep breath. Fear flooded my mind at my close friends' predicament, with all their children to support! What would become of them all?

Alfred returned with a handful of freshly picked and quickly washed mint. "That smells divine!" I said, hoping to lift Annie's spirits and set a happier tone for refreshment.

Alfred pulled up a wooden chair that had traveled with them through several previous house moves. "Yes, I do love fresh mint," he replied, as he offered us each a sprig for our water.

As I sat there enjoying my mint water, I thought to myself. Here sits one of the most world-renowned men of science, with barely a penny to his name and a family to support. He has published, jointly with Charles Darwin, a highly successful narrative based on his travels to Southeast Asia, where he carried out research on animals among the islands of the Malay Archipelago, determining what is known as the Wallace Line, the invisible but definite boundary between the islands that separate the fauna of Australasia from that of Asia. He has written several scientific papers and is an established naturalist, yet here he sits in front of me, with no income, save that of a small family inheritance. Something must be done, or they will face ruin. But what, exactly?

We chatted lightly about his work in Spiritualism and their

garden as we finished the cake.

"Well, I am off to return to marking and grading examination papers. Mustn't keep the students waiting," he said. His meek comportment told me how dire his situation was.

I departed soon after, unsettled by the visit. I could hear Lady Lyell's caution to me about Spiritualism, that it was not true science and to stay away from it, in my ears as I made my way back to the station.

"Your worth as a woman of science is just beginning, is begging to be born," my father insisted as we sat at Sunday dinner around our fine dining room table at home in Paddington. Henry had taken the train to Manchester for a trial in which he was representing a client, and our new tenant had taken dinner in her room, ill with a respiratory condition. It was just Mother and Father, who looked at me across the table.

"I have my doubts about that, Father," I said. "I am not sure I have the same support as an author that I had as Sir Charles's literary assistant. Might I read you a letter I have received from Mr. Darwin today to that end? I would like to ask your opinion about it." I took the letter out of my pocket and unfolded it, carefully, and began to read it aloud.

Down, February 11, 1876

My dear Miss Buckley,

You must let me have the pleasure of saying that I have just finished reading with very great interest your new book. The idea seems to me a capital one, and as far as I can judge very well carried out. There is much fascination in taking a bird's eye view of all the grand leading steps in the progress of science. At first I regretted that you had not kept each science more separate; but I dare say you found it impossible. I have hardly any criticisms, except that I think you ought to have introduced Murchison as a great classifier of formations, second only to W. Smith. You have done full justice, and not more than justice, to our dear old master, Lyell. Perhaps a little more ought to have been said about botany, and if you should ever add this, you would find Sachs' 'History,' lately published, very good for your purpose.

You have crowned Wallace and me with much honour and glory. I heartily congratulate you on having produced so novel and interesting a work, and remain,

My dear Miss Buckley, yours very faithfully,
Ch. Darwin

Father gaped at me in disbelief. "Can you imagine," he said softly. "Receiving a letter like that from Charles Darwin himself. It is unimaginable."

I looked at Father across the table. "Mr. Darwin is quite supportive of my book, isn't he?" I had just come from my room to our Sunday supper after writing a testimonial for Sir Charles. The pressure and pain of his loss gushed over me like a gigantic wave. I would next send the testimonial to Mr. Darwin, Mr. Wallace, Mr. Huxley and others for their approval, which would in itself be something of an achievement for me.

Our hope was that the testimonial would be well placed in several prominent publications as a small testament to our friend and mentor.

"Absolutely. Incredibly high praise, Arabella. You are already a published author," Father said, scooping a heaped spoonful of mashed potatoes on his plate to accompany his steaming pork loin. "My guess is that the scientific fraternity will jump at the chance to support an author taught by Sir Charles." Father was a force for good. He had to be, given his line of work. I chose to listen closely to him.

"Yes, perhaps," I responded, hesitantly. "But do I have any right to be an author? Outside of historical books, I mean. I want to write books for science with my own expansions and elaborations of their findings and have discussed this with Mr. Darwin, and he approves."

"I can see why he would welcome someone who writes so clearly in support of him as you. Perhaps you must be your own mentor on this issue. What would you counsel someone just like yourself to do?" Father asked, softly and wisely.

I quickly said, "Counsel someone else, like myself? I seriously doubt there is another person alive in my situation, Father. A woman attempting to become an author without academic credentials, and in competition with a sea of men?" I looked at my parents' faces. My mother sat motionless and unreadable, lips tightly pressed. My father waited for my further response. "Nevertheless, I would say that repaying Sir Charles and educating others are paramount in my life, and therefore I would counsel myself to listen to what my heart demands. My heart demands that I write about science in a way that is beautiful and full of poetry and imagination."

Father cocked his head to one side, chewing his pork loin and nodding wordlessly. My mother continued to sit silently. Finally, Father squared his shoulders to me and said, "Choice opportunities are hard to find in this world. You have done well. You have paved a path before you with the Lord, and it seems a fine path. To disregard it seems wasteful."

I replied, "I cannot disagree, Father."

Suddenly, Mother chimed in. "Perhaps you could disguise your work by using a pseudonym or some other writing device that would enable you to be more acceptable to society." Advice I had heard before, of course. Her tone conveyed a thinly veiled warning.

The following day, I was anxious to meet Henry and to get out of the February cold. I burst through the doors of the winter garden at the Langham Hotel in Marylebone, which was filled with lunchtime patrons, busy and bustling with barristers, judges, clerks and other well-dressed men. I looked around for my brother, who, upon his return from Manchester, had agreed to meet me for lunch in the winter garden, one of my favorite spots. I glanced at the beautiful clock outside as I went in: I was late. I looked around the tall green palms and tables covered in white linens, searching for my brother. The maitre d'hotel recognized me and flew to my side to assist. I saw Henry sitting, somewhat impatiently, in a booth about eight tables away from the front door. He returned my light wave with a stiff nod and nose-up gesture, the kind that a man gives to another as acknowledgement without wanting to make a display of it.

I attempted to approach his table but was forced to wait for other patrons to pass as they were being seated. I noticed Mr. Prescott and a group of three stodgy looking middle-aged men sitting at a table to my right, by the door.

"Good day to you, Miss Buckley," Mr. Prescott said in an annoyed tone, as if having to pass the time of day with me was disturbing his immensely important conversation.

"Gentlemen," I replied, standing at my full height. I would not let his dismissive tone impair my day in the least.

After an uncomfortable pause, he cleared his throat. "Miss Buckley, may I present my colleagues from the Consolidated Bank?"

"How do you do?" I smiled as the introductions were made. "Are you enjoying your luncheon?" Glasses rang in a tinkling sound in the background as waiters in black trousers, white shirts and stiff black bow ties whisked by. Smells of roasted meats and freshly baked bread filled my nostrils. I was so hungry that my mouth started to water.

"Yes," said one of the men, Towson, who wore a brown woollen waistcoat and jacket. "But it is a sight here with the crowd, do you not agree?"

"Oh, yes. Quite busy today as most days," I replied, amicably.

Another man, Mr. Reed, was seated next to Mr. Prescott. "Buckley. That name sounds so familiar. Have we met before?" he asked me.

As I started to respond, Mr. Prescott interjected, "She is the vicar's daughter—the one at St Mary's Paddington."

The man looked confused. "No, I do not attend church in that parish," he replied, deep in thought.

"Perhaps you have read or heard of my recent book, *A Short History of Natural Science*?" I asked sincerely. But I seriously doubted if any of these men were familiar with such a work, much less a publication from a woman.

"Miss Buckley has written a history book," Mr. Prescott said, flatly, as if to put a dismissive disclaimer on my work.

"Why, yes!" Mr. Reed exclaimed. "That's it. My daughter was reading your book," he said, pointing a finger up in the air in amazement of his discovery of my authorship. His words gave me a thrill that I tried to play down a little.

"Wonderful! I hope she found it enjoyable," I replied.

"Yes. A good day to you, Miss Buckley. We were just discussing bank business..." Mr. Prescott interjected, rudely.

Ignoring Mr. Prescott, Mr. Reed continued. "My daughter said that the book is quite a fantastic summary of the history of the natural sciences, which many adults would benefit from reading. Maybe even you, Prescott," and with that he laughed heartily, slapping a gray flannel knee that stuck out from beneath the table.

"I believe that is my brother signaling me to join him," I said rather quickly, reading Mr. Prescott's surly expression. "It was a pleasure meeting you."

As I swished away in my long, green taffeta skirt and bustle with matching jacket, I heard Mr. Reed saying, "A genuine author at our table. That book is top rate, I'd say."

I walked quickly to Henry's table, dodging a waiter, and sat down in a plush gold cushioned chair opposite him. I pulled off my gloves, one finger at a time, and folded them neatly on the table beside me, happy in the knowledge that Mr. Prescott had heard directly from his colleague that the colleague's daughter had read my book and enjoyed it.

"Sorry to be a little late," I sighed. "I narrowly missed being run over by a carriage and four just outside—and then by Mr. Prescott and crew inside. Thank you for meeting me, Henry."

"Of course. I saw Mr. Prescott on the way in. Don't fret about him. His bank is facing more competition than he would like, and it's one crisis after another for banks these days, which is probably why he is such a curmudgeon." He placed his napkin in his lap. "Now, what is it that demands your attention so much that you could not mention it at home?"

"Two things, really." I poured out my concerns about the Wallaces' finances to him as we ordered our pea soup and fillet of sole.

Henry swallowed a mouthful of soup from his spoon after

the waiter brought our first course. "It seems to me that those scientific types have civil stipends," he said. He saw the quizzical look on my face and explained. "You know, a monthly sum to live off as they continue their contributions to the greater good of humanity through science. Does Wallace not have a stipend from the government?"

"No, he does not have any stipend. Henry, you are a genius!" I exclaimed. "A stipend would be perfect. But how can he obtain one?"

Henry looked down at his bowl and thought for a moment. "A declaration of accomplishments to the right people in high offices," he said. "The Prime Minister, I expect. Recommendations from renowned people of science to validate a list of his accomplishments. Mr. Darwin could help with this, obviously. Testimonials from others of his peers. A compilation of such pieces would create a recommendation to request a stipend. I have no idea about any specific protocol or process. These are only my conjecture as to what it entails." But Henry was very knowledgeable about many things, so I took his conjecture to be as solid as granite.

"Mr. Wallace is far too humble to create such documentation about himself," I replied, searching Henry's face for guidance.

"Then you must create the documentation yourself."

"Yes, I see," I said slowly, considering the difficulty of such a task.

"And the second concern? You said there were two," Henry asked.

"Yes, the second," I said, pulling myself away from considerations of stipends. "The second is more of an announcement rather than a concern. I have decided to become an authoress of science books, with Mr. Darwin's permission. And Father also approves!" I exclaimed.

"I see congratulations are in order!" Henry said, genuinely

happy for me, taking a sip of his white wine. I noticed his impeccable manners, his thoughtful pauses, and his ability to listen. His handsome face and thick waving light brown hair. How I loved him, my brother! He was always there for me as a friend and as a guide.

"Thank you," I said. "And Mary Treat has requested my help with editing her new science book. Me! Mary Treat, from across the Atlantic. She is a respected American entomologist and botanist who does research for Mr. Darwin on North American species, and is beginning a writing career of her own."

"Yes, of course. I am very familiar with her," Henry said sarcastically, rolling his eyes. I knew of course that he had never heard of her.

"Do not joke. She is becoming very established. Mother and Father are getting, well, a bit older and I am concerned about my ability to provide for myself in my own later years. A question for you is, should I accept her work?" I leaned in as I asked the question, demanding his full and serious attention. "If I accept, it is as if I am declaring that I am again a literary assistant in one way and not a serious author, as I desire. Do you not see? Because, I believe, through my writing, I am more than a literary assistant and more than an editor. I believe that I am myself a woman of science, capable of more than simple editing!" I was on a rant now, poor Henry.

"Yes, I see. I see that you have grown far beyond the boundaries of your first situation. And far beyond the boundaries typical of polite society."

"And so?" I demanded as the waiter set our plates of fish and lentils down before us.

He picked up his fork. "What is it exactly that you are capable of doing more of? Spell it out for me, to be clear, and then we can better understand the problem." He was detangling the issue just as a lawyer should.

I sat thinking for a moment in order to relay the clearest grasp of my mission as I could to Henry, my most trusted ally. Then I went ahead and explained it to him—that I wanted to convey the teachings of science to readers at large, and to do so in an accessible way that connected with their faith and did not threaten it. I spoke for several moments and stopped, waiting for Henry's reaction.

"And so, be it," came Henry's answer.

I looked at him, quite astonished that it seemed so easy for him to reach such a monumental, even outlandish, conclusion. Still, I felt a sense of calm sweep over me with his words. The decision was quite simple. Of course, I would accept serious offers of scientific work. But I would also pursue my own writing. I already had a published book and had started my first scientific work in my head. It would be based on my lectures. A write up of my lectures comparing natural processes to the magic of fairyland, as if science is a land of magic and fairies that create nature, through the hand of God.

"Yes, I think I agree," I said. "Why stay still or go backwards when moving forward will repay Sir Charles and Mr. Darwin in a much grander way, on a much larger scale? The fish is delicious, don't you think?" I asked, trying not to devour mine too quickly.

"Yes, however, you must consider the implications of becoming a more public and prominent author. Have you thought of that?" Henry's chewing seemed to become faster, more intense. His eyes were dark and piercing.

"Yes, I would have financial stability and ..."

Henry interrupted. "I am referring to you becoming a public figure, one whom people would want to know more about and admire. How are you going to get round this public figure having an unseemly affair of the heart with a married man, especially as the daughter of a vicar and the sister of a prominent barrister?" He emphasized the words "married" and "vicar' in a way that made me wince. "And let us not forget the incident with the ever-watchful Mr. Prescott," he finished, with a slight jerk of his head in the direction of Mr. Prescott's table.

Not knowing what to say, I sat, lips pressed together as I stared the remains of my fish on its lovely pink flowered porcelain plate. The ornate silver fork I was holding began to quiver as I realized my hand was shaking.

"You are saying that I should end it with Thomas." I murmured forlornly.

"Yes, exactly. End it with Thomas. Before you two ruin both of your reputations and mine. He keeps you on a string that might as well be a noose for your career. Do you understand? The authoress with dark secrets of her own? The tawdry tales the papers could tell! Can you imagine?" My normally placid brother was seething. "Look, I do admire Thomas, but I do not admire what he has drawn you into, especially when he doesn't know yet that you are about to pursue something that few people, especially women, have the heart and brain to accomplish. Do you not see?"

"Plainly. Yes, I do see it. Plainly." My plate sat untouched for the remainder of the meal.

Henry and I had just finished some lively games of Whist in the parlour with our oldest sister, Elsie, who had come to London for a rare visit, one rainy Saturday afternoon. We had had to play German style for two, as there were only three of us, taking it in turns to sit out. I took the opportunity to ask if I could take advantage of them being a captive audience. They both seemed pleasantly amused, and Mother and Father were gone for the afternoon, so I gauged that they might be in the right state of mind to provide a reaction to a fresh and solid draft of my new scientific book.

"May I read to you my draft of the opening of my latest work, '*The Fairy Land of Science*'?" I asked. "I do think my opening is rather convincing and enjoyable, based on the reactions of the attendees at some of my lectures."

"You know I am not a science lover, Arabella, but I would adore being the first to hear a passage from your new book!" Henry exclaimed, delight shining in his eyes as he walked from the card table to sit before me as I opened my leather folio and took out my papers.

"I would also be delighted," Elsie echoed as she moved to the sofa.

"As an example," I began, "I wrote this particular passage to provide a larger picture of science—that is, to demonstrate how every element of science is interconnected and all of that science is connected through a divine being. I will read it now."

> *"...Watch the water flowing in deep quiet stream or forming the vast ocean; and then reflect that every drop is guided by invisible forces working according to fixed laws. See plants springing up under the sunlight, learn the secrets of plant life, and how their scents and colors attract the insects. Read how insects cannot live without plants, nor plants without the flitting butterfly or the busy bee, out of all of this springs the wonderful universe around us...Can you help feeling a part of this guided and governed nature? Or doubt that the power which fixed the laws of the stars and of the tiniest drop of water—that made the plant draw power from the sun, the tiny coral animal its food from the dashing waves, that adapted the flower to the insect, and the insect to the flower—is also molding your life as part of the great machinery of the universe so that you have only to work, and to wait, and*

> *to love? We are all groping dimly for the Unseen Power but no one who loves nature and studies it can ever feel alone or unloved in the world...You may call this Unseen Power what you will—may lean on it in loving, trusting faith, or bend in reverent and silent awe; but even the little child who lives with nature and gazes on her with open eye, must rise in some sense or other through nature to nature's God."*

"Bravo!" Henry clapped, vigorously. I gave a small but happy curtsey in return.

"Wonderful. Might we have a bit more?" Elsie asked.

"Yes, indeed. Even I, the most ill-equipped human for science, would like more, darling sister. If there is more, please, read on!" Henry urged emphatically, his hand outstretched in a sweeping motion and a large smile covered his handsome face.

"Why yes, I do have more." I went to a table by the window, opened the drawer, and pulled out a magnifying glass. Then I opened my folio while still clutching the magnifying glass. "Chapter 2 is 'Sunbeams and The Work They Do.' Allow me, please, to read this small section to explain my purpose in writing this book by way of example."

> *"In order to see how powerful, the sun's rays are, you have only to take a magnifying glass and gather them to a pinpoint on a piece of brown paper, for they will set the paper alight. Furthermore, Sir John Herschel tells us that at the Cape of Good Hope the heat was even so great that he cooked a beefsteak and roasted some eggs by merely putting them in the sun, in a box with a glass lid!"*

I placed the magnifier in a beam of sunlight, and it shone brightly beneath. I looked up at my siblings. “I am the magnifying glass! Do you see my meaning? Mr. Darwin, Sir Charles, and their colleagues are the sun. I will harness their energy and set the public alight with it,” I said, triumphantly. I will illuminate the future of science!”

Chapter Seventeen

Life and Her Children

1 St. Mary's Terrace,
London

January 1879

When my old friend Mrs. Fanny Salter invited me to a dinner party, I thought I would enjoy the affair immensely. I dressed in a beige, lightly beaded satin evening dress with a bustle and small train, trimmed in tiny pearls. I sat at the sumptuously laid out dinner table, chatting away. My dining partner to my right was Mr. Haycock, Fanny's brother. Casually he asked what I had been doing earlier in the day.

"I was at the Reading Room at the British Museum engrossed in my new book, still a work in progress, called *Life And Her Children*," I responded quite happily.

I had been working all day in the Reading Room of that great domed library with Mr. Garnett, who had become a dear friend. As Mr. Haycock spoke, I thought briefly about Mr. Garnett—how interested he had been in my writing, and how he had helped me find the materials I needed in the Museum, both written and exhibited. He was the most smiling, most friendly, and most strangely attractive, erudite man, despite his yellowed teeth and bristling red stubble of a beard.

His large, kind eyes often looked away while speaking, but they were so round and compelling when they finally did connect. His eyes! Those magnetic eyes!

I found myself thinking about Mr. Garnett quite regularly and not strictly in a platonic, professional way but not in a lurid way either. Was he simply a distraction from thinking about Thomas or was he becoming something more to me? He was happily married, after all, and he had six children. I had received many invitations to his home for family dinners, which I loved, and felt as if I was one of the more favored guests there. But Mr. Garnett was more of a friend than anything, wasn't he?

When Mr. Haycock mentioned one of my books, my attention snapped back to his presence.

"I know your book *A Short History of Natural Science* has been a fantastic success. What was it that the *Post* said about it? Something to the effect of, "There is no use in further editions as there are already too many copies sold as it is. Something to that effect, I believe," Mr. Haycock said, satisfied that he had recalled the review.

"Thank you. I have had many parents tell me that my most recent book, *The Fairylands of Science* has been useful in their own religious teachings, which is my greatest reward," I beamed back at him.

"And what is this new book about and when can we expect to see it?" Mr. Haycock asked, curiosity written all over his face.

I was quite happy to reply to see if I could even further engage his curiosity. "The new book offers glimpses of animal life from the amoeba to the insects. Today I sketched land leeches of Ceylon racing to attack some creature," I said, with an airy wave of my hand.

"Interesting," he mused. "I wonder if your readers will be able to, shall we say, admire these worms as much as you do?"

"Of course, they will," I replied quickly, "because I open the book with a poem that has always been a guidepost for me by Coleridge:

"He prayeth best who loveth best
All things both great and small;
For the dear God who loveth us,
He made and loveth all."

"Yes, quite so, Miss Buckley!" Mr. Haycock returned his eyes to his plate, looking down as if the worms were intruding on his lamb and crossing over onto his peas. Now looking incredulously at me and looking sideways at his plate, grimacing.

"As a reminder that even jointed spiders, crabs, scorpions and shrimps, admittedly frightening, have their own sort of glory and beauty in their evolved frames and abilities. I plan to include over one hundred sketches of my subjects in the book, including spiders, crabs, and all sorts of related creatures," I said.

"Sketches of scorpions and spiders," Mr. Haycock echoed, now looking incredulously at me and with a clear aversion to his plate.

Shortly after dinner, a much-restored Mr. Haycock turned to me again, tapping me on the shoulder. "Excuse me, Miss Buckley. A Mr. Samuel Butler wishes to make your acquaintance." He tilted his head in the direction of the doorway.

What is *he* doing here, I asked myself. *Ironic that I am working on leeches and spiders today. Speak of the devil.* To me, he resembled a scorpion, dressed in an all-black suit.

Slowly I rose from my chair and steeled myself to be prepared for a likely attack from someone who had become one of the worst critics of Mr. Darwin the world had seen, someone I was loathe to converse with. Mr. Darwin was my mentor and now my livelihood. And, like Mr. Huxley, my professional and personal relationship with Mr. Darwin was to be defended in all ways. I imagined myself wearing the body armor of a spider as well as having the venomous bite, should I need it.

"Miss Buckley, may I present Mr. Samuel Butler, formerly of New Zealand?" Mr. Haycock said with formality. "Mr. Butler and I attended Shrewsbury and St Johns together. He is also an author. Perhaps you are familiar with his work?"

I curtsied. "Good evening, Mr. Butler. Of course, we are acquainted. We both attended séances with Alfred Wallace, my good friend, a few years ago," I said, intending to establish a polite and cordial atmosphere. Behind us, other dinner party guests milled about the parlour in close proximity.

"Miss Buckley, but of course we are acquainted through our works and interest in evolution—and the human's ability to inherit memory, as well," Mr. Butler glibly stated.

"Yes, Mr. Butler," I replied. "Congratulations are in order. I have read your latest work, *Evolution Old and New*, and have noted your very opinionated views." I hoped that I sounded polite and neutral, but inside I was fuming. How dare he criticize Mr. Darwin's theory of evolution in that book as being inferior to others, such as Buffon and Lamarck! I seethed when I recalled his recent journal notice challenging Mr. Darwin.

"And it is I who commend *you* on your children's writings, Miss Buckley. You do the world a great service by educating the very young," he said with a demeaning tone, looking down his nose.

"Yes, well, I do base my work on scientific fact, which is critical as a person of science," I lobbed back.

He raised an eyebrow, eyes narrowing. "Speaking of science, has Darwin read my book, do you know? I sent it to him and would very much like a meeting with him to discuss what he thinks of my future publication prospects. I have been to

Down House before, in '72, to discuss my book *Erewhon*."

"I have not spoken to him about your latest book, so I really could not say," I responded, tempted to toy with him and his so-called "science." In truth, we had discussed several of his works, the giants and I, and had dismissed him as being an amateur, fraudulent, and not at all complimentary to Mr. Darwin's position and data on evolution. We found his work critical of Mr. Darwin in unflattering and unscientific ways. He was not *one of us*, shall we say.

"I do think Mr. Darwin has clouded the understanding of evolution, would you agree, Miss Buckley?" he asked, his head held high and his beard, which resembled a black triangle coming to a point under his chin, jutting out. His beard shone from abundant pomade; I could smell the sickeningly sweet scent as he drew nearer.

"Absolutely not, sir," I retorted quickly. "The world has found the theory of evolution because of him. A theory that will live in the annals of history."

Butler vehemently disagreed. "As one of Darwin's claqueurs, you are all continually crying out that he should have the credit of having discovered evolution—not because he discovered it, but because he popularized it," he said. "He ought rather to have the credit of persuading people to believe in it, though he got them to think they believed in a distorted and impossible form. He found a discredited form of truth, which he manipulated so much that it became an accredited fallacy. This is what he did, and it is all he should be credited with," Mr. Butler asserted, spittle flying out of his mouth. Other guests noticed his emphatic speech and began to give him sideways glances.

"Had you been part of Darwin's inner circle—and I believe that you did repeatedly try to be—you would not be saying so," I replied, cooly. "Obviously you hold a grudge against him. Now, if you will excuse me, I must return home as I have an early morning meeting tomorrow with my London publisher about my latest book, for which I am being pressed for a completion date." *Oh, how delightful it was to say that to this pompous man*! "If you will please excuse me," I repeated, smiling up at him and with a quick turn, I walked away.

I will not stand there and argue with a fool, only to allow him to have the last word, I scoffed to myself. I made my way towards Fanny, kissed her on the cheek, politely said my goodbyes, and left immediately.

Henry came in from the cold streets of London one evening a few days later and I asked if I could see him in the parlour after dinner.

"How are you, Bella? Your writing continues well, I hope?" he said, pecking me on the cheek.

"Yes, good news!" I exclaimed. "My friend, Mr. Garnett, from the Reading Room, has given me the latest issue of *Nature* magazine, and I have a featured review in it. May I read it to you, please? I am so very excited about it!" I was gushing.

"By all means!" He leaned over my shoulder to see the journal in my hand.

"It says here, 'We praise the book's goal of showing how things far more wonderful than those related in fairytales are daily happenings around us. This realm may be entered by any one with eyes.' You see, they agree that educators need to widen scientific knowledge and understanding to wider audiences!" I said excitedly.

"Go on, what else does it say?" Henry urged.

"Oh, yes. 'Acquiring the observational and technical skills necessary for understanding the sciences is akin to developing superior senses and glimpsing the structures and forces hidden beneath the surface of things.'"

"Bravo, my sister the authoress strikes at the core of the lack of education!" Henry said, using his arm like a sword striking at something evil in the air.

I laughed. "Yes, I am a knight with a pen. My pen is as mighty as a sword!" I declared, also waving my arm about, giggling like a schoolgirl.

"In all seriousness, children and people all over the world will be looking at science altogether differently because of you," Henry lauded.

"I do hope so," I said. "I am continuing that mission as we speak." I smoothed my skirt down over my legs and Henry sat down next to me.

"Given that, may I ask where you and Thomas have left things? You and I have not discussed him in quite a while," Henry said in a serious tone.

"Yes, in fact, you are sitting in the exact spot where Thomas and I last discussed the topic. It was just before he returned to New Zealand after his daughter's wedding." I paused, trying to decide how much to share with my brother. "After our lunch, Henry, I realized that I must go forward to spread the word of science that the giants had begun. I knew I could illuminate Darwin and Wallace for others like perhaps no one else could, building a band of learned followers long after the deaths of these great men. But I could not do so bound to a tawdry string, as you rightly said. I began to agree with you, Henry, my dear brother, that my connection with Thomas, if found out by the public, would hurt my chances of future publications," I said, patting his leg.

"Yes, exactly," Henry agreed.

"So, I told Thomas that I had decided long ago to truly pursue science and make it my mission for life, and could not, in all conscience, continue with him knowing that the public would not approve of such a relationship between me and a married man," I sighed.

Henry looked stunned. "That must have been incredibly difficult for you, Bella. I am sorry," he said softly.

I drew in my breath, "It was for the best. Besides, I had my friends to rely on. I converse daily with my dear friend Mr. Richard Garnett. So much so that I intend to acknowledge his kind assistance in the preface of *Life and Her Children*. I have been spending my evenings at his home at his and his daughter Olive's invitation, and I continue to see the Wallaces and their dear children. I am especially fond of their daughter Violet."

We sat in silence for a moment. I pulled out the locket Thomas had given me from my bodice and opened the secret chamber.

"That was the last conversation I had with Thomas," I confessed. "And the pain I felt then I still feel now, months later." I looked inside the secret chamber of the locket at the tiny note written on faded and yellowed thin paper with a tiny blue flower.

1864

MY SOUL NOW KNOWS WHO IT LOVES.

YOURS IN DEVOTION,

THOMAS

Henry's eyes widened. "He gave you that locket? A very kind trinket from a fond time. But, as you said, Sister, you are better without him. I must go now and give my regards to Mother and Father before they go to sleep. I will bid you goodnight. And, I must say, I am emphatically proud of you." With that, he turned and left the parlour with me smiling after him.

I sat in the comfort of the sofa cushions, locket in hand, wondering what Thomas might be doing now. Where was he and who was he with? Was he happy? Would I ever speak with him again?

I thought back to the conversation we had sitting in this very room, where I sat at this very moment. I sat here when I told him I could not continue our relationship any longer as I stared down at the tiny scroll and its endearing message. I played out our last moments together over and over in my head.

"Must you go back to Timaru? Why not stay here in England and resume your medical practice or buy a sheep farm here, for that matter! Have you ever considered staying here?" I had asked him.

"We have been through this before, my love. I cannot stay, for I have duties and responsibilities in Timaru." He gently stroked my face.

"Yes, of course." I said, trying to gather steam for what was an incredibly difficult conversation. Thomas had grown to be the love of my life, but the confines of our relationship were tearing me to pieces. "In that case, I am sure you will understand when I tell you that this will be the last time we will see each other. Our relationship goes against every moral fiber of my being. I feel like a kite on a string. Up and down. I am sorry to tell you that I no longer want to be a part of this."

"But I love you."

"Yes. And I you. But it is a lonely love for me."

"Is there someone else?"

"No, certainly not. I believe I am very much past the marrying age by now. I find, as I have since the start of our relationship all these years ago that I prefer my work to this 'here today and gone tomorrow' relationship. My mission in life is and has been to work in science, to be a published author. I am now in the public eye. And you are still a married man. I hope you understand my predicament."

"I do not clearly understand, no. It pains me to no end to know that I am the source of your unhappiness; that much is clear. Do you feel your mind is immutable, unchangeable?"

"Yes, quite definitely. I am so very sorry," I said, firmly and rather coldly. I recalled feeling coldly about him and the pain that he had put me through on that day. However painful, it was the right decision for me. My memory of that last meeting continued.

"In that case, I will abide by your wishes," he had said. "I am grievously saddened by your decision. I wish you to take the cameo ring that I had made of you and that I wear. You remember it, don't you? It is the cameo I had made during my last departure from London."

"It is a beautiful cameo, but you should keep it."

Thomas ignored me and continued. "I was so forlorn over leaving and potentially losing you, that I thought of almost nothing else. When we stopped in the Bahama Islands, I saw a local man carving cameos from conch shells. He and I discussed your likeness, and the next day, before we sailed on, he sold me this cameo of you and I had it set in the gold ring I wear today. Please take it. I do not think I could bear to look at it again, knowing our relationship has broken."

"Thomas, I do not know what to say..." My eyes watered and my throat became swollen with grief.

"Say you will keep this and remember our fond times, our mutual love, and our laughter." He smiled. "It will make me feel better knowing you have something of mine."

"I still wear the silver locket you gave me almost every day." I tried to smile back. "See? I have it on now. I will keep the locket and I want you to keep the cameo. Please."

"Very well. Did you find the secret compartment in the locket?" he asked forlornly.

"No, you never mentioned that. It has a secret compartment? Where?" I asked, curiously searching its crevasses.

"Let me open it for you." He drew me near so that we could both investigate the locket. "You simply press the pearl latch like so, and it pops open. Another layer of locket behind the first." He smiled. He was so close I could see the tiny details of his lips and smell his breath. I cast my eyes downward as I knew what would happen if I looked up, and I would be only too glad to feel his lips on mine. *I must pull out of his gravitational attraction. I must pull away now, before it is too late*, I urged myself.

Inside the second layer of the locket was a small note and a pressed flower. "Is that a Forget-Me-Not?" I asked.

Thomas cleared his throat and stoically said, "Yes, it is. I found it pressed in a shop and thought you might like it. The small blue flower still had remains of the yellow pollen on its stamens. A truly beautiful gem of nature, it still had most of its light blue colour. But please do not read the note now," he said emphatically, reaching over to try to stop me from reading.

"Of course, I will read the note now!" I declared. He rolled his eyes in protest. The note was curled up into a tiny scroll. I unrolled the small, yellowed slip of paper and read it to myself.

1864

My soul now knows who it loves.

Yours in devotion,

Thomas

"You felt deeply for me, all those years ago, when we first met?" I asked him, returning both the scrolled note and the Forget-Me-Not back safely inside their secret place in the locket.

"Yes. But we must put all that behind us now. I am reminded of the popular song about Polly Perkins of Paddington Green. How does it go? Oh, yes." He began to softly sing a song that was made popular in the 1840s and is still quite recognizable now. As he sang, he stroked the side of my face with his open palm.

"I am a broken-hearted milkman, in grief I'm arrayed
Through keeping of the company of a young servant maid
Who lived on board and wages, the house to keep clean
In a gentleman's family near Paddington Green.
She was as beautiful as a butterfly and proud as a queen
Was pretty little Polly Perkins of Paddington Green
She'd an ankle like an antelope and a step like a deer
A voice like a Blackbird, so mellow and clear
Her hair hung in ringlets so beautiful and long
I thought that she loved me, but I found I was wrong."

He paused. "I do not remember the second verse," he said, sadly.

"The first verse was sufficient to make your point. But you are wrong. I do love you but not the way of life that comes with you."

"I see. Keep moving on with your work, as it is of keen value to the world. And to me. I mean that. And I shall keep going as well. Goodbye, my love. I will think of you always." He hugged me tightly and took hold of both my hands briefly before he walked out of the parlour, out the front door, and down the street, slowly, tipping his hat to me as he knew I would be watching him leave.

Nothing to be done. I had to end it and that was that. I must continue to move on. I assured myself I had done the right thing. Why then, was I so haunted by our last conversation?

Chapter Eighteen

A Thorny Request

Down House,
Kent

October – November 1880

Charles Darwin set off for his early afternoon walk around the Sandwalk with his third son, Francis, now aged thirty-two. He was born and grew up in Down House and was now himself a botanist. Francis had come to visit and work with his father on experiments dealing with plant movements, specifically phototropism. Together, they had written *The Power of Movement in Plants,* to be published that same year. Charles Darwin carried his walking cane in hand. Today, Mr. Darwin senior was determined to unravel the disturbing situation of his dear friend, Alfred Wallace, whom he had known even before the time of the publication of *Origin*.

"It is quite fresh out today. Are you sure a walk is a good idea, Father?" Francis asked, looking up at the ominous grey clouds. Built much like his father, Francis himself had no problem with a vigorous walk in cold, wet weather himself.

"Yes, yes! Today and every day. Despite the wind and chill. Let us be off." Their proper footwear crunched the small round white stones along the Sandwalk as they briskly set off.

"I am hoping you can hear me out on an issue I must devote my time to today. It involves considering a request from Miss Buckley," Mr. Darwin said as they passed the gardens and the fruit trees.

"What type of request, may I ask?" Francis inquired as they reached the field and turned the corner to follow the path around to the left.

"She presents a thorny problem, not of science, but of people, which I find the most difficult kind of problem. I do wish the world would allow me more time with my plants and earthworms!" Mr. Darwin exclaimed.

"I see. Who are the people in this thorny problem, Father?" Francis asked, concerned. "They must be friends, or Miss Buckley would not have mentioned it to you."

"Yes, quite right. Where my friends are involved, I must allow them due time and consideration, mustn't I? Hopefully, our time on the Sandwalk will reveal a solution to me." The two marched on past the Chestnut trees.

"Perhaps I can assist if you start at the beginning. What is the problem at hand and who is involved?" Francis asked with trepidation.

Mr. Darwin hesitated. "When I think back to the beginning, I was very surprised that Miss Buckley approached me about the difficult financial conditions the Wallaces are facing. It is right that she is an advocate for them, but it surprises me that she has chosen to put her neck out so far and so urgently on their behalf. Why does she do this, do you think?"

Francis shook his head. "I could not say. Perhaps it is Mrs. Wallace who influences her?"

The Darwins had entered the wooded section of the Sandwalk, and Mr. Darwin sat on a fallen log. Francis remained standing, looking down at his father. "No, I do not think that connection is powerful enough," Mr. Darwin said. "She and Wallace share a grand exuberance for learning and for evolution. I believe it is her admiration for Wallace and his accomplishments in learning that compels her take up their cause. Her suggestion is to create an award for Wallace that would come with an annual pension, which would solve their financial problems. A brilliant proposal, I daresay. She suggests that she herself write most of the request and then hand it over to me to bring before the powers-that-be. Her confidence in my abilities to make this magic happen is flattering. She asks me for help; however, I fear that I alone cannot make this happen."

"How amazing of her to even begin thinking about such a plan for Wallace! I mean, that is truly magnanimous," Francis declared.

"Yes, and had I been more in touch with the Wallaces, perhaps I would have thought of it myself," his father returned. "Miss Buckley is to the point. She sees a problem and she initiates action. She is a wonder. She has been a generous friend to the Lyells and the Wallaces. To everyone, really. Her kindness is, well, astounding. That she would put forward the amount of effort a plan like this requires is quite unusual," Mr. Darwin sighed.

"I agree completely. What do you plan to do and how can I be of assistance?" Francis asked thoughtfully.

Mr. Darwin, suddenly distracted, pointed to a spot near the log. "Is that a colony of ants coming out of that Fir tree? I must get closer." He bent down to a dark crack in the Fir tree. "Yes, they are busy harvesting sap for their queen. I wonder if they are using slave ants as part of their labour? We must return and gather a sample!" He returned to his seat on the log.

"Miss Buckley, father…" Francis prompted.

"Ah, yes. I am not sure what to do next. I must think of an

appropriate course of action. Of course, your mother, like Miss Buckley, puts in a lot of effort on my behalf and those of our family daily. If not for her, our family and my own writing would suffer dearly. How is it that women can operate on so many different levels and functions at once? If baffles me," Mr. Darwin wondered aloud.

"Too right," Francis agreed. "Most men would not consider such multiple and laborious undertakings, being consumed by their own lives and single projects."

Mr. Darwin nodded. "My own heart and soul care for worms and nothing else in this world. Why, Chester just wrote to me saying sometimes a single fact in the life of one person has been the turning point of events that have influenced the whole kingdom and even the world. Perhaps, if I resemble most men, burrowed down as we are in our work, this is why we neglect our own families, or so they might say. Perhaps aiding Wallace will change his fortune and the world's. After all, he has the ability to do so," he said, his finger pointing skyward.

"Perhaps it is Miss Buckley's religious upbringing that gives her this calling." Francis suggested.

With certainty, Mr. Darwin replied, "No, I think it is more central to her own being than that. Perhaps it is in fact mutualism, handed down from her parents. Yet I doubt that she sees this in herself—she doesn't realize that she is, in fact, a shining example of mutualism, her favorite extension of natural selection! That she is in fact collaborating on behalf of the Wallaces to improve and save her species. What an extraordinary situation! Neither Huxley nor I could have done better."

"I know that you and she discuss books—hers and yours. What is your opinion of her recent book *Life and Her Children*? Does it not parallel your own work on the origins of the backbone?" Francis looked down at his father with great admiration.

"Yes. I applaud her passages about, what was it? She called it the 'great backboned family.' Those were particularly good. I recall reading something like, 'The history of the various branches of the great backboned family has been one of a gradual rise from lower to higher forms of life, and this is the mode in which the Great Power works, not by sudden and violent new creations,'—which is a nod to Lyell, of course, which pleases me to no end." He nodded with satisfaction. "Glimpses such as these provide the best evidence I have found of a guiding force, which is inherent in all her works. Her first chapter reminds me of *Origin* when she declares, 'All living beings obey the law to increase, multiply, and replenish the earth from the day when first into our planet from the bosom of the great Creator was breathed the breath of life.' Perhaps I will alter that last sentence of *Origin* to reflect a bit of this relation of the Creation and the Creator," he mused.

Francis shook his head. "Father, you amaze me. How do you recall all those passages, in someone else's book, no less?"

Mr. Darwin looked about his surroundings. "Ah, my dear wood. My favorite part of the Sandwalk! It is like walking into a magical play with thousands of characters, each acting their part. Miss Buckley is right about that! The rabbits and birds barely hurry out of my way—they are so used to my jaunts." Both the Darwins chuckled. "But back to the question," Mr. Darwin said, clearing his throat. "Miss Buckley's gumption in her authorship and now with the Wallace pension proposal are—well—innovative and extraordinary. She is a rare talent. In truth, she writes of evolution with much dexterity. I shall tell her this by way of encouragement. Who knows how many new science minds her work may inspire? And if other men of science have a problem with her success, in my mind they will need to augment their own skills. She is a new force in both the science and the authorship arenas. They must adapt as her determination is unmatched."

Francis added, "Of course, she is correct in saying that anyone who reads Wallace would agree that his many published papers are commendable."

"True. True," Mr. Darwin agreed, nodding his head. "Yet, sadly, it seems apparent now that decisions made long ago about the authorship of *Origin* are plaguing him in ways I had no foresight to see at the time. We all agreed, Lyell, Wallace and myself, that, with my research, I would be the sole author of *Origin*, despite Wallace's abundance of meticulous data. Was I wrong to accept that solution when he came out in such a shocking manner with almost my exact theory of natural selection in his own work? Perhaps if we had both been the authors, he would not be in the position he finds himself in now. His poor wife and children! He is practically poverty stricken with no hope of employment. Their predicament troubles me, Frank. I would like to whatever I can to help!"

"I can see that it does trouble you, Father. But you did the best you could with what you knew at the time," Francis soothed.

His father sighed. After a pause, he said, "Ah, the Chestnuts have littered the path a plenty. Where is my knife? I want to score the nuts to see what, if any, changes there may be in them." He produced his knife and began digging into a Chestnut. "Hmmm. Nothing significant. My legs feel quite strong today, my boy. Yes, the path is better than the cures the physicians supply, which do not aid my stomach ailments in the least. Damn illness!" He lamented, tossing the nut into the woods.

"Have you made known Miss Buckley's request to Mr. Hooker or Mr. Huxley?" Francis asked.

"Yes, I did confer with Huxley. He fears that even if we could get a memorial for Wallace signed by a few first-rate men, it might yet be extremely difficult to get a pension for him, on account of the scandalous manner in which these pensions are distributed. Certainly, Huxley and I would want Wallace to hear nothing about our efforts, in the event it is denied. But how can I move forward if even Huxley, who knows and admires most of Wallace's work, is fearful that there is nothing to gain?"

"Perhaps you should change Huxley's mind about the possibility of a pension, to get him more agreeable to the proposal? We could perhaps think of a way to get Huxley to support and lead this effort." Francis suggested, balling up his fists with excitement.

"Yes, but how?" Mr. Darwin wondered out loud. He straightened, leaving the Chestnuts behind. They continued walking, passing vines, lush bushes, gnarled trees, and tangled branches.

"You need a few first-rate men, Huxley had said. What about starting with Sir John Lubbock? He is close by as our neighbor." Francis cocked his head in the direction of the field that Sir John owned.

"We are on very cordial terms now after our former differences," Mr. Darwin said thoughtfully. "And he *is* a neighbor. Plus, we have shared books during dreary winter months. Yes! I will have your mother invite him and his wife for dinner, and I will ask him if he is willing to be one of the backers. If he is, then I will tell Huxley and see if having one first rate man on our side will change his mind. Excellent thinking, Frank!" Mr. Darwin said, clapping his son on his back.

The two men had emerged from the woods and were back to the start of the Sandwalk.

"That is one circuit around the Sandwalk, Father. I will mark it with a stone." Francis bent down and placed the stone on the spot where stones had been placed by the Darwin family for decades. "There, that is the first. Now, on to the second," Francis said, happily. "What shall we discuss next?"

Mr. Darwin smiled. "I will write to Miss Buckley to satisfy her determination on this project. But I need to do so carefully, carefully. I will certainly ask her not to awaken Wallace's suspicions about this plan or to our purpose here. She is a woman of integrity and will oblige us by complying with this request, I am certain. I feel that she fills a bit of the emptiness left by the Lyells, for me and the Wallaces. She and I miss them sorely!" he admitted, stuffing his hands into his coat pockets.

"Your next steps comprise a very logical approach to gain ground on two fronts at once, Father."

Charles Darwin replied, "Yes, I am satisfied. For now."

Chapter Nineteen

Backing Darwin

1 St. Mary's Terrace, Paddington, London; Down House, Kent; British Museum, London

1880 – 1881

"Telegram for a Miss Arabella Buckley!" A young boy on one of those new bicycles, a curious contraption that seemed to encourage death on wheels, shouted as he slid to a stop in front of our family home.

"Telegram?" I said, coming down off our front porch where I happened to be standing, enjoying the spring day, and turning to look at him in surprised disbelief. I had only just become aware of the use of telegrams for personal correspondence but had thought they were mainly for emergencies. "Who would want to send me a telegram?" I said to the boy, reaching out to take the envelope.

"Don't know, Miss," he replied with a smile as he tipped his charcoal grey uniform hat, set his feet on the pedals, and pumped his legs against them. The bicycle flew away down the street. My hands shook in anticipation of what dreadful news must wait inside. I opened the envelope and unfolded the pale yellow paper within.

EASTERN TELEGRAPH COMPANY

Received at London Paddington Station

April 2, 1880

Urgent news Election lost Wife dead in Buckfastleigh 29 3 80 Much to discuss with you Selling Grampians Returning to England permanently Sail when Grampians sells Letter to follow.

Fondest Regards Thomas

I reread the telegram. Then I reread it again, the breath knocked out of me. I held on to the porch rail, only staying on my feet with difficulty. My head was spinning, and my eyes brimmed with tears. My life was about to radically change, forever, it seemed.

OCTOBER 1880

Over the next few months, my work kept me busy, but it did seem like a lifetime, however, until Thomas finally sold the Grampians' sheep run in New Zealand and sailed for London. I retained my sanity by editing Mrs. Treat's book. I also worked on several editorial projects for Mr. Darwin, including on his new book about moving plants, which was fascinating.

Absorbed in my work, one morning I happened to glance at an advertisement in a journal that caught my attention. A closer look revealed an ad that referred to the release of Samuel Butler's new book *Evolution, Old and New*. An article accompanied the advertisement. *Oh, not this same anti-Darwinism again*, I thought and began to read the article. Among other things, it accused Darwin of stealing the idea of evolution from Darwin's own grandfather.

I was livid, alarmed, and completely disgusted. I felt compelled to go to Mr. Darwin immediately and directly to figure out how to put an end to this slanderous accusation. I packed a light bag and set off for Downe to see Mr. Darwin and investigate this alleged crime further, knowing full well that it was very likely Mr. Darwin had no idea whatsoever about the accusation that Butler had made against him. When I arrived, I found him in his usual spot, the greenhouse, busy at work with several samples of deceased earthworms.

Mr. Darwin was fully devoted to the study of earthworms to investigate forms of movement and the complexities of sensitivity. He wanted to explore how earthworms adapted to varying conditions to examine what they could sense. He aimed to determine where a plant stopped and an animal began—that is, to determine the boundary between animals and plants, which was also the book he had just finished. A key implication from this research was the origin of the nervous system. He and I were discussing these issues for my own book, *Life and Her Children*. In which, in my own poetic style, I referred to the nervous system as a wondrous web of neurons and synapses that linked simple creatures to the greater world of sensations—from the gentle caress of breezes to the roar of thunderstorms.

Our greeting was quite warm and cordial, as it had been for years. I loved spending time with this legend, and while he was showing his age these days, he remained every bit the warm-hearted genius I had always known.

"You have returned. And so soon after our last meeting this summer, July was it not?" he asked, barely looking up from his work, dressed in a white laboratory coat, wielding a small pair of forceps in his hand as he hovered over his victims.

"Yes, I was here on the eighteenth of July," I recalled. "I was visiting Lady Lyell's sister-in-law. I had a very nice dinner with them."

"It was good of you to see them," he said, with a slight nod of his head.

"Yes, I am pleased to keep in touch with them as they remind me of the Lyells, whom I miss dearly. But Mr. Darwin, something concerning has come up, which is why I am here."

I hated to break his concentration, which could be an enormous contribution to the world, forming right in front of me. He was so content in his peaceful setting, doing his life's work with no one to disrupt him from the outside world. Here, he had only the world of science to be concerned with. I could almost see the ideas swirling in the air above his head, waiting to be born, to be set down to paper. But his genius would have to wait.

"To get to the point, Mr. Darwin, I have some rather disturbing news about Mr. Samuel Butler that requires me to clarify certain claims he is making about you. Several distasteful claims that I would like to dispense with as soon as possible," I said, making my way around him to sit at an open chair near his working bench.

Mr. Darwin looked up immediately when I spoke Mr. Butler's name and replied, "You know, Mr. Butler is rather a strange person. His manners have been a bit odd: after the publication of *Erewhon*, we asked him here, in fact I believe he came twice, but somehow or other neither Mrs. Darwin nor myself were drawn to him or felt any kind of connection. You know how many people I am obliged to have here, and with my health, visitors are a strain upon me, so we did not ask him anymore. I am afraid Mr. Butler has been offended by this and attacks me in consequence. According to Frank, Mr. Butler wrote to him recently saying that re-reading *Origin* made him aware of the antagonisms between my book and Lamarck's theory of evolution, and that he consequently eliminated from his own book *Life and Habit* all support for 'natural selection"—to make it square with the Lamarckian view. But now, he hopes to make *Life and Habit* an 'adjunct' to my *Origin*, since he was supporting the theory of evolution and thought 'natural selection' and evolution were synonymous. It appears he is both testing his ideas out on Frank and hoping Frank will embrace his ideas and promote them to me. Not an enviable position for my son!"

"I should think not. Nor for you to be tied to Mr. Butler." I held myself back from complaining aggressively about Mr. Butler because I did not want to overstimulate and perhaps worsen Mr. Darwin's stomach distress. Gently I said, "And now, after all that, he has insisted on creating a dispute about the *Biography of Erasmus Darwin* that you have astutely written. He claims that he sent you a copy of his *Evolution, Old and New* shortly after *Erasmus* appeared." I tried to relay the facts of the controversy as clearly as possible.

"I see" was all Mr. Darwin said as he mulled over the thorny timing of the facts so far.

"He claims that several new passages—written by Krauss—in your *Erasmus* are borrowed from *Evolution, Old and New* written by Kraus without acknowledging him. Worse still, he claims these passages put your sanity in question as it appears to the public as if you are championing your grandfather's version of evolution over your own." I added gingerly. "In sum, that you have taken your own theories of evolution from your own grandfather." I cringed.

"Perhaps he should turn his attention entirely to novel writing," Mr. Darwin offered, putting down his foreceps.

I smiled. "He asks you for a public apology."

"I know nothing of what my collaborator in this work,

Krause, has written, and I was never responsible for his portion of the writing of my grandfather's biography. I was only responsible for my small portion," Mr. Darwin responded clearly, giving me the impression that I had had all along. Mr. Darwin was in no way knowledgeable of or responsible for any of this acrimony and confusion.

"I, of course, know that. I know you had no hand in this whatsoever. Continue on as you have been and do not give him the satisfaction of any response," I advised.

"Exactly what Mr. Huxley says on these types of controversies," he replied, scoring a sample of a worm with his scalpel.

I would stand by Mr. Darwin, no matter what the costs. And I would address Mr. Butler at the next opportunity.

That opening came some days later when I spotted Mr. Butler again in the British Museum.

"Mr. Butler, a word please." I said in an adversarial tone that I intended. I motioned for him to join me in a corner of the large entrance hall, away from those around us. Make no mistake, Mr. Butler would get his comeuppance.

"Oh, Miss Buckley. How charming to see you again," he purred like a cheetah about to pounce on an unsuspecting antelope.

"I have been to Down House to consult with Mr. Darwin about the Krause controversy. Mr. Darwin knows nothing about any new portions of the Krauss work, as he was only responsible for his own small portion. He had no responsibility at all for Krause's work. I believe Mr. Darwin completely. He has no relation to this petty accusation."

"I hardly think plagiarism by an author like Krauss is a petty matter," Mr. Butler barked back at me.

I steadied myself. "Mr. Darwin has a noble character and credits anyone he works with for their contributions. I should know. I am one of them," I retorted.

"See here, Miss Buckley, I fail to see that this "controversy," as you call it, is any of your business."

"Sir, you are a malicious, self-serving man who is clearly trying to tack himself onto the coattails of a famous and noble man. It is also clear that you are a man in controversy only with yourself," I replied, smiling as best as I could.

"Is that so? What is clear to *me*, Miss Buckley, is that you are a silly, tattling, log-rolling, mischief making woman!" He turned and stormed out of the entrance hall, passing through the gilded doors to arrive safely outside the museum.

My heart was racing. *What a pretty spat*. I thought, Run if you must, Mr. Butler, but Mr. Darwin will be vindicated, you can be sure of that.

Soon after *Life and Her Children* was published, I had a most unexpected and glorious letter from Mr. Darwin that I treasured.

Down, Bechenham
Nov 14, 1880

My dear Miss Buckley

I am very much obliged to you for sending me your new book, the appearance of which is most elegant. I have read the two first chapters and shall hereafter read more, but just at present I have a lot of papers to read on account of work in hand.

I think that you have treated evolution with much dexterity and truthfulness; and it will be a very savage heretic-hunter who will persecute you. I daresay that you will escape, and you will not be called a dangerous woman. Your plan seems to me an excellent one, and who can tell how many naturalists may spring up from the seed sown by you.

I heartily wish your book all success. At p. 4 I think you ought to except utter deserts, for I believe they support nothing.

I believe that you might make an equally interesting book for the young about Plants.

Pray believe me, my dear Miss Buckley, yours sincerely.

Ch. Darwin

I have dispatched my paper about Wallace to Huxley and have spoken again to Sir John Lubbock.

That Mr. Darwin said I treated evolution "with much dexterity and truthfulness" was a dream come true. As I looked around my room, I realized that I was in fact an author, a popularizer who has been given credit by Charles Darwin himself. I had accomplished the goal I had set about for so long to achieve. Now I just had to pull the pieces of my life together that did not fit onto the printed page.

Chapter Twenty

Saving Wallace

Erasmus Darwin's House, London

November 1880

On a chilly November morning a few weeks later, I rushed to meet Mr. Darwin at his brother Erasmus's house for an update on our efforts to secure a stipend for Alfred Wallace.

"Good morning, Mr. Darwin," I said. "I know you are off very shortly to see your publisher about *Plants*, but I did want to bring you up to date about my conversation with Mr. Wallace concerning the award. I thought speaking with you directly would be quicker and a bit easier." I knew how our frequent correspondence and numerous letters back and forth had been wearing on Mr. Darwin's nerves of late.

"Yes, hello, Miss Buckley. Thank you for coming. So many letters and papers! Yes. Do tell me. Would you like a cup of tea?"

"Yes, please. It is all right as far as Mr. Wallace himself is concerned. I told him that you and Mr. Huxley thought him entitled to a government pension *if* it could be secured."

"And what did he say?" Mr. Darwin asked, nervously. He motioned to a maid for the tea.

"At first he hesitated, but when I represented that such men as Joule and Faraday had received similar awards, he said, 'I confess it would be a *very great relief* to me, and if such men as Darwin and Huxley think I may accept it I suppose I may'—and he also added, 'I really have some claim, for most naturalists and travelers on their return from a foreign country have been given some post or situation, and I have tried for one in vain.'"

"I see," Mr. Darwin said, nodding. "That is good news."

"Yes, it certainly is. Mr. Wallace also said a friend suggested it to him some time ago, but he rejected the idea; but now that it comes from men like yourself and Mr. Huxley who can appreciate his work, it makes a difference. I could not get the memorial lists, but when I said to Wallace that you would have only a few good names and suggested the Duke of Argyll, he said he is just the man who would probably give his name with pleasure! So, he was happy with that," I concluded with relief.

"The crucial factor in all this is his understanding that this award is not guaranteed. Do you think he understands this, Miss Buckley?" Mr. Darwin asked sternly.

"He quite understands that the result is very doubtful, and indeed he said very little about it. I also suggested to him that he should not dwell upon it," I said, nodding.

"Right. Well, at least we have the application underway," Mr. Darwin said, stressing the word *underway*. "From my short conversation yesterday, I am more than ever sure that your generous efforts, if they succeed, really will confer a great boon on Mr. Wallace and relieve him of anxiety."

"Thank you, Mr. Darwin."

The tea arrived and the maid poured it out.

"Please let me know if I can look up anything more for you for the award," I said.

We sipped our tea in silence, like two old friends, mulling

over the course of events.

Finally, Darwin spoke again. "Thank you, Miss Buckley, for helping to gather all the information needed for the major claim, which seems to be that he has opened up our knowledge of the whole flora and fauna of the Malay Archipelago. Quite an accomplishment."

"And his application of this knowledge to the understanding of the geographical distribution of animals," I added.

"And his share in the question of the *Origin of Species*—" Mr. Darwin stressed. "*That* above all. Good heavens, how pleased I am!"

We sat and savored those worthy accomplishments, willing them into motion.

1 St. Mary's Terrace Paddington, London, 1881

Tired from a long day at the Reading Room, and worn out from my long continuing wait for news from Thomas on his next steps, I hauled myself and my bag up the stairs to my room. I sat down at my desk and was welcomed by a pile of letters waiting to be opened. I rifled through them and spotted one from Down House. As usual, whenever I received a letter from Mr. Darwin, I tore it open immediately. I could hardly believe what I read this time.

Down House, Beckenham

January 4, 1881

My dear Miss Buckley,

The memorial for Mr. Wallace was dispatched this morning to him, accompanied by a private note from me.

The Memorial was drawn up chiefly from the materials forwarded to me by you and was corrected by Huxley. I enclose the list of signers. The Duke of Argyll, to whom I wrote answered most courteously, and said that he had already written to Mr. Gladstone on the subject. Heaven knows I hardly ever wished so much for anything in my life as for its success. I suppose that I shall receive only an official answer, but if it gives any indication, I will inform you. I wrote to all the signers and received from almost all a letter in return, saying how strongly they approved of the Memorial and wished for its success.

Your discretion will tell you whether it would at some time please Mr. Wallace to hear who have signed and how cordially the signers expressed themselves.

I know that I should be proud to be supported by such men.

I am glad it is all over. I can truly say that I have done my best; but as my boys would express it "it has been an awful grind" – I mean so many letters.

Believe me, my dear Miss Buckley.

Yours very sincerely,

Ch. Darwin

I clutched the letter to my chest. My dear friends the Wallaces were saved! Justice and Mr. Darwin prevailed!

Chapter Nineteen

Mine!

1 St. Mary's Terrace,
London

March 1882

Thomas had sent word to me at the vicarage that he had arrived in London for the final time, safely, and that he would pay us a call that very afternoon at three o'clock. The sun was high and clear in the sky, but few people were about in the street as I peered through the front window, trying to catch a glimpse of him arriving. An old man with a heavy limp passed by on the street, causing several dogs to bark. A woman in a brown frock and cream-coloured shawl hurried on her way to somewhere, a large basket under her arm. The minutes ticked by at what seemed a glacially slow pace as I waited impatiently for him to arrive.

What would we say to each other, now that his wife was dead? *Perhaps he has changed in this long absence,* I thought. Of course, I still loved him despite my decision several years ago to put an end to our relationship. But it had been a very, very long time since we had spoken those words of love. *I was dreadfully tired of missing him, of the long absences. But I must stand my ground and be firm about the terms of our relationship. I cannot simply jump back into being tied to his string.* I looked through the curtains and out the window again, searching for a sign of him. I paced back and forth in the entryway of the vicarage like a caged lioness, separated from her mate.

When his cab pulled up, I raced to the front door and flung it open. He leapt out of the cab and ran around it; his lean and lithe body turned the corner with an ease and grace quite uncommon for an older man. In that instant, I knew he still loved me, and nothing had changed. Without thinking, my body took over, and any thought of proper etiquette vanished. I flew down the stairs, barely touching them, on my way to the street below.

I ran to him, holding up my skirts. He ran to me and swept me up in his arms.

"Arabella! Oh, my dear, sweet Arabella," he cried out, hoarsely. "How I have missed you," he said, his eyes full of tears.

"And I you!" I echoed. We gazed into each other's eyes for a split second and then he pulled me to him and kissed me, his lips on mine in the most loving union. I wished our embrace would never end as our bodies and minds were finally together and no longer merely a dream. Knowing that he would not be returning to New Zealand and that he had apparently not only forgiven me for dissolving our previous relationship, but still loved me as he once had seemed a miracle.

The feel of my arms around his muscular back in our embrace was foreign but electrifying. I could feel taut muscles moving under his jacket but longed to feel his skin to mine. Although brief, I hungered for that sensation of his body under my hands and arms, longing for it as if I was starved of food and water. I did not want to let go for anything or anyone.

Not caring who might be watching, he pulled back from

our embrace and took my hands, both of them, in his own, which were large, strong, and calloused. He lowered himself to one knee and took off his hat and placed it under his arm, his eyes never leaving mine. He quickly smoothed back his thick, dark blonde hair. I was completely astonished, my eyes searching his face to try to comprehend the meaning of his movements.

In a low and solemn voice, he said, "Arabella Burton Buckley, you are my soul's calling. Your love is all that sustains me. I cannot wait one more minute to ask you what I have wanted to ask you for more than twenty years. I have come here today to declare that the stars are now aligned for us. So, I ask you. Will you do me the supreme honour of becoming my wife?"

Astonished, stupefied, and open mouthed, I took a second to gain comprehension of the moment, his question, and the complete look of passion on his face.

"Yes!" I said, pulling my hands from his and cupping his clean-shaven face. "Yes, a thousand times, Thomas, yes!"

He rose from his knee, and we kissed until he had the propriety to pull me up the steps and into the house.

"Is your family at home?" he asked, looking about the parlour.

"Mother and Henry are gone for the afternoon. Father is ill upstairs, being tended by the servants," I replied quickly.

"Very well. I would like to ask for their blessing. But perhaps my proposal would be better met by your family if you had a ring on that finger," he said, as he held out my left hand. "I would like to take you to select an engagement ring this very minute," he said, his eyes twinkling, looking down on me.

"Now that you mention it, my greatest desire would be to wear your cameo ring as my engagement ring," I said. "It is a ring for your smallest finger, but it fits nicely on my wedding finger. It reminds me of your incredible fidelity and commitment to me. I will treasure it, and I think no other ring or stone would come close to the conviction of love that we have for each other. Anything else would be a vacant vessel," I murmured, my heart swelling to bursting, tears in my eyes. I felt complete gratitude and sent a silent prayer to God for delivering Thomas to me in so many ways.

"Then you shall have it. He took it off and gallantly placed it on my ring finger. "And I hope you will wear it proudly in honour of our pending union," he smiled. We sat on the sofa in the parlour, holding hands, whispering in each other's ears. Mother and Henry's absence was turning out to be quite convenient. Had Henry, once I told him of Thomas's pending arrival, arranged to take my Mother out for the afternoon? It seemed likely. Henry was a good brother!

But I had to think practically, even now, too. "In terms of the wedding and date, my dearest, what are your opinions and what plans should we make?" I asked.

"You sound a bit alarmed. Is there something you are worried about?" Thomas asked.

"It is only that Father's health is precarious at the moment, and a wedding announcement would be rather poorly timed. My book is also nearing publication, and I would want to have that neatly delivered to the publisher prior to getting deep into wedding details. "

"But darling, I think that I have found a fabulous place for us to live. I want our life to move forward as quickly as possible," Thomas urged.

"I see. Yes. Continue your search for home and hearth," I said, beaming, "and let us think about the proper timing for all concerned. We will share our good fortune with those closest to us for now, even though we both want to shout it from St Mary's steeple!"

His green eyes had not aged. They shone with keen brilliance and a fervor that was an unending love in his heart.

I worked like a fiend to finish *Life* before my own life drastically changed. I had come a long way with this book, writing about shapeless and sluggish amoeba through the advanced Cuttlefish and making many points to justify the statement that I made when I began, namely that by giving the prize of success to those who best fight the battle of existence, Life educates her children to fill their place in the world.

Frequently I checked my work with Mr. Garnett as he was my primary editor. We always met at the same table in the Reading Room at the British Museum where he worked. At the end of one session, I asked him directly about his opinion of *Life* and how it would meet its purpose. With pages and pages in front of us, I pressed him, "Is it succeeding? Did I adequately show the transition from the tiny lime-builders and their beautiful shells to the first advance that we perceive in sponges, as one of the architects of individual existence?"

"Yes, you clearly articulate how species move from feeble to the rudiments of senses that afterwards become so keen," Mr. Garnett said soothingly, knowing how anxious I was about the writing and my urgency in completing it.

"Yes, but will the reader understand how the nerves, eyes, and ears of the jellyfish enable it to live a free and independent life? And that in the starfish and its companions, we advance even further? Is that clear to an ordinary man, woman, or child, do you think?" I asked him.

He avoided eye contact, as he usually did. His red stubble reminded me of the red glow of a sunset. "Yes, I believe that line of argument is well done."

"My themes that expand upon Darwin's work are very important to me, and by that I mean mutualism. "As on this page," I pointed, "when I discuss how in the higher mollusca where we find something like maternal care in the Cuttlefish, and here how the Scorpion and Earwig care for their young...? What do you think about how these passages come across to the reader?" I asked, trying to sound neutral.

"I believe any reader will be amazed at your insights and will read your work as wonderful," Mr. Garnett replied sincerely.

I looked at him with sincere admiration. No other editor understood my purpose as well as he did. "Oh, I am so relieved. You have no idea," I said, heaving a heavy sigh.

"I am sure *Life* will do very well commercially," Mr. Garnett said, putting the pages back in their correct chapter order. He was used to managing anxious authors, in his work with other literary figures from the Reading Room and from his own personal experience writing novels.

I sat back in my chair. "For me, it is more than that," I told him. "Most insects never live to see their children born, and those which do generally leave the care of them to others. It is the relation of parents to children—it is family love. My hope is that future science will be able to trace out the history of vertebrate animals to the rise of higher feeling and collaboration. Then we may learn that the struggle for existence, as Darwin has specified, is also able to teach that kind of higher devotion, as in mother to child. Mutual help, mutual sympathy is what will ensure the survival of the human race. That is my firm belief."

Chapter Twenty-Two

Farewell From Westminster

1 St. Mary's Terrace, Paddington and Westminster Abbey, London

April 1882

"Charles Darwin is dead. After his collapse on the Sandwalk from the stroke, he lived for two weeks. His last words were, 'Thank you for all you have given me' to his family. Hetty was by his side, Francis, and Emma, of course," I said to Thomas, starting to cry. "The world has lost much in him and owes much to him. I cannot bear it. A world without him."

"You have lost much but we will bear it together, you and I," Thomas soothed as he stroked my hair.

I struggled to regain my composure. "I have been invited to the funeral."

"Where is it taking place?"

"It has been moved from St Mary's in Downe, where he and Emma wanted him to be buried, to Westminster Abbey. Many of his colleagues, especially Huxley and Lubbock, rallied against internment in Downe due to his stature in the world, and Emma acquiesced, and the Dean of the Abbey was happy to agree."

Thomas added in a somber tone, "To be buried in Westminster Abbey is the highest honor that can be bestowed to a British citizen."

I blew my nose into a handkerchief. "Some twelve family friends and I will see him to his final resting place. It is right, despite Mr. Darwin's original wishes, to be buried with royalty and the best of the world's scholars. He was scientific royalty, you know. People will want to visit his resting place. To me, there will never be anyone as brilliant as he was. Or as kind." Tears streamed down my face. My insides were a huge, empty black caldron. Cold and never to be filled again.

"Then it is your job to tell the generations to come that he was otherworldly in his talents and contributions. You must continue your writing, espousing his theories and explaining them so future generations appreciate and understand his insights."

"Yes, now more than ever," I sniffled, with new determination growing in my heart.

CHARLES DARWIN'S FUNERAL, WESTMINSTER ABBEY, APRIL 26, 1882, 12 P.M.

The grey day matched the dark mourning dress of those of us who were to follow the coffin assembled at The Chapter House, presenting attendants with a card that allowed our admission. On this day and hour, committees adjourned, Parliament virtually emptied, judges put down their gavels, and Londoners from all walks of life set aside their labors and trooped to the Abbey. From embassies, scientific societies, and ordinary science lovers, people came. The skies were cool and heavy, but they still came. I turned from my vantage point at the front of the Abbey and saw the throngs of many heads that were there, for I was in front of the Abbey with Emma and the family at the front of the hallowed church.

Almost with the grandeur of a state occasion, the greatest intellects and minds were brought together to honor one they could scarcely have dreamed of becoming themselves. One they had read with fascination and awe. And I *knew* him and had known him well. I had the extreme honour and privilege to call him my mentor and friend. I swore that I would keep sacred every second I could remember of him and his wisdom. My mission now burned within me as never before. As I saw his coffin resting on the thick and ancient paving where kings and queens were buried, I said to him, under my breath, "You will live on. Your work was not in vain and will not die. You will reach generations to come. You will live on."

I saw Charles Darwin's life celebrated just a few feet from another of the greatest sources of inspiration, Sir Isaac Newton, at the north end of the choir screen. While Mr. Darwin began by studying religion, he became agnostic as an adult. Yet now he rested on one of the most holy grounds in the world, which honors his legacy of science and in faith, which, as he and I had discussed many times, may not be mutually exclusive after all.

Chapter Twenty-Three

A New Life

The Reading Room, The British Museum;
Regent's Park, London

July 1883

"There you are! I have been awaiting your arrival. I have news! A word in my office please," exclaimed Mr. Garnett, who had been on my mind more and more lately. I was always glad to see him, my trusted friend and confidant. I pushed my feelings for him back in my mind as I was still not sure what they meant. I was more comfortable that way.

I pulled off my rain cloak and stuffed my matching gloves into its pockets before hanging the garment on the coat rack beside the large glass swinging doors of the British Museum's Reading Room. My face was flushed from my vigorous walking. Mr. Garnett's face, flushed as well, seemed to match mine and I had no idea why since he had not been walking briskly.

"What type of news? I asked curiously, as I opened my portfolio and began to pull out a brown, leather-backed book. "Overdue," I noted, nodding to the book in my hand. "May I renew its loan, or have I exceeded the number of times I am allowed to renew?"

"Never mind that now," glancing at the book. "I have a

book review that will interest you." He delivered a wry smile, looking down into my face.

"Well then, I am all ears. Who is the author? Where was the review published?" I reached over to pull the source out of his hand, but he quickly pulled it back.

"Not just any review, and not just any author. Just published in *Popular Science Monthly*." He opened the journal. "And placed second after a review about a new book about J. S. Mill and his father, no less."

"Do tell! It sounds interesting. Who is the author?" I asked.

"You are, Arabella. You are the author," he said with a rare, broad smile spreading across his face.

"Me?" I asked incredulously, completely surprised.

"Listen to this." Mr. Garnett's face lit up like a child opening a gift wrapped in fancy trimmings as he read:

> "The Winners in Life's Race*: Or,* The Great Backboned Family *by Arabella B Buckley, Appleton & Co. As a popular scientific writer, the position of Miss Buckley is now assured. Her knowledge is sound, her judgment trustworthy, and her power of elementary exposition much above the common standard. Her first book,* A Short History of Natural Science, *was needed and was well done.* The Fairy Land of Science *was also excellent.* Life and her Children *struck into the new biological path, and gave an interesting account of the invertebrates, or the lower forms of living creatures. The present work is a continuation of it into a higher field, although the present is an independent and self-explanatory work.*
>
> *The work we now have from Miss Buckley was much demanded. We wanted a popular book on the vertebrates, the backboned family from the historic or evolution point of view. This made necessary unusual*

> *qualifications in the writer, and implied a knowledge of geology and palaeontology, as well as natural history. Miss Buckley had been for many years the secretary and special student of Sir Charles Lyell and had therefore the best opportunities to become familiar with those branches that have now become indispensable parts of biology."*

We both looked at each other in amazement and we clasped hands, rejoicing, in a bond of laborious work and effort required to create *Life's Race*. An outsider looking on might have claimed to see love in our relationship, and he would not have been wrong. We both truly loved our work and how we had worked together. To receive a glowing review in a prestigious popular science journal was the pinnacle of our collaboration thus far.

"The review includes a quote from you on your method but then elaborates on evolution. Listen to this part," he said, skimming his index finger down the page.

> *"This acceptance of the evolution standpoint, this tracing of the stream of life along the great course of terrestrial changes, this marking of the epochs of advancing organization in the ascending movement, and this tracing of genetic relationships, all concur in giving a new and impressive significance to the idea of unity in the great scheme of life and give to natural history a new element of almost romantic interest. Miss Buckley has given attractiveness to the subject by her wealth of information, the clearness and the simplicity of her descriptions, and she has heightened the effect by the skilfully conceived and finely executed illustrations with which the volume is filled."*

I was speechless. I looked at Mr. Garnett with eyes as wide as saucers.

"Congratulations, Arabella. You have officially broken down the door as a female author. You have arrived," Mr. Garnett said, beaming.

"Thank you, Mr. Garnett! And thank you heartily for your research assistance and editorial advice!" I clasped his right hand in my right hand and gave it a squeeze. We were both thrilled and excited. Then our hands dropped, awkwardly.

"Speaking of romantic," I said, clearing my throat and lowering my voice even further, "I have accepted him, you know."

"So, I heard. Mr. Butler informed me," Mr. Garnett replied, laying the journal on the table. "Again, congratulations are in order," he said, looking down as he toed the floor.

"Thank you. He has been a long-time family friend, as you know," I replied, also looking down at the floor.

Suddenly, he turned to face me. Mr. Garnett was quite a handsome man, dressed in his dark trousers, white shirt, and pin-striped jacket. His large, intelligent eyes burst with expression. "Arabella, are you quite sure that stodgy old doctor is worthy of you?" he asked softly. "You do not have to marry, you know. Your books will provide for you. Marriage is not all *"Twilight of the Gods,"* you know. What I mean is, marriage is not all romance and beautiful words like I wrote in my book, *Twilight of the Gods*."

"Easy for you to say," I said, a bit too defensively, but so be it. "You, with your long-term, loving wife and six children, the epitome of the perfect well-bred society man!"

"But is that why you marry him? Because of society? You are at a height in your career that most men could only dream of, and you could go much higher still, I daresay," he replied with vigor.

I looked at him earnestly and said, "My father is extremely ill, as you know. Mr. Darwin..." I had to swallow so that the lump in my throat would not prevent me from speaking. "Mr. Darwin has passed. Sadly, I expect that soon it will be only Mother, me, and Henry my brother at home. I must think about my future. A sustainable future."

"But what about Henry? He is a well-established barrister, is he not? You could easily attach you and your mother to him as a guidepost, if not only for society's eyes, could you not?" His own eyes questioning mine intensely. "What if you cannot continue to write as a result of being a wife?"

"I think Henry deserves more than merely serving as a guidepost. I can continue to write equally well as a married lady. Thomas has agreed to this stipulation," I said firmly but gently, regaining my normal tone. "I am not done with science yet, my dear friend."

JULY, REGENT'S PARK, LONDON

"I have brought you here for a reason," Thomas said a few days later as he and I lazily strolled through Regent's Park's regal gardens, along a lane of flowers and garden ornaments. I wore a straw bonnet with light green silk ribbons that matched my green day dress. The sun shone brightly, and the flowers lifted their heads to meet its rays. I imagined the fairies from my book, *The Fairy Land of Science*, peeking out at me from behind the ferns and rose petals.

"Let me see. Is it because we are going to study pond frogs in the lake, to uncover their habits, their prey, their mating activities…?" I asked, playfully.

He put a finger to my lips. "No. I brought you here to tell you about some fabulous news." He looked deeply into my eyes as the sun warmed us.

"Fabulous news? What fabulous news?" I asked in a combination of excitement and anticipation.

"I have found the most amazing place for us to live!" Thomas said, turning and squeezing me about the waist.

"Is it in Marylebone?" I asked, curiously.

"Come and sit down here on this bench and let me describe it to you. It is not in Marylebone, my love," Thomas said gingerly.

"Oh, well, is it somewhere near Paddington?" At this point, I assumed it was somewhere close to my current home.

"No, it is not here in London, my love," he said slowly.

"What? Where, then?" I asked, very surprised.

"First, allow me to describe the house, and then I will reveal its location."

"Very well," I said. "I do hope it is a beautiful place."

"It is! It is incredibly lovely, with a long and fascinating history." Thomas moved very close to me. "It is a large farm with a main manor house that has a quiet, elegant charm. It is nestled in a large acreage of open ground. Very near it is a village called 'Sheepwash,' about one mile's walking distance, and our nearest neighbor lives in another manor house like ours, called Upcott Barton. I get the sense that the history of years of previous owners is still fragrant in the house."

I could see that Thomas was trying very hard to win me over with his description of the house and that it was very important to him. It was not like him to ramble on at length about a house. I continued to listen, growing more and more apprehensive. He told me it was two storied, with five large bedrooms and four reception rooms. And a library—he knew that would warm me up to the prospect. He explained that the house was built in 1832 on a property that was owned by a key advisor to William the Conqueror himself.

"Incredible, is it not?" he said. "A key advisor to William the Conqueror roamed the exact property. And the history continues up to present day!"

"William the Conqueror?" I asked, incredulously, turning to look at him full in the face.

"Yes, is it not exciting! I know how much you love history, and our manor not only shares in the history of the estate, it also comes with its own spirits!" Thomas said, triumphantly, his arms now crossed across his chest. "Yes, that is right. I said spirits."

I was afraid to ask but proceeded to ask anyway, "Spirits?"

"Yes, for your spiritualism, darling."

Once again I found myself speechless. It was a lot to take in.

"Charming country life at its absolute best, darling!" Thomas explained. "Centuries-old pubs. An ancient church named...something or other."

"I see. Did you say, 'spirits?" I did not want to dampen Thomas' enthusiasm for his find, but this had me taken aback.

"Yes, darling. Spirits. As in ghosts. The house is large enough for entertaining guests and the library is already stocked with books. We will have several outbuildings to provide for our needs and there is also a small mill on the property.

"Whose ghosts come with this property?" I asked, regaining my balance. Perhaps this could be a different tactic toward proving spiritualism. And perhaps I could try to make contact again with my dear sister Jane, with more success than I had had at that long-ago séance at Mr. Wallace's.

"I believe a civil war soldier on a horse was mentioned. But darling, pay attention to the features of the house, if you would." Thomas prepared to go on with his description, explaining more about the grain mill and the amount of farmable acreage. "I would serve as overseer to the operations, given my sheep farming expertise," he said, "which the current owner thinks will be invaluable. It is perfect for us!"

"I may have missed this key point, but where is this Shangri-la of which you speak?" I asked, a hint of fear in my voice.

Thomas looked at me and reiterated that critical detail. "Ah. It is in Sheepwash. In West Devon."

"Forgive me, Sheepwash? I am not familiar with that locale." I was truly worried now.

"It is in West Devon, a reasonable journey to Exeter and the Royal Albert Museum, which is a grand country center of the arts and sciences, just on Queen Street. I have made inquiries and it is full of stuffed birds and other animals that you may need there for your writing. A giraffe is there to greet you as you enter! Can you imagine? Oh, Arabella! It will be perfect for your writing; do you not see?" I started to reply but he would not let me; he was too enthusiastic. "You can write to your heart's content there. I only ask that you write under our name," he added, his eyes assessing mine. "That is, Fisher."

"Yes, of course. That is our married name. But Sheepwash? Is that not a bit remote?" I wondered aloud. If I remembered correctly, the village was near Torrington, site of one of the decisive battles of the English Civil War in 1646.

He shied away from my question. "Did I mention the lush, rolling green hillsides? Think of how much there would be for us to discover there! And I would help run the property." He paused, considering. "The Widow Fleming owns the house. She would let it to us for seven to fourteen years and keep on the farmer and staff as well as the head of the granary. That means, my darling, if you do not like living there, we can certainly move somewhere else, and we will not be hampered by ownership. Is that not ideal? And, of course, we would be closer to Rose and her family in Plymouth. I promise to take you to see them any time you like."

"Well, yes," I said. "I would enjoy that. But it still sounds a bit far removed..." I trailed off.

"But that is the point, is it not?" he pressed. "It is quite remote and perfect. Tranquil. Room to breathe, fish, ride, hike. Anything we like. So, do you think you could come to love it?" he asked, hopefully.

I could see his heart was set on the place. Yes, we would be living on a medieval haunted estate in the middle of nowhere. But we would be together. That was all I really cared about. "Yes, I think I can," I said. "As long as I am living as husband and wife with the love of my life."

He kissed me. "Upcott Avenel is the name of the manor house," he said, wistfully, as his arms encircled me.

"Upcott Avenel it is then," I said, laying my head on his shoulder.

Chapter Twenty-Four

Time Belongs to No One

1 St. Mary's Terrace,
Paddington, London

August 1883

"I am seventy-four years old and my time to meet our Lord has come," Father said to me in a rasping whisper. His long-term respiratory ailment had shackled his lungs, making each breath a struggle. The skin on his face had become red, crusty, and cracked. I could clearly see the veins on his bony hands, which had once been strong enough to lead a large congregation and our family but now appeared fragile and weak. He was limp with exhaustion. The doctors had long since given up any interest in treating him.

My siblings and I took turns watching over him in his bed, while he lay completely still under a white coverlet. "Arabella, take courage. Take courage. The Lord will provide." Those were his last words to me as his life slipped free of his meager body. He lay in death with a calmness I had never known. Like a forest covered in a deep snowfall, completely silent and still but with a graciousness that must have been his rise to heaven.

A profound emptiness took over me. In the days that followed, it trailed me daily and practically hourly. I would turn to speak to him or remind myself of something important that he would want to know, only to remember that he was gone. Gone. My lifelong ally and partner was gone. I carried him with me in my thoughts and heart, but his absence gave me the feeling of falling off a high cliff. Endless falling.

But amidst my grief, I tried to create a sense of wonder and beauty. I took solace in what I had written in my book, *The Fairy Land of Science*, which had taken me far in my journey, with my father at my side. I wrote of how the fairies of our magical world must know death well, as we humans did. For death was a part of nature and a natural cycle of life and rebirth. Fairies knew that even as one life ended, another was just beginning, just like in their home, the garden, whereas one flower's season ended, another's began. Thus, the beauty of the garden would endure.

I imagined a winter fairy garden, for it was January, where the flowers had hues of azure blue, topaz green, and pristine white with frost crystals sprinkled on the petals. Sapphire blue flowers grew next to long, clear ice flows. In this surreal and otherworldly garden, in the glow of a faint blue light, a sense of my father's gentleness and peace filled my heart. I could feel the sway of the flowers and tall grasses in my mind and see the sprites and fairies that lived in the garden, and even though my heart was heavy with sorrow, I felt connected to my father through the magic of this winter garden and knew his spirit would live on through me. Of all the prosperity I had had in my life, I knew the best part of all was that I was lucky enough to have had him as a father and that no one could take that away from me.

Chapter Twenty-Five

I Said I Will

The Reading Room,
British Museum, London

March 1884 –
three days before my wedding to Thomas Fisher

"It is getting late, and we must leave now or miss our omnibus entirely," Mr. Garnett said as he looked down at his portfolio, clasping the latches slowly.

"Yes," I said. "I am afraid this will be my last time walking with you to the station." I tried to sound cheerful, but my voice cracked, and my hands seemed to protest as I tried to put on my gloves gracefully.

"Oh, we will see each other after the wedding, do not fret about that. I know you have plenty of future work for me in that head of yours." His eyes looked into mine, a bit pleadingly, only for a second or two, before he stiffly put on his hat and turned for the enormous revolving door, portfolio in hand.

"I am afraid, Mr. Garnett," I burst out, surprising myself as well as him. "Very afraid that I am making a huge mistake." I said to his back. "You think I am too. I can tell that you do."

He stopped at the great wide entrance to the reading room, his hand on the railing of the revolving door. He slowly turned around to see me and said, "Not true. From my own experience, I know there are many kinds of love, and you have a special kind of love with Dr. Fisher. That makes him worthy of you, in my mind. You will be well taken care of, and we will still have many chapters ahead of us, you, and I, in our own way. You gain him but do not lose me in any way." He smiled. "Now, let us go quickly before we are left standing in the dark with no way home, shall we?"

TWO DAYS BEFORE MY WEDDING;
1 ST. MARY'S TERRACE, LONDON, MARCH 4, 1884

I sat at my desk in my room at One St Mary's Street for one of the last times as my wedding to Thomas loomed over me. With all the preparations done, all I had was time to sit and wonder at all my decisions. Was I doing the right thing? Mr. Garnett had assured me that I was and I revisited our last conversation over and over again in my mind to reaffirm what I was sure were just last minute jitters. How I wished I could talk to him again. But that would be inappropriate, of course. He had become more to me than I would ever acknowledge to anyone. Marriage or not, he had touched my heart and had a secure place there. I decided to write to him to at least give him a sign of what he meant to me and how his last words had touched me deeply.

Dearest Friend,

You see I cannot get on without you. Miss Beatrix Potter writes today asking me to send her a list of the books I would like to possess that she may choose one to give me. Do suggest a few. I cannot think of names except "Darwin's Variation of Plants and Animals." A book on "Philosophy, Buddhism—or of history would do—What is Freman's Tea Great Religion" is it worth having? You were very good today and I am grateful to you for it. I shall certainly have to accumulate quotations and remarks—Once a week will not be enough unless I keep up each day.

Yours as ever, ABB

OUR WEDDING DAY, ST MARY'S ABBOTT, KENSINGTON, LONDON, MARCH 6, 1884

I had said, "I will." And now, after the marriage ceremony itself, I heard nothing. The grand and elegant aisles, four of them, stretched out before Thomas and me like grand long avenues of life yet to be traveled, and I was filled with a powerful fountain of joy that sprang up through my head, and reached the vaulted ceiling, filling the church with a spiritual ebullience I had never known. The altar, nave, and gloriously coloured stained glass rising to the ceiling behind me were resplendent, reverberating in my jubilation. I had just clearly and loudly said, "I will." Two more powerful words could not exist for me in the English language as I began my walk into a new life with Thomas as my husband, as a married couple. I heard nothing more, even though I saw an ocean of smiling and nodding faces of family, friends, and colleagues, all there, dressed in their finery.

Just moments earlier, Henry had walked me down the

aisle. "I told you Thomas's intentions were completely honourable all along," he quipped and winked to break the nervousness of the day. I laughed. I had chosen Henry to do me the honour of walking me down the aisle in my father's absence. After Father's death, a new vicar was chosen and our family had to relocate and we decided to join St. Mary's Abbott. The church was considerably larger than St. Mary's Paddington and therefore the walk to the altar in this large and newly rebuilt castle of a church seemed to be as long as a city block. He looked so grand in his wedding clothes, and no one was prouder than me to have her younger brother, one of the most favoured lawyers in London, on her arm.

We passed Rose Heriot, her husband, Mackay, and their children, sitting in the first rows of pews. The older children, Thomas, fifteen years old, Granville, thirteen, and Lilian, twelve, looked intrigued and fascinated by the grandeur of the church and the day. Eric and Oscar, ten and four, respectively, sat gazing off absently but were sitting quietly. I was thrilled to be receiving children as part of the marriage package! I had spent time in Bath where the Heriot's were living because of Mackay's military posting, and caring for the children, especially the younger boys, and bonding with them and Rose. They were now a family of my own.

I smiled at Mother, the queen of the chess board, as we passed her and my siblings: Elsie, the oldest, William, Julia, Charles, Robert, and Arthur. *Mother must be relieved* was all I could think of as I processed forward. Today was her "check" move for the win summing up all the chess board moves she and I had made over the years. Yet, her expression was not one of "check," or an exalted win. I could not quite capture the look on her face. I expected triumph but instead saw a pinched face fighting for control over her emotions. She seemed sad when I thought she would be supremely happy at my appropriate choice. I am sure she missed Father dreadfully, especially at this moment. But perhaps she would also miss me after all these years of having me close at hand.

The pews had come alive with them, our guests, the fury of bobbing heads in colourful hats and waving in a commotion of vivid brilliance of life at its most animated. The organ reverberated the tune "The Prince of Denmark's March," which some called "Trumpet Voluntary," which I knew was playing even though I did not hear a single note, as I selected this exact tune for our wedding march back towards the cloister and church entrance where we departed for our new life.

"Sound, sound, sound the trumpets
Fill the air with loud hosanna!
Joyful sounds of music
Proudly ring His name."

But I heard none of this, either. My mind was locked into this moment, which I had no idea would be as intense as it was. I had said, "I will." I was, after more than twenty years of devotion, finally married to Thomas, the man who had made my soul come alive with a power I had not known possible and with such a joy that I found it impossible to describe. I was his wife, and no other woman could claim this title. I was only thinking of him as I walked in my wedding gown, only aware of my inner thoughts and my clutch on Thomas's arm in his black woollen wedding coat.

We passed the arched limestone pillars on either side of us that reached to the vaulted green ceiling, arm in arm, as if in slow motion, and with no sound. His arms belonged to me now. Mine to hold in public. Mine to cherish now with no more intervals of mourning his absence, waiting for his return after years of absence. My arm, connected to his, and his arm connected to his body, which I was free to explore, to learn from, to wrap around. Our linked arms were but the beginning of bodies that melted into one. We two had become one.

I had long been interested in human sexuality as a topic, though I had never indulged in it myself. Reading about it was my sole source of education and preparation for our impending union, now very close at hand. Dr Allbutt, in writing *The Wife's Handbook* years earlier, had said husband and wife should maintain a happy state of mind during sex. I should hope so, I thought to myself as my slippers padded along the long aisle.

But what if our union resulted in a child? Despite our advanced ages, me at forty-four and Thomas at sixty-seven, it was still a possibility. Thomas had assured me that, come what may, we would welcome a child if one was created. He also suggested that he could use a condom made of sheep gut and tied with a ribbon at the base. Or I had read in *The Wife's Handbook* that we could use a pessary, something shaped like a round dish cover, the dome of which was made of thin, smooth India rubber which would collapse at a touch. And, as I understood it from my reading, the hollow portion of the pessary was intended to cover the neck and mouth of the womb during intercourse, so that no semen penetrated the womb. I preferred these options to that method often used in the upper classes—a sponge attached to a ribbon and soaked in alum and water as a spermicide. Thomas said he would procure the needed devices.

Given my scientific knowledge of mating, I looked forward to Thomas "awakening" me and somehow, I knew that our union would be both physical and emotional, rather than only emotional, as some early educators recommended. I could not wait for us to be entwined in each other's embrace and was curious as to how the events of the act itself would unfold. It was only natural to be thinking of and curious about the evening of the wedding day, I told myself as I glided down the aisle on Thomas's arm.

As we stepped out into the light of day, alone for mere moments given the hundreds of guests behind us with the organ still playing, I looked up at his face as he turned to me, eclipsing the strong sunlight overhead His face was the most handsome I had ever seen and I felt enormous satisfaction that I would be seeing it every day from now on. He kissed me full on the lips, fervently and passionately, and I again tried to imagine what would happen next on our wedding night. I knew at that moment that he felt the same exalted joy that I felt, as if God had achieved another miracle, a triumph in our union.

After the wedding breakfast, the carriage took us to Mayfair. We had booked a quiet, luxurious suite in a small hotel tucked away from the bustle of London. The front desk was quiet, and the footmen took our luggage to our room, which we were assured by the manager was at the end of the hall on the first floor.

"Yes sir, Dr. Fisher. Your room is at the end of the hall, where I can assure you total peace and quiet," the hotel manager said, his eyes fixed on his paperwork with no sideways glances at what he must have known—that Thomas and I were newlyweds.

"See to it that we are not disturbed. No one knocks on our door, understood? I do not care if the building is up in flames, even. No one comes near our door. If we want food, I will notify you. Understood?" Thomas asked, politely but sternly. I had to stifle a smile that was creeping over my face.

"Indeed sir. Understood." The manager pulled at his collar. He was clearly becoming nervous at being solely responsible for our contentment.

I entered our suite of rooms and took in the lovely lavender scented candles and petals placed about in lovely cut glass dishes. The décor was sumptuous and pampering, I noticed as I glanced around the room. But what captured my mind was the bed, beckoning me to begin my married life.

Neither of us spoke. The dam that society had created, a dam that had held back twenty years of pent-up yearning and longing, finally broke. Without any adolescent coyness, we were a torrent of constant movement, each to the other, with no nervousness or hesitation. My husband's mouth, fingers, knees, and hips directed, guided, steered all of his powerful manhood that led the way, searing me, and my body willingly followed and flowed. Oblivious to time, light moon and stars, or corporeal needs, our bodies found our unique rhythm, truly becoming one in a fiery passion through the night.

Chapter Twenty-Six

Troubled Life

Upcott Avenel, Sheepwash
Devon, UK

June 1884 – 1887

We arrived in Sheepwash after our belongings and household were set up and arranged, which was a blessing, because upon arrival our carriage became hopelessly stuck in the thick mud. The country lane devoured the wheels of our carriage and my boots, sucking them right off my feet. Thomas carried me over the threshold, both of us covered in mud, laughing.

The mud was a new reality, especially for me. Just a few weeks ago, we had been living in London, one of the most sophisticated, urbane cities in the world full of railways, fashion, and museums. Now we were surrounded by farms, walking paths, livestock, and mud. Lots of thick mud everywhere. And there were sheep. Many, many sheep. And with sheep come droppings. Lots of sheep's droppings.

The manor house, painted ivory and situated near the Torridge river, was a lovely design with four bed chambers, high ceilings, intricate woodwork, and grand fireplaces. Given the house was relatively new, nothing much had been changed since it had been built, which was adequate for us. Thomas was satisfied with the extensive outbuildings which provided for all our needs.

Being together was a completely new reality for us both. Together meant the incredible softness of warm bodies touching for hours in a day, which was a delight to get used to. I no longer had to wonder what Thomas was doing or where he was, which was something of a strange but glorious feeling. Any time I wanted to speak with him, he was there. By my side.

But more than anything, I was thrilled to be learning about and sharing this new life with my husband. We had only been married for a few short weeks, but we savored every day given the years we had waited. We spent our days exploring the grounds and gardens, listening to birds, reading by the fire, and laughing at how different our lives had become.

"I want to hear what you think of the birds, my dearest. I know how you love them," Thomas whispered in my ear late one night as we lay tangled in our bed clothes.

"At dusk and at dawn, they sing to each other, so joyously and so vibrantly. It makes one feel quite close to God." I whispered back.

"So, you do love it here then, don't you?" He turned his head to look at me and held my chin softly with his fingers.

"Yes. I do. And the air is clean and fresh. No soot. The greenery is more plentiful than I could have imagined. The quiet. It takes getting used to. Time as well. It is as if time has stopped here and nothing changes," I mused.

He smiled. Within minutes he was in a complete and peaceful slumber.

Our married life began in earnest many months after settling into our manor house and I began what had been and what I hoped would continue to be the backbone of my life: steady writing. But the distractions of my new household quickly began taking their toll. I hoped putting these frustrations down on paper would sort them out in my mind. The only person I felt I could turn to now was Mr. Garnett, as I did not want to convey any complaints to "the Doctor"—as Thomas was referred to in our house now.

November 20, 1884

My dear friend,

Your long, pleasant letter was very welcome, and I hope this time to write you a more cheerful one in return. First, I must tell you I have set to work steadily. I have always had rather a difficulty in disciplining myself in work—getting my nose to the grindstone. But I do hope I shall bring myself to it here, for it ought to be the backbone of my life—We have had some perfect days lately, such as the country only can give, and I have felt much more happy. But to you, to whom I complain everything I must say that my difficulty is that I recognize or fancy I do, that I shall be happier in proportion as I think into the little details of country life, and this disturbs me. Mrs. Swan, the housekeeper, is quite happy; for feeding the dogs, salting a hen, making the bread, arranging the stores, etc., give her activity full scope and she feels herself useful. I could find plenty of these small things to do and fill my day with things and by being thus more in harmony with my surroundings way would solve my problems; but if I do, my perception of other things will be dulled in proportion. With watering, weeding, etc., my day is soon gone and what is more my mind's concentration will be gone too....I have forgotten to tell you that we have four cats and they lay all curled up together in a large chair.

Yours with sincerest friendship,
Arabella B. Fisher

I had tried to make a start on a book about plants, as Mr. Darwin suggested to me in 1880, following his book about moving plants published two years earlier, and I had drawn many pictures detailing sections of my writing. But the subject matter seemed to bore me now where it once had interested me, and I lacked my usual enthusiasm for writing. I was in a quandary, lost without a set and solid writing topic. I floundered as I never had in my life, both on the writing topic and in my new surroundings. I was so lost I was talking to the Doctor and writing to Mr. Garnett about the cats and the spiders, the flies, and birds they caught, sounding like a batty old lady rather than an established authoress. What was wrong with me? Was this what marriage was like for women?

I tried to think of Mr. Darwin as a means of inspiration. I missed our meetings so! I reminded myself of how he had lived at Down House, and I tried to emulate his daily routine and his work habits that had been so successful for him. I tried to routinely go out into the garden as he did. Mr. Darwin much enjoyed wandering slowly in the garden with Emma or some of his guests or sitting on a bench on the lawn. He often sat directly on the grass, so I often did this too, like a child would. I also remember Mr. Darwin lying at the foot of a big Lime tree.

During one of my attempts to borrow Mr. Darwin's habits for inspiration, I went to our garden and laid down under a Lime tree nearby. I sank my fingers into a patch of soft emerald coloured moss and instantly felt a cool calmness sweep over me. I gazed up at the lattice of tree branches above me, randomly scattered against the blue sky. No wind moved the branches, but I swore that I could see them moving regardless. How could I explain in writing that branches moved without wind to a child or even to an adult, for that matter? The tiniest branches were woven together in a wooden lace that nature assured me was much more than random. Birds, my favorite beings, flitted from branch to branch, singing their precious songs. Their heads popped this way and that knowingly, as if they were trying to tell me all that they knew about the trees' abilities. I was deep in concentration about trees moving on their own, reaching out to communicate with other trees and the clouds when Thomas walked by on his way from a shooting event back to the house.

"Whatever are you doing lying on the ground, Arabella?" He asked, somewhat pointedly, looking down at me, as if I was wasting time. "You will be covered with ants before you know it."

"Yes, that is the hope, dear, because ants explain much about science." I laughed as he walked away, shaking his head. "Mr. Darwin loved ants," I called after him, laughing.

The Doctor and I drove out on the moor most days when the weather cooperated, and we even went as far as to be able to see Cornwall way off into the distance. The scenery here was more beautiful than any other I had ever seen in England. Such lovely trips broke up the household chores and enabled us to get to know the townspeople, all of which was most beneficial to me. However, these distractions also interfered greatly with my writing, but I had hoped they would liven up our atmosphere and encourage us to talk of something besides our cats. Frequently, the Doctor was very much troubled with a bad cough and was not able to go out driving or shooting, and therefore, my writing suffered continuously as I had to take care of him.

I concluded that I must do something to get back to writing on a regular basis. I decided to write to Mr. Wallace, my old friend, whose daughter Violet had visited with us on occasion and was such a delight that she had stayed longer than expected, to ask him about my writing dilemma and to inquire if he knew of any writing opportunities that would suit me. As luck would have it, he referred me to an interesting opportunity that would set me back on course, at least in terms of my writing.

My new project was to be a short book for beginners on the history of England called *The History of England For Beginners*. Not a science book as I would have preferred but an educational book nonetheless. Finally, a project I could easily sink my teeth into, from Palaeolithic man, to how the English came to be, I thought. Thankfully, the writing began to come more easily to me out here in the country, in my library. My pen flew. I scanned the gilded bindings that lined Upcott Avenel's small library with charming floor to ceiling inlaid shelves. I admired both the lovely sight and scent of the mix of tomes, some old and from previous residents, and some belonging to Thomas and me.

I decided to write to Mr. Garnett to hurry along any resources he could send me for the history book. No one could ever understand the way I wrote but him. I told myself that I must read each reference piece and then the moment after I read it, I must write it.

April 4, 1886

My dearest friend,

We returned from Buckfastleigh last Tuesday bringing Mrs. Heriot and Lily with us. Please let me know what you have today of the period that is coming in my book (Georges). Hints and suggestions are of far more use to me when they are ahead of my work, when once my thought is set, I cannot go back. I hope I shall manage after all to spend some time at the British Museum when I come next. That is if you can collect some good and not too lengthy works for me to study the time of the Georges…what I want are good standard histories from which I can take events vividly drawn, such as are important to children. I have touched up James 1 and Charles giving a little more life to Hampden, Pym, Vane, etc. This part of the history will be very difficult and must be extremely sketchy. I wish it were done, for I feel it is beyond me. Even Gardiner in his child's history has double the space I have.

Did you see in the Pall Mall Gazette that Mrs. Grant Duff recommends my History of Science among twenty books for young people?

Yours with sincerest friendship,
Arabella Buckley Fisher

UPCOTT AVENEL, 1886

"Toss books from these shelves into the fire as if they were logs! Horrendous!" I muttered. Could the history of Upcott Avenel be true in that some lurid old uncle, obviously uneducated, and most likely in the drink, used some of these works as firewood? How many of Sheepwash's books had suffered similar fates? A heinous crime in my way of thinking. But it is believable given the lack of education in the area.

As I sat at the center table, clutching my shawl around my shoulders, swaths of looming black, dejected feelings clouded my mind as my lectures stared back at me, spread across the table, my nib in hand and a stack of nude, unmarked paper at the ready. Frustration ate away at my focus. I was more driven than ever to continue with my writing, as I had received many positive reviews and accolades for my previous four books, yet despite my desire to continue to write and provide help to readers in need, I had begun to realize that I was in trouble. Despite refusing to allow my marriage to the Doctor to impinge on my career, in point of fact our life in Sheepwash was doing exactly that. Life in the country was preventing me from continuing what had become my well-established career. That was exactly what was happening. I seemed unable to stop it.

In the two years at our new home at Upcott Avenel, a mile

from Sheepwash, the tiny village closest to us still consisted of only a few houses and two pubs. I was amazed by how Thomas still felt at home, comfortable here right from the first day. For I was not. He was happy amongst the sheep run and farmers, of course. I, on the other hand, was completely adrift, cut off from anything familiar, from the intensive intellectual conversations that I had lived and breathed all my adult years in London prior to our marriage. The manor house seemed to me like a small ivory, early yellow ship, bobbing up and down among rolling fields of green, never going anywhere. Never changing. I was lost in a sea of acres and acres of undulating green fields.

I recalled a discussion Thomas and I had had at Regent's Park one cloudy afternoon prior to his departure for New Zealand, long ago. I had asked him what life on a ship during a long voyage at sea was like. Now I knew firsthand. Of course, he had chosen for us to live in Sheepwash! Sheep and sport were the life he had lived most of his time prior to our marriage. The life he knew and enjoyed! Why, he even loved life at sea!

I began to note how he had benefited from the decisions, while I had not. Where he loved hunting and fishing and had ready-made friends who loved these sports, I had no one with whom I could share my literary interests. Whereas he was accustomed to the harsh realities and stench of farm life, the only wildlife I had observed in my previous life came stuffed in a museum in a carefully curated exhibit. My life had consisted of lively debates over recent scientific findings at the Reading Room with Mr. Garnett, or time spent with "the literary ladies" visiting an art exhibition. Now my activities were confined to reading and writing letters to those who knew and cared about such things, especially Mr. Garnett.

The gloomiest part of living at Upcott Avenel was not the lack of culture or interest in literature, however, but the lack of human sound and the void that had grown inside me—a darkness that I struggled to contain and hide from Thomas. I was used to and longed for the familiar clacking carriage wheels made as they spun by, shouting, and people walking by my windows arm in arm, rushing by on their way to some event, and my family living in the house or at least making arrangements to visit. But here, in the most remote area I could ever imagine, nothing rushed by, or clacked, or shouted. The deafening silence drained my energy to write and saddened me with its nothingness. I decided to look for other places to live before the country drowned me completely.

For me, country life had lost its bucolic charm and was in complete contrast to the hushed conversations that I had loved in the Reading Room in the British Museum, filled with other authors and friends any minute of the day. I missed exchanging lists and opinions in person with Mr. Garnett. While I of course wrote many letters about editorial notes, illustrations, and the like, my work here in the library was a daily struggle, and my trips to the vibrancy of London far too seldom. I tried to create reasons to go to London, but hated to leave the Doctor, who was now advancing in years and who had become more concerned about me leaving home for any amount of time, given his illnesses.

More than that, though I hated to admit it, my marriage to Thomas had begun to fall into a stale routine very quickly upon arrival. I had not realized during our courtship how different our interests would be on a day-to-day basis, living under one roof, in isolation from everyone except our household servants. More recently, my husband's frequent respiratory illnesses began to include long coughing fits, and I was now expected to nurse him instead of focusing on writing. His illnesses could last days at a time. When he was in poor health, I was expected to drop everything. When he was in good health, it seemed all he wanted to do was join the shooting parties in Sheepwash or join one of many fishing expeditions in the area by the river. I quickly became bored of hearing how his shooting was better than the other neighbors', even though I was glad that his successes buoyed his moods, which had become more and more distant and sullen.

Why had he become sullen and often sedentary? I wondered. Was it the solitude of the country environment, his health, his advancing age, the cold, leaden clouds, or all of these in some combination? I assumed it was the latter but had never expected these issues would appear so soon after our marriage. I did try to entertain us both by inviting family to visit or whomever I could find to dine, but despite these well intended and sometimes rewarding efforts, we both retreated to our corners of the house afterward to resume our individual lives. Our life now was definitely not the life I had hoped we would have together.

As a result, I felt disappointed and angry at him and at myself that I was left to manage the house while he was regularly out all day shooting and then went out again at night as well drinking only to be ill the next day or week as a consequence. When I made my concerns about his absences known to him, he didn't seem to care very much. I imagined his sports were to him what my writing was to me, and I prayed he would never ask me to give that up. So how could I ever ask it of him? I felt like a torrent of hot, dark emotions that would boil over at any moment. I told myself I was still in an ongoing period of adjustment to marriage. But how long would this adjustment last?

Chapter Twenty-Seven

Through Magic Glasses

Upcott Avenel, Sheepwash
Devon, UK

1888 – 1890

Despite these disturbing and nagging thoughts, I had undertaken what I hoped would be an easy work-from-home project that my editor and I agreed would be an exciting and valuable addition to my literary collection: a sequel to *Fairyland* comprised of lectures I had given to children and their parents in St John's Wood Church Hall in London. Then, once I had established my rhythm and writing cadence in my new country environment, I hoped to take on another book, one of some scientific significance, that would continue to weave together the presence of a higher deity and science. I dreamed of still more works after that, books that could continue to support public knowledge of evolution. Repaying Mr. Darwin, Sir Charles Lyell, and Mr. Wallace for all they had taught me was still my utmost desire and a goal that I vowed to continue achieving.

Thomas popped his head in the library. He was wearing his fishing attire and carrying his tackle box in one hand. "Darling, I am off for some fishing. The water is running high, and we want to get to Torrington quickly. Do you mind?" he asked, though we both knew it mattered not what my response would be.

"Of course not," I said. "I am having difficulty with my writing again. If I could only get the old feeling that I know something others want to know, I know I can get on. It is this feeling of merely making books that stultifies me."

"You will get on a streak soon, dear. You always do," he said, absently, buttoning up his jacket.

I replied, "Sometimes I think I ought to give up writing. Until I really have something to say. But I dread sinking into apathy. At one time I seemed to have so much I wanted to write about. Now, I struggle just to think of a single paragraph." I was in a kind of mental agony and wanted him to help me by providing at least a minor amount of sympathy as he had showed me in the past, but he had none to offer.

"Give up writing? But then how would you occupy yourself?" Thomas asked, looking at me quizzically, as if he had not seen my struggle here in Sheepwash before.

"Well, certainly not with fishing and shooting," I said, sarcastically. "You best be off, dear. Be careful." I rose to give him a quick peck on the cheek to make up for my short reply. But as I returned to my chair, I thought, the last four years of intellectual stagnation were telling on me.

With significant effort, I swept away the distracting and annoying thoughts that bothered me. My task today was to begin the book, which is the most difficult part of writing a book, even if you know exactly how to do it. I used the opening that had warmed and excited so many audiences before. I wrote from memory, and—glory be!—it all came back to me so easily that my pen could hardly keep up with the river of words that flowed from my mind. My pen scratched the paper as it flew down the page.

CHAPTER 1

The Magician's Chamber By Moonlight

The full moon was shining in all its splendour one lovely August night, as the magician sat in his turret chamber bathed in her pure white beams, which streamed upon him through the open shutter in the wooden dome above. It is true a faint gleam of warmer light shone from below through the open door, for this room was but an offshoot at the top of the building, and on looking down the turret stairs a lecture-room might be seen below where a bright light was burning. Very little, however, of the warm glow reached the magician, and the implements of his art around him looked like weird giant skeletons as they cast their long shadows across the floor in the moonlight.

I smiled as I recalled the audience's *ooo's* and *ahh's* at this point in my lectures when I had delivered them in 1878. I adored being privileged enough to be the one filling interested minds. Now, with this book, which my publisher and I had agreed would be titled *Through Magic Glasses*, I hoped to reach thousands of people from all classes eager to learn about science. My aim was to write about and reach out to artisan classes while teaching evolution tied to a higher being. No small feat! I continued writing in the silence of the library, those leather tomes watching over me, reminding me to keep my focus.

I inhaled the strengthening scent of the library and began writing about the first magic glasses: the telescope, beginning with the farthest view magic glasses could provide, and then moving to the closest view, the microscope. These topics came naturally to me. My one true happiness coming from living in the country was the darkness of the nighttime sky. Without city lights to illuminate the sky, the stars and planets were quite easy to observe. So, I built a small observatory around a used telescope that I had purchased. To my complete delight, the rolling action of the observatory's wheels enabled me to turn the telescope around the night sky and identify numerous moons and stars. I used this firsthand knowledge in my book as well as frequent requests for information and references from Mr. Garnett back in the Reading Room at the British Museum.

I gripped the nib pen as my lectures flowed from my mind and out onto the page.

> *The small observatory, for such it was, was a circular building with four windows in the walls, and roofed with a wooden dome, so made that it could be shifted round and round by pulling certain cords. In the center of the room, with its long tube directed towards an open shutter, stood the largest magic glass, the TELESCOPE.*

A thought occurred to me as I completed that last sentence. Perhaps if I augmented life here at the manor, made it livelier, that is, my feelings about being here would improve, and then possibly my writing would flow more easily, I thought. But how? Suddenly, I realized that noise and sound were what I craved. Human interaction and the hubbub of life in motion. "A church choir," I said out loud as I laid down my pen and rose from the table. "Yes, a choir of local people and a focus on music!" I loved the idea and returned to my chair to devise a plan for who to invite and how to invite them, what the vicar at St Lawrence would say, and how to involve him. "He can choose the hymns to be performed and I will arrange the practices and performances. I will appeal to all ages and genders. We can teach music, through the choir, to everyone, regardless of education. A brilliant and practical solution!" I felt better already.

Occasionally, I accompanied Thomas to The Half Moon Inn, a charming, several hundred-years-old tavern in the center of Sheepwash and on the west side of the village square, perpendicular to St Lawrence's church. Directly across from the tavern was the actual sheep washing well, created around a natural spring used to wash the sheep driven to this centrally located sheep market, the largest in the Tavistock area.

Thomas and his sporting cronies would loiter around the ancient fireplace where the tax man was said to have set up shop a century before, drinking pints and telling tales of the ones that got away. Meanwhile, the ladies' parlour resided in a long hall adjacent to this pub and was entered through a separate door. Here, we ladies were allowed to drink tea and pass the time with needlework or sharing the town news and gossiping with other women. I had learned that many of the women here were involved with the booming glove making business in the building across from the well, either that or they worked on local farms with their families. I enjoyed their hearty mannerisms and laughter, but I longed for the academic and philosophical discussions I had enjoyed in London.

I sat in the ladies' parlour and thought about Mr. Garnett while several of the local ladies discussed their plans for an upcoming holiday. Even after all these years, I wondered what it was Mr. Garnett felt for me and how I felt about him. He had always been happily ensconced in his married life and had become a father several times over during the years I frequented his Reading Room. I thought about all the times I stayed until closing time, hovering over his desk, my bonnet always on, while he wrapped up for the day. Then we would walk as far as the bus stop together. Was this friendship or something more?

During one of these walks, we happened across Mr. Butler strolling in the opposite direction. His direct and piercing glare told me that he disapproved of my walking alone at night with Mr. Garnett and clearly thought Mr. Garnett and I were something more than friends. I worried that given his caustic nature, he would mention seeing us to Thomas, either before or after our marriage, since he and Thomas had been friends in New Zealand. I don't know if Mr. Butler ever mentioned seeing Mr. Garnett and I to Thomas. Regardless, I still needed and desired Mr. Garnett's opinion and resources if I was to continue my work, which I planned to do, despite all that Sheepwash did to try to derail me. Besides that, Mr. Garnett and I both valued 'thinking people.' *Nothing unseemly about that.*

Writing to Mr. Garnett made me feel less isolated. So I excused myself from the ladies and sat at a corner table to begin my letter to him with news about a recent visit from authoress Antonia Zimmerman, my good friend, who had thankfully been to see us Upcott Avenel in recent days.

January 4, 1885

My Dearest Friend,

I have been very glad to have Antonia with me and plenty of games of chess. Her visit has been a very great pleasure. We have driven out almost daily. Necessarily, I have not done much work, but I feel that I shall get on when we are alone again. As soon as I have finished this chapter, I shall copy it and send it to you for criticism. I hope it is interesting.

Mr. Powell and his wife dined with us. They are nice people who will come in and take us as we are and hold interesting conversation. Mr. Brown, the rich Australian merchant and acquirer of Buckland Filleigh called with his daughter. He seems a shrewd and wide-thinking man. I even think that if I can offer to such men as conversationalists, I might venture to invite Beatrice Potter Webb down some day, by which you see that my ambition is begging to soar.

Your ideas and mine about religion are very much the same really. You say that if justice requires immortality then it follows as a matter of course. To me, it seems that nothing can be plainer than that it is required by justice, therefore, it must be a fact Q.E.D.

Yours in sincerest friendship,
Arabella Buckley Fisher

March 1889

Attendance at the choir practices that I had initiated was already dwindling, much to my dismay, and our concert was to be held in just a few weeks. My best participants were two fourteen-year-old girls with lovely contralto voices, along with several tenor farmers. All had difficulty reading music, but we managed. St. Lawrence's was not available for our practice; so we had to meet at our neighbor's manor house, Upcott Barton, which was the home of one of the farmers in the choir and he graciously agreed to host us there. Upcott Barton had a central room large enough for our choir: it had once been used as one kind of ancient meeting place, perhaps for priests from the chapel. I dragged Thomas with me to the practice, as I did not want to be wandering around our neighbor's isolated property alone at night.

I had to persuade and cajole Thomas until he finally agreed to come with me. "Oh, do please come with me to the Barton tonight for choir practice," I said to my husband. "You know I do not like to be out on that lonely road at night, far away from everything."

"The Barton is the only reason I would agree to go. Choir practice!" He sniffed.

The Barton included an ancient chapel, or what was thought to be a chapel, because a *fleur de lis* was engraved at the top of the building. Thomas loved looking about the Barton's rookery, stables, and outbuildings as well as viewing the original wood set into the walls from the 1500s.

When we arrived, we joined a handful of parishioners including a handsome visiting Baptist minister in the manor's central room. Thomas excused himself after he said his pleasantries and we commenced with our practice. The group painfully struggled through the hymns for an unexpected reason. The Baptist minister had apparently come to make advances on the two fourteen-year-olds, Milly and Bessie.

Bessie asked me, looking at the tiled ceiling, "Is this where the knights of the round table held their meetings?"

"The building is very old, but not that old, Bessie dear," I explained with a silent sigh.

"Bessie, I would gladly be your knight. Come closer to me and I will share my music with you," the Baptist minister said, patting his leg as if Bessie was a lap dog. He could not stop flirting, first with Bessie and then with Molly. The girls' giggling was so pronounced that they disrupted the entire practice. Bessie, flattered by the attention, flew to his side and sat altogether too close to him for my comfort.

"Let us begin, please. Turn to page 252 in your hymnal," I said, rather loudly.

The minister disregarded my words and said, very cheekily, "I hear this very manor has been haunted for hundreds of years by soldiers who died here in the civil war!" Bessie let out a squeal and her hand flew to her mouth in lurid excitement.

Then I saw the minister, who luckily was only visiting our parish for a short while, pat the girl on her behind. I had heard from Dr. Patterson, the local doctor, that sexual relations among the younger locals were flagrant and prevalent, and I was beginning to see what he meant.

When the long, dismal hour of practice ended, I went out into the darkness in the front of the house to the apple orchard. Quite large, this orchard produced the most delicious yellow gifts when in season. The mud tugged at my boots while I walked, but I was quite enjoying myself, walking through the trees, when all at once I became aware of a strange movement in the mist beyond the trees. I had heard the stories of civil war ghosts that inhabited Upcott Barton, from Thomas and other locals, including the current owners. For that matter, my own staff at Upcott Avenel said Avenel was also haunted, but if it was, having lived there, I was sure

I would have seen a ghost if there was one to be seen.

I was certain that the movement I saw was my mind conjuring up these stories from its recesses, but I could not help but be intrigued and therefore ventured farther. I called out, turning my head from side to side, "Thomas, is that you? Where are you? Our practice has concluded." No one answered. I stood completely still in the darkness and waited. Over the years working with Alfred Wallace, I had tried my hand at being a medium with no results, so I had little hope that I could in fact lure any spirit that might be nearby now. But I continued walking towards the rookery, where birds were kept that would end up in pies and casseroles.

"Is anyone there?" I whispered, lightly touching the side of the rookery as to not frighten the birds. I slowly walked around the building in total blackness. The birds inside fluttered and flapped. The smell from their droppings was overpoweringly repugnant and I pitied the pour soul whose task it was to look after the birds and use their offal as garden fertilizer. I hurried away.

Then, as I looked up past the rookery, I saw something in the shadowy mist—it was a pale form of something the size of a person, but I could not say exactly what it was. Fascinated, I moved a few steps closer to get a better view. I could not get my eyes adjusted to see exactly what it was...The figure moved slightly farther away as I approached. A few feet more and I would be able to see it clearly, I thought.

I could not believe my eyes as I watched the figure slowly glide towards me in the darkness. The dark figure was shrouded in mist, with a flowing, tattered cape that seemed to be made of moonbeams and its grey hair was wild and unkempt. I felt my blood run cold as I realized I was about to come face to face with a ghost. My voice froze in my throat. My feet were blocks of ice. I could not move at all. I wanted to scream, to run away, but my feet would not budge. As the figure grew closer, it reached out a bony hand towards me. But then, as it was almost upon me, I saw that it was not a ghost at all, but an old beggar woman who I had seen sleeping in the churchyard once before. She gave me a toothless grin and said, "Spare a meal for an old woman, mistress?" I realized I had been taken in by my own imagination.

I tried to hide the fact that I was startled and breathless from Thomas as we sat in the carriage on the ride home. He assisted me as we climbed in and did not seem to notice my distress. But I could not stop thinking about ghosts and spirits. If only we could connect and communicate with the afterlife! Perhaps ghosts are in fact real and trying to tell us something. To warn us perhaps.

As we rumbled home in the carriage, I was surrounded by darkness and shadows, lost in my thoughts. My mind drifted to the world beyond. How mysterious and just out of reach the world of ghosts and spirits was to me. I was fascinated with the unknown and the unknowable, just like Alfred Wallace had been for years. He and I were still in touch and discussed what little was known about Spiritualism, mostly by letter these days. What lay beyond our mortal toil? In my Christian upbringing, heaven and the afterlife were ever-present topics while we were growing up and in our age of scientific exploration and discovery, the unknowable was becoming known on a daily basis. So why not the afterlife? If only I could unravel the secrets that lie hidden in the hard and permanent line that separated our worlds! I was drawn to knowing like a moth to a flame.

Life was so tiresome and dull, apart from my encounter with the "ghost," that the arrival of a piece of good news so overjoyed me that I quickly wrote of my excitement to Mr. Garnett.

5 May 1889

I have a piece of news for you, possibly great. It is only a possibility…I have not trusted myself even to think of it. On Thursday we went to see Walreddon, a house formerly occupied by Sir Thomas Secombe two miles out of Tavistock. It has 1000 acres of shooting, and of course good fishing and is situated just above Virtuous Lady Mine where the Walkham and the Tavy meet. It is a rambling old house built in the reign of Edward VI, too large really but I think I could make it comfortable. I am a little afraid of expense but the Dr and Mrs. Swann think it need not be much greater than here. And he takes kindly to it. I cannot feel sure whether he does so merely because he feels I do not like the loneliness here and I feel rather selfish, but I believe if we are ever to move we must do so now and as he gets older I dread this place. Is it wrong, do you think, to try to get something for oneself?

Yours in sincerest friendship,
Arabella Buckley Fisher

Chapter Twenty-Eight

Life Together

Branscombe,
Devon, UK

1885 – 1893

"When I was in Timaru, I often rode twenty miles on horseback just to play a game of cards with Samuel Butler," Thomas laughed, looking down at my gloved hands as I shifted uncomfortably in the carriage. We had taken the train from Tavistock to just past Exeter and then rented a carriage for the remainder of the journey. The long ride on cart paths that presumed to be roads to the Beer cliffs in Devon was arduous and numbing my backside, with constant bumping and jostling. Thomas drove the chestnut pair and I sat beside him. We had tethered an additional pack horse behind the carriage to carry equipment and supplies, and this horse rotated in when one of the front horses needed a rest.

"I may never understand what you see in that bull headed brute of a man!" I exclaimed distastefully, as I looked at the thick hedgerow we were passing. "It is getting towards afternoon. Are we nearing our stopping point in Branscombe? We are staying at a farmhouse you have let in the village, correct? Close to an inn, you said? I hope we reach it in time for a walk before supper. I need to spend some time on my feet, walking!" I said.

Thomas looked at me and gave me an empathic smile at my obvious discomfort. "We are turning on the country lane leading to the village just now, my lovely. Not long now," he said soothingly.

"What do we think we will have for weather?" I asked, skeptically looking around the roof of the carriage and upward at the wisps of clouds floating by.

"Are you a fair-weather sailor?" he asked, one eyebrow arched, humored by my worry.

I immediately said, "Yes, I am, and I hope you do not think less of me for it."

He chuckled. "I think our weather will cooperate with us. And if we make good time, it will not be a concern." His soothing words and tone reassured me, but given his frequent illnesses, I hoped the weather would oblige, that my husband would remain warm and dry, and that we would not have to remain inside, bound to our chairs during the trip.

We could have chosen to stay at the lively sea front town of Sidmouth for our accommodations for this journey to Beer, which had become a popular, well-heeled destination for the wealthy, and which I had enjoyed during our time there on our honeymoon. But Thomas preferred the quiet, unspoiled, uncrowded, timeless villages of Devon. I supposed our destination would be similar to our own farm in Upcott, with an abundance of land and woods to please Thomas, while I would have to make do without interesting society. I had many additions and revisions on my list to make for my seventh book, *Wildlife in Woods and Fields*, which I continued to work on now under my married name. I also had in mind another book about birds, my ongoing love since childhood. Given the natural environment we were headed into, with birds aplenty, I figured that I could gather information about them on this trip, as well. "*Who needs the shops and galleries with their crowds of people in Sidmouth when I have all of nature before me!*" I told myself, somewhat unconvincingly.

I was happy enough to be on our excursion, but the isolation of our lodgings and our current way of life continued to bother me. The enormous consolation was that my current loneliness was now going to be short lived. I had found a solution to end my isolation permanently. But at what cost? Over the last many months, the loneliness of Upcott Avenel had overtaken me, and I had decided that I could not continue living there any longer. I had taken up an extensive search for a more suitable home for us both but had found nothing available, until recently. Now, I was so excited about the possibility of this new home, I found it difficult to think of anything else. I ruminated over a letter I had sent to Mr. Garnett about our perfect find, the manor house at Walreddon, as we made our way on narrow roads with a patchwork of green fields for company.

Was I being selfish for wanting this drastic change? Would Mr. Garnett agree with me and see the benefit to me and my writing in a new location closer to educated minds? Even if he did, that wasn't the real issue. The real issue was my husband's opinion. Thomas was the decision maker, and he was also, increasingly, my responsibility. I only hoped this journey would benefit the both of us, mind and body.

Thomas had become somewhat sedentary and was ill even more than usual in recent days. I was hoping a change of scenery would improve our time spent together. I was also anxious to see the result of a dramatic cliff fall from the eighteenth century, with its white chalk columns and ledges. I wanted to study the evolution of the site, to look at what vegetation had taken over, how animals had adapted to the resulting landscape, and the exposed new face of the fall. The latter interest was out of respect for what our dear friend Sir Charles Lyell would have been excited to examine. My plan was to sketch the fall, take copious notes, and summarize my findings for future articles, books, and lectures. I hoped Thomas would join me on expeditions, hunt for fishing lure items along the paths, and then create the lures for the hours he would spend knee deep in frigid streams nearby. For me, seeing the fall firsthand, even though it occurred one hundred years ago, would be priceless. My blank notebooks and sharpened pencils were at the ready, eager to compile their new facts and findings of the magical fairyland of science the fall created.

"We are truly fortunate, to be here on this research expedition." I looked to my left and up into Thomas' beautiful eyes. I took his hand in mine to breach the gap and to encourage him to enjoy the trip.

"The fortune is mine." He smiled back, revealing deep dimples at the sides of his mouth.

"The only unfortunate thing is my backside. And maybe a kidney that has been knocked loose deep in my innards from these dreadful roads." I clasped his free hand in mine. "Dearest, I have had a letter from Lilian, and she is quite well," I said, with a lilt in my voice.

Thomas responded absent mindedly as he steered the horses around a hole in the road. Breaking a wheel would be an enormous delay, which meant we had to manage the horses carefully. The upside, however, was that the horses were not overly taxed and therefore we saved time resting them. Thomas was very skillful at planning and managing our resources carefully so that we would arrive safely and on schedule.

"Oh?" he said. "Does my granddaughter write to you often?"

"Yes. She has made a request that I think is a sound one." I hesitated.

"What kind of request?" he asked, his eyes on me with full

attention, his chiseled chin pointing down with serious intent.

I held my breath for a moment and then calmly said, "She would like to have a change of scenery from life at the barracks. With us. In Sheepwash and then in Tavistock. That is, she would like to come and live with us. She is eighteen now, as you know. And she is quite a talented painter."

The wheels of the carriage continued to grind down the dried-mud lane. At the same time, I could almost see the wheels in Thomas' head turning. "I see. You have corresponded with her about this previously, it seems."

"Yes, we have tossed the idea about. Our thoughts are that she would stay at least two years. Then, we would reevaluate her interests then as to whether she would continue to stay or move to another situation," I said, clearly.

"I see," he said, mulling the idea over and taking off his hat briefly to run his fingers through his hair.

"You know how I love family about," I said. "I was raised living with family, and I do miss it. We are a bit remote on the farm and I would love to have her company. It would give me great pleasure and purpose, you see." My eyes searched his as he briefly took them away from the road ahead to perhaps see how much I wanted this substantial change to our lives.

"She would need to help out around the house with chores as well. Understood?" He stated flatly—no room for discussion on the topic.

"Yes, clearly that would be part of the arrangement. Given that, are you willing to accept her request?" I asked, hopefully.

"If she understands that she would need obey our rules, I do agree. Yes, in fact, I think it is a fine idea," he said, smiling under the brim of his hat. "I would say that daughter of mine made a fine choice in her brave Captain Mackay Heriot and that their Lilian is of fine stock. Yes, I want to help both Rosie and Lilian out if we can. Military life with Mackay cannot be easy. Perhaps military life is a bit restrictive for a young woman."

I was delighted. "I will reply to Lilian's letter with the good news and also write to Rose and Mackay immediately to confirm that Lilian's parents are completely committed as well!" We sat admiring the country scenery. The road turned into a long thin lane that meandered steeply downhill, curving first left then right, with beautiful flowers distracting us. Purple Butterfly Weed was in bloom, looking like large bunches of purple grapes at a distance, in tall bushes that bobbed and dangled in the wind.

"For heaven's sake! Would you look at that!" I exclaimed. Around a bend in the road was one of the oldest churches I had ever seen. The sign says it is St Winifred's Church. Oh, it looks positively ancient! We must return to take a look inside. I am sure it contains amazing artifacts." Thomas slowed the horses so that we could examine the church from the lane.

"Is that Saxon herringbone work, just there?" I pointed to the front of the church.

"I believe it is. It is a beauty, to be sure. I have heard that it is over one thousand years old," Thomas agreed. "Heyah," he said, softly, urging the horses onward with a light tap of the reins.

"This lane is called 'Mill Lane'," he said after a pause, as we dodged the occasional carriage or horse rider. "It leads us to an old mill and bakery from the last century. We could stop briefly and look round the mill and have luncheon at the bakery, which is quite good, I am told, if you like."

"I would adore a stop and a break. Yes, please." I said, trying to sound like I was no longer complaining.

On our left, we passed a thatched forge. It too looked to be over one hundred years old. From our seats in the carriage, we could see that the forge produced traditional ironwork tools and gates. A few fire baskets hung from the inside of the forge, and we saw several black ironwork candlesticks sitting on a table inside.

"They seem to do lovely work," I noted, giving a friendly wave to the two men laboring inside.

"Perhaps we will give them a visit later and see what they have in the way of walking sticks," Thomas suggested.

"Oh yes, sturdy walking sticks would come in handy, with these gigantic hills!" I agreed, enthusiastically.

Our carriage rolled on, adding somewhat to the ruts in the now-dry road surface made by previous carriages and horse hooves. We came to a turn in the lane. Just off to the right, we saw both the bakery and the mill. Since the bakery was closest and we could not ignore the alluring smell of what seemed like freshly made scones, we tied up the horses and I fairly sprang out of the carriage.

"That wonderful smell! Is it not heavenly?" I declared as we walked down a path toward a two-story stone house with a lovely back garden. We went down several steps and into the front doors and were greeted with a lovely display of baked goods ready for sale and a chipper baker.

"You alright?" he said, wiping his hands on his white apron. "Would you like something here or to take away? All made today here in my own oven."

"That is a sizeable oven," I said, admiring the oven from the bakery display.

"Me and my brother make at least one hundred and thirty loaves a day," the baker said proudly, putting his hands on his hips.

Thomas and I ordered the coziest of lunches and sat outside at a rectangular table for two: thick brown mushroom soup, large slices of soft bread, with crunchy crusts, a fine black tea, scones with raisins and thick clotted cream.

"Perhaps not up to London standards, but passable, do you not agree?" Thomas quipped as we tucked in.

"Every bit up to London standards. Can you imagine? Out

here in the middle of the country? Such fine baking!" I cried out, taking a delicious bite of my scone.

After our most comforting lunch, we walked around the old granary mill works, admiring both the building and its outputs. It was nestled in a small valley, somewhat hidden from view by grasses growing all around. A mill worker showed us where to tie up our horses and encouraged our use of the water trough and grassy slope for their needs. Thomas rested both hands on the plank fence. "What ingenuity our forefathers had to design and build this massive operation!"

"I quite agree. It is like traveling back in time to see this. Just look how quickly the wheel turns, powered by the stream below. Very ingenious."

Our quick tour was just enough time to physically recover from the journey and then we continued downhill, down Mill Lane, towards our rented farmhouse. I was anxious to be settled there and looked forward to greeting several staff whom we had hired to unpack, cook, clean, and wash for us, as well as a guide who came with donkeys and horses, and otherwise make sure we were taken care of in this country setting.

We passed white cottages with thatched roofs adorning each side of the lane, along with white post fences and cheerfully painted windows that looked out over heavily sloped fields carpeted with dark grass between the hedgerows. Each cottage had an original name, such as "Thatched Barton." Trills of girlish laughter came in on the breeze and over the hedgerows, apparently from a gay afternoon at one of the cottages. We exchanged glances, and I shrugged my shoulders as if to say, "I do not know where the laughter is coming from, but it makes me curious!" Thomas smiled benevolently. The blackberry bramble held thousands of tiny red berries in its boughs, waiting for the sun to ripen them. And the 'hoo' song of the pale grey doves off in the distance added to the country's crisp and charming welcome.

We continued down the hill to find more houses now closely lining the lane. I saw one tavern called The Mason's Arms. "Where is the village, Thomas?" I asked, looking about.

"This *is* the village. The bakery, the mill, the forge, and now The Mason's Arms. The village," he said, opening his arms as if presenting me with a grand scene.

"Not exactly Sidmouth, is it?" I asked, looking around and trying not to sound disappointed.

"No, thank God, it is not." We slowed at The Mason's Arms. "We can dine here later tonight. It looks quite charming and old. Yes, I say it looks quite suitable." Thomas said, happily to himself. We continued on, up a slight hill where, to our left, was an elegant and large white wooden farmhouse surrounded by a tall forest.

"Here we are. Your castle, madam." He tipped his hat and leaned over to kiss my cheek.

"Oh Thomas!" I fairly sighed. "It looks beautiful!"

The two-story farmhouse rested perpendicular to the lane and surrounded by a lush forest of trees. It had very tall windows with painted frames and stucco walls. Several outbuildings created a large circle around the back, forming a large open and grassy area in the middle and giving an estate-like look to the property. I ran inside.

Thomas chuckled and shook his head as he handed the lead to one of the stable boys.

Beauty was everywhere I turned in Branscombe, Devon, with its shingled white beaches flanked by curvaceous red clay cliffs, believed to date back hundreds of millions of years. Dotted hillsides with lush green trees and then by wide open, undulating grassy green hills dreamily completed the exquisite view. After a few days of splashing at the beach with its flat, cold indigo and turquoise waves, we decided to pack up the donkeys and journey to Beer Head to explore the white chalk cliffs and the rock fall from years ago. I couldn't wait.

The path along the coast led us up a steep grassy slope, easy enough for our donkeys, Gorse and Wort. With the step of each hoof, they established a cadence, their heads bobbing up and down in a steady rhythm. Thomas and I smiled at each other in anticipation of the view from the top. The wind was brisk but warm. The sun was high in the sky, and I was enjoying life again. *If only we did not have to wait so long for this,* I thought. *I rue the wasted adventures we could have had.* But I chose to set those thoughts aside.

The path turned into a sandy mix together with small rocks, ran left and then ascended through several gates, which our donkeys navigated easily. The terrain slope had increased, and I was more than thankful for the surefooted donkeys we rode. Upward and onward, we came to a slope that was almost completely vertical and faced the sea. We looked up at it, intimidated. This time, our smiles were a bit more nervous. "I will lead Wort up first, taking advantage of these footholds that almost form stairs," Thomas said. "Then you ride up, astride, and lay flat on Gorse, evening out your weight and therefore making it easier for him to climb. Is that agreeable for you, darling?"

"Yes, I believe so," I said, hiking up my skirt and sheath so that I could sit astride.

"It will only be a few moments of slight discomfort on your legs, and you will have a strange feeling of going very much up in the air. But it will be over quickly and there is sure to be less steep terrain ahead. Best not to look down," he advised.

"Right," I said to both Thomas and Gorse. I gripped the front of the saddle with both hands, leaned against Gorse's back and held on tightly with my thighs. Gorse followed Wort readily, so I had no need to squeeze my thighs or urge him onward in any way, for which I was thankful.

Every few moments, I would lift my head as blackberry brambles passed by. I tried to see how far ahead Thomas was. He was only about three donkey lengths ahead of me, and we progressed slowly and carefully. However, it was a dreadfully long way up. At about one third of the way, I started to tremble from fright. I dared not look down towards the sea churning on the rocks below as I knew it would seem miles away. Periodically, Gorse would stumble ever so slightly, heightening my fears.

"There's my brave, bricky wife!" Thomas called out. "You are making fine progress, Arabella. Keep going as you are."

Just then, about halfway up the steepest climb of my life, on a donkey no less, Gorse slipped, lunging and buckling in such a manner that even though I held on as tightly as I could, I was no match for the force of his weight. In a terrible panic, I flew off Gorse's back and into the brambles several feet down the path. I landed on my side, luckily, with an impact I had never before experienced. My breath was knocked out of me, and I gulped for air but only for a second. I heard Thomas shouting. I could not move. I was frozen in fear, knowing what would happen should I slip any further. It would surely mean an excruciating death.

But after a few moments I realized that I could hold on to the bottom of the brambles, which made me feel a great deal safer. I also began to realize, and I caught my breath again, that the path was only wide enough for one donkey, one person. Thomas would not be able to make it to me before the bramble broke and I careened down the side of the cliff. With this newfound motivation to save myself, I pulled up to a sitting position, not looking over my shoulder at the deadly drop. The dry, sandy, and rocky soil was treacherous and loose, but I managed to pull myself up to a stand with the aid of the brambles, thorns imbedding in the sides of my arms and my wrists.

"Are you badly hurt?" Thomas called through cupped hands.

"No, I am alright," I called back. I was not in the least bit "all right," but saying so enabled me to find the steps to climb back up to Gorse, who appeared as if nothing at all had happened as he chewed on a budding yellow flower of his namesake plant.

I grabbed on to Gorse saying, "Easy boy. Just a tumble. Up and onward. Good boy."

After a few tries, I managed to reseat myself in the saddle. Exhausted, I laid my full weight on Gorse's back and rode up the remainder of the cliff like a dead weight. When we reached the summit, I slid off the donkey and into Thomas' waiting arms.

"Where does it hurt, my love?" He asked, searching my clothes for blood, bumps or both.

"Everywhere!" I said, panting. Then I let out a combination of a laugh and a sigh as I took in the view of the sea. Peregrines and Sea Gulls flew at eye level, some even below us. We were so high up; the shingle on the beach was invisible and one colour. The view of the beach and enormous sea was as beautiful as I could have ever imagined in my most colourful, elaborate dream.

"Incredible!" I said with wide eyes and a full heart. I then looked around us and found we were on another steep slope, but this time the slope was a grassy field. Cows and sheep munched on the soft grass, and the scene calmed me.

"Yes, you are," Thomas echoed. He patted Gorse's flank and ran a hand down the animal's legs to check for injury.

Given my scratches and bruises, we decided to spend the night in that grassy field, out in the open, on top of the cliffs between Branscombe and Beer. I could not face the thought of going down the menacing cliff and did not know how we would accomplish that. Thomas unpacked a small tent and the cheese, ham, bread, wine and fruit we had brought along, as well as several large warm blankets he had brought in case we needed them. How right he had been!

Luckily, he had also brought along salve and bandages for just such an occasion. "Allow me, please." Thomas removed my clothing down to my shift and examined me fully. He anointed my wounds and reported his findings.

"Nothing broken, punctured, or dislocated. You will have some nasty bruising and possibly some swelling. For that, I prescribe more wine," he said, lovingly.

"I do forget sometimes that you are a physician." I laughed and then winced at the pain in my ribs on my side that hit the ground.

"You will be plenty sore," Thomas noted. "We may have to linger up here for a couple of days until you feel a bit stronger. Can you manage that, my love? It is getting dark. Cover up in this blanket."

"The stars are magnificent here. I am glad we decided to stay," I replied, feeling a bit lightheaded and less sore. It was also quite romantic, I had to admit.

That night, our adventure rekindled our bond, as I had hoped it would, and we enjoyed to the fullest our long-awaited rewards of married people.

The next morning, to my surprise, I was not very sore from my fall, and I was determined after a bit of breakfast to move on, along the field at the top of the cliff to Beer Head and the rock fall site. We gathered up our belongings and the flat field at the top of the sloping field was exactly what I needed.

"Nice and flat," I said with ironic cheer to Thomas, surveying the field before us.

"Yes, indeed," he said, laughing.

The view from the top of Beer Head was stunning and daunting.

"I imagine few human beings have ever been up at this altitude before," I said, letting the wind blow my hair and skirts. We were able to get quite close to the edge of the headland because the brambles had formed a bit of a fence on the very edge of the cliffs. Seagulls soared in the sky above and below us over the sea.

We rode a bit further, and to our amazement, the white chalk columns from the fall stood before us. The white column and cliff edges were the magnificently carved marble male statues posed in a museum, standing before us with all the physique and pride of a nude David, striking and strong against the velvet background of the sea.

We clambered down the cliff on the winding path amongst the rubble and crumble of the fall. Mother Nature had done well to recapture the fallen rock with her mosses, ferns, and trees a plenty. We walked and slid down the fallen rock slowly, so that I could sketch a fern here and a cracked open rock there. Bees had taken to the lower-level flowers peeking out from between the rock bed. I caught one with a linen napkin as a sample to compare it to a bee at the top of the cliff. I noticed ants and beetles between and under rocks that we turned over. I felt my notebook rejoice as I filled it with information, drawings, and questions to pursue later.

We made our way all the way to the shingle beach, where it was low tide, and to our delight rock pools had formed. A pretty Brittle and then a Cushion Starfish scurried away from us.

"Come see this!" Thomas said, almost gleefully, his brown boots shining and wet. He had found a beautiful Strawberry Anemone tucked between a large rock and the shingles. Its tentacles were waving in the current, mimicking the wind's force on land. A lovely dance, I could barely pull my eyes away from the motion and colour explosion. Sidling next to the anemone was a shy, broad-clawed Porcelain Crab. Thomas and I watched them for several minutes, then embraced each other in our mutual admiration of the bounty of natural wonders we had discovered.

We moved down the beach to a wider section, where the seaweed covered boulders were mixed with the white pebbly shingle. We headed to the prize of our journey, the most scenic section, described to us as a group of small promontories creating tiny coves linked by sea caves and caverns, the largest of which looked like a large arched open doorway or isolated hall passage. Surrounded by sheer white cliffs, this "hall" or open doorway was a magnificent natural sculpture. Over it jutted an enormous chalk wall, like a building, extending horizontally to the beach and over the hall, giving grandeur to the entire structure.

We walked towards the breathtaking formation wordlessly and in awe. He vanished, no longer standing strong where he once had been but was replaced by a hazy form and then erased. When we reached the hall, Thomas examined the rim and determined it safe for passage. He moved through the arched open door with his hands out to his sides, in full admiration. I ran my hands along its striated chalk lines. We forgot all about wet shoes, my bruises, rising tides, fatigue, distance, and time. I felt at the height of happiness in my life, other than those magical achievements with Sir Charles and Mr. Darwin.

The brilliant sunshine mixed with the dark shadows along the boulders and inside the hall blinded me and created the most peculiar sensation. My eyes stung in the bright light and could not adjust quickly enough to see clearly in the shadows. Only a moment earlier, I saw Thomas go through the hall, but in the mix of light and shadows, I could no longer see him. It was as if he had vanished, no longer standing strong where he once been but almost replaced by hazy form and then erased. I had stepped into the light, and he into the shadows. And in that moment, I felt the shock of what it would be like to lose him—of falling helplessly into an emptiness beyond words. I shuddered. Despite our troubles, despite the years of distance and misunderstanding, he was my rock. He had been and would continue to be the wind beneath my wings.

Chapter Twenty-Nine

From Light to Shadow

Walreddon Estate,
Whitchurch, near Tavistock, UK

March 1893 – January 1895

We moved into Walreddon after six years of searching for a place to live that was in less of an isolated location. I began to feel better about the decision, which was largely mine, and I started a letter to Mr. Garnett to give him the news.

March 19, 1893

My Dearest Friend,

Walreddon is a grand old place full of historic relics. Mrs. Heriot is delighted with it, and in many other ways, I begin to feel it is the finest place. General Heriot ran up from Plymouth for a few hours on Sunday, and Mrs. Heriot and Lily are here today… We feel sure that the Royal Arms are Elizabeth's, and this pleases me. They are a very quaint lion and unicorn with Honi Soit etc.

and three small lions and three fleur de lys in the two opposite corners. The date over the porch we believe is 1591 at which time the house was evidently restored. Parts they say belong to Edward the Third…I am going next week to try to write the article on Sir Charles Lyell which must be sent to America in a fortnight.

One of my favorite spots in the entire Walreddon estate was the rose garden off the kitchen in the back of the house. The roses were meticulously spaced and posted by Simon, the gardener hired by Thomas, a trusted young man who also seemed to revel in the roses with me. On occasion, he would bring me a chair to sit on so that I might write in the garden when the weather cooperated.

Lady Courtenay had brought me into the Women's Liberal Unionist political organization in Tavistock. I found it very easy simply to roll down the hill from Walreddon to the main street in town to attend these meetings. There, I could shop as I liked in the ancient corn market square, visit the town museum in their new town hall, and enjoy the river walk on Abbey Bridge, surrounded by medieval walls with other passersby. All in all, I found it a much more invigorating environment than Sheepwash!

I sat in our small parlour writing letters on my new typing machine while Thomas sat tying fly lures in a chair.

"Your machine is quite loud, dear. All that *tap, tap, tapping* is just awfully loud!" Thomas complained.

"I quite agree with you. And it hurts my eyes and cramps my thoughts as well. I think I shall write with my own hand," I said, in agreement.

Thomas gave a sort of grunt of approval, squinting at a thread and a bead on a hook-shaped reed.

"My eyes are a little better today," I added. "I have had a good deal of pain in them lately." I attributed this discomfort to treatments the doctor had been giving me—and to the occasional glare that I still struggled with. "Some days I can see quite well and others not at all. I have had to refuse to be secretary to the Women's Liberal Unionist Association, which just opened in Tavistock. I go to a meeting today after extracting a promise that I shall not be pressed into public work at the present" I said. I was hoping for a little sympathy from him.

"All right" was all Thomas said in reply, given his concentration on his lure.

"Do not forget that the photographic convention is meeting, and we are to have a party up here for them on Tuesday. I do hope the weather turns out. Perhaps we could have them take some photos of Walreddon, dear. What do you think of that idea? To have for posterity?" I asked.

"Posterity will not care or remember us, dear," Thomas said without looking up, squinting at the work in his hands.

After nearly two years, Walreddon had restored my energy and excitement to carry on my writing. My writing backbone had returned, and my intellectual stagnation had abated. I was able to come and go to London quite easily from the station in Tavistock. Therefore, seeing Henry, and my other family, as well as Mr. Garnett, became a more frequent part of my country life. However, the Doctor became more and more fidgety about my going anywhere and leaving him behind due to his marginal health.

On a cold day in January, Thomas entered our bedroom striding across the floor, his gait a little stooped, with purpose, as if impatient to begin his day. He was dressed in outdoors wear and said, "Darling, I am just going about the property to check on things. Not enough for me to do here these bleak winter days, I am afraid…" He trailed off as he came around the door and found me soaking in a large, white, porcelain tub, completely naked, the water line hitting my body below my rib cage, my arms draped wide across each side of the back edge of the tub like those of a young and glamorous London actress, smiling at him. He stopped and his eyes leveled at my full, rounded breasts rather than lighting on my face, I noticed.

"Do I startle, my dear?" I asked, coquettishly. I laughed, raising one knee above the water line and looked down at the water, suddenly sheepish at my antics.

"I'll say!" Thomas said, lustily. "I would join you, but I am off to tour the exterior of the house and the gardens to see if all is well. Simon is out in the rose garden picking up after that fallen tree. We might as well pick up any remaining leaves as well." He eyed me with great interest. "I must say, your loveliness has not changed in all the years of our marriage. You delight me, my darling." His adoring eyes softened his face and looked at me with the gaze of a much younger man.

"Always a pleasure to hear." I said, softly, my eyes taking stock of him. Despite his age, he still cut a fine figure with his broad shoulders and narrow waist. His hair was grey now and his fingers had a bit of a gnarl on them. Still, even though he had shrunk a bit from his younger years, he had retained much of his physicality. I had always admired his upper body strength that created his rugged appearance. He was strong in all ways but also gentle when we were abed, which I appreciated. Yes, I had done well to marry him, I thought to myself, even though he bored me at times with his talk of shooting and fishing. And it is not every seventy-five-year-old man who still appreciated his wife.

"Right then," I said, smiling. "I am taking off the chill here in front of the fire and then I have correspondence to take care of in the front sitting room. I do love my baths here at Walreddon, you know. I will see you at luncheon?" I brushed a creamy soap, smelling of mint, up and down my right arm, my eyes still on him.

Thomas grinned. "Yes, after two years here I believe I am quite fond of Walreddon as well. And, too bad this old house has so many draughts or I would be lucky enough to find you still here when I returned," he quipped. "Yes, luncheon. I am off. I love you, dear." He turned and strode back towards the door.

"And I you, dear." I lilted back as he went down the hallway. I often worried about him. Over the past six months, he had begun suffering what we referred to as "spells," periods of disorientation where he would forget where he was, become lost outdoors and even in the house. All this on top of his frequent colds and flus. Was it because he needed time, given his advanced age, to assimilate into Walreddon and was still familiarizing himself with the grounds and house? I thought about saying something to him, but he seemed so exuberant, I did not want to spoil the excitement of his day.

Still, I was concerned. Only a month before, he had been confined to his chair with a respiratory illness, and even now remained somewhat frail from lack of exercise. I hoped that Simon, our groundsman, would stay somewhat close at hand. I trusted that he would, since I had discussed the Doctor's frailty and these spells with Simon only days ago.

I dressed in a maroon day gown and black slippers. Since I was not going out, the day called for cozy indoor attire. I glanced out the second-floor window and down on the back courtyard below—and found gloomy, heavily overcast clouds and brisk winter wind. Thomas was such a sturdy outdoorsman; he seemed almost impervious to the weather. Still, I worried.

I sat at the front of the house in the small sitting room off the front entrance, my preferred source of light at this time of day when reading or writing was required. I pulled out my writing tools—nib, ink, paper, blotter, and pen that I liked to use, and bowed my head in earnest to begin my first letter. I searched for the recipient's address in my weekly pile of letters.

I had only organized a couple of thoughts, when I heard a muffled, small yelp coming from outdoors, far behind the house. I stopped my work and listened for clues as to the source, but none came, so I returned to begin my letter, assuming it was one of the workers frustrated with some chore or tool that might be malfunctioning.

My head bent, I leaned towards the enormous fireplace that contained the largest pieces of granite I had ever seen. I refocused on an important update via letter to the Liberal Party, of which I was now the Vice President. I had not been able to resist this appointed position, which, indeed, I had vied for as a newcomer to the area. Thomas' agent had endorsed me and parents at the Kelly College where Oscar, our studious grandson, now a student there, were willing to as well. As I sat at a gorgeously carved table resting on a gray flag-stone floor and under a painted ceiling of Tudor crests and roses, the letter required my full focus and concentration. I sat where the light was brightest this cold and dreary January morning.

My fervor for writing had reawakened at Walreddon. What a relief, especially after I had struggled so much at Upcott Avenel! I had made several trips to see my publisher and my writing had gone as planned, despite being busier than usual with visitors (Sir John Hall, the former Prime Minister of New Zealand, had paid us a welcome visit to chat about all things New Zealand, to our delight) and my work with the Women of the Liberal Party. I had agreed with my publisher to republish another version of *Moralities of Science* in shorter form, with the intent of capturing a larger audience who might have less of an appetite for the longer, more philosophical version. And I had discussed a series of smaller, more digestible works that my publisher at Cassell recommended for readers who preferred shorter works. We called it the series *Eyes and No Eyes* and planned for it to be based on the adventures of three children, Peter, Peggy, and Paul, living in the woods, by rivers, and in fields. By using the river, stream, and field setting, I could include my favorite beings yet again—birds and insects, namely—and reposition them around the lovely settings that I actually now inhabited myself.

As I reflected, I understood with new insight how difficult our nine or so years at Upcott had been. I had never really gotten over my loathing of the solitude of country life as compared to living in central London. Still, I did have fond times in Sheepwash. I did love the walk down the field and up the next one to St Lawrence's church each Sunday for services, when the deep mud permitted. Flashes of fond and cherished memories of Avenel flew across my mind. The manor house library. Men sitting outside the Half Moon pub in Sheepwash happily drinking pints of ale, the gaiety of the sheep market where women also sold handmade gloves and bakery items. I genuinely missed sitting in front of the great wide fire in the great room in the manor house whose light I used to write my books, even though the fire in front of me now was equally grand, if not more so.

But Walreddon was better for so many reasons—one of which was our darling grandson. Oscar's boarding school, the Kelly College for military children in Tavistock, was so close to home. We could be involved with him on holidays now, and we could look after him while Rose and Mackay were at home in the Newton Abbot now after his retirement.

How Oscar loved the estate! He was especially fond of the riding and generous paddock facilities and the grounds which afforded him unlimited excursions. He would often ride with the hunt or for pleasure with Thomas. The manor house itself was itself full of adventure as well. On one occasion in his bedroom, he discovered that on the far left of the giant fireplace, which was so large that he could venture inside it and not be burned, there was a peep hole that must have been used as a lookout place during medieval times, for spying or security. The hole allowed the occupant to see who was approaching from the front of the house and along the side, from the stables. Oscar was delighted at this remarkable find. I smiled down at my paper thinking of how I considered Oscar my own grandson.

Returning my attention to my morning work, I reviewed my letter, satisfied with the content and the penmanship of the first page. I had just reached for a second page of paper when I heard it—a shout. A loud shout—more of a shrieking. The sound of someone who is truly terrified. Was it Simon, from the garden? The low tone definitely came from a man. Thomas would never shout like that. That is, I had never heard him do so. Then, I heard stifled voices and the footsteps of multiple people scurrying about. Something was wrong.

After a few seconds, it was Simon in fact, rather than our cook, Ethel, who was the head of the household but apparently away at the moment, who came panting into the sitting room, which was highly unusual. He spoke from the doorway, hat, coat and gloves still on. Thomas had insisted we did not require any butler as we no longer hosted guests, so Simon was the head of the household if Ethel was away. I was standing in alarm at the noise and turned around to see him. I had no words in response to the agony on his face.

"Madame, you must come at once. Immediately. It is Dr. Thomas. He has fallen ill. Please, follow me, immediately," he begged.

"Oh, God," I said.

Simon was a sinewy and lithe young man whose intelligence about herbology, and landscaping had proved very useful. I knew Simon to be a quick thinker and I trusted him, as did Thomas. My heart started pounding in a strong and ugly way. My nose and eyes burned in alarm. I followed Simon through passageways to the back of the house and the small entryway that boasted of a seal of a lady in waiting to the queen by the massive arched back door. Judith, a maid I had come to love dearly, stopped me and jammed my arms into one of my heavy coats, given the cold wind outside.

"What is going on, Judith?" I asked swiftly. She said nothing at first, her white cap placed neatly on her head covering brown curls. Her eyes were cast down her lips pressed tightly together, the way a highly trained maid who was no fool would when trouble was about.

"I am afraid Dr. Thomas is truly very ill, Madame," finally came her answer. When she looked up, I saw that her eyes were full of tears. The hair on the back of my neck stiffened, and I swallowed hard. "I must go," I said urgently. Thomas was clearly in grave danger.

Simon swung the thick wooden back door open wide as it if was made of a light cloth and led the way for me left, down a few stairs and through the back courtyard. I glanced to my right to see if anyone was about. The great wide door of the Old Barn was open, and I could just see one of the black wrought iron candle holders swinging from the arched ceiling, swaying slightly. Nothing seemed amiss there.

We ran down the stone pathway toward the twelve-foot-high hedges that served as a wall to the courtyard. A high arched door led us to a smaller "stable courtyard" with a black granite fountain and a series of six horse stalls. This seemed to be where we were headed. Only one stall was occupied, the last one, and as no one was planning on riding today, the remaining horses were kept in the paddock where they would be warm and fed. Why were we hurrying towards the horse stalls? I called after Simon with his long-legged gait to ask, but he did not seem to hear me. He kept going towards the first and closest stall, which was open, with no horse in it.

Then, I saw a figure, a man, in a black coat who was lying on his back, draped across the low bench at the end of the stall. It was Thomas prone on the bench. I ran to him and knelt by his head and gently wrapped my left arm around his head and my placed my right hand on his face. I felt nauseated–something was terribly wrong with him.

"What has happened? Has he fallen?" I looked sharply up into Simon's eyes, asking for answers. Jimmy, the meaty looking, red faced young stable boy, was also on hand. Jimmy looked dumbly down at me, as if he was looking at nothing more than a box of stable tack.

"Jimmy says that the Doctor was out walking a few minutes ago and came through the gate toward the stables and simply fell to his knees on the grass," Simon said, helplessly, both his arms out and palms up as if to say that was all either of them had to offer. "I was not here to witness what happened." Simon looked down at Thomas. "Jimmy did right by running around the house to the rose garden, where I was picking up fallen tree branches and leaves to fetch me as quick as he could."

Jimmy gave a helpless nod. "The Doctor fell" he said, shrugging his shoulders.

"Thomas?" I cried to him in a wail. I put my ear to his chest, listening for a rise and fall. I waited, praying to God with every ounce of piety I had. An overwhelming sense of oddity came over me as I saw no movement at all. Only stillness. "Thomas?" I called to him again, this time more loudly. "Thomas?" I repeated, urgently. I grabbed his wrist and felt by his thumb side to check for a pulse. My hand shook as it told me the grim answer. There was no pulse. I slowly laid

Thomas's wrist back down by his side. Simon stood at his feet, watching me conduct the grim process I felt he had surely conducted himself with the same grave result.

"Has he passed, Madame?" Simon asked slowly and softly, his voice cracking, his red hands wringing his woollen hat in his hands. Thomas had hired Simon when we first arrived at Walreddon in the early spring of 1894. I imagined Simon felt extreme sorrow, as he and Thomas seemed to more than enjoy passing time outdoors together in the gardens and by the lakes, working to keep the property in good condition.

I was totally disoriented. Hadn't Thomas seemed in good spirits only an hour earlier when I had last seen him? What had his last words to me been? We had been flirting, hadn't we? And then he had said something about not having enough to do and therefore he would be taking a walk around the property to oversee the upkeep and maintenance of the estate and would be back within a few hours. Now here he lay before me, a bluish tinge around his mouth and fingertips, posed in the most graceful, immobile calm I had ever seen him in. I had never seen him so still, so frozen. I was stunned to see him now so motionless when in life he had been anything but. In life, he was in constant motion, as if he created all energy and light around him. As I gazed down at him trying to comprehend this new stillness, I was overcome with loss in what now appeared to be the finality of silence in the shadow of his death.

In stunned agony, I forced words up through my throat and out of my mouth to break the silence. "Yes, Simon. It appears he is gone" was all I could say as I sat next to Thomas in shock on the cold bench. I stood up and kissed my husband's lips while I held his face in my hands. I bent my knees and laid my face on his chest and smelled his still soap-tinged body. I willed myself to imprint his scent and the feel of him in my mind, permanently, like a tattoo. I clutched his upper arms to hold on to the last bits of his warmth. I heard myself barely utter, "Oh! Oh!" several times but my words sounded eerily like someone else was whispering them. *All I want is for you to be alive, even for a few more minutes. Thomas, I don't want to live another minute of this life without you.* This was all I could think as I lay on Thomas' chest for what was surely the last time. The last time I would touch the only man I had touched and loved my entire life.

His black woollen coat scratched my wet cheek. Due to the bitter cold, the tiny clouds of mist that came out of my mouth were painful, leaving my throat raw. No clouds of mist came from Thomas' mouth or nose. *He feels nothing,* I thought. Nothing ever again. Death is so very final.

"My deepest condolences, ma'am," Simon whispered solemnly as he and Jimmy stood behind me at Thomas's feet.

Chapter Thirty

Conquering Another Day

The College,
Glasgow, Scotland

Late 1880s

"Science chose you?" Samuel Butler asked incredulously. "What do you mean, 'it chose you?'" He had closed in on me and was leaning down towards my face, his eyes glaring. I glanced around us in the auditorium at The College, Glasgow after my lecture of *Progress of Life on Earth* to see who might be listening to our acidic conversation.

"I mean, I worked to help others," I said. "First the Lyells, then Mr. Darwin and many more. You, Mr. Butler, have belonged to no literary school, no scientific theory, and spawned no followers that I know of. Who have you helped? Who do you belong to? You are an amateur critic, a dilettante dabbling in evolution and religious thought. In our day, you are either a religionist or a Darwinian or, like me, a traducianist who combines the two, but you sir are none of these."

"You are a woman of no real education. A charlatan. A... A..." he stammered. "What is more, I know you carried on some type of love affair with Richard Garnett!"

Taken aback, I gasped. I quickly said, "I know of many different types of love, Mr. Butler, as I am most sure you do, given your, shall we say, proclivities?" His heavy black eyebrows shot up, realizing my meaning.

I dismissed that line of thinking with a quick wave of my hand. "You come here on what is to be my most prestigious invited lecture to denigrate my work? You have followed me for thirty years, snooping about, asking questions trying to glean information from me or trying to supplant me, constantly jealous of my work. You ask how I have achieved my success?"

"Yes, how did you gain access where others did not?" he reiterated, clearly agitated. The years of unrequited struggle to gain access to Mr. Darwin and his colleagues and to gain their approval had eaten away at him bit by bit, taking away his decorum and parts of this sanity.

"My success has come in the form of bridging worlds, Mr. Butler. Bridging divides. Something you know very little about, I dare say. I come from an unprivileged world that yearns for the power of the privileged society that you come from, Mr. Butler—that power being knowledge. My gift was that I diligently put art and words together for those that could not to provide science for everyone. They call it "popularizing" or creating meaning for the masses. For me, Mr. Darwin was the pedestal of scientific achievement, and I wanted the world to see him as I did: as a luminary. It is all quite simple. For current and future generations, I made it my mission to write about science and evolution in a way that illuminated Mr. Darwin." *And in the process, almost by accident, I created a rather wonderful life for myself*, I thought but did not say so to him.

For once, Mr. Butler said nothing. His dark brown eyes tried to bore holes through me, but I refused to let them. I turned, chin held high, and took hold of the handles of my portfolio. Without another word, I walked briskly out of the auditorium, leaving Mr. Butler gaping after me. The force that had chosen me was still the wind at my back. I left, fortified to conquer another day.

Epilogue

An Old War Horse

3 Coburg Place
Sidmouth, UK

1928

Now almost completely blind, I move about the library and shops of Sidmouth by wheelchair and with the help of Lilian or an assistant. All my old friends here and in London are largely gone. Alfred Wallace and I stayed in touch and his children visited me as I lived on and off in London and here in Sidmouth various times, but he went to our Lord years ago on November 7, 1913, and then his dear Annie three years later in 1916. His legacy lives on. How I miss them both and our work together, especially the séances!

I do enjoy listening to my cast of readers that come to me to read aloud, and I have my true luxury, my wireless, which sustains me by connecting my mind to the bigger world when my eyes cannot. How the Doctor would have marveled at the wireless! And the automobile, for that matter. What a pity that he did not live long enough to see these miracles.

I imagine him listening to political broadcasts while sitting in his chair in the paneled drawing room by the fire, despite him being gone now for over thirty years. How fast the time went! Our time together was a small slice of my life, but one I hold dear. As our marriage continues in my mind after his death, I know exactly what the Doctor would say and do at any given time. I imagine the conversations we would have had over my moving to Brook Cottage in Tavistock after selling all our carriages and home items from Walreddon. He might not have understood how I could not live in the manor without him. I was in quite a lot of anguish to leave our servants and the manor behind. The cottage was quite near his favorite fishing spot, the one where he caught the five-pound trout that time.

He would have loathed the events leading up to and the outcomes of the Great War as a terrible waste of life, time, and money. He would have been sick with worry for Rose's boys, but ironically and perhaps thankfully, Oscar passed away before he was forced to enter that horrid fight. I had Oscar buried in the same plot as the Doctor. He died falling off his horse, riding when he was too sick and should not have been out. I have a place for myself in that same grave site. I plan to join them when the time comes. That is, my name will be in the space that remains on the tombstone.

My dear friend Richard Garnett passed away on April 13, 1906, and was buried on the eastern side of Highgate Cemetery. But not before he and a woman named Violet connected on their mutual love of the writer Shelley and apparently more. Oh, but his family was livid! He was busy working to the end. I had a letter from him and replied to it just months before his death. How I miss him! I decided that our love was a true love but a platonic love. I still think of him and how he and he alone helped me get through difficult times.

Lily moved back to Newton Abbot with her parents, Rose and Mackay, after about a year with Thomas and I but returned to Sheepwash and Waldreddon to visit. She now lives with me in my white house here on Coburg Street and she remains unmarried. I plan to leave everything I have to her. She is more than comfortable and wants for nothing. She was a joy to me during my lonely days at Sheepwash and at Sidmouth. Just as she is now.

I see some of Henry's children on occasion. He had a lot of them with his young wife and late in life. He was such a successful barrister that he became a judge and then was offered a peerage. My brother!

The evening sun lights my room, but all I can see are shadows moving most evenings. My vision is very poor now and so I must make do with the shadows and shades of grey. "Mrs. Fisher, it is time for your radio program to begin," Agnes, my evening assistant, reminds me, breaking into my thoughts like a bright spotlight on a foggy morning. Lily is out for the evening with friends.

"Oh yes, I am quite excited for this one. The broadcast is by Sir Arthur Keith, the President of the British Association for the Advancement of Science, you know."

"No ma'am. I am not familiar with him," Agnes replied in a bored tone.

"Oh, well then, please position me close to the radio and amplify the volume, will you please?" I said, getting out of breath, as I forced my aching knees and back to stand upright and cross the room to sit by the radio with Agnes's aid. When I hear the introductory announcement, my heart leaps out of my chest. The topic of this broadcast is none other than Charles Darwin.

Sir Arthur Keith begins speaking. "The subject of my address is Man's remote history. Fifty-six years have come and gone since Charles Darwin wrote *A History of Man's Descent.*

How does his work stand the test of time? This is the question I propose to discuss with you tonight in the brief hour at my disposal."

"If he says it does not stand the test of time, he is an absolute fool. An utter fool," I said out loud. Agnes was busy clanking my dinner dishes on my tray taking them away to the kitchen.

"Yes, ma'am," she said, her voice trailing off as she left the room. Her shoes made a faint clacking on the floors, which comforted me, given my poor eyesight. *Good to know someone is nearby.*

Sir Arthur Keith continues. "In tracing the course of events which led up to our present conception of Man's origin, no place could serve as a historical starting point so well as Leeds. In this city was fired the first verbal shot of that long and bitter strife which ended in the overthrow of those who defined the Biblical account of Man's creation and in a victory of Darwin. On December 23, 1858—sixty-nine years ago—the British Association assembled in this city just as we do tonight; Sir Richard Owen, the first anatomist of his age, stood where I stand now. He had prepared a long address and surveyed the whole realm of science; but only those parts which concern Man's origin require our attention now."

"Get on with it, man. Get to the gist of Darwin's theory of man's descent as it stands today," I urged.

"Owen poured scorn on the idea that man was merely a transmuted ape. He declared to the assembled association that the difference between man and ape was so great that it was necessary, in his opinion, to assign mankind to an altogether separate order in the animal kingdom. As this statement fell from the President's lips there was at least one man in the audience whose spirit of opposition was roused—Thomas Henry Huxley—Owen's young and rising antagonist."

"Hmmpff. I would say so. Mr. Huxley abhorred the man.

Thought he was an idiot," I replied to the radio as if President Keith was speaking directly to me.

"Two years later, in 1860, when this association met in Oxford, Owen repeated the statement made at Leeds as to Man's separate position, claiming that the human brain had certain structural features never seen in the brain of anthropoid apes. Huxley's reply was a brief and emphatic denial with a promise to produce evidence in due course—which was faithfully kept.

Two days later our protagonists had a spectacular fight—the most memorable in the history of our Association—in which the Bishop of Oxford, the representative of Owen and of Orthodoxy, left his scalp in Huxley's hands. Huxley settled for all time that Man's rightful position is among the primates, and that his nearest living kin are the anthropoid apes."

"Indeed! Huxley always was a defender of Darwin and his best bulldog!" I cheered. I remembered back to the evening of my first reception at Sir Charles' home where Lady Lyell invited Mr. Huxley to tell that exact story. How young and brilliant they all were then! How cavalier Huxley had been as he toyed with me at that party! Luckily it was I who had gotten the best of him that time! I was so young and fortunate to be in that circle. I knew it then, as I know it now.

"My aim is to make clear to you the foundations on which rest our present-day conception of Man's origin. I must now address another issue which Sir Richard Owen merely touched upon, but which is of supreme interest to us now. He spent the summer in London, just as I have done, writing his address for Leeds and keeping an eye on what was happening at scientific meetings. In his case something really interesting happened. Sir Charles Lyell and Sir Joseph Hooker left with the Linnean Society what appeared to be an ordinary roll of manuscript, but what in reality was a parcel charged with verbal high explosives, prepared by two very innocent looking men—Alfred Russel Wallace and Charles Darwin. As a matter of honesty, it must be admitted that these two men were well aware of the deadly nature of its contents, and knew that if an explosion occurred, Man himself, the crown of creation, could not escape it destructive effects.

"Why is he ploughing through all this ancient history, fine as it may be? Everyone knows this. I was not there on scene yet for all that, but oh, I wish I had been!" I lamented.

"Owen examined the contents of the parcel and came to the conclusion that they were not dangerous; at least he gave no sign of alarm in his presidential address. He dismissed both Wallace and Darwin, particularly Darwin, in the briefest of paragraphs, at the same time citing passages from his own work to prove that the conception of Natural Selection as an evolutionary force was one which he had already recognized."

"The pretentiousness!" I exclaimed.

"As I address these words to you, I cannot help marveling over the difference between our outlook today and that of the audience which Sir Richard Owen had to face in this city sixty-nine years ago. The vast assemblage which confronted him was convinced, almost without dissent, that Man had appeared on earth by a special act of creation; whereas the audience which I have now the honour of addressing, and that larger congregation which the wonders of wireless brings withing the reach of my voice, if not convinced Darwinists are yet prepared to believe, when full proofs are forthcoming, that Man began his career as a humble primate animal, and has reached his present estate by the action and reaction of biological forces which have been and are ever at work within his body and brain."

I heaved a heavy sight. "At last, please do get on with it."

"Let us turn our attention to the little village of Downe where Charles Darwin completed his book, *The Origin of Species* in 1859, which was to affect a sweeping revolution in our way looking at living things and to initiate a new period in human thought—the Darwinian period—in which we still are. Without knowing it, Darwin was a consummate general. He stocked his arsenal with ample stores of tested and assorted fact. Having established a treasury of biological observation and an advanced base, he moved forward on his final objective—the problem of Human Beginnings—by the publication of *The Descent of Man* (1871). Many a soldier of truth had attempted this citadel before Darwin's day, but they failed because they had neither his generalship nor his artillery."

"A general! You can tell that Sir Keith did not know Mr. Darwin at all! A ludicrous comment for so gentle a man as Mr. Darwin," I fumed. "He would not have enjoyed that analogy, to be sure. If he was a general, what was I? Not a soldier, like a man, out on the front line. No, I was more like a war horse." I chuckled. "I was behind the scenes but a critical part of carrying the load. I carried my share of the load, and I did not shy away from fire, did I?"

"Will Darwin's victory endure for all time? Let us look at what kind of book *Descent of Man* is. It is a book of history—the history of Man, written in a new way—the way discovered by Charles Darwin…"

"Correct! Mr. Darwin did write in a new way to appeal to those in the non-science world. He began all his writing with this premise in mind—a premise that we both agreed with and that I assisted him with, through our many dialogues and my edits of his work. I carried on our premise through my own writing, clarifying his theory in ways everyone could understand. I espoused his theories and made it my mission to popularize them and him through my books, lectures and papers to repay him and to provide help to those who wanted to learn. In this way, I brought Mr. Darwin to the world. *I illuminated him for others. I illuminated Charles Darwin,*" I thought to myself with deep satisfaction and pride.

"...Charles Darwin wrote *Man* by gathering historical documents from the body and behaviour of Man and he compared them with observations made on the body and behaviour of every animal which showed the least resemblance to Man. He took into consideration the manner in which the living tissues of Man react to disease, to drugs, and to environment; he had to account for the existence of diverse races of mankind. "

The address continued. "Fifty-six years have come and gone since that history was written; an enormous body of new evidence has poured in upon us. We are now able to fill in many pages which Darwin had perforce to leave blank, and we have found it necessary to alter details in his narrative, but the fundamentals of Darwin's outline of Man's History remain unshaken. Nay, so strong has his position become that I am convinced that it never can be shaken."

"Hurrah! Hurrah for Mr. Darwin! For Emma, the children! For Mr. Wallace, Mr. Huxley, Mr. Hooker, the Lyells, and the lot!" I cheered in my hoarse voice. My cheering caused my throat to constrict and to unsettle the fluid in my chest, causing a coughing fit. I sipped my tea to quell my coughing, so that I could listen to more of the address.

"Why do I say so confidently that Darwin's position has become impregnable? Since his death we have succeeded in tracing Man by means of his fossil remains and his stone implements backwards in time to the very beginning of that period of the earth's history to which the name Pleistocene is given..."

"And how is it that Darwin so well-known after all these years?" I asked myself out loud. "How are his theories so impregnable, and why are we still in a Darwinian era? Partially because of my writing. Me. A woman. I was able to converse with Darwin admirably. Francis Darwin often said how fond Mr. Darwin was of talking about my books. Probably because they were inclusive of his theory! In that way, and through me,

Darwin must have seen what is possible for womankind to achieve." I recalled his kind words in letters he had written to me about *A Short History of Natural Science* and *A Fairyland of Science*! How I treasured those words. "Ultimately," I continued, "I must have demonstrated to him that womankind is not so different from Man in intellectual activity! *Another way I illuminated Mr. Darwin—in his observations of the capabilities of women!"*

"...The evidence of Man's evolution from an ape-like being, obtained from a study of fossil remains, is definite and irrefutable, but the process has been infinitely more complex than was suspected in Darwin's time..."

"Exactly as Mr. Darwin and I discussed in edits of *Man*. Evolution is not merely about the physical characteristics of the body or brain, but also the collaboration required within and between species that enable life to continue. I will be most interested if Sir Keith includes this in his broadcast," I ruminated.

"...The differences between the mentality of Man and ape, they are of degree, not of kind. ...There is so much that we do not yet understand. Can we explain why inherited ability falls to one family and not to another, or why we will be able to assist in the evolution of new types or Man as we do in new types of motor cars? If we are to understand the machinery which underlies the evolution of Man and of ape, we have to enter the factories where they are produced—look within the womb and see the ovum being transformed into an embryo and then into a babe...One of the ways into the machine is via the activities of Starling's discovery of hormones, opening up new vistas to the student of Man's evolution. How Darwin would have welcomed this discovery!"

I finished my tea and sat back in my chair. The broadcast was wrapping up. "In a brief hour," Keith continued, "I have attempted to answer a question of momentous importance to all of us. Was Darwin right when he said that Man, under the action of biological forces which can be observed and measured, has been raised from a place amongst the anthropoid apes to that which he now occupies? The answer is yes! I am content to follow Darwin's own example—Let the truth speak for itself." As Sir Arthur Keith's speech concluded, the crowd at the auditorium erupted with applause in appreciation for not only his riveting speech, but most likely for Mr. Darwin himself.

I was so fortunate indeed to have worked with him, I reflected. So truly fortunate. I pulled my favorite crocheted wool lap blanket up higher on my chest and checked to make sure my newest book *The Nature of the Physical World* by Sir Arthur Eddington was on my to-be-read pile for Agnes in the morning. My dear friend's daughter, Alice Zimmerman, will be stopping by to read it to me tomorrow. The book was about his set of lectures on quantum physics and man's place in the universe, and fascinated by the topic, I could not wait to dive into it.

Shifting my weight to lessen the pain in my aching joints, I thought, Mr. Darwin truly has stood the test of time. He illuminated mankind and probably would continue doing so for time eternal. *And I illuminated Darwin.* I had the good fortune to help in handing to successive generations the torch of new knowledge. And through this, I repaid as best I could those to whom I owe more than I can ever express. *And what a rich life it has been.*

I heard a Skylark, our favorite bird, sing a beautiful trill of notes outside my window and I said to it, "Goodnight, my love."

Afterword

Bernard Lightman

Author of Victorian Popularizers of Science: Designing Nature for New Audiences
Professor, York University, Toronto

Arabella Buckley (1840 – 1929) wasn't known to those working in Victorian studies until the middle of the 1990s. Literary scholars were the first to pick up on her, followed closely by historians of science. One reason why she received little attention until the last quarter century was because until the 1980s, women were not seen as having played an important role in the history of science. Feminist scholars helped us to realize that women had been erased from the historical record when it came to science because they had been excluded from institutions of higher learning and because they had been seen as being incapable, by their very nature, of thinking scientifically. By the time scholars began to examine Buckley's writings, there was already an ongoing attempt to recover the contributions of women to science.

Another reason why Buckley attracted little interest in the past was because popularizers of science as a whole were largely neglected. They were seen as unimportant disseminators of scientific theories already discovered by the real scientists. And they were usually presented as figures who distorted or simplified science so that an ignorant reading audience could understand ideas way over their heads. This view has been challenged vigorously by scholars who now see popularizers as crucial communicators who grasped how to effectively convey scientific ideas to an eager public who wanted to know the larger meaning of new discoveries like evolution. What did it tell us about humanity's place in nature? About traditional religious beliefs? And about our long-term future as a species? Popularizers, we now realize, played an essential role in explaining what science meant to the vast sea of Victorian readers. There were many popularizers during the Victorian period. What makes Buckley important?

One reason why Buckley became the subject of research has to do with her place in the Victorian scientific community. She became secretary to the eminent geologist Charles Lyell in 1864, which brought her into contact with the most important men of science, including Charles Darwin, the biologist Thomas Henry Huxley, and the co-discoverer of the theory of natural selection, Alfred Russel Wallace. Buckley became friends with all three. According to Darwin's son Francis, Buckley was one of the few women that Darwin regarded as his friend. Since Darwin revered Lyell, and saw that Buckley was providing Lyell with excellent secretarial assistance, he valued her as well. Buckley was also friendly with Huxley and on occasion was a teatime guest of his wife, Henrietta. But it was Wallace with whom she had the closest bond. She was his most intimate and confidential friend in the early 1880s. They shared a fascination with spiritualism, even though Darwin and Huxley would have been horrified if they found out about Buckley's interest. Spiritualism, to Darwin and Huxley, was a grave challenge to their conception of the naturalistic foundations of science. Despite her attraction to spiritualism, Buckley had strong connections to Darwin and his inner circle by virtue of her position as Lyell's secretary. Examining her life gives us some insight into the important men of science whose views on evolution were so influential in the mid and late Victorian period.

After Lyell's death in 1875, Buckley decided to embark on a career as popularizer of science. She became a prolific scientific author who wrote ten books on science, many for children. She established enough of a reputation for herself that she was one of the few women invited to lecture on scientific topics. This is a second reason for appreciating Buckley's historical importance. Although the Victorian public read the books written by Darwin, Huxley, and Wallace on evolution, they also read books on the subject by popularizers like Buckley. Buckley had a gift for interpreting complex scientific ideas and making them understandable to members of the public, including children. Popularizers like her, as much as the Darwins, Huxleys, and Wallaces, were responsible for helping readers to grasp the larger significance of new scientific discoveries like evolution.

Above all, Buckley was an imaginative writer, particularly when it came to conveying scientific ideas to children in the form of fairy tales. In *The Fairyland of Science* (1879), she drew upon her audience's love of fairy tales to insist that science had introduced new fairy tales that were just as enchanting as the old ones. In "Sleeping Beauty," the spellbound inhabitants of a castle are frozen until the valiant prince kisses the princess, and everything comes to life again. The modern scientific tale of frozen water, spellbound by the enchantments of a frost-giant until a sunbeam sets the water free, was just as magical. Buckley maintained that there were hundreds of fairy tales in science. The stories of science were similar to fairy tales because in nature, as in fairyland, things happened suddenly and mysteriously, due to the magical actions of invisible fairies ceaselessly at work. The forces in nature, which Buckley wished to refer to as fairies, were, to her mind, more magical and beautiful in their work than those of the old fairy tales. She told stories about the fairy's heat, cohesion, gravitation, crystallization and chemical attraction, and about how these science fairies did their work in nature in sunbeams, gases, water, sound, plants, coal, and beehives. Any common object, Buckley believed, whether it be fire or water, for example, had a history that could reveal nature's invisible fairies if the reader only used their imagination. Buckley's *Fairyland of Science* was popular and influential. Published by no fewer than seven publishers in both England and the United States, the last edition appeared in 1905.

In some of her other books Buckley focused specifically on the theory of evolution. A third reason that scholars began to see Buckley as important has to do with interesting way she presented this subject. Take, for example, her *Life and Her Children* (1880) and *Winners in Life's Race* (1882), a two-part examination of how evolution had operated in the development of the major forms of life. In these books Buckley outlined an evolutionary epic that began with the lower forms of life and ended with the production of humans. Buckley's books are populated with unlikely heroes who courageously use their natural advantages to survive the struggle for existence. Each animal group, even those that were more primitive, possesses some special advantage that enables them to spread their children over the world. Sponges had their cooperative life and their protecting skeletons, while jellyfish were like lasso-throwers who had poisonous weapons to capture their food. All forms of life preceding the more highly evolved vertebrates were depicted by Buckley as inspirations to the human reader for their heroism under fire.

But Buckley's evolutionary epic was not just about the weapons and defenses that nature had supplied all animals to compete in the struggle for existence. The more important theme running throughout both books was the family bond uniting all life. Buckley placed more emphasis on cooperation than on competition. Particularly when it came to the more advanced forms of life discussed in *Winners in Life's Race*, Buckley focused on the evolution of true sympathy, based on the love of parent for child, starting with the bony race of fish, through reptiles, birds, and mammals. To win the race, the vertebrates learned that unity is strength. For Buckley, this indicated that the evolutionary process had both a religious and a moral dimension. Buckley did not see Darwin's theory of evolution as leading to gross materialism. She saw no contradiction between the theory of natural selection and the notion that an unseen power guided the evolutionary process toward a moral end. In her evolutionary books, Buckley aimed to give her readers a glimpse into the workings of a divine being over the course of the whole process of evolution. Buckley's use of an evolutionary epic to bring together science and religion gives us insight into how, in a post-Darwinian world, evolution could be integrated into Christian forms of thought.

Buckley is one of the most fascinating and important popularizers of science in the Victorian period. Yet very few of her letters have survived, and there is no substantial biographical study. It requires the creative imagination of a novelist to derive reasonable conclusions from historical facts to fill in the blanks of Buckley's life for us. Only then can we truly appreciate Buckley's contribution to the development of science in the Victorian age.

Glossary

Characters, Places & Terms

List of names by chapter, and further notes on people, institutions, and other matters mentioned in the text.

In order of appearance, fictional characters are shown in *underlined italics*.

Chapter 1: A Woman at the Podium

Sir William Hamilton (ninth baronet, 1788-1856): a noted Edinburgh philosopher and metaphysicist. Given that Sir William had passed away at the time of this presentation, it was likely presented by one of his colleagues.

Sir Joseph Dalton Hooker (1817-1911): Botanical explorer and researcher in many parts of the world, including the Himalayas and Antarctica; director of the Royal Botanic Gardens at Kew in west London from 1865, and president of the Royal Society, 1873-1878. He made significant contributions in plant taxonomy (classification). He was a close friend and collaborator of Charles Darwin. With Sir Charles Lyell, he encouraged Darwin to develop and publish his theories on evolution and natural selection.

Herbert Spencer (1820-1903) An English polymath active as a philosopher, psychologist, biologist, sociologist, and anthropologist, Spencer originated the expression "survival of the fittest", which he coined in *Principles of Biology* (1864) after reading Charles Darwin's 1859 book *On the Origin of Species*.

Samuel Butler (1835-1902): Author and novelist; wrote controversially on many different subjects. His best-known works are *Erewhon* (1872) and *The Way of all Flesh* (1903). The latter, essentially a critique of Victorian values, is also a fictional autobiography. Although enthusiastically accepting evolutionary theory at first, he later sharply and bitterly differed from Darwin. Between 1859 and 1864, he was a sheep farmer in New Zealand, where he was Thomas Fisher's nearest neighbour. Butler was a prominent figure in the Victorian literary scene and his work helped to challenge traditional beliefs about science and religion.

Chapter 2: More than a Pawn

The Buckley family: Arabella's father was John Wall Buckley (1809-1883), a minister of the Church of England, and vicar of St Mary's, Paddington in London. Previously they had been in Brighton, Sussex. Her mother was Elizabeth Burton Buckley (1808-1889). Her siblings were Elizabeth (Elsie, 1833-1917), William (1835-1888), Jane (1837-1874), Julia (1839-1924, who became Mrs Clauson), Charles (1842-1912), Henry (1845-1935, lawyer and judge, who later became Baron Wrenbury), Robert (1847-1927), and Arthur (1849-1937).

Frederica Rowan (1814-1882): besides being secretary to Sir Francis Goldsmid (1808-1878, Member of Parliament and barrister), she was the author of a *History of the French Revolution* (1844); and also wrote for Chambers' Library for Young

People. Proficient in several languages, she was also a translator, with some work commissioned by Queen Victoria. George Eliot, who met Frederica in 1852, described her as 'a learned lady in spectacles.'

Chapter 3: Into the Gullet of Science

Dr Thomas Fisher (1817-1895): Born in Linwood, near Market Rasen in Lincolnshire. In the 1840s he married Eliza, his first wife, after completing his medical training. He was established in medical practice in Buckfastleigh, Devon by 1846. From 1854 to 1882, he lived, apparently apart from his wife, in New Zealand; as a medical practitioner, sheep farmer and aspirant politician. Eliza died in Buckfastleigh in 1880, and he married Arabella Buckley in 1884.

Collections of Natural History at the British Museum: these were located at the Museum in Great Russell Street, Bloomsbury in London. The Natural History Museum in South Kensington, which was opened in 1881, took these Collections over and greatly enlarged their scope.

Ammonites: Extinct marine molluscs with flat spiral shells; some were very large. Commonly found as fossils.

William Pengelly (1812-1894): Geologist and amateur archaeologist, born in Looe, Cornwall. He was one of the founders of the Devonshire Association for the Advancement of Science, Literature and Art, and a Fellow of the Royal Society.

Sir James Brooke (1803-1868): after assisting the Rajah of Sarawak in putting down a rebellion, he was himself awarded the title of rajah in 1842. As an explorer, he was well-known to people like Wallace and Lyell. He was knighted in 1848, and eventually retired to Torquay.

Angela Burdett-Coutts (1814-1906): She became the richest woman in Britain after inheriting £1.8 million from the Coutts family fortune in 1837, besides having an annual income of £50,000 from the Coutts bank. She devoted her life and inheritance to philanthropy. She became Baroness Burdett-Coutts in 1871. A friend of Rajah Brooke, she became his financial backer.

Chapter 4: The Man and the Mission

Natural Selection: The process by which living organisms adapt and evolve over time to better survive and reproduce in their environment. This concept was developed by Charles Darwin in his theory of evolution, which states that the fittest individuals within a species are more likely to survive and pass on their advantageous traits to future generations. Natural selection is a crucial component of the theory of evolution and is responsible for the incredible diversity of life on Earth, as adaptation is infinite in its scope.

Galapagos Tortoise (or Turtle): is a species native to the Galapagos Islands. These turtles can live for over 100 years and are the largest living tortoise species in the world. They are known for their unique ability to store large amounts of water in their bodies, allowing them to survive for months without drinking. The Galapagos Turtle played a significant role in the development of Charles Darwin's theory of evolution, as he realized that different species of the turtle had adapted to their specific environments.

Floriography is the language of flowers, a symbolic code used to communicate emotions and messages through the giving and receiving of flowers. This language was popular in the Victorian era, when certain flowers were assigned specific meanings and used to convey complex emotions that it was not socially acceptable to express verbally. Floriography has been used in literature, art and culture; and its fascination continues.

Regent's Park is one of the largest parks in central London, England. It was designed by John Nash in the time of the Prince Regent (later George IV) in the early nineteenth century and features numerous gardens, lakes and sports facilities. Regent's Park is also home to the famous London Zoo, which houses a vast collection of animals from around the world.

Whist: a very popular family card game in the eighteenth and nineteenth centuries. It is a trick-taking game for four players using a standard deck of cards. The so-called 'German style' (which did not originate in Germany) is a variant for only two players instead of the usual four.

Charles Dickens (1812-1870): The most popular Victorian novelist. His character *Bob Cratchit* was the impoverished clerk of Ebenezer Scrooge in *A Christmas Carol* (1843). Bob was characterized by hard work and a humble nature. Despite working long hours for little pay, he remained optimistic and kind. He can be taken as representative of the struggling working man of his time.

Instincts are innate behaviours that are present in all animals, including humans. These behaviours are genetically programmed; and help animals survive and thrive in their environment. Examples of instincts in animals include migration, courtship rituals, and hunting techniques.

Tess: The Lyells' young Cornish maid here is fictitious.

Sophia Nisbitt (born 1806): She was listed among the Lyells' servants in the 1871 Census, and is here taken to be the cook. The Lyell servants listed in the 1871 Census were George Swann (age 47), Sophia Nisbitt (65), Charlotte Beville (37), Eleanor Newberry (53) and Anna Trudgitt (21). All were born in the Home Counties.

Mrs. Emma Darwin (1808-1896): Wife and first cousin of Charles, and daughter of Josiah Wedgwood II, of the Staffordshire pottery family. She played an important role in his scientific work as a talented artist and musician, providing support and encouragement to her husband. Emma was also a devoted mother to their ten children (of which three died in childhood), and was known for her kindness and generosity.

Conchologist: a person who studies shells and molluscs. This field of study is important in understanding the diversity of marine life and the role of molluscs in their ecosystems.

Darwin family: the seven surviving children were William (1839-1914), Henrietta (1843-1927), George (1845-1912), Elizabeth (1847-1926), Francis (1848-1925), Leonard (1850-1943) and Horace (1851-1928). Elizabeth was a skilled artist, creating detailed illustrations of plants and animals which were used in her father's publications. Francis (Frank) became a prominent botanist as Sir Francis Darwin. He collaborated with his father in several publications and contributed to the study of plant physiology. He also served as president of the Royal Botanic Society and made significant contributions in horticulture. Leonard became prominent in eugenics, serving as president of the Eugenics Society which advocated policies intended to improve the genetic quality of the human population. This had a very dark side, manifest in Nazi Germany; and is now discredited. Leonard also contributed to the study of biometry, the statistical analysis of biological data.

Down House: Home of the Darwin family in Downe, near Orpington in Kent. Subsequently a girls' school, it was restored to its former condition by English Heritage and is open to the public. The village (but not the House) was renamed 'Downe' to avoid confusion with County Down in Ireland.

Linnean Society of London: Founded in 1788, this was the first specifically scientific association, named after the famous Swedish botanist Carl Linnaeus. The Society promotes the study of natural history and taxonomy (the classification of plants and animals), and is known for its extensive collections of botanical and zoological specimens. The Linnean Society also publishes scientific journals and also organizes lectures and events for its members and for the general public.

Backgammon: a board game for two players that has been played for over 5,000 years. It is a game of strategy and chance in which the players must move their pieces around the board and try to bear them off before their opponent. Backgammon has been popular throughout history and is still played today in homes and clubs around the world.

Hooker: see under Chapter 1.

Sir John Lubbock (1834-1913): son of Darwin's neighbour in Downe, and becoming the fourth baronet of that name after his father's death in 1865. He was a banker, politician, archaeologist and naturalist, contributing to the field of entomology (the study of insects); and in his writings a popularizer of science.

He created Baron Avebury in 1900. In Parliament, he was an advocate for education and social reform. The 'accusations' were in the preface to his *Prehistoric Times* (1865), where he claimed that Sir Charles Lyell had quoted verbatim from Lubbock's earlier work without due acknowledgement.

Vice-Admiral Robert Fitzroy (1805-1865): Earlier in his career he was captain of *HMS Beagle*, the brig which circumnavigated the world in 1831-1836, with Darwin on board as his 'companion'. He was governor of New Zealand, 1843-1845, and unpopular for favouring the Maoris. After 1854, he turned to meteorology, inventing the barometer and founding the Meteorological Office in London. He became vehemently opposed to Darwin's theories.

Darwin's work on domesticated animals: This was eventually published as *The Variation of Animals and Plants under Domestication* in 1868. Darwin believed that domestication was a form of artificial selection and that the process of domestication could provide insights into the natural section in wild species.

Chapter 5: A Curious Specimen

Erasmus Alvey Darwin (1804-1881): Charles Darwin's brother and a resident of Marylebone, with whom he often stayed when visiting London. In the 1871 Census, he was staying with him in Queen Anne Street.

Our grandfather Erasmus: Erasmus Darwin (1731-1802) was the grandfather of Erasmus and Charles; and was a prominent physician, philosopher and naturalist. He made significant contributions to the study of botany, zoology and geology and was a proponent of an evolutionary hypothesis before his grandson.

Chapter 6: Darwin's Reception

Johannes Brahms (1833-1897): One of the foremost composers of the age. He began writing string quartets in 1859.

Franz Liszt (1811-1886): Hungarian pianist and innovative composer. As a virtuosic performer, he toured Europe during the 1840s to wild acclaim. He was one of the most famous musicians of the nineteenth century, and is considered to be a major figure in the Romantic era of classical music. A large part of his writing is for the piano, renowned for its technical difficulty and emotional depth; and continues to be popular today.

Anton Rubinstein (1829-1894) was a Russian pianist, composer and conductor, more famous in his lifetime than subsequently. He is remembered for his virtuosic performances and his contributions to the development of classical music in Russia. He was a founder of the St Petersburg Conservatory, and was a mentor to many prominent musicians, including Petr Ilich Tchaikovsky. He composed his ten string quartets between 1855 and 1881, as well as works for other instrumental combinations.

A cravat is a type of neckwear that was popular in the 18th and 19th centuries. It is similar to a necktie but is wider and more elaborate, often featuring intricate knots and folds. The cravat was worn by men of all classes and was considered a symbol of elegance and sophistication.

Margaret Gatty (1809-1873) was a Victorian author and naturalist who wrote several books on natural history, including *British Sea-Weeds* and *Parables from Nature*. She was known for her ability to write about scientific topics in a way that was accessible to a general audience and was a pioneer in the field of marine biology. Gatty was also a prominent advocate for women's education and founded a school for girls in her hometown of Ecclesfield.

Charles Babbage (1792-1871) was a 19th-century mathematician and inventor who is considered to be the father of the computer. He designed the first mechanical computer, the Analytical Engine, which was capable of performing complex mathematical calculations. Babbage's work laid the foundation for modern computing and his legacy continues to be felt today.

Alfred Wallace (1823-1913) was a 19th-century biologist and explorer who is known for his contributions to the theory of evolution. He independently developed the concept of natural selection, which he presented to Charles Darwin in a letter in 1858. Wallace's work was instrumental in the development of the theory of evolution and he is considered one of the most important biologists of the 19th century.

Thomas Huxley (1825-1895), Richard Owen (1804-1892), and Samuel Wilberforce (1805-1873) were all prominent figures in the 19th-century scientific community. Huxley was a biologist and advocate for Darwin's theory of evolution, while Owen was a paleontologist and opponent of evolution. Wilberforce was a bishop and theologian who famously debated Huxley over the validity of evolution at a meeting of the British Association for the Advancement of Science in 1860.

Mary Somerville (1780-1872) was a 19th-century mathematician and astronomer who was known for her contributions to the study of science and mathematics. She was one of the first women to be recognized for her scientific work and was a prominent advocate for women's education. Somerville's work helped to pave the way for future generations of women in science.

Elizabeth Catherine Thomas Carne (1817-1873) was a 19th-century geologist and banker in Penzance, Cornwall who wrote scientific papers about geology. She was the first woman accepted to the Royal Geological Society of Cornwall. She wrote two books that drove her opinions that the class system was a destructive force in civilization, groundbreaking works at the time, especially for a woman. One of the few women bankers of her time, she led her bank to be significantly profitable for fifteen years, more profitable than many male-led banks. Elizabeth and her family were generous philanthropists and Elizabeth herself funded and started at least three schools. She also funded the land upon which Penzance's new town hall was built. For more information about Elizabeth Carne, please see the historical fiction novel about her, *The Light Among Us: The Elizabeth Carne Story, Cornwall* by Jill George with John Dirring.

Bodmin Moor is a large moorland in Cornwall, U.K. The moor is known for its rugged landscape, wild beauty, and ancient monuments, including stone circles, standing stones, and burial mounds. Bodmin Moor is a popular destination for hikers and nature enthusiasts, and its unique flora and fauna make it an important conservation area.

Spiritualism is a religious movement that emerged in the 19th century and emphasizes communication with the dead. Spiritualists believe that the spirits of the dead can communicate with the living through mediums, who act as a conduit between the two worlds. Spiritualism gained popularity in the Victorian era and was often associated with progressive social movements, such as women's suffrage and the abolition of slavery.

Mediums are individuals who claim to be able to communicate with the spirits of the dead. They often use various techniques, such as trance states, automatic writing, or Ouija boards, to facilitate communication with the spirit world. Mediums have been controversial figures throughout history, with skeptics claiming that their abilities are fraudulent or based on psychological tricks.

The Free Love Debate was a public discussion that took place in 1858 between feminist activists and traditionalists over the issue of free love. The debate centered on the idea that individuals should have the right to love and marry whom they choose, without the interference of the state or society. The Free Love Debate was a groundbreaking event in the history of the women's rights movement and helped to pave the way for greater freedom and equality in relationships.

Chapter 7: Arabella, A Force of Nature

Frederic Chopin (1810-1849) was a 19th-century composer and pianist who is considered one of the greatest composers of the Romantic era. He was known for his emotive piano compositions and his innovative use of harmony and melody. Chopin's music continues to be popular today and is often studied by music students around the world.

George Eliot (1819-1880) was the pen name of Mary Ann Evans, a 19th-century novelist who is best known for her books *Middlemarch* and *The Mill on the Floss*. Elliot was a prominent figure in the Victorian literary scene and was known for her realistic depictions of rural life and her exploration of social issues.

John Stuart Mill (1806-1873) was a 19th-century philosopher and political economist who is known for his advocacy of individual freedom and social reform. He was a prominent figure in the Victorian era and his ideas on liberalism, democracy, and utilitarianism continue to be influential today.

Chapter 8: The Long Goodbye

Geological Evidences of the Antiquity of Man is a book written by Charles Lyell that was published in 1863. The book examines the geological evidence for the existence of prehistoric humans and argues that humans have been around much longer than previously thought. Lyell's work helped to pave the way for the study of human evolution and the development of the theory of natural selection.

The Avenue Gardens is a section of Regent's Park in London that is known for its beautiful gardens and walking paths. The gardens were designed in the Victorian era and are home to a variety of plant species from around the world. The Avenue Gardens is a popular destination for tourists and locals alike and is often used for events and festivals.

Chapter 9: Spiritualism As A Science

Mary Marshall (1842-1884) was a 19th-century spiritualist who claimed to have the ability to communicate with the spirits of the dead. She was known for her work as a medium and her ability to provide comfort and solace to those who had lost loved ones. Marshall's work helped to popularize the spiritualist movement and her legacy continues to be felt today.

Jane Burton Buckley: Arabella's older sister. See Buckley family.

Chapter 10: A Threat to Darwin

Rose Fisher (1847-1938): Thomas Fisher's daughter by his first marriage. Thomas left Rose in her mother's care and went to New Zealand when she was only five or six years old.

Mackay Andrew Herbert James Heriot (1840-1918): Rose married Mackay and they lived in barracks as Mackay's career in the military required. He became a Major-General upon retirement.

The Evangelical Christians Alliance Lady Hope was a 19th-century religious organization that was founded by Lady Hope of Carriden. The group was committed to promoting evangelical Christianity and social reform and was involved in a variety of charitable and educational projects. Lady Hope was a prominent figure in the movement and was known for her work as a social reformer and philanthropist.

Richard Garnett (1835-1906) was a 19th-century librarian and scholar who worked at the British Museum. He was known for his work in the field of bibliography and his contributions to the study of English literature. He kept letters and ardent follower of the author Shelley. Garnett was a prolific writer, for example in the fantasy genre, and his works on literature and bibliography continue to be influential today.

Chapter 11: Fortune Favors the Bold

Descent of Man is a book written by Charles Darwin published in 1871. The book explores the evolutionary history of humans and argues that humans share a common ancestry with apes and other primates. *Descent of Man* was a groundbreaking work that helped to popularize the theory of evolution and had a profound impact on the fields of anthropology and biology.

Mutualism is a type of symbiotic relationship between two organisms in which both parties benefit. Mutualistic relationships are common in nature and can involve a variety of organisms, such as plants and pollinators, or animals and bacteria. Mutualism is an important concept in ecology and has helped to shed light on the complex relationships that exist between different species.

Traducianism is a theological concept that argues that the soul is transmitted from parent to child at the moment of conception. Traducianism was a popular idea in early Christianity and was often associated with the doctrine of original sin. The concept of traducianism continues to be debated by theologians today and remains an important topic in the study of Christian theology.

Chapter 13: The Throes

Typhoid is a bacterial infection that is spread through contaminated food and water. The disease is characterized by fever, fatigue, and abdominal pain, and can be life-threatening if left untreated. Typhoid was a major public health concern in the 19th century and was responsible for numerous outbreaks around the world. Today, typhoid is treatable with antibiotics and is much less common than it once was.

Insectivorous Plants is a book written by Charles Darwin that was published in 1875. The book explores the phenomenon of carnivorous plants, which capture and digest insects for nutrients. Darwin's work on insectivorous plants helped to shed light on the complex relationships that exist between plants and animals and contributed to our understanding of the evolution of different species.

Chapter 16: The Fairyland of Science

A popularizer of science is an individual who works to make scientific concepts and ideas accessible to a general audience. Popularizers of science can take many forms, including writers, educators, and activists. Popularizers of science are important because they help to bridge the gap between the scientific community and the public and can help to inspire the next generation of scientists and innovators.

Mary Aelia Davis Treat (1830 – 1923) was a naturalist and correspondent with Charles Darwin from the United States. Her contributions to botany and entomology were so extensive that six species of plants and animals were named after her, including the amaryllis.

Chapter 17: Life and Her Children

Fanny Salter was a 19th-century artist and illustrator who was known for her work on botanical and natural history subjects. She was a close friend of Charles Darwin and collaborated with him on several projects, including his book *Insectivorous Plants*. Salter's illustrations were praised for their accuracy and attention to detail, and her work helped to popularize the study of botany and natural history.

Chapter 18: A Thorny Request

The Power of Movement in Plants is a book written by Charles Darwin that was published in 1880. The book explores the phenomenon of plant movement and the ways in which plants respond to various stimuli, such as light and gravity. Darwin's work on plant movement helped to expand our understanding of the complexity and diversity of the plant world and laid the foundation for future research in the field.

Chapter 19: Backing Darwin

The Biography of Erasmus Darwin is a book written by Charles Darwin that was published in 1879. The book is a biography of Charles Darwin's grandfather, Erasmus Darwin, who was a prominent physician, naturalist, and philosopher. The book examines Erasmus Darwin's life and work, including his contributions to the study of evolution and his influence on the younger Darwin's own ideas.

Chapter 20: Saving Wallace

The Duke of Argyll was a 19th-century politician and naturalist who was known for his work on the geology and natural history of Scotland. He was a prominent figure in the Victorian scientific community and was a member of the Royal Society. The Duke of Argyll's work helped to expand our understanding of the natural world and his legacy continues to be felt today.

Chapter 22: Farewell from Westminster

Westminster Abbey is a historic church located in the heart of London, England. The abbey has been the site of numerous coronations, weddings, and funerals throughout British history, and is the final resting place of many notable figures, including Isaac Newton, and Charles Darwin. The abbey is also known for its beautiful architecture and stained glass windows, and is a popular tourist destination.

Chapter 23: A New Life

Twilight of the Gods is a book written by Richard Garnett that was published in 1888. The book is a collection of myths and legends from around the world, including Norse mythology,

Greek mythology, and Indian mythology. The book explores the themes of heroism, love, and the struggle between good and evil, and has been praised for its vivid storytelling and literary style.

Sheepwash Devon is a small village located in the county of Devon, England. The village is known for its beautiful countryside and history as the regional sheep market with a natural spring to wash sheep for sale. It has been a fishing and hunting location for centuries. Sheepwash Devon is also home to several historic buildings, such as St Lawrence church and The Half Moon pub.

William the Conqueror (1028-1087) was a Norman duke who ruled England from 1066 until his death in 1087. He is best known for his victory at the Battle of Hastings, which led to the Norman Conquest of England. William was a skilled military strategist and a powerful ruler, and his reign helped to shape the course of English history.

Chapter 25: I Said I Will

The Heriot Children: Thomas (1869 - ?), Granville (1871 – ?), Lillian (1872 – 1953), Eric (1874 - ?), Oscar (1880 – 1903).

The Wife's Handbook is a book written by Dr. Thomas Clifford Allbutt that was first published in 1880. The book was designed to provide women with practical advice on a wide range of topics, including health, hygiene, and household management. The book was popular among middle-class women in the Victorian era and helped to promote women's education and empowerment.

Chapter 26: Troubled Life

Walreddon Manor is a large estate about two miles from the center of Tavistock. It is one of the earliest sites of settlement in the area and the mansion itself was built in the middle of the sixteenth century with the plaster arms of Edward VI in a ground floor room, suggesting the original date for the building within three years of 1550.

Chapter 28: Life Together

Sidmouth is a lively coastal town located in the county of Devon, England, known for its scenic beauty and historic charm, Jurassic beaches, and is a popular shopping destination for tourists and holidaymakers. Arabella lived in Sidmouth a few times and spent her final days here, possibly because Sidmouth was home to many intellectuals.

Branscombe is a small village in Devon near Beer and the chalk cliffs in Devon, England. It is located at the end of the longest village street in the U.K. called Mill Street which is dotted with cottages and historic buildings from the fifteenth century, such as a mill, a bakery, and a tavern called The Mason's Arm's that is now a restaurant and hotel (that we highly recommend!). We do not know if Arabella and Thomas visited Branscombe, but they did visit several of the nearby places as mentioned in her letters, such as Buckfastleigh, Sidmouth, and Plymouth, and given her interest in geology, it is reasonable to think that she visited here to examine the beauty of the cliffs.

Chapter 29: From Light To Shadow

Simon, *Ethel*, *Judith* and *Jimmy* are all fictional characters.

Epilogue: An Old War Horse

A wireless was the term used for a radio in the early days of the invention of radio communication.

A peerage is a hereditary title of nobility that is granted by the British monarch. There are several different types of peerage, including dukes, marquesses, earls, viscounts, and barons. Peerages are often granted to members of the aristocracy and are usually inherited by the aristocracy, but are sometimes granted to commoners as a recognition of achievement and merit. Henry Buckley as Baron Wrenbury is a prime example of this. Peers are entitled to certain privileges, such as a seat in the House of Lords and the right to use specific titles and honors. Peerages have a long history in British society and remain an important symbol of social status and prestige.

Sir Arthur Keith (1866-1955) was a 19th- and early 20th-century anthropologist and anatomist who was known for his work on human evolution. He was a prominent figure in the scientific community and was a member of the Royal Society. Keith served as the president of the British Society of Science from 1918 to 1919 and his work helped to shape our understanding of the origins and development of human beings.

Alice Zimmerman was a 19th-century women's rights activist who was involved in the women's suffrage movement. She was a member of the National Union of Women's Suffrage Societies and was a prominent speaker and writer on women's issues. Zimmerman's work helped to promote women's education and empowerment and laid the foundation for future generations of women's rights activists.

Afterword

Arabella Burton Buckley (1840-1929): Born in Brighton, Sussex, in 1840. By 1851, the family had moved to St Mary's Vicarage, 1 St Mary's Terrace, Paddington in London. In 1876, after working for Sir Charles Lyell until his death in 1875, she began her writing career as a popularizer of science. In 1884, she married Dr Thomas Fisher. They lived at Upcott Avenel, North Devon; and then at Walreddon Manor near Tavistock. Thomas died in 1895; and she moved into Brook Cottage in Tavistock, later returning to London to live. After 1921, she had retired to Sidmouth in East Devon, where she died from influenza in 1929.

Sir Charles Lyell (1797-1875): pioneering geologist; his *Principles of Geology* (1830) went through twelve editions by 1876. In 1833 he married Mary Elizabeth Horner (1809-1873), who became Lady Mary Lyell when he was knighted in 1848. His eyesight was failing when Arabella went to work for him. He was created a baronet in 1864.

Charles Darwin (1809-1882): After sailing around the world as researcher on HMS *Beagle* (1831-1836), his ideas on evolution and natural selection slowly emerged over the next twenty years to result in the publication of *On the Origin of Species* in 1859.

Thomas Henry Huxley (1825-1895): Biologist and controversialist; in public debate in 1860 defended Darwin's theory of evolution against Bishop Wilberforce, its most outspoken critic. Like Darwin and Wallace, he had voyaged extensively across the world. He married Henrietta Anne Heathorn in 1855, whom he had met in Sydney, Australia. Aldous Huxley, the novelist and author of *Brave New World,* was his grandson.

Alfred Russel Wallace (1823-1913): Biologist and entomologist who spent several years exploring and collecting in Brazil and what is now Indonesia. He reached similar conclusions to Darwin on evolution. He gave his name to the Wallace Line, drawn through the islands of Indonesia, which shows the sharp boundary between the fauna of Asia and the fauna of Australasia.

References

Frequently Used Resources

Sources of Letters

The Darwin Correspondence Project, Cambridge University, UK.

The Library of New Zealand.

The Life and Letters of Charles Darwin, Vol I and II edited by Francis Darwin 1887.

Northwestern University Richard Garnett Estate McCormick Special Collection.

Harry Ransom Center at the University of Texas, Austin.

Alfred Russel Wallace: Letters and Reminiscences by James Marchant (2018).

Reference Books

A History of the Descent of Man, Charles Darwin February 24, 1871.

Charles Darwin, A Reference Guide To His Life and Works by J. David Archibald (2018).

Down House: The Home of Charles Darwin. Tori Reeve. English Heritage Guidebooks 2009.

Victorian Populizers of Science by Bernard Lightman (2007).

The Notebooks of Samuel Butler, Volume 1 1874 – 1883 by Hans Peter Breuer (1984).

The Origin of Species, Charles Darwin (1859).

Arabella Buckley Fisher's Publications

Darwinism and Religion, *MacMillan Magazine*, May 1871

A Short History of Natural Science (1876)

The Fairyland of Science (1879)

Through Magic Glasses (1880)

Life and Her Children (1881)

Winners in Life's Race (1882)

History of England For Beginners (1887)

Eyes and No Eyes Series (1903)

Author's Note

The moment I met Arabella Buckley via my research I felt that her contribution to society was so significant that it could not be measured; therefore, I was compelled to write the first story ever about her. Imagine a humble daughter of a vicar interacting with and becoming a discussant with the world's most famous scientist: Charles Darwin! Arabella to me is a prime example of a woman on whose shoulders we stand on today and whose successes paved the way to change roles for women for decades. That is why I chose to write about her—to inspire women in today's world to press boundaries like she did and to accomplish the impossible.

You will want to know what is real versus imagined throughout the novel. In general, I tried to use as many facts as I could and my research was extensive. I turned over every book, letter, link, and site. I used her letters for everything: facts about settings, her reactions to various things and people, places she went, her likes and dislikes. All the Darwin letters are exact historical fact. I may have shortened a letter or two of Arabella's to Mr. Garnett, but the words are hers exactly. Where I didn't use her letters, I leveraged the Darwin letters or facts from Sir Charles' or Alfred Wallace's memoirs (who didn't mention anything about her by the way) or other historical books. I did use real excerpts from her books to demonstrate what an amazing writer she was, as you can see.

I did visit each location in the novel, some several times, which was some of the most fun I have ever had. I seriously think I was born and lived in the U.K. with my ancestors in another time, another world.

For me, it is easier to describe what I imagined as those pieces are fewer than the many real pieces. I don't know any details about Arabella's mother and father other than their birthdates. Their roles could have been reversed in terms of support. I thought it realistic to think her mother would want a socially acceptable role for her. Likewise, I do not know how supportive Henry, her younger brother, was of her career, but living in the same household, I hope he was supportive as I have portrayed.

Now to the big one, Thomas. It is true that she knew Thomas as a long-term family friend. I tried and tried to figure out how and by what means he was a long-term family friend, but John Dirring and I could not discover these facts. If you find out, please let us know! Therefore, I extrapolated from the facts and went backwards to form their relationship. That is, if she, a Londoner, agreed to live deep in the countryside of Sheepwash with him, she must have been in love with him in some very significant way. Why else would she, a financially stable, well networked woman agree to marry him? She very well could have lived under Henry's wing but didn't. Her friend, Beatrice Potter, the revolutionary thinker, social historian, and activist better known as Beatrice Webb (not the cute country animal children's books writer), wrote that Arabella was not in love with Thomas but agreed to a marriage of convenience. But I believe Beatrice was also very jaded and it is a known fact that she had relationship difficulties of her own. Certainly, Arabella's letters to Thomas' friends intimated a loving relationship from her own words. We will never know for certain, but most of the information tipped me towards concluding that Arabella and Thomas had a loving relationship. I therefore found Thomas' history as a surgeon in London and backtracked to determine his timelines and there you have it.

The Lyells did give receptions and parties, but I did put words in Thomas Huxley's mouth about the Free Love Debate which was an actual debate at the time. Huxley was outspoken and sometimes had a biting wit as described so I thought he would enjoy having a bit of fun at the party with Arabella.

Please note the jewelry that Arabella is wearing in the photo portrait I have included. You will notice a large silver locket like the one I describe Thomas giving her and look at her ring finger on her left hand. Does this not look like the setting a cameo would sit in? I bought several antique cameos with similar settings to see what they would look like in person and to see what the setting would look like if the cameo was removed. The ones with similar settings do look remarkably like that ring she wears, so I included it in the story. My guess is that she wears it without the cameo so that it looks more like a wedding band. The rings she wears is striking and unusual, much like her.

Mr. Prescott, the grouchy neighbor, is fictional, but the trouble at his bank was not. I imagine he represented the thinking of the time that women writing books was not socially acceptable.

A key premise to the entire novel is that at some point, I believe, Arabella and Charles Darwin must have discussed her interests in writing and publishing books popularizing his theories. None of this is written down anywhere but given it was rare to actually write something down including women during that time it is not surprising. The parallels of their writing are uncanny. When he writes *Descent*, she writes an article praising it. When he writes about "the great backbone family," she writes her own book about that too. When he writes about plants, he invites her to write a book about plants as well. And, she is one of twelve people invited to his funeral to sit with the family, I believe because she is so endeared to the work of Charles Darwin. Therefore, I believe that she must have discussed this "mission" of popularizing science and his work with him, and I wrote about these discussions throughout the book.

I don't know for a fact that Charles Darwin and Francis Darwin spoke about Alfred Wallace's pension, but it is reasonable to think they might have given that Francis was there working on the book with Mr. Darwin during the time of the many letters and anguish over the Wallace's situation.

The Fishers did go on many trips to various local places, such as Buckfastleigh, where Thomas lived with his first wife, Plymouth, where the Heriots lived, etc. Given the geological and natural beauty of Branscombe, I imagined that they might have gone there for the reasons described in the Life Together chapter. All the setting details of that chapter are real, except the names of the donkeys.

Lady Hope of Carriden was a real person who did object to Darwin's theory of evolution, but the letter is fictitious. She purported to visit Down House and visit him on his death bed but his family claimed this to be false.

Séances were prevalent during this time and in this section of the book the characters who took part and the process are real, but the conversations are imagined, of course.

I did imagine the bathtub scene. Hey, she was still young, right ladies? I don't know the exact circumstances of Thomas Fisher's death, but there was no inquiry and he was healthy and sitting in his chair the prior December, according to Arabella's letters.

Arabella did speak on the topic of Progress of Life on Earth at the Edinburgh Philosophical Institute in September of 1883, but I don't know if Samuel Butler was in the audience. From what I have learned about him, he probably was.

My sincere hope is that I have done Arabella's poetic writing and courageous life justice, weaving facts together in a way that make her life and the contributions she made to our world unforgettable.

Acknowledgments

Never have I had a project so fill me with so much wonder and joy as this novel. I would like to thank the key players on my team for their support and assistance. First and forever in my gratitude and heart is Melissa Hardie of Penzance, Cornwall, who ran the Hypatia Trust before her death in 2022. She concurred with me about the mission of this book, that a first ever story about Arabella and how she illuminated Darwin was compelling, and I hope readers agree.

I had two early reader friends, Susan and Gwenn, who I adore, who agreed to read the early slop, so thank you to them for giving the early directional review.

Thank you to the very generous owners of the Upcott Barton and Upcott Avenel for sharing the details of their homes with me. A true highlight of my research for this novel!

I also had several manuscript reviewers, thanks to and including my friend, Rosa L., Chris C., Jeanette L., Mary B., Gwenn B., Roderick M., and Bernie L., for their insight and terrific recall of facts and issues.

I sincerely thank Bernard Lightman for his insight and advice on this project, given his advanced expertise in Darwin and Arabella, and for the afterward that he contributed. It grounds the story so well!

Next, to my historical editor and friend, John Dirring who agreed to join me for another novel after our first, *The Light*

Among Us: The Elizabeth Carne Story, thank you for the historical accuracy and sage advice for this novel. John and I visited Down House in Downe, Kent, and the Mason's Arms that those sites to our list of literary adventures.

A new friend entered my team for this novel, Roderick Martin, the trustee/manager of the Tavistock Museum, and he provided a never-to-be-forgotten tour of Walreddon and Tavistock, including Thomas' grave site. When you find gems like John and Roderick, who help provide the authenticity to the novel, you are truly lucky as an author.

Fellow Victorian lover, Caroline Smith, editor, had the job of pouring over drafts to say, "more, more, more" and therefore helped to deepen our experience of Arabella, Thomas, Darwin, and the Giants that have lived in my head and now on paper, so many thanks to her. I was also incredibly lucky to find soul sister editor Stacia Pelletier on this journey. Her edits turned the novel into the dream state that I hoped for, so I truly thank her for all her expertise. I can't thank John Dirring enough for creating the polish and accuracy he has provided through hours and hours of diligence on this novel.

Thank you to my ever-patient family, my husband, and children. And to my mother, who did not get to read the ending but who cheered me on at every step, my countless, neverending thanks and eternal love.

Finally, I know you, as a reader, have many options of books to read, so thank you so very much for choosing this story about Arabella. I hope she takes you to great places.

About the Author

Jill George, Ph.D. is a historical researcher and Industrial Psychologist specializing in the Victorian era London and Cornwall, UK. She writes historical fiction novels in these eras. Her love of writing drives her to rebalance history based on women's successes and the men who supported them. She travels frequently to London, Cornwall, and Devon to do hands-on research of each site mentioned in her books. Her next novel, the first in a series, will be *A Hopeless Dawn: The Novel*, based on a painting from 1870 in the Tate museum, London by Frank Bramley. The book is a historical gothic romance thriller set in Port Quin in majestic Cornwall, U.K. Many photos of Jill's research trips are on display in the gallery on her website: www.jillgeorgeauthor.com and on Instagram @jillgeorgeauthor. Come see! Jill lives in Pittsburgh, PA USA with her teenagers (son and twin daughters), husband, and many pets.

Book Club Questions

1. Have you ever wanted to write a story, song, book, paint, take photos, draw, or create some other form of art? What does creating feel like? How does it change you? How does art change others? What stopped you or prevented you from going forward with your art? How can you move forward now?
2. In this novel, how did writing change Arabella? Those around her?
3. How did Arabella's novels impact her readers? Future generations?
4. What does this novel have to say about types of love? How many types of love do you have in your life? Do different types of love satisfy different needs in your life?
5. How did Arabella overcome role barriers as she achieved success?
6. What role did men play in Arabella's success? How can women best leverage men to help them succeed?
7. Arabella's faith played a key role throughout her life and in her writing. How does faith help you in your successes or how could it play a different role?
8. What barriers that Arabella faced are still prominent for women today in the twenty first century? Why?
9. What do you most admire about Arabella and her mission? What do you least admire about her and why?
10. What are your opinions of Samuel Butler? Was he a villain? Did Arabella loathe him? Why or why not?

Made in the USA
Coppell, TX
05 September 2024

36815351R00215